Foul Matter

Books by Joan Aiken

FOUL MATTER
THE GIRL FROM PARIS
THE WEEPING ASH
THE SMILE OF THE STRANGER
THE FIVE-MINUTE MARRIAGE
LAST MOVEMENT
VOICES IN AN EMPTY HOUSE

A CLUSTER OF
  SEPARATE SPARKS
THE EMBROIDERED SUNSET
THE CRYSTAL CROW
DARK INTERVAL
BEWARE OF THE BOUQUET
THE FORTUNE HUNTERS
THE SILENCE OF HERONDALE

JUVENILES

THE STOLEN LAKE
THE SHADOW GUESTS
A TOUCH OF CHILL
  AND OTHER TALES
MIDNIGHT IS A PLACE
THE SKIN SPINNERS: POEMS
ARABEL AND MORTIMER
NOT WHAT YOU EXPECTED
GO SADDLE THE SEA
ARABEL'S RAVEN
STREET: A PLAY FOR CHILDREN
THE MOONCUSSER'S DAUGHTER:
  A PLAY FOR CHILDREN
THE GREEN FLASH
  AND OTHER TALES

WINTERTHING:
  A CHILDREN'S PLAY
THE CUCKOO TREE
DIED ON A RAINY SUNDAY
NIGHT FALL
SMOKE FROM CROMWELL'S
  TIME AND OTHER STORIES
THE WHISPERING MOUNTAIN
A NECKLACE OF RAINDROPS
ARMITAGE, ARMITAGE
  FLY AWAY HOME
NIGHTBIRDS ON NANTUCKET
BLACK HEARTS IN BATTERSEA
THE WOLVES OF WILLOUGHBY
  CHASE
THE KINGDOM AND THE CAVE

Foul Matter

JOAN AIKEN

Doubleday & Company, Inc.

Garden City, New York

1983

Grateful acknowledgment is made to the following for permission to reprint their copyrighted material:

Excerpt from Dylan Thomas, "Under Milkwood." Copyright 1954 by New Directions. All rights reserved. Reprinted by permission of New Directions Publishing Corp.

Library of Congress Cataloging in Publication Data

Aiken, Joan, 1924–
Foul matter.

I. Title.
PR6051.I35F6   1983   823'.914
ISBN: 0-385-18371-2
Library of Congress Catalog Card Number 82-45536

Foul Matter

1

Begin, then, Sisters of the sacred well . . .
John Milton, *Lycidas*

How many more onions shall I cut up before I die is a thought that intermittently comes to entertain me when I am embarking on yet another of those dishes made from leftover lamb which begin with a chopped, sautéed onion. All cookery takes off from a chopped onion, my friend Elly once said. She also said that gracious living always seems to entail getting up at 6 A.M. Both statements are true. One of my lovers once remarked that my hands always seemed to smell of raw onion (that was long ago, before I learned about dipping them in cold water immediately). I apologised, but he said he liked it; reminded him of gardens and greenhouses and potting sheds. Larry. I wonder what ever became of him? He had the most touching, innocent profile; nothing but downy curves. Not unlike a duck.

Here I sit, in the Campus Tavern bedroom, thirty feet long by twelve feet wide. The style of decoration is Spanish Gothic—massive polished wood frames for mirrors, wooden lampstands, carved wooden tombstone slab heads for the two immense double beds, each big enough for an orgy of hippopotami; floor lamps tall as the Statue of Liberty; a folding screen of wooden panelling (dog-shit brown, toffee brown, spuriously shiny) across the far end of the room, concealing sink and shower; striped yellow-and-rust curtains (to match the bedspreads) cover the glass-panelled front end of the room, which opens on to a roofed courtyard the size of a parade ground.

A leaflet, *How to Survive a Hotel Fire*, is thoughtfully placed by the bedside lamp.

No daylight or fresh air can ever enter this room; sociologists of a later epoch will deduce that it was one of those incarceration cubicles designed to demoralise the prisoner and speedily disintegrate his personality.

I phone Room Service and wait some time.

"You may want to keep your room key in your pants pocket or on the night stand . . ."

"Ah, we don't deliver to rooms till 7:30 A.M.," Room Service told me when they answered my call, in joyful denial of the twenty-four-hour promise on the menu. No use to protest that, for me, it is now 3 P.M. European time.

"If there is any evidence of smoke in the room, roll out of bed and crawl to the door . . ."

I wait until seven-thirty and try again. "Melon, coffee, and omelet." "We have no melon." "But the menu says melon in season. When is the season for melon if not summer?" "Sorry, we do not have any melon. Would you like juice instead?"

This dialogue makes me think about what George used to call the Bubble.

The Bubble is the cartoon mirage that floats above your head, promising perfection; the Bubble is the transcendant opposite of reality. The Bubble told me that Mitchison, Nevada, would be a small, picturesque mountain town, about the size, say, of Ronda; that the Campus Tavern would be an agreeable, compact building, chalet-style perhaps, within walking distance of Mitchison University Campus. Instead, Mitchison appears to cover about a hundred square miles of flat land, with rectangular concrete buildings, separated, each from the other, by a complex system of freeways and thruways; no human foot ever touches this land, you may pass from point to point only by automobile, helicopter, or balloon. And the Campus Tavern I have already described. Its huge, silent areas are defended from each other by bulletproof glass screens and locked doors.

"Feel the door with the palm of your hand. If the knob is hot —don't open it."

When I was a child, nothing ever worked for me. My attempts to follow instructions from books—how to make paper fans, Indian headdresses, dollhouse furniture—always ended in total failure. Chocolate vending machines invariably rejected my coins, or proved to be empty; special offers closed just before my letters reached them; or the object, if it did arrive, was insultingly smaller than, inferior to, the picture in the catalogue, and was sent in the wrong colour. Nothing ever came up to expectation. By the age of twelve I was wholly resigned to disappointment. No Bubble could deceive *me*, in my teens or twenties.

It is only during the last few months (God knows why) that, mysteriously, my hopes, my expectations, have been aroused once more.

Suppose that Daniel's child were still living, not drowned; alive (he would be thirteen now), cared for, reared by strangers ignorant of his background? Little Finn, the smiling fair-haired boy. Dare I consider this possibility?

More and more I find myself doing so.

Dan's son, Ingrid Christ's son; how wild, struggling, and sorrowful a mix of genes must his small frame encompass—poetry, deceit, ambition, love, genius—above all, the urge to self-destruction. Both his parents killed themselves. If I could ever find little Finn, if I could devote myself to his welfare, would I be able to redirect that violent urge in him towards energy, life, happiness? Who should know better than I how to do this? I have been on nodding terms with death since age nineteen. Death holds precious little mystery for *me*. During the last sixteen years I have eaten death for breakfast, Hoovered it out of my rugs, dug it from my flower beds, mixed it into my sauces, mowed it off my little sloping patch of lawn.

During the last sixteen years I have learned one thing for sure. The world is a frightening place, people are chancy, unreliable, their opinions based on hearsay; facts can't be proved, everybody tells a different story. But at least food is real. If you feed people, that's doing something definite.

"Fires generate heat, smoke, and panic, so hold onto the hand-rail for protection against being knocked down by exiting occupants . . ."

Luckily I have never been afraid of fire.

The conference does not open until three-thirty. Each menu of every meal has been planned, down to the last olive and butterball; catered for, scheduled, checked, and double-checked. I have no duties just now, I need do nothing but wait. I can lie here in this dim, ugly, silent, dispassionate limbo, and take stock.

Just before coming away from England I went to see Anthony Roche. The interview was acutely gritty and painful.

Closing one's house must always be a sad process—even when it is for a period of no more than a month's absence. Objects reproach, mutely: clean cups on their hooks, clear desk top, pillowcases washed and hung up to dry, books aligned tidily in shelves, wistaria and roses wooing the eye with glowing ruby, clusters of wistful grey-blue; all will be faded, withered, choked among weeds by the day of return. If that day ever comes. Any departure is a foretaste of death.

I think of Aunt Thisbe, who always unwinds every toilet roll completely (she buys the stiff, shiny, upper-class kind, durable as papyrus, eminently suitable to receive monkish chronicles, Egyptian hieroglyphs, or testamentary dispositions), and writes in red Biro on the last section: "Stranger, if I am dead by the time this leaf is reached, remember Thisbe Angela Churchill."

"Why don't you say, 'Pray for the soul of Thisbe Angela'?" I was once moved to ask when, with a certain diffidence, I had flushed away her admonition.

"*Soul*, Tuesday?" Thisbe is the only person who still calls me Tuesday. "You know me better than *that*, I should hope," she said trenchantly. "In what way do you possibly imagine that another person's prayers could benefit my soul? Always supposing that I have one? Only one's own efforts can have any effect."

"Oh, I don't know. Other people's prayers might help—lubrication—like a five-thousand-mile service."

"Pish!" Aunt Thisbe belongs to the generation that really said Pish. "I suppose you have been picking up notions from that Catholic friend of yours."

Aunt Thisbe, by osmosis, for I don't confide in her, knows a certain amount, more than most, about my private affairs. But she is generally several years out of date. She has a lot to think about—the Social Democratic Party, Amnesty International, Pimlico Borough Council.

I said, "Actually I don't see him any more. Not for five years— since Hugh died."

"I would have thought—after the death of his wife—that he would be glad of your company."

"It didn't work that way."

"Just as well," she growled. "You might have become too attached—he was an interesting, well-informed man. Though I can't imagine your marrying a Catholic. Mind," said Aunt Thisbe unexpectedly, "you *ought* to marry again."

"Marry Anthony? He'd as soon marry Madame Mao. And I'd sooner."

"Don't be silly, Tuesday. You couldn't marry Madame Mao."

I closed the house. Threw away unused milk, left note for milkman, put chicken fat in the coconut for the blue tits, glancing up from my small, walled garden, up the thorny slope at the castle battlements, gap-toothed in the sky, high above my chimney pots, where, as usual, starlings scrabbled and jabbered. Carried out my travel bag and closed the front door softly, so as not to disturb the Listeners inside. Why feel guilty when I leave house and garden to themselves? They may be glad to see the back of me; there must exist different orders of being in each enclosure, who come into their own at the times when I am not there.

> Shut the door, count and run
> Now the silence has begun:
> Who's that sitting in my chair?
> Who comes softly down the stair?
> Who lies sleeping in my bed?
> By whose voice were these words said?

One of Ingrid's early poems. *Children's Games,* she called it.

Dear little ancient house. Watch Cottage. I always turn to look back at it with love. White, compact, weatherboarded, tiny, it stands in dignity below the brambly Castle Mound, at the head of a short, steep, cobbled cul-de-sac, Watch Hill, which leads down into Bastion Street. There's no place to put a car, the houses are jammed like teeth in a narrow jaw, so I keep my Citroën at the station garage, where it lodges, expensively idle, sometimes for weeks together. The train journey to London is just as quick, and one can read, or talk to other people.

A venerable wistaria scrambles over the front of Watch Cottage. The two tiny front flower beds, caged with iron hoops, overflow with campanulas and geraniums.

Three worn stone steps lead to the faded blue door with its brass knocker.

The first time I saw it was the day before my wedding.

"Going away again?" Old Miss Crutchley, setting out her milk bottles at Number Two, sees my bag. Her articulation is all vowels; teeth not yet in for the day.

"For a month. To America."

"Cooking for another of your conferences?"

"That's it. Doctors they are, this time. I believe Brezhnev's own doctor is going to be there."

Nowadays I don't exactly do the cooking myself, but it comes to the same thing so far as Miss Crutchley is concerned. Besides, I generally do provide a festive dish for a special meal.

"Doctors? Big eaters, I daresay. Mind you feed 'em well— they'll give you another medal! And I'll water your geraniums for you, love, if the weather's dry."

"Thank you, Miss Crutchley, you're very kind."

"You bring me all those strawberry and cheese tarts, dear. I always say, what use is it in life if we can't do each other a good turn?"

Aproned, slippered, she turns back indoors. Old Miss Crutchley. When she dies, her little house will be snapped up by some young executive pair.

On down the steep hill; the town of Affton Wells displayed below my feet like a backdrop in flint, brick, and tiled gables. Tudor at the core, seventeenth and eighteenth century on the perimeter. Grey saltmarsh beyond, receding to the English Channel.

And now, instead of bearing left, as has been my wont, I turn right into Monmouth Street, where the handsome Queen Anne houses begin, and the avenue of sweet-scented lime trees set into the wide brick sidewalks, and the dignified, white-pillared Monmouth Hotel, and the offices of the more gentlemanly professions: doctors, architects, ecclesiastical commissioners, lawyers.

This, for me, is the most direct route to the railway station. But during the last five years I have been taking the longer way, through Shadow Twitten and Quakers' Row.

Big, four-storeyed, and impressive, the flint-built, stone-dressed frontage of Roche, Quimper, and Durrenmatt, whose premises for years I have taken such pains to avoid passing. The wide-panelled black front door, with its thick, clean mat, stands open on this summer day. I put my head into the receptionists' enclosure, partitioned from the hall by a breast-high polished walnut barrier, and give my name.

"Miss Churchill. Mr. Roche is expecting me at nine-thirty."

"I should know *you*, Miss Churchill, I should hope!"

Miss Knowles, elderly, moustached, and spectacled, beams in welcome. "Though it's *ever* such a long time since we've seen you. Mr. Roche is expecting you, I know, if you care to walk up."

Once inside, you realise that the Queen Anne frontage is only a facade. Sloping stairs, trodden hollow by generations, doorways built for dwarves, reveal their earlier origins. Anthony's office is situated three flights up. By seniority he would be entitled to something lower down, but he loves the view, a dramatic one down over the town walls and the flat grassy park known as the Severals, enclosed by plane trees and girdled by the river Aff.

Antarctica would seem like a thermal region compared to the atmosphere in Anthony's room.

I had forgotten—strangely enough—his towering height. A fine figure of a man (as Aunt Thisbe would say), massively proportioned, with strong nose and chin, muscular neck, resonant voice, deep-set eyes. More than a touch of grey, now, in his thick bushy brows and upspringing black hair.

When I was a child I divided people, no matter what their age, into Us and Them, children and grown-ups. Anthony would always have been one of the grown-ups.

Dan's black eyebrows were more beautiful, though: soft and glossy, like paintbrushes; you always wanted to stroke them. I think they were what first made me fall in love with him.

"Good morning. Won't you sit down?"

Anthony's voice, his whole bearing, was stiff with outrage and dislike at this infringement of his five-year privacy. He gestured at the black-leather-upholstered chair in front of his desk. And I thought, That hand used to adoringly cradle my breast, that voice —deep-toned, faint touch of Irish about it—had the power, even on the phone, to make my heart melt like a candle.

Anthony is able to trace his descent clear back to some character who came over with William the Conqueror. His ancestors have been settling tribal disputes in County Cork for seven hundred years. And, I daresay, intermarrying with quite a sprinkling of the indigenous Celts through the generations. He has inherited all their propensity for grudge and grievance.

I could easily remember almost his last shouted words at me— in this very room, as it happened, "You're nothing but a *harlot!*"

"Oh, come off it, Anthony! Who are *you*, to pass judgement, if I may ask?"

But my words went unheard, and what difference would they have made? He was in such a tearing passion, his hands shaking uncontrollably as he stubbed out yet another cigarette, that I seriously wondered whether he might not brain me with the heavy glass ashtray. And anyway our discussion (if it could be called that) had terminated, there was nothing more to be said, so I left the room, with Anthony still in full peroration, and had not seen him since. Now, glancing politely about me, I noticed one difference in his office, otherwise quite unchanged: the ashtray was gone.

"You've given up smoking!" I exclaimed.

He glanced at his watch.

"I haven't a lot of time. If you wouldn't mind—" Painstakingly patient.

"Oh. Yes. Well. It's like this." I found it hard to get started, particularly in view of his unconcealed suspicion and hostility. I said, "I have begun wondering—it has been in my mind a good deal lately—whether Daniel's son might possibly still be alive."

"Daniel's son."

"The son of Daniel Suter. My husband."

Anthony was being deliberately unhelpful. He knew perfectly well what I was talking about. He had been Dan's friend in the first place, they knew each other before I knew either of them, they met in a train somewhere, fell into conversation, found they both hailed from Affton Wells, and settled to a discussion of the South-Eastern Arts Council, its parsimony, pigheadedness, and heinous usage of the Cinque Ports University. Dan was always falling into talk with strangers on trains and thus forming lasting friendships; so, when he and Ingrid wanted a divorce, he naturally turned to Anthony for help. The divorce, in the event, had not come about, but it was after Ingrid's death that Anthony tidied up the legal loose ends, such as there were. And had continued to do so, after Dan's own death. Two or three debts, complications from his past had, in course of time, come to light, which Anthony dealt with for me in his characteristic way, with speed, energy, efficiency, and ruthless honesty.

"Do I have to pay this grisly character, Anthony?"

"Dan was your husband, wasn't he? You inherited his estate?"

"A thousand pounds of insurance and nine hundred pounds of debts."

"You are in a perfectly good position to pay the debts now," Anthony pointed out.

Which was true. By then I had gone back to work for Daisy Dairy Products and risen to Director of Marketing. Also Vanessa, my mother, had settled on me, her only child, the rights to all her Greek drama translations, which had won her the Epidauros Prize and brought me in a tidy annual sum. So I paid off all poor Dan's seamy debts and bled a little, inwardly, as each was revealed.

If minds can be covered with scar tissue, mine is like a patchwork vest.

"You may remember, perhaps," I said now to Anthony, regulating my patience by his, "that Daniel and Ingrid had a baby, little Finn. He was six months old when Dan and I married."

"Of course I know *that*," he replied rather sharply, as if I were accusing him of senility. "But the child was on the boat when it went down."

"There was never any proof of that. His body was never washed up—when the other two—"

I swallowed and stopped.

Anthony looked at me with intense distaste.

"And what in the *world* would give you the notion, after all this time—twelve years—"

"Thirteen. I was twenty-two when I married Dan."

"—that the child might still be alive? Why—for instance—wouldn't the authorities have been notified—if a child had been washed up—?"

"Somebody might have preferred not to."

"And an unknown child was just accepted into a community without question? What Gothic romance put *that* idea into your head?" he inquired acidly.

I hesitated before answering him.

In fact there *had* been some of the trappings of Gothic romance.

When I first moved into Watch Cottage the house contained no telephone (it had belonged latterly to a ninety-eight-year-old eccentric who had retired there from Trinidad and peacefully starved himself to death). For my work a telephone was an urgent necessity, but in those days a delay of nine months was nothing out of the common before the post office got around to granting the frantic prayers of would-be subscribers. But I had learned expertise in the pursuit of my profession: I pestered the GPO by letter, card, and phone box calls; I was in front of the Regional Telephone Office counter day after day, cursing, threatening, and pleading; as a result, in a record-breaking three weeks, my phone was scrambled in for me by a pair of what appeared to be moonlighters working after hours; two ends of wire were tied in a granny knot among the jungle of wistaria outside the front window, a hasty hole was bored through the white planking, and Watch Cottage became connected to the outside world. It was intended to be a temporary installation, but nobody ever returned to approve or improve the rather makeshift connection. Consequently, on the debit side, and doubtless a deliberate punishment meted out in retribution for harassing the post office out of its due process, I had to put up with the fact that in windy weather my line tended to go dumb, or become crossed with other lines; thus I picked up all sorts of riveting conversations between total strangers about their illnesses, children's misdoings, professional problems, habit of smuggling watches from Switzerland, feuds with neighbours, and plans for Christmas.

Once or twice I suggested to the GPO that they ought to do something about it, but, since the service was satisfactory on the whole, I did not devote the same energy to the matter that I had in the first place when it was a question of getting the phone installed; besides I was bitterly lonely at that time in spite of, or because of, my various lovers, and it became an entertainment, furnished a kind of ghostly companionship, to participate as silent witness in the lives of these unknown people. It was a frill on the edge of life.

Until the day when, last year, I picked up the receiver to call the Gas Board, and heard two women talking.

First came various gruesome surgical details. One of the pair was suffering from the after-effects of a dental operation; extraction of wisdom teeth, maybe.

". . . They still keep picking splinters of bone out of my jaw. I shan't be able to eat for another week. I must have lost at least nine pounds."

"Well, congratulations. I can put that *on* in a week. Too many professional lunches, that's my trouble," drily responded Number Two, whose sympathy had been perfunctory at best. "When do you plan to get back to work?"

"Oh, not for some days yet."

Both had decidedly upper-crust, horseback-riding accents; those full, ringing British tones that carry the details of their owners' opinions and domestic concerns clear across a crowded restaurant. St. Anthony himself would not have withstood the temptation of listening in to them, and I'm no St. Anthony.

"So: what about Robert?"

"My dear! He was shattered, because Neil had got at him, threatened to commit *suicide*, in his *bath*, I fancy. Robert wrote a letter about it."

"Did he?" The other now sounded really interested. "Fancy that! I'll drop round some time for a cup of coffee and then I can read it."

"Oh, all right." Lack of enthusiasm here. Well, poor thing, she has her painful jaw, I thought, she won't want to be bothered with droppers-in. "We do have these boys here, you know," she went on in a demurring manner.

The line crackled—it was apt to do that—for a moment or two, and then came back, clear as a bell. The louder of the pair, Professional Lunches, was now saying, "But what about Daniel's second wife? You mean she never *knew* that his child was still alive?"

"No, how could she? After all, if you think, there was no way in which she could have found out."

"Wouldn't she have tried to find out?"

"Why should she? He was no concern of hers. She had her own life to lead. And, anyway, what would give her the idea? She'd naturally assume him to be dead."

"But if she had loved her husband?"

"Hmm. I'll have to think a bit more about that. I might be able to make some use of it."

"Make some use! I should think so! It's the *key*. There's a real angle here. You know, I think there could be a packet of money in this one."

"You really think so?" Hopeful; greedy; eagerly questioning.

"Certain of it."

And then—just at that moment—I had to go and cough—I was at home convalescing from flu—and one of the women said sharply, "Is there anybody else on this line?"

I kept mousy quiet, but Sore Jaw said, "Well, anyway, I'm supposed to gargle every hour. I'll call you again soon when I know more about how it's going."

"So long then. See you very soon."

Wait! Wait! I wanted to cry, what was all that about Dan's second wife, and the child? But—tantalisingly, irretrievably—they had vanished into the ether, leaving me clutching the white Bakelite receiver as if it were a hot line to the banks of the river Styx, the ghostly fields of Tartarus.

For several months I brooded about this conversation. I didn't rush precipitately into action. I was cautious. But at length I decided it would do no harm to write to Dan's mother and ask if I might go to see her. Mrs. Suter had always loathed me, as much as she did her first daughter-in-law, and no doubt still did, though I had long since paid back the four hundred that Dan borrowed from her as a down payment on the boat *Valkyrie*. Plus interest. She never acknowledged it, though I knew it had been put into her post office account. As when I informed her about Watch Cottage, she didn't answer my letter, but I went to see her anyway: a long dismal journey on the Northern line, out past a lot of suburbs with Saxon names like Thane Acre and Edwell's Wood, but wholly un-Saxon appearance. Unending red-brick wilderness.

Then a half hour's walk from the Dodman's End tube station through more and more melancholy streets of little neglected houses. And finally, disappointment.

"No. Sorry. Mrs. Suter doesn't live here now."

A fat mop-headed woman, who ought to have been jolly to match her girth, but had eyes cold as frozen peas.

"She'd gone before we moved here. Don't know how long. No, she never left no forwarding address; or not with us. You could ask at the post office. But we've been here close on two years."

Now I noticed that the house and garden looked much more unkempt than they had on my previous, infrequent visits. Thin, sour, disillusioned, joyless, Dan's mother found her only satisfaction in keeping her house grimly neat, her garden glaring with hideous unnatural flowers, Perspex-coloured dahlias, gladiolas, begonias. She had sweetpeas like cheap cotton candy, and roses the colour of plastic curtain material. But now the garden was trampled and straggly, with bare patches.

I made inquiries at the post office, but it was only a tiny sub-office, selling sweets, tinned soup, and papers as well; they hardly remembered Mrs. Suter and were wholly unhelpful. I checked at the doctors' surgery and the Registrar of Deaths, but found no indication that Dan's mother had fallen ill or died; why should she, she was only fifty when he was drowned, he had been her only child, born when she was nineteen. It had been a shotgun marriage, her husband was an alcoholic, she had to do most of the earning, and the father died when Dan was thirteen. No wonder she was so bitterly, jealously possessive. Though her love for Dan had been self-defeating. He couldn't stand her, and I couldn't blame him.

Ingrid's poem "What big false teeth you have/Grandmother dear!/Will you teach Rapunzel/to burn off her hair?" had been written about Mrs. Suter.

No neighbours knew anything about her, but that was not surprising; she detested the suburb where Dan had installed her; she never made friends.

Mrs. Suter had moved away, vanished from Dodman's End, as she had a perfect right to do. I wondered if she might have moved back to Affton Wells, and searched the phonebook; there were upwards of thirty Suters; it was a common local name, but none of them was Mrs. Edith Agnes, nor E.A. And none of them knew anything about her when I tried calling to inquire.

I could hardly blame her for not keeping me informed of her move; I hadn't taken a lot of pains to keep in touch.

The next step I took, after considerable thought, was to advertise.

I put messages in *The Lady, The Times, Exchange & Mart,* and a couple of weeklies famous for their personal columns. "I would be interested to receive any information relating to the present whereabouts of the child of Daniel and Ingrid Suter," and gave my address, Mrs. Suter, c/o Barclays Bank, Victoria Station,

London SW, using that name because I didn't want to make myself the target for a lot of nutters.

There had, however, been a few paragraphs about me in the papers when I received my decoration in the Birthday Honours, and a TV interview mentioning where I lived. I'm in the phonebook under Churchill, C., for I reverted to my maiden name twelve years ago. I suppose it wouldn't be hard to find out where I am, if somebody wanted to.

And evidently somebody had. For after a few months—although I did not have a single answer to my advertisements—I began receiving anonymous letters.

One of these I now silently passed across his large gleaming desk to Anthony Roche. He took it with a look of disgust, as if he could almost see the typhoid germs hatching from the grubby card, on which were pasted words cut from newspapers.

HA HA YOU LITTLE BITCH WOULDNT YOU JUST LIKE TO KNOW WHO HAS THE CHILD.

He surveyed it for a while in silence, then asked, "What about the envelope? Handwritten? Printed? Typed?"

"No. Someone has been to quite a lot of trouble."

They had indeed. You can buy gummed labels with your name and address printed, but not less than a thousand. So someone, somewhere, must have nine hundred and ninety-one labels with my address: Ms. Clytie Churchill, Watch Cottage, Watch Hill, Affton Wells, East Sussex. I showed one to Anthony.

"How many of these have come?"

"That's the ninth. All the same. I didn't keep the others."

"Postmark?"

"Central London. They tend to arrive towards the back end of the week, Thursday to Saturday."

He went on scrutinizing the card in his hand. The expression on his face indicated that this was just the kind of sordid, messy business I might be expected to land myself in. Well, he's right, I thought.

I said, because I really detest bad feeling, and if he was to help me with this problem, I wanted to establish *some* kind of rapport between us, however slight, "You're looking tired, Anthony." And he shouldn't be, it was early on a Monday morning. I went on, "How are you keeping, these days?"

"All right." His tone was brusque, dismissive. None of *your* business, thanks very much, and pray keep your distance. Then I flushed, remembering, too late, the terms of his appalling Last Will and Testament, and the savagery with which I'd been informed of it. But surely, by now, he must have revoked that rancorous document and made another? Knowing Anthony as intimately as I did, though, I could not feel confident as to this.

Would he think I had been inquisitively probing, that I wanted an up-to-date statement from him on his condition of health and expectation of life? Oh damn, damn.

To switch the current of his thought I said hastily, "Do you think I ought to show those cards to the police?"

"No, it isn't the kind of thing they'd want to deal with. No threat has been made, no one is trying to extract money from you."

"But suppose they do?" I remembered the overheard conversation. "*I think there could be a packet of money in this one.*" And a thousand labels meant that someone was settling down for a long siege.

"If they do, *then* it will be time to call in the police."

"In the meantime, how should I act?"

"Well—" He laid the card down with fastidious fingers. "We must assume that the intention at present is simply to annoy and distress. Somebody, somewhere, must be waiting and watching for your reactions. There'd be little point in doing it if they couldn't see the effect it was having."

That was a nasty thought.

"Like obscene telephone callers? Hoping for hysterics, so the quickest way to choke them off is to laugh at them."

"I wouldn't know about that," said Anthony glacially.

Another black mark against poor Clytie, who is wholly immoral, gets into messes, natural prey of extortionists, blackmailers, and lubricious telephone callers.

"So—you think—the—the person who is sending these things must be somebody whom I regularly see, in daily life? Otherwise there'd not be much point . . . ? But who, who in the *world* would nurse a hideous grudge like that—behave in such a way?"

"You are the only one who can answer that question," said Anthony, dry as the Gobi Desert.

I tried to rack my brains, but his stare unnerved me. Well, certainly, my life has not been lacking in event. When I was nineteen I had a real enemy, a woman called Eleanor Foley, a Lesbian paranoid, who hated me like poison, tried her damnedest to murder me, planned to kill her own brother as well, and was incidentally responsible for the deaths of three other people, two of them my greatest friends. Eleanor, had she been alive, could certainly have sent me such messages—would have been happy to do so—but she had died long ago. There was no doubt about her death. And, since that time, though I have conducted my personal relationships in a fairly unfettered—some would say a regardless, irresponsible—manner, I wouldn't think it could be said that I have done anybody any real *harm*—not to elicit a hatred, a venom, like this.

Hastily, I ran over the circle of my friends and colleagues. No possible candidate at Cuisine Churchill; my business affairs are all transacted in a strictly businesslike way; I rely on my staff; when choosing them I look for buoyancy, resilience, and cheerful spirits, as well as culinary talent, and I am seldom misled, so that we are a very congenial, harmonious group; and in my private life . . .

I thought of my two dearest friends, Elly and Chris. Elly I have known since schooldays, and Chris since, at age twenty, we both attended a grisly speedwriting course. I was recovering from three violent deaths, she from three years at the London School of Economics. Elly, Chris, and I have seen each other through marriage, death, and terrible times, know all there is to know about one another, meet casually or intimately several times a month, and are still deep friends, despite all. Could either of them conceivably go wild, become subject to such an aberration—?

No.

It is all too long ago.

I said to Anthony, "I honestly can't think of a soul."

Then a really grotesque thought struck me.

The one person in my entire circle of acquaintance who had ever made his outrage, fury, and detestation of me perfectly plain, unqualified, and vocal was sitting right there opposite me.

"You have poisoned my whole existence—retroactively. The very thought of you makes me sick to my heart. Because of you I shall never be able to like, respect, or believe in another woman. You have crippled my faith in people—even my faith in God. Oh, I can't stand the sight of you! You have even debased my memories of Rose—damn you, damn you!"

That was when I had known it was time to get out, fast. You can't argue with emotion at that flood level. But five years had passed since then. Five is a mystical number. We slough our physical selves, undergo total bodily change in seven years; debts are wiped out, squatters' rights become valid, wooers win maidens' hands. Surely five years ought to provide some statute of limitation for moral debts; at least they should have been set on one side for reconsideration?

Could Anthony be concealing nine hundred and ninety-one labels in his desk drawer? Could he have gone off the rails to such a degree that he began sending me vitriolic anonymous letters? If so, it was certainly a delicate and appropriate bit of irony that I should have turned to him for help, in spite of our shattered relations.

But no: Anthony could not have committed such a malignant act. After all, he was a Catholic, he went to confession through thick and thin.

Or did he now? What did I really know about Anthony these days? He had never married again, I knew that. People said it was a terrible pity.

"Do you still go to confession, Anthony?"

I could imagine myself chattily putting the question, and knew it was time to leave.

"So you think there's nothing to be done?"

"Nothing for the moment. Wait and see what happens. Very likely the whole thing will die out. Whoever it is will become bored, if there is no visible effect."

"How about trying to trace the label firm?"

He shrugged. "I could try. But little printers do them; they come and go like mushrooms."

"Well," I said, "it will be easy enough for me to do nothing. I'm just off to the U.S. for a month, maybe longer." So you see, I added internally, this consultation is not an attempt to resume our interrupted acquaintance. I'm off to fresh woods and pastures new. Clytie is a free agent, pray remember that.

"Going away on a job?" he inquired politely.

"Catering for a medical conference." I hoped to detect a wistful expression in his eye. Anthony used to be crazy about my egg patties. I make them with puff pastry, parsley butter, a touch of Parmesan, and a touch of caviare. He always came around to Ordnance Mansions on Friday evenings, and could eat ten or a dozen, straight off.

But now he merely said, "Oh well, that's excellent. Ten to one the nuisance will have died down by the time you come back. What happens to your mail when you are away?"

"Somebody forwards it. Would you mind," I asked with some diffidence, "if I left instructions for any letters with printed labels to be sent to you?"

After a short hesitation he answered, "Very well. I can see you wouldn't want to be bothered with them while you are feeding the doctors."

Detecting more than a touch of irony in his tone, I stood up in a businesslike way, thanked him for his time, and got myself through the door before he was able to come out from behind his massive desk—supposing he tried; I didn't look back to see.

Down the shallow, much-trodden stairs, remembering the last time, blind with tears; and remembering other, earlier times, on my way in to consult him about this or that point in connection with Cuisine Churchill, Ltd.; at one era the very hollows of those stairs and the massive old baluster rail were endowed with such a potency, such a significance for me that now, seeing them, feeling them, for a moment I was wholly translated back into that earlier state of mind.

It's over, it's done. Forget it. What's gone is gone. Humpty

Dumpty can't be put together again, and you are on an even keel; professionally flourishing.

There was one thing I hadn't been able to bring myself to tell Anthony. I suppose the habit of regular confession makes divulging such intimacies easier? But I had long fallen into habits of privacy, and this was so disgusting—like finding a maggot in one's own infected wound—that I was unable to speak of it. A great pity, as it turned out.

I picked up my travel bag from the receptionist's office and ran on down the hill to Affton Wells station, which is an architectural delight all on its own, being built in a lavish series of noble curves, like some baroque musical clef clasping its signature on the three staves, or tracks, that sweep away in different directions, taking their course to London, Hastings, and Brighton.

At the bookstall I paused to tell Mrs. Fisher that I would be away for a month and to cancel my daily and weekly papers; then down to the long, curving platform.

My first sight of this station was when I stepped off the London train with Dan, on a bright blowy day in October.

He had brought me down from London to look at a house, the house where he was born and spent his childhood.

2

Where were ye, Nymphs, when the remorseless Deep
Closed o'er the head of your lov'd Lycidas?

When I first met Daniel Suter, I was in a state of shock. Travelling on a train from Cornwall, where too many appalling things had happened to me, far too suddenly, en route for London, which, so far as I was concerned, gaped empty as a Black Hole. In Cornwall I had lost my dearest friend. She had been shot in mistake for somebody else, by a poor crazy wretch who had then himself been killed, falling off a viaduct. So there was nobody left alive to blame or console. I had also lost the chance of love; had removed myself, with utter reluctance and agony, from the proximity of a man I'd have gone to the stake for. Unfortunately he didn't need anybody to go to the stake for him; he needed nothing like that; he needed to be left alone. I'd not have been good for him, and, young as I was, and luckily for him, I realised that. He was simple, I'm complicated; I'd have ended by doing him a lot of damage. We won't even mention his name, if you please.

I was nineteen.

So there I found myself, sitting in the goddam train, which wouldn't arrive at its destination for six hours. Six hours of creeping, painful emptiness. I was like a snail whose shell has been ripped off, raw and bleeding from nape to heel. All my past had been violently snatched away; nothing was left but vacancy ahead. Also—never mind the figures of speech—I had a broken leg in a heavy plaster cast, and was obliged to drag myself about with difficulty and some pain on a pair of arm-wrenching crutches. God only knew how I'd cope with the necessities of existence while on the train; negotiating the narrow corridor to the W.C. was, for instance, not going to be practicable, I could see that.

We crept through damp, hummocky Cornwall, and on as far as Devon.

Meanwhile I discovered, reading *The Times* (which had been bought for me by the kind woman who drove me to the station), that yet another friend of mine, a man I had known for several years and had, indeed, latterly gone to bed with, had died, drowned, in a transatlantic yacht race. So *he* would never be coming back; not that I had expected him; we had parted on rather formal terms. But he was a thoughtful, honest person, and I liked him; why, why, had *he* been selected to die, I demanded with rage of the empty air in the empty carriage? How much are we expected to take? Do they think it amusing, somewhere, to see us writhe like squashed bugs?

My solitude in the vacant apartment was the only thing I had that seemed of any value, so I was even more enraged when, at Exeter, another person got in to share and disperse it. The train (it was morning, midweek) had seemed by no means crowded; why the devil couldn't this person find himself somewhere else to sit?

There were dried tears on my cheeks and I wasn't going to wipe them away or trouble to make any kind of social pretence for the incomer; I hunched a shoulder against him as he established himself with his luggage on the opposite seat. Denying his existence, I peered determinedly through the grimy glass while Exeter's suburbs went clanking past. My *Times* slid to the floor and I paid no heed when the stranger quietly picked it up again and laid it on the seat by me.

I had settled into a dull apathy of misery and was beginning to hope that it would be possible to ride out the next five hours in this condition when, after twenty minutes or so, Daniel opened communication by remarking calmly, "I recognised you, of course, as soon as I looked through the window. You wrote that novel, didn't you—*Mayhem in Miniature?* Aren't you Aulis Jones?"

This gambit did jerk me a short distance out of my anguished numbness; it was the very last thing I expected. Yes, he was right; I was Aulis Jones, or at least those were the names I had used for the purpose of my shocking book, written as a fling of defiance to annoy grown-ups and teachers when I was seventeen. Aulis is my middle name, due to my having been born midway between Athens and Thermopylae, and my mother being a Hellenophile; Jones was *her* middle name. But most people at that time called me Tuesday; Aulis, not a name I favour, was employed only on solemn occasions, passing-out ceremonies, funerals, and legal documents.

At that moment I did not at all care to be reminded of my book, which had earned me a certain amount of notoriety two years before, and about a thousand pounds, recklessly spent long since; no publisher had expressed the slightest interest in my second novel, *The Last Cup of Coffee in the World*, and I hadn't yet found time to write my third. Hadn't, indeed, much expectation of ever wishing to do so; writing, I had decided, wasn't my outlet, it wasn't physical enough, it didn't ride me like a vocation. There's a Chekhov character—Trigorin is it? I suppose Chekhov himself, really?—continually driven by something inside him that says, "I must write, I must write"; that isn't my feeling at all. I write, as I learned to roller-skate, in order to leave no area unexplored. But one doesn't wish to roller-skate all the time.

"It was a very funny book, I enjoyed it a lot," added this intruder who had thrust himself into my carriage.

"Good," I said, and would have returned to my inventory of the backyards of Taunton (a dismal town) but my companion needed to talk. Had, in fact, obviously selected me with particular care as a confidante; indeed, now I came to take stock of him, I recognised with gloom a face that had given me a searching stare through the window at Exeter; he had been walking along the platform looking into each carriage in search of somebody; me, apparently. I daresay we all send out signals to each other all the time. I was not aware of having done so, but he, in a state of high tension himself, must have picked up my vibrations.

I have a keen, atavistic sense of smell. By professional practice —all good cooks depend on their sense of smell—it has become yet more delicate—but even then it was sharp enough. Other people's body odours, undetectable to the average nostril, convey loud clear messages to me. I can detect instantly when somebody is nervous, distressed, or unhappy; people emit different essences at those times. I can tell when a person I know has passed through a room, ten minutes after. When I am myself under stress I know that I send out a faint metallic emanation like the scent of a steel knife just removed from hot water. If I am ill the hot-water smell becomes much more pronounced, no matter how often I bathe, shower, or splash on cologne. Some people when happy send out a charming fragrance like the perfume of a ripe wheat field on a warm day, or bread baking.

Anthony in bed had a smell like roasting chestnuts; George rather sharp and acidic, French mustard is the nearest I can get to it.

The smell of approaching death is also quite unmistakable.

So now I was immediately aware that this man opposite was suffering from strong emotional stress, resentment, and anxiety; he exuded a faint but perceptible mineral tang, like crushed rock.

"Are you going to write another novel?" he asked; out with queen's pawn.

"Look," I told him, "I'm prepared to believe you mean no harm, but I am feeling like hell at present; a great friend of mine died last week, and I just read in this *Times* that somebody else I know has been drowned; and I don't feel like talking, do you mind?"

"But, you know," said this persistent character, "drowning's not a bad way to go. If I had any say in the matter, I reckon I'd choose it."

"My friend didn't *want* to die," I snapped at him furiously. "It wasn't a question of choice," and then thought, what did I know about the matter, really? and, secondly, that this was rather an abrupt conversation to be holding with a total stranger.

I gave him a more exhaustive survey. After which I was obliged to admit that I didn't dislike his looks: a narrow, clever face, with a considerable degree of charm; high, well-shaped forehead, humour in the line of the mouth, good teeth, beguiling (*what* a word, but it did describe them), beguiling hazel eyes, and soft floppy dark hair.

And those eyebrows. Ah, poor Dan.

"Look," he said persuasively, "I'm not trying to pick you up, my intentions are strictly honourable and wholly blameless. I'm not a wolf. I'm *married*, if you want to know, I have a wife, she's a writer, too, like you. But, to be honest, I'm in a fairly desperate state myself, I badly need someone to talk to on this journey. And I thought you looked—well, sympathetic and responsive. After we get to London, if you like, we need never meet or speak again. I won't even tell you my name. I'm a neurotic kind of sod, actually, I know that! I don't want to put a burden on you, thrust my troubles into your life. But I just can't face the prospect of a long journey without some congenial person to exchange ideas with."

All this, of course, was highly characteristic of Dan, who lived in a perpetual cloud of glory, loved to romanticise himself, to be the dark stranger; and in my depleted state I fell for it. He was quite a lot older than I, in his late twenties, I guessed (in fact he was twenty-eight), interesting, he seemed, quick-witted, sensitive, but above all I realised that he, too, was in a bad way, there was something serious the matter with him, his sufferings were as acute as my own; and so I began to listen to his story; at least lending an ear to his problems carried me out of my own paralysing despair.

Poor Dan, he did suffer, not a doubt of that; but just the same he wanted a discerning audience for his tale. Not just any old ear would do to pour his woes into, he required a distinguished one, and mine, since I'd written a book that was mildly notorious and had my picture in the Sunday colour supplements, was the best he could find on the ten-thirty Penzance to Paddington train. "Don't-ee marry for money, but go where money is," would be an adage to fit Dan like a glove, if you substituted celebrity for money.

He loved to be around well-known people, especially in the realms of art or literature; he liked cultural name-dropping; unpublished, so far, himself, he made straight for those who had got into print, and cultivated them with as much assiduity as flowers in a desert settlement. I must have seemed a heaven-sent windfall to him on that sad train.

Once assured of my listening ear, he didn't trouble me much for responses, but poured out his soul; I had his whole life story between Taunton and the terminus. His dead, alcoholic father, his jealous, overpossessive mother; his three years of service at sea. "We're a naval family, generations of us," he explained. "Some of my ancestors were admirals, it was just assumed automatically that I'd go in as a midshipman"; the horrors of life in the Navy, nuttier, more sadistic, more rigid, regimented, puritanical, and doctrinaire than Kafka's craziest dream; the terrifying eccentricities of captains who, lonelier than anybody in the world, have to remain shut up, secluded in their cabins, anchorites of the Establishment, for month after month. One had seduced him; another subjected him to atrocious mental torture; a third fell abjectly in love with him and then went out of his mind, throwing raw eggs at the purser and singing obscene variations of hymns.

I began to be really engaged by this recital (which bore the glossy patina of much use); compared with such adventures my own seemed quite commonplace.

"Why don't you write it all down?" I suggested. "It would make a tremendous novel."

But, unfortunately, of course, he had; Conrad, Melville, Masefield had been his models from twelve to twenty; only, for some reason, no publisher would take his book. He had tried twenty. The libel angle probably scared them off, he said.

Later I discovered that was not the reason. Poor Dan was incapable of writing a clear simple sentence when it described his own experience. His book was turgid stuff. Odd, because his professional copy was straightforward enough, and his conversation so persuasive.

Bruised for life, he had rushed out of the Navy and into journalism. He still intended to be a man of letters, and had become involved with small superior magazines of the kind that publish your story but don't pay you for it; then, from a point of vantage as a creative writer (in an advertising agency), he had worked his way into writers' workshops, and seminars, and weekend courses on Identification, and Subjectivity, and Sexual Politics, and Existential Methodology. He had been invited to write a book on creative technique in fiction. He was going to represent Great Britain at an international writers' conference in the Seychelles. He had a grant from the Arts Council to do research on orphaned writers.

All this impressed me greatly; it seemed a far more intellectual approach to literature than my own simple notions about writing books.

"What about your wife?" I asked. "Didn't you say that she was a writer too?"

"Oh, God, yes."

She, I learned, was why he was in this state of tension and despair. It seemed she had just tried to kill herself. He had been obliged to abandon a course on creative writing at Exeter University, where he had been lecturing on the Heroic Myth, in order to dash back to her bedside in St. Mary Abbotts hospital.

"*Suicide?*" I was aghast. "But why?"

Even in my own state of utter wretchedness, I found it hard to conceive a point of such desolation that one would wish to give up entirely; not to have sufficient curiosity to want to see what lies around the next corner; not to feel that, if life is so terrible now, surely there must be room for improvement?

He began to tell me about his wife, Ingrid. Aristocratic forbears, Danish, mother died, father married again; family trouble, unloving stepmother, hostile stepsister, father now dead; she had married Dan and come to England in order, I gathered, to escape from this unhappy background.

"What did you say her name was? What does she write?"

"She's a poet. Her name is Ingrid Christ."

It seemed faintly familiar. I had seen a slim volume, perhaps? Or even a couple, with the imprint of some quite prestigious publisher?

"But why try to *kill* herself?" I asked Dan. "What made her want to get out of the *world*?"

I felt personally troubled by her act, as if I had been giving a party and one of the guests disdainfully glanced about and turned to leave before even first drinks or sticks of celery were handed.

A wary look came over Dan's face. He said: "She has always been that way. She's a poet—you know what that means. She really sweats blood over her poetry; each time she writes a poem it's like pulling out a piece of her gut and offering it to mankind. All poets are the same," he added sourly.

"I've never met one." But, thinking over those whose lives I could recall, I supposed he might be right. Poets are a driven, frantic lot—they die young, they kill themselves with drugs, with drink, with guns. But why? Surely they have special privileges?

"It doesn't work that way," said Dan. "She believes that the world owes her *everything*, in return for what she produces. And nothing that anyone can ever do for her will be enough."

He did sound aggrieved. However, being a poet's husband can't be any bed of roses, I supposed. Sappho never had one, Browning and Wilfred Meynell were poets themselves, so knew what it was about. Very likely poor Dan felt excluded from the Orphic mysteries. Or expected her to write her poetry about him and felt snubbed when she didn't. Or thought he was misrepresented by what she wrote.

"When we were first married it was all different. She trusted me then," he lamented. "I thought I'd be able to reconcile her to life—make her happy."

Now, of course, I know what a fatal mistake it is to marry somebody thinking that you are going to change their life.

"What is her poetry about?" I asked.

"Mostly about death."

"What's it like? Can you say some?"

"*Say* some?" He sounded as put out, as affronted, as if I'd asked for a look at his toenails. Englishmen don't recite poetry on trains.

"Well, but can't you remember *any* of it? Not a single line?"

"No. Not offhand," he answered briefly, and went on to describe the terribly difficult relations between Ingrid and his mother, after he had come out of the Navy. He had met Ingrid, it seemed, in Copenhagen, on some naval occasion, was bewitched by her patrician bearing, and married her as soon as he could extricate himself from the service of his country. Back in England, he had persuaded his mother to sell the little house where he had been born and brought up, in a small Sussex town, to buy one closer to London, which the young couple could share, in order that Dan might work for a Fleet Street publicity agency, and Ingrid meet London poetry editors.

But of course the arrangement proved disastrous; aristocratic Ingrid and middle-class Mrs. Suter had not one thing in common; there had been fierce quarrels and a speedy separation of the parties. Dan's mother had been especially bitter over losing her house in a town where she had lived all her life and had acquaintances, if not friends, and getting in return only solitude and anonymity in a huge, featureless London suburb.

"Are you *sure* you can't remember any of Ingrid's poetry? If you think of one, even one verse, one line, do say it," I put in, becoming bored with dismal old Mrs. Suter, anxious to get back to Ingrid, wondering what means of suicide she had tried, and why the attempt had not been successful. Had it, perhaps, been one of those not-serious demonstrations that psychiatrists classify as a Call for Help? Was anybody helping Ingrid?

"Everybody thinks her poetry is quite first class," Dan informed me with pride, as if she were a restaurant and he a Good Food Guide awarding her crossed knives and forks. "She's had wonderful reviews by Leavis, Prendergast, Empson, Lauterpacht—she's had poems in the *Paris Review* and the *London Review* and the *Atlantic Monthly—*"

"And you can't think of a single line?"

"No, I can't," he said flatly.

"Well—what does she look like?"

"Very, very beautiful. Tall. Fair."

The very reverse of me, I thought. In every particular.

"Classic beauty," Dan went on, warming to his subject. "Like a Norse goddess. Like Garbo. Like Liv Ullmann."

Both? But, anyway, just how I had imagined her. To me the name Ingrid *sounded* beautiful—like calm granite sculpture. Like tranquil water in stone pools. She had all that—the poetry, the beauty, a devoted husband, critical acclaim—why in the world did she want to die?

"Do you have children?"

His face shut like a trap.

"Ingrid doesn't want a child."

I said hastily, since this appeared to be a mined area, "How old is she?"

Instead of answering, Dan suddenly declaimed:

> *My wilful corpse, as I lie sleeping*
> *Takes stubbornly the air I grieve*
> *And thus with breath keeps warm the coffin*
> *Which I would give my life to leave . . .*
>
> *Thus waking day by day I find me*
> *Exiled again from my dark trance;*
> *Eve, Adam rise in me to battle*
> *Pluck up their weapons and advance—*

"There! You see, you *did* remember some!" Powerfully struck by the suddenness of his oration, for which I had ceased to hope, as well as by the lines themselves, I pondered them for a while in silence. They were not at all the kind of thing I had expected from the various clues Dan had let fall. I had imagined that Ingrid would take a more obscure, gnomic line; cryptic, mystical in utterance; not such a plain statement.

"Are they all like that?"

"No," he said vaguely, as if searching in a foreign market for an object he had little expectation of finding, "but they are all very . . . strong."

I received a sudden distinct impression of Ingrid; as if she herself had spoken through him to me. I *felt* her—powerful, caged, conscious that her forces were somehow being misapplied, yet unable to redirect them. But, surely, a person with all that vigour inside her would be able to find a way out other than self-destruction?

What factor is it in us that gives some the purpose to battle on and survive, while others concede defeat before the game is half over, rush on to the finale, succumb without putting up any kind of fight at all? Are such people naturally drawn to one another?

Dan gave me an apple and ate one himself. While we munched, he told me a bit about places he had visited while in the Navy. He had a shrewd, observant eye, could hit off a place or person in a couple of witty phrases; I thought he probably made an excellent journalist (as, indeed, he did) so long as he stayed with straightforward description or analysis. It was only when he began trying to express ideas, particularly his own, that he went agley.

How very hard he was working to impress me, I thought unkindly, observing with detachment his animation, the way in which he gestured with his well-shaped muscular hands, crossed and uncrossed his long legs, leaned forward forcibly to emphasize a point.

Dan's urge to impress was compulsive; it hardly mattered to him what audience received his performance, once he got going, provided there *was* an audience. Even then I was aware of this, but it amused me. I felt a kind of friendly compassion for him because he was bothering to put on all this production for me, and, had he but known it, I was predisposed in his favour already; at least that part of me, poor tattered fragment, which was still engaged with life and what it had to offer. I found Dan compatible —funny, charming, and pathetic. His faults were spread before me like a map, I disregarded and forgave them. Parallel to this feeling ran my strong idiosympathy—is there such a word?—for Ingrid; I felt I knew that girl and deeply wished her well; I thought she had probably committed a bad mistake in marrying Dan and now perhaps regretted it, but I hoped they still had a chance to make a success of their life together. And anyway, for heaven's sake, she didn't have to *kill* herself—did she?—to get away from him.

"Is she a good cook—Ingrid, I mean?" I asked, interrupting him in mid-flow. You can tell such a lot about people—everything, really—from their attitude to food.

My friend Elly is a superb unimaginative cook, my friend Chris an atrocious but interesting one; you could read either of them from the way they deal with an egg.

Dan started off into a panegyric about smorgasbord, but then quickly reverted to what a terrible cook his mother was; resentful at having to do it at all, bored, parsimonious, addicted to margarine, tinned peas, tomato soup, and wrapped bread. Dan's approach to all subjects seemed bounded by his mother, she rose like a cliff in every direction. It was remarkable, I thought—really interesting—that he had managed to rescue himself from her by marriage to Ingrid, only to run back, head-first, into the trap again.

But Ingrid was probably quite equal to her mother-in-law if matters came to a direct confrontation.

Presently, looking out of the window, I was astonished to realise that we had reached the western suburbs of London; absorbed by Dan's recital I had been unaware of the passage of time. My journey had proved infinitely less painful than I had any right to expect, and for that I felt gratitude to Daniel, though aware that his motives were entirely self-interested; it was not for *my* benefit that he had entertained me, simply because he needed distraction from his own distresses.

"Well—" He stood up, took down his bag from the rack. "Just as I expected, it's been good talking to you. I knew, when I first looked at you, that you'd be very receptive."

Receptive, yeah. Receptive as a bomb crater.

"Is somebody meeting you? Can I get you a cab? Sure? As a matter of fact, I really ought to rush—I promised I'd get to the hospital by six."

"I do—I do *hope* she's all right."

Almost I said, "Give her my love." I felt that I knew Ingrid quite intimately; as if she were my perplexed sister, the sister I didn't have.

"Oh—thank you." Polite but heedless already; he was no part of me any longer, I was not for him. Then he had gone, thrusting his hasty way through the evening crowds.

Nobody *was* there to meet me, of course; how could there be? I had to wait until a carriage cleaner arrived, with broom and trash can, to help me out of the train, with my crutches, plaster cast, and rucksack. By now the platform had emptied, the hurrying travellers were all gone, and so were the taxis.

Three years passed before I met Dan again.

From time to time, however, I remembered that intimate, one-sided conversation. Occasionally I would come across one of Ingrid's poems, in the *New Statesman* or *TLS*; I used to cut them out and keep them. They all, to me, seemed to carry the same urgent message: a demand to be let out of the cage, to be set free. Were they any good? I'm no expert, I couldn't judge. I liked them, but they made me anxious. Sometimes she figured in a short news story; she had taken part in a protest, received an award, appeared on a panel. The stories sometimes mentioned that her husband was a journalist; from which I concluded that she was still married to Dan.

Meanwhile, time passed, as the train journey had done. You don't recover from agony. The fissure is still there in your substructure, but the rocks settle together and roots of trees bind up the cracks. I took various courses, worked at various jobs, met my friend Chris Ellenwater, now Chris Davenport, shared a flat with her in Beaufort Street, where we lived mostly on curried rabbit and black-currant purée, because we were abysmally poor; Chris had a boyfriend, Ferdi Kundera, a Hungarian flautist, who used to drop around sometimes with a bottle of red wine, but he was very poor, too, the wine came from Algeria, and his relationship with Chris was a very low-pressure one; indeed, we were all too hard-worked and undernourished to do much more than just get on with our lives. I had become interested in cooking; I did private catering, people's dinner parties, in the evenings, to eke out

my scanty salary as a field worker (which meant faking ques-
tionnaires on housewives' doorsteps) for Daisy Dairy Products;
and so that was how I met Dan again.

My boss, a kind lady who believed in giving young talent a
chance, specially when it meant getting cheap service, had asked
me to organise and prepare a publicity dinner in our office suite,
given in honour of some visiting Dutch margarine tycoons. It was
a buffet occasion. All the dishes had to be made with marge, my
chief told me; otherwise, within our budget limits, I might have a
free hand.

To my astonishment, there was Daniel among the guests. He
was no margarine tycoon, I felt certain, though he seemed entirely
at his ease. He looked just as I remembered him. For several
reasons, I decided not to approach him. Firstly, if he were there
under false pretences, I wouldn't be the one to expose him;
secondly, he might not remember me; thirdly, I had read some
sad news, a few months ago, which made me pity him deeply,
and pity is not something easily expressed at a party.

But to my surprise he saw me and came straight over.

"Hallo! You know, I felt sure we'd meet again someday! What
an extraordinary conversation that was. What a lot we said."

What a lot you said, I thought.

And I said, "Don't tell me you're a margarine tycoon?"

"No, I cover stories like this for the *Londoner's Diary*. And
you?"

"Oh, I work here, at Daisy Dairy. In fact I cooked this meal."

"It's very good." He sounded surprised. "Don't tell me it's all
done with margarine."

"No. It isn't. But don't put that in the *Londoner's Diary*. I
economised on the wine instead. Didn't think they'd notice."

They hadn't.

"Are you still writing? Listen, let's meet, shall we?" he said
eagerly. "How about tomorrow evening? Are you free?"

Our acquaintance rolled along from there. Dan often said, "I
felt as if we'd been *led together* again." We rapidly discovered all
kinds of odd coincidences about each other; our birthdays fell on

the same date, our telephone numbers were the same but in reverse order, we shared dreams at night, or came out with identical remarks, we had read the same books, seen the same films. For a short period of time our psyches were threaded, laced together, as if some random wind from space had entwined us.

Of course he talked at immense length about Ingrid, who had killed herself three months before.

I had read about it in the papers.

Thirteen weeks previously they had had a baby. She had had a baby. Planned, agreed on, no problems about the birth, a son, little Finn, a beautiful child, Dan delighted, Mrs. Suter proud, everybody happy. A week after coming home from hospital, mother and child doing well, Ingrid had taken her car, a Porsche won with the proceeds of a poetry prize, driven herself to Kent, driven herself and car over the white cliffs of Dover. The same way that she entered England, she left it for good.

The baby had been deposited for the day with Dan's mother; Ingrid said she wanted to attend a lecture on prosody. Typed a letter for Dan to find, explaining that she had had enough of life. It didn't suit her and she wanted no more of it.

"I always knew she'd bring it off sooner or later," said Dan. "Always. It was like living on the side of a volcano."

"But what had gone wrong? Her poetry? The baby?"

"Well, her last batch had been sent back by Creevey and Creevey, the publishers who did the other books. They just said it was a bad time for poetry. Ingrid hadn't tried sending them anywhere else. The baby . . . Well. She looked after him capably enough. But she said she didn't love him. Couldn't. Found she had no maternal feelings. Milk and nappies and all that disgusted her. It would have been better, she said, if Finn had been covered with fur. Ingrid was very fond of cats."

"So where's the baby now?"

"With my mother, of course." Dan sounded surprised. "She's devoted to him. It has quite changed her life."

Dan and I began going out regularly. In fact we couldn't see too much of one another. Each filled a hole in the other's existence. We enjoyed the same shows, dishes, magazines, liked walking in the same countryside. Through me, Dan was introduced to the world of classical music; thunderstruck, he discovered what a pleasure he had been missing. The first Brandenburg Concerto that he heard knocked him endways; after that he couldn't hear enough Bach. He came to our flat in Beaufort Street and met Chris, and through her Ferdi Kundera; we did lots of things all four together, going out to Proms or on Putney Heath; staying in, cooking spaghetti, and listening to records. We all went to the Dartington music summer school for two happy weeks that July; Ferdi was playing there professionally and procured tickets for us.

Dan took me to see his mother, and the baby, now coming up to four months, at the dismal little house in Dodman's End.

Mrs. Suter, of course, greeted me with total aversion and mistrust. One Ingrid had been quite enough in her life. To be sure, I was English, at least, but what sort of a name was *Clytie*?

She was a thin, cardiganed, scooped-out woman, with brownish-greyish lanky hair scraped into a bun, and a sallow face like a slice of melon. Her eyes were pale, watchful, suspicious; she seemed wholly different from Dan in every way. I speculated a good deal as to what the alcoholic husband could have been like. Could it have been from him that Dan's optimism and buoyancy derived? To say that Mrs. Suter was reticent about her deceased husband would be a major understatement. Just occasionally there would be some passing mention of "your dad" in a remark to Dan; the tone was always derogatory, dry, sour, dismissive.

Sometimes it did occur to me to wonder a little at the extremely resilient way in which Dan had bounced back to normality and hope after his devastating experience with Ingrid. Her death was so recent: only four months, only five months in the past. My own traumas were now three years behind me, but still I had nightmares, still searched, hopelessly, in crowds, for faces that I would never see again; still woke, very often, in the mornings, with a heart like lead and throat stiff with tears, still dissolved, helplessly, at certain pieces of music. Dan was helping to heal me, but I knew I was a long way, yet, from total recovery; I did not delude myself about that.

But, I suppose he had been living with the threat of what finally happened for three years; for him, in a way, it had begun to happen a long time ago.

Mrs. Suter disliked my coming to Dodman's End; I could see that; but she could not resist showing off little Finn, and if my presence was the price she had to pay for Dan's visits, very well. Dan was proud of the child, too, but he found going to visit his mother a detestable bore, and once a month was quite often enough to his way of thinking.

Little Finn was indeed a beautiful child: downy, peaceful, smiling, brown-eyed and silky-fair-headed, he lay thoughtfully gazing at his toes or at us; he seemed like some celestial Correggio baby, arrayed in light. He never cried; took his bottle, Mrs. Suter informed us proudly, like an angel; betrayed no awareness of the tragedy in the background, of his grievous loss.

Like Ingrid, I could not feel any maternal instincts stirring in me; had no instinctive yearnings towards cradles and diapers; but it was impossible to see little Finn without being bowled over by his radiance. It did seem exceedingly sad that he should be obliged to spend his childhood under the governance of sour Mrs. Suter, living on margarine, tinned peas, and wrapped bread in that cold ugly little house at Dodman's End.

I thought that he ought to be with Dan. Dan would make— wouldn't he?—a loving, lively father. Very different from mine, who had been an archaeologist first, and a parent only a long way further down the scale; and had, anyway, died of dysentery on a dig long before I was old enough to have much rapport with him.

"How can you be happy about leaving little Finn with your mother?" I asked Dan.

"Oh, why not?" He was quite blithe about it. "The kid's too young to mind; it's doing Mother a hell of a lot of good; gives her something to care about, think about. I couldn't look after a baby, could I now?"

Dan had a flat, a kind of loft, near Covent Garden, handy for Fleet Street; soon I was spending a good many nights in it, and had helped civilise it, for on my first visit it held only a camp bed and a tin trunk, besides his clothes; in a frenzy, after Ingrid's death, he had given up the room they had in Earls Court and sold or given away their furniture.

By degrees it emerged that he had been planning, at the time we met again, to live on a boat on the Thames, moored at Hammersmith, or in the Pool of London. Sailing was the chief passion that he and Ingrid had in common; they had first met in some Copenhagen yacht club, and so long as they could go on boating trips together, haul in halyards, splice booms, or whatever you do, all was well; Ingrid, I began to see, had an image of herself as a golden sailor boy, a Viking lass, and while Dan shared this image, all went well. Domesticity was what brought them to grief.

In pursuance of his aim of living on a boat, Dan had recently bought one; which was why, as I soon began to realise, he had practically no money in spite of earning a good Fleet Street salary; the boat, *Valkyrie*, sucked it up like blotting paper. Somehow his aim had been deflected, he had failed to buy the houseboat he was after, and had instead acquired a seagoing sloop in rather poor repair. This was very characteristic of Dan, who had an air of dashing expertise that camouflaged a strange randomness in his life pattern; he could very easily set out to buy a horse and come back with a gross of shagreen leather spectacle cases, and would then be able to give you excellent reasons why the shagreen cases were a better buy.

So he had this boat, *Valkyrie*; and we were to take a wedding trip on it, for somehow, before long, without much said, it had become established that Dan and I were going to be married.

Everyone thought it an excellent plan. Chris was pleased, because then she could share the Beaufort Street flat with Ferdi; my aunt Thisbe, who had invited Dan and me to a formal dinner in her huge, pitch-dark apartment in Ordnance Mansions, Powdermakers Way, Victoria Street, appeared greatly taken with Dan, who was politically alert, a lively talker, and gave her back as good as he got; Thisbe wrote my mother that for once I had taken a sensible step, and Vanessa cabled her approval and congratulations from Easter Island. My friend Elly wrote from York that it was high time I married and settled down; twenty-two was a good age for matrimony. She herself had taken the plunge at twenty and never regretted it.

The only person thoroughly opposed to our nuptials was, needless to say, Dan's mother, for I was proposing to throw up my job at Daisy Dairy, begin free-lancing instead, and thus be able to take care of little Finn, who would live with us as soon as we returned from our sailing trip. Where would we live? No firm decisions had been reached about that. Dan thought we ought to have a house. Where would the money come from? Never mind. In the meantime we would camp in the Covent Garden loft.

Candidly, I didn't look forward to the sailing trip. I hardly know one end of a boat from the other, and will be happy to leave matters that way. I tried not to let my lack of enthusiasm become too plain. Dan's romantic heart was set on sailing round the Kent coast from Gravesend, where the boat was moored at present, and up the river Aff to Affton Wells, the town where he had grown up.

"I'll show you the house where I was born," he said with a yearning look in his eye. "But whatever you do, don't tell Mother where we are going, she'd never forgive me. She's still mad at me for making her sell the house and move to Dodman's End."

I could hardly blame her. Who in his right mind would want to live in that ugly nondescript spot? But I said, "Why in the world doesn't she move back, since you don't live with her now anyway?"

"Oh, she couldn't afford to," he said carelessly. "House prices have shot there since we left."

And Dan, I guessed, had spent a large part of what the Affton house fetched when they sold it; money poured through his hands like sand.

Then, all of a sudden, he decided that it would take too long to sail so far, all the way round the coast of Kent and a chunk of Sussex, up the shoaly Aff River. Instead, we would spend our week's honeymoon sailing in the Thames estuary.

I was relieved. That plan, I thought, sounded more within my compass.

"We'll go down to Affton before, by train, a day trip," Dan
said. "That way, it'll be easier to keep it dark from Mother."

We were to be married on Monday, October 7. So we went to
Affton on Sunday, October 6.

It was a halcyon day; golden October weather. Chestnut leaves
turning yellow; dahlias and Michaelmas daisies still blooming in
the little steep gardens. The town of Affton Wells glittered like a
pile of coffee sugar on its hill above the railway station, with the
castle crowning all. Sheep, tiny as cottonseeds, nibbled far away
on the green marsh.

I was feeling buoyant and joyful. My first recipe book, *All
You Can Do with an Apple*, had just come out, and, that very
day, had a short but good review in *The Observer*; I began to feel
confident that I could combine looking after little Finn with
making enough money from free-lance cookery to counterbalance
Dan's extravagance.

And Affton was such a handsome town! A splendid place for a
day trip. I had never been there before; hardly even knew of its
existence. It is very salutary and exhilarating to discover a gap in
one's knowledge and have it so satisfyingly filled.

Dan rushed me about the town, showing me the house where
the mystical poet James Herriard lived in the seventeenth century, the Shambles, the pub where Charles II had lunch, the
slope Dan had slid down with his friends below the castle keep,
the confectioner's shop where he stole his first packet of Wood-
bines while a friend distracted the shopkeeper, the river wharfside
where, even now, Dutch barges still occasionally moored, the
Upper Severals, a paved colonnaded area where very nasty mineral water could be purchased and drunk in paper cups, the Fif-
teenth-Century Bookshop, and the Flower Market.

He was in tearing spirits; happy as a schoolboy. He seemed to
have thrown off all cares. What thoughts can have been going
through his mind? To my dying day I shall ask myself that question. How very different our lives would be if we could hear each
other think. Privacy, somebody said, is the essence of civilisation.
It is also the essence of concealment, treachery, betrayal, outrage.

We had lunch, roast beef and Yorkshire pud, at the white-pillared cosy, stuffy Monmouth.

"Now we'll go and look at Watch Cottage," said Dan.

He was really excited. I could feel his hand tremble in mine as we climbed up winding cobbled Bastion Street and turned into even steeper Watch Hill. Nobody was about, not a soul to be seen. Sunday afternoon sloth and calm pervaded the air. The little white-boarded house sat tranquilly above us at the top of the short, narrow cul-de-sac street; snuggled in wistaria it seemed peaceful as a broody Leghorn hen.

"I *wish* you could see inside," said Dan, wistful, peering through a window. "The rooms are panelled in white match-boarding. And there's an arched window over the stairs at the back; very pretty; and the kitchen looks out on a little paved courtyard."

He tried the front door.

"Dan! What ever are you *doing*?"

But the door was locked. He even pressed the bell and knocked; but nobody answered, and his face took on a closed, clouded look.

"Well . . ." he said. "Someday we'll buy it back. When your name is as well known as Isabella Beeton, and I'm writing *Times* leaders, we'll be so rich that we can afford to live here and travel up to London every day. The town has a wonderful train service."

"Then why in the world didn't you—"

But there's no use pursuing might-have-beens. That's one thing I *have* learned.

From that moment the day began to go downhill. The sky had greyed over, and the air turned sharp; Affton Wells lost its charm and became a dull, chilly English country town, wrapped in Sunday tidiness and ennui. We hurried back to the station as if the devil were on our heels.

What *can* he have been thinking?

Is it possible to hold two intentions, mutually and wholly contradictory, at one and the same time? Your mind can do a whole lot of different things at once: instruct your feet to climb stairs, make heart beat, recite Keats's *Ode to Psyche*, and think about plans for supper. So I suppose it may be capable of making mutually exclusive plans. I even found later that Dan had written to a house agent's firm, asking them to let him know if Watch Cottage ever came on the market.

That night we had dinner with Mrs. Suter; a grim meal. We had offered to take her out, get a baby-sitter for little Finn, but she wouldn't hear of such a plan.

"One of the last evenings I'll have him; do you think I'd leave him?" she said.

That set the tone for the whole occasion. She was not proposing to be at our wedding next day, for that also would have entailed leaving little Finn. Of course the ceremony was going to be very quiet, a registrar's office, to avoid any publicity, for, after all, not much more than six months had elapsed since Ingrid's death, which had been extensively reported in the press. There would be only six guests: my friend Elly and her husband, Hugh; Chris, and Ferdi Kundera; Anthony Roche, Dan's lawyer, whom I had not yet met, and his wife. Dan did not seem to have any other friends he wished to invite. "Oh, they're just business acquaintances," he said, when I suggested one or another with whom he had seemed on excellent terms. I certainly had no objections; I preferred a quiet affair. Aunt Thisbe said she would come if she felt up to it, but she detested weddings, so I had little hope of her.

Mrs. Suter spent that Sunday evening putting me through a catechism on the subject of baby care. If she had been marking me out of a hundred I would have scored about thirteen.

"It's easy to see *you've* never had anything to do with children," she said acidly, as I fumbled question after question.

Well who has? I thought, unless they are a professional nurse or teacher. For most mothers, their own baby is the first they have met; how much experience did you have, pray, at age nineteen, when Dan was first put into your arms?

But this thought did not appear to have struck Mrs. Suter. She eyed me with less and less favour, more and more gloom.

Little Finn, of course, was asleep by the time we arrived. When Dan suggested waking him, his grandmother nearly burst with outrage, so, after a brief peep, we tiptoed back down the narrow squeaking stairs. The house always smelt of stale floorcloths and lavatory air freshener and disgustingly scented furniture polish.

"Well, I reckon we'd better be getting along," said Dan at last. I breathed a sigh of intense relief. "So long, Mother." He dropped a hasty kiss on her thin, sallow cheek. "We'll send you a postcard from Southend or Rochester."

Rochester was where we were due to spend our first night, moored in the Medway.

Dan and his mother: there they stood saying goodbye to each other. If they had worn duellists' masks, their thoughts and intentions could not have been more hidden from each other. Nor, indeed, from me.

She bade us a perfunctory, cold good night; almost slammed the door on us in her anxiety to be alone with her grandchild while yet she might.

Next morning, at eleven forty-five, we were married to each other in a registry office like the inside of a shoebox. Then we went to have our wedding lunch at the Chelsea flat of Dan's acquaintance Thelma Batey. Thelma herself would not be present. A movie critic for the *Guardian*, she had gone off to attend some Italian film festival and offered her place for our party because she knew we were hard up and it would, she said, be homelier than a restaurant; she had heard that I was a magnificent cook. (She was not, in fact, a very close friend of Dan's; he had so few.)

For once, I was not enthusiastic at the chance of cooking a festive lunch; to tell the truth, I would far rather have been taken out on my wedding day, even if only to sausage-and-mash in a pub. And I didn't care for Thelma's flat; if we were to have a party, I thought Dan's loft quite good enough. It was going to be a devilish nuisance, afterwards, getting the apartment cleaned up again before we went off. Thelma was a terrifyingly house-proud lady in her mid-forties; everything in her abode was kept shining clean, perfect like new, aseptic, wrapped in a plastic cover. But Dan was charmed by all her silver and glassware. Luckily for me, my friends Elly and Chris thought the plan a pleasant one and co-operated over the wedding lunch, Elly providing a huge cold pigeon pie, which she brought all the way from Yorkshire, and Chris a number of delicious ready-made salads from a vegetarian epicure shop (Ferdi ate no meat); while I produced wine, cheese, and dessert.

The party was rather slow in getting underway. We all stood about uncomfortably, though Dan made a great fireworks display of gaiety. Perhaps the thought of Ingrid washing about at the foot of Dover cliffs, only six months drowned, weighed on us all. Patches of silence tended to swell like bubbles, and some desperately silly remarks were made.

My two best friends were both looking very beautiful, I thought: Chris in a black velvet suit she had made herself that emphasized her sumptuous shape, and a twist of black lace with a white rose in it over her silvery blond hair. Elly wore a dress that had belonged to Hugh's grandmother (since her own grandmother was lost in the mists of the Russian past); a dress of shot satin, dead-brown and purple, with a huge topaz brooch at the high throat; she made an alarmingly distinguished figure and I could see that Dan, under his hectic gaiety, was a little afraid of her. Elly's husband, Hugh, a big lanky Yorkshireman, was not well known to any of us, and Dan had not met him before; Anthony Roche knew nobody except Dan; Anthony's wife, Rose, was very young and shy; and I was desperately nervous about the possibility of food being spilled on the horribly valuable Chinese carpet, or Thelma's Waterford glass and Royal Worcester getting broken.

But Hugh, bless him, had brought a crate of champagne, and the ice was beginning to thaw, when, from the flat below, began the wildest, most ear-splitting racket that any of us could possibly have imagined.

"What, in God's name, can be going *on* down there?" demanded Elly, astounded. "It sounds like two orchestras composed of raving maniacs."

It did, really. One could distinguish musical instruments—drums, basses, saxophones—but they were not following any time or tune, merely playing as loud as possible, as fast as possible, a series of loud discordant noises.

It went on and on. We could not hear each other speak.

Ferdi, who was always very obliging, went down to investigate, and came back sadly to report that it was the members of a Paraguayan—or did he say Patagonian?—instrumental group. The downstairs flat belonged to one of them, this was their weekly practice time, and they had not the slightest intention of stopping. They had the habit of playing from noon to four. Was this Thelma's little joke on us? I wondered. Or did she not know about the band? Maybe she was always out at that time.

Meanwhile the noise below redoubled in volume, as if to demonstrate the group's resentment at any suggestion of interference.

The next thing that happened was a violent altercation between members of the wedding party. Some were for calling in the police, on the grounds that the noise was an outrage and it would be a service to the whole neighbourhood to have it stopped. But others (Anthony Roche was of this faction) held that any hostile act against the group would probably rebound disastrously on our absent hostess, who had to go on living with the downstairs tenants; we ought to consider her interests and bear with the nuisance as best we could.

It's queer, now, I can't remember very clearly who was on which side. I can remember Chris, white with rage, almost flinging her champagne glass in some male face. I can remember Elly, arms folded, tapping her elegantly shod foot with irritation, her English becoming louder, faster, and more idiomatic as it does when she is thoroughly roused. I don't remember which side I took myself. I was too miserable, dashing around, topping up people's champagne glasses, watching like a hawk for bits of pigeon pie on the carpet, witnessing the ruin of my wedding party.

In the end, Dan did the sensible thing—or so it seemed at the time; he went down and invited the group to come up and have a drink. Up they came. There were six of them. They looked like primitive gods with long, string-coloured faces and huge protruding eyeballs; they wore grey flannel suits, spoke little English, and seemed unimpressed by Hugh's Bollinger, which they swigged down as if it were lemonade. They stood round creating a strange and rather sinister imbalance in our own group, which had not been well balanced to begin with. It was like introducing much too much strong, thin stock into a doubtful sauce at a late stage.

How they did stare at Chris in her luxurious, taper black velvet, and Elly, glowing bronze and lilac! And then, suddenly, they went wild. They danced, sang, leapt about, ate huge quantities of the food, laughed like hyenas, and started breaking up the place.

"For God's *sake*, what do we do now?" snarled Elly. "This was *your* idea," she said furiously to Dan, who looked abused and distraught.

Hugh, suddenly, took the initiative, acting with terrific speed and decision. He shot down to the street, found a policeman, brought him in, got the Patagonians under control, and dispatched them back to their own quarters.

No, he and Anthony said to the baffled cop, no, we would not lay any charges. That would be up to the owner of the flat. But what about all the breakages? We'd settle up over that, with the lady herself, when she returned. If she wanted to make a complaint about the people below, that was up to her. The cop departed, wholly unsatisfied. We began, dismally, to tidy up the mess.

Hugh looked at his watch; he had London business to transact, an appointment at two-thirty. Anthony also had a date with a client; but before leaving he helped us draw up a list of damages.

Then suddenly Dan exclaimed, as if struck by inspiration: "Look, Tuesday, you must need some peace and quiet after all this. I've had a bright idea. You don't want to be bothered with the nuisance of getting *Valkyrie* downriver from Gravesend. You're tired, you had all the business of getting the lunch, on top of finishing-up at your office last week" (which was true); "why don't you girls go to the pictures or something, and then Tuesday can catch a train down to Rochester and meet me there this evening, about seven, say?"

I was a little taken aback. After all, this was our wedding day;

that morning we had promised to cherish each other till death did us part. But everyone else seemed to find it a sensible suggestion, after the fiasco of the lunch.

Ferdi said that he would go down to Gravesend with Dan and get the boat ready for sailing.

Dan, with Anthony's help, wrote an effusive note of apology to Thelma, asking her to send us the bill for damages. (Thank God, I thought, I'd just had the publisher's advance for my *Apple* book.) Then all the males departed, Anthony leading Rosie, who looked back at us with huge pitying eyes, as if she'd have liked to stay, but was swept off by her large forceful husband.

Elly and Chris and I in silence surveyed Thelma's flat, which, despite our best efforts, still resembled Passchendaele.

What an omen for one's wedding day.

"Dan was right," said Chris. "We can't do any more. Let's go to the pictures."

So that was how I spent the rest of my wedding afternoon: with my two friends, going to a revival of the French movie *La Ronde*. Oh, those cunning Europeans, how they disguise sentiment as irony, irony as sentiment. Just occasionally, still, one hears that lilting waltz tune in some programme of period music; it always gives me the most terrible pang.

Despite everything, I was so full of hope on that day.

After the movie I said goodbye to Elly and Chris, thanked them again for their presents (Elly, the twelve-volume Oxford Dictionary, Chris, a handsome French stewpan), caught a train to Rochester, and walked from the station to the yacht basin.

Dan's boat hadn't arrived. I went away and had a drink at a pub, came back, went away and had an omelet at a café, came back, went away and had a cup of coffee at a truck drivers' sandwich kiosk near the docks; came back, went away, wondered if I should call the police, or who; spent a miserable night at a bed-and-breakfast place where the bed felt and smelt like a sardine tin and the breakfast consisted of tinned spaghetti-and-tomato on toast with ketchup on the side and powdered milk in the tea; returned to the yacht basin, still no sign of Dan, Ferdi, or *Valkyrie*.

Seriously worried, at last, I did go to the police, who called coast guard patrols up and down the coast; nobody knew anything, no one could tell me a single helpful fact. I didn't know what to do with myself.

When I am miserable and terrified I don't want friends or company; fear and anguish to me seem like a disgusting illness, one feels shame at exposing one's condition to anybody else. So I didn't phone Elly, who would be back in Yorkshire by now, believing me gaily embarked on my honeymoon voyage. I didn't call Dan's mother, partly out of consideration, because I didn't want to scare her unnecessarily if there were some simple explanation for Dan's failure to turn up, but mainly because I couldn't endure the thought of her I-told-you-so cluckings and croakings.

In the end I went back to the flat in Covent Garden because the police had told me to stay on the end of a telephone, and I huddled there for another twenty-four hours while nothing happened.

Then, nothing still having happened, it occurred to me for the first time to phone Chris. You'll think I was abysmally stupid not to have thought of her before. Well, I was stupid; I was numb and bemused with prescience of disaster.

When I finally did call, to ask about Ferdi's return, I thought Chris sounded very strange.

"Where in God's name are you?" she said.

"Back in Bedford Buildings . . . Has Ferdi come home?"

"No, he hasn't," said Chris. Her voice was bleak and shocked.

"Did—have you had any word from him?"

"Yes, a card; posted from Gravesend. It said, 'Dearest Chris, thanks for everything. You won't be seeing me again. Don't miss me. You were too good for me. I wasn't worth much.'"

"But—*what*—? But I thought— I don't *understand*. I thought you were both going to—"

"So did I," said Chris. "But apparently we weren't. Oh well; there's as good fish in the sea . . . so they say."

"Do—would you like me to come round?" I asked doubtfully. But Chris and I are alike in many ways; she, too, prefers to lick her wounds in private.

"No, I don't think so, thanks. I'll get in touch after a while. But I hope—I hope you soon have news of Dan. Let me know. Or I'll give you a call in a few days."

Both of us, I suppose, were struggling not to be aware of the truth, which stank all around us like the smell of rotten onions.

After a week the boat turned up, seacocks open, drifting, three-quarters submerged, off the Goodwins.

The bodies of Ferdi and Dan were subsequently washed up on the Kent coast, somewhat waterlogged; identifying them was horrible; and Death by Misadventure would have been the verdict if they had not both been so full of brandy and phenobarb.

So then I did have to get in touch with Mrs. Suter. And then she told me that Dan had gone back to her house on the day of the wedding and picked up little Finn.

"He said the plans were changed," she kept repeating. "That you weren't going on any boat trip after all. He said—he said—"

She looked at me with cold, venomous hatred, as if she could hardly believe in my existence, and spat out: "Go away! Clear away from my house and don't ever, ever come back! *You* aren't Dan's wife. The only wife he had wasn't much good and she's dead. But you are just scum. I'll contest his will. You can be sure of that! You shan't get a penny of his money—not a single penny! Don't you think it!"

God knows, poor woman, what she thought he had, stashed away. I knew Dan well enough, after only three months, to be certain that he would have left nothing but debts.

Mrs. Suter's thin freckled hands shook like cobwebs as she gathered her cardigan closer round her angular body. She was breathing in ragged gasps.

"If it weren't for *you*—you little nothing—my grandchild would still be here—where he ought to be—"

"Dan never said anything to me about a change of plan. I didn't know he meant to come for the baby—"

"Of course he didn't tell you!" she sneered triumphantly. "*You* meant nothing to him. *You* were just a convenience."

She had turned frighteningly pale, blue-lipped and breathless. "Are you all right?" I said, alarmed at her looks.

"Never you mind! Never you mind how I am! Just you go away and stay away."

So I went. It occurred to me to wonder whether she had heart trouble, whether Dan had known about that. Could that have been why he decided to marry me? Because he knew his mother wouldn't be able to look after the baby for very long?

But then, why take Finn himself, if the plan was that I should be left to cope? Had he suddenly changed his mind? With Dan, of course, that was quite on the cards.

My speculations went round and round.

Little Finn's body was never recovered. He was only six months old, and small for his age; and there are hundreds of square miles of water in the English Channel and the North Sea.

Dan's simple will left everything to me. Mrs. Suter never did contest it; I imagine she consulted a lawyer who made her see that she would be wasting time and money. I inherited Dan's clothes, a few books, a box full of unfinished newspaper articles, the typescript of his novel about life in the Navy, a suitcase containing Ingrid's poems, notebooks, and papers, and a few copies of her two slim volumes, *The Broken Anchor* and *The Rat Wife*. I wondered if these things ought to be returned to her family in Denmark, and wrote to Creevey and Creevey, her publishers, asking if they had any Danish address. But they knew of none. Ingrid's dealings with them had all been subsequent to her arrival in England and marriage to Dan. The Authors' Society was equally unable to help. Ingrid's own parents were dead, I knew from Dan, there was only an unloving stepsister who would presumably not have any great interest in the poems; so, for the time being, I constituted myself Ingrid's literary executor and kept them.

I looked at a few of them. There was one called *Sailor's Wife*, which began,

> *Earthman and airman come safe home at nightfall*
> *To soup and the hearth, fire and the plumped-out pillow*
> *While my man—*

That was enough for me. I shuffled the pages together and put them back in the folder.

Abandoning the Covent Garden loft, I found a bed-sitter in Putney. It was a glum room, but big, and had a window looking out on to the river, which I liked. I used to spend hours sitting by that window, not thinking, not reading or listening to music, not doing anything, just sitting, watching the water sliding past, tide high, tide low, and the reflections dovetailing in and out, snaking from one bank to the other.

Dan had loved water. "When we're rich we'll buy a house right on the beach," he used to say. "So we can lie in bed at night and listen to the waves breaking. There's nothing better. Or we'll have a cottage in the country with a brook running through the garden. Finn must be able to swim by the time he's three."

Dan's plans were so often mutually contradictory. For, besides the house on the shore, the house by the brook, he was also going to buy back Watch Cottage. "It was a terrible mistake leaving that place," he said. He was going into Parliament as a Liberal; but also we were going to emigrate to New Zealand, which he had fallen in love with while on a naval visit; Finn was to grow up in idyllic rural surroundings, far from any thought of the bomb. Dan was going to edit a yachting monthly; but also we were going to sail round the world forever.

The final conclusion with Ferdi was, I suppose, his escape, or solution, to all these ambivalences.

For months I felt a bitter resentment on Ferdi's behalf; nice, brown-faced, curly-headed boy, years younger than Dan, uprooted, a refugee, Dan had no right to drag him down into his private whirlpool.

But after innumerable talks with Chris on the subject, I began to feel more acquiescent about it.

We had begun seeing each other regularly; she used to come and sit with me by my river window and we'd talk and smoke, listen to Beethoven quartets, crushing that terrible calm hope out of the quintessence of despair, and we would go over and over the lives of our two lost creatures until we began to feel that we had made a little sense of the catastrophe.

"They did love each other," said Chris. "I can remember Dan's face when Ferdi was playing Bach. Translated. Translucent. As if at last he'd found what he was looking for."

"Yes . . . That's true . . ."

"Dan was Ferdi's first real English friend. He was like an elder brother."

"Just because you are fond of your elder brother you don't have to join him in a *death pact*," I said furiously. "Why couldn't the silly asses go off to Brighton or Tahiti?"

"You have to get it in perspective," Chris explained. Her expression was austere. She has immense tolerance and restraint. Even when someone has dealt her a deadly blow, she will take time to think all round the act, so as to discover their motive, and whether there was due cause or justification for it; insanely impatient over trifles that wouldn't worry me for a single moment, she has a wry, wintry, disillusioned philosophy which floats her safe past rapids where others would founder. She is an extremely strong person; Ferdi had clung to her with instinctive knowledge of this, although on the surface their relationship was all nonsense, wisecracking, and jokes.

"You can't *make* somebody let go if they don't want to," she went on. "They have to be ready for it themselves."

I hoped she was right. I still hope so. Dan had a tremendously compelling, persuasive personality; when he really wanted something he went after it like a laser beam.

"But why take little Finn along?"

That was always my stumbling block, I simply couldn't fathom his motive there.

Chris stubbed out her half-smoked cigarette and took another.

"Dan loathed his mother—right? He didn't want the baby brought up in that ambiance. If he thought his mother was likely to become ill—maybe die—"

"But I was there. I'd have looked after Finn. Dan could have trusted me."

"He had no real claim on you."

"He might have trusted me," I repeated wretchedly. Oddly enough it was this lack of trust that wounded me most: that Dan had not thought me capable of bringing up his child. The will had not mentioned little Finn at all. No guardian had been named.

"Don't you see," Chris said with patience, "Dan was judging you by his own standards. Which is all any of us can do really. He knew perfectly well that *he* would soon have found some way of shuffling off the responsibility. He assumed you'd do the same. And he wanted to deal a final slap at his mother."

"I expect you're right . . ."

"I'm sure I'm right." She stubbed out another cigarette.

"You're smoking much too much, Chris."

"So are you."

"We'd better eat something."

My bed-sitter had a gas ring, and there was a sink and cold tap on the landing. For months the only food I brought home was those Swiss powdered soups that you mix with water, and packets of crispbread. Night after night, that was what we ate. Then we'd go out and wander along by the river, and finally I'd walk Chris over Putney Bridge to the underground station. We each of us lost over twenty pounds in weight that winter.

At last Chris said, "This won't do. We have to give up smoking. And I'm going to a marriage bureau."

"What?"

"I've decided to get married," she said. "Marriage seems to suit Elly. And I'm going to set about it in a perfectly businesslike manner, as if I were my own French eighteenth-century bourgeois ancestors arranging a suitable *parti*."

Chris does, in fact, have French forbears, Huguenots who migrated to East Anglia. Her parents were killed in a multiple motorway pileup and she was reared by cousins, which may account for her disillusioned outlook. The cousins did their best, but their best was not a good one.

"What kind of person do you intend to marry?"

I still wasn't taking her quite seriously.

"I shall make out a list of qualifications."

And she did, there and then. "Not English, for a start. I prefer Continentals."

"Why?"

"All Englishmen are basically homosexual. At bottom they fear and dislike women. And can you wonder? Most of them don't have any dealings with women till they are about eighteen. If then."

"Oh, come on! Hugh's not queer."

Hugh was Elly's husband.

"Well—Hugh's the exception. 99 percent of Englishmen."

"Okay. European. What else?"

"Over thirty. With his own business. Reasonably well off."

"Musical? Literary? Sense of humour?"

"No, no. Those are luxuries. I can manage without them. But he *must* be *articulate*. I'm not ever, ever again, going to live with one of those manic-depressive, up-and-down tongue-tied children of nature who can't express what's at the back of their moods. It's going to be all cards on the table from now on."

"European, thirties, professionally thriving, articulate. What else? What *kind* of profession?"

"I don't give a rap. He can be a hangman, so long as he's good at it, and takes a proper pride in what he does. What I want," said Chris, "is someone *reliable*."

Before poor Ferdi she had had a whole string of moody, romantic seaweedy lovers; they could all see that Chris made the perfect rock to wrap themselves round.

She stood up, shook herself, and peered in the spotted mirror which hung in a dark corner of my depressing room, then scowled at what she saw. Chris has fine naturally blond hair, which springs back in a high plume from her high intelligent brow. Her skin is always a pale bisque; at that time it was deathlike in colour. She said, "I look like something that's just been prized out of a sarcophagus. And so do you. Come on, I got a rise from those skinflints"—she was working in the social welfare department of a London hospital—"we'll go out and have a Chinese dinner. And then I'm going to write off to the Evelyn Farmer Agency for their form, and I shall give them your name as well."

"Oh, heavens, no, Chris. I don't want to be bothered with a

whole lot of strangers wanting to impress me with their charm and earning capacity. I'd rather do a Cordon Bleu course."

"Nothing to stop you doing both," said Chris. "Put your coat on."

So that was how Chris and I came to have a lot of bizarre experiences. We never went out on double dates, but we used to meet once a week to compare notes.

Besides the agency, egged on by Chris, I began to answer some of the more conservative personal ads in the *New Statesman*, and thus I encountered Reggie the Flagellator, a sweet fellow, apart from his proclivity, which I made plain from the start I did not share; while Chris had her little run-in with the man who advertised for a collaborator in Pearl White dramas. Chris always thought she'd like to try her hand at detective fiction, so got in touch with him, but it turned out that what *he* had in mind was the real thing, and she had to extract herself with speed from a situation that threatened to hurtle head-on to disaster. Luckily Chris is a stalwart well-muscled girl, and quick in the uptake too; she soon had his measure.

After that she gave up the ads, and the matrimonial agency, which, right from the first, had become of purely academic interest; she had only continued out of a sense of duty because, she said, she wanted her money's worth and it seemed absurd to call a halt, make up her mind too hastily, without a full and thorough survey of the field.

But in fact her mind *had* been made up, right from the start. For the very first man she met through the agency was George Dombrad, who later changed his name to Davenport.

3

Meanwhile the rural ditties were not mute
Tempered to the oaten Flute;
Rough Satyrs danc'd . . .

In the mornings I do Yoga, from seven till eight.

At that time of day, almost anywhere in the world, you may find classical music on the radio. It comes cheaper, I suppose; also, pop and rock listeners do not wake until later. The Naturajasana, a balance position with which I always begin, goes well to Bach; the harmonious balance of his music assists one's own equilibrium. For the Naturajasana you must raise your right arm, bend your left knee, and bring the left foot up backwards until your left hand, reaching behind you, is able to grasp it. Then, balancing on your right foot, raise your head and look upwards. Hold the position as long as possible. Then lean slowly forward like a ship's figurehead. Hold again.

This exercise clears the nasal passages for the day, besides giving poise and calm. Repeat on the other leg. I follow it with four other standing positions, the Tree, the Triangle, the Leg Clasp, and the Stork. Then down to sitting: the Half Lotus, the *Janusirasana* or Swan, and Back Stretch or *Paschimottanasana*. Presently, down to lying: the Side Raise, Back Raise, Shoulder Stand, Plough; still lying, the Cobra, Locust, and Bow; then I stretch up into the Cat, and on to the *Ardha Chakrasana*, bringing the closed hands up behind the shoulders; then slip down into the Cow, combined with neck and face exercises; then I move on to the Twist or *Ardha Matsyendrasana;* each position developing naturally out of the last; then into the Cat again, or some other limbering movement; and finally back into the Lotus, for ten minutes of meditation.

Hotel bedrooms are ideal for Yoga; as a rule there is generous floor space, mostly carpeted, adequately clean; and, staying in a hotel, one's mind is at ease, at leisure, not distracted by fluff under the dressing table and thoughts of housework; somebody else will be making the beds and providing breakfast.

My bedroom in the Campus Tavern was perfect: half an acre of dog-brown carpet, and Pachelbel's Canon on Radio Mitchison.

As always, I found a paper clip; I have found paper clips everywhere, even in the Parthenon. Suggested to a friend of Dan's, a film director, that he make a film about a man with an ambition to pick up a ton of paper clips, from streets in world capitals, but he wasn't attracted by the idea. My father was a naturally silent man; I recall very few of his utterances. One concerned the ubiquity of paper clips; even among the foundations of Colchis, which he had been excavating, he found a paper clip that must date from 2000 B.C. Another of his rare dicta was a rhyme that he made up, about a parrot called Polyglot who travelled around North Africa with us for a while. I suppose my parents felt a parrot would make up in some degree for my lack of normal childhood and playmates:

> *Our parrot is so slow in wits*
> *She eats the perch on which she sits*
> *Reflecting not that she must fall*
> *When there is no perch left at all;*
> *To check which habit, the Almighty*
> *Provides a perch of lignum vitae.*
> *This rhyme is for my daughter Clytie.*

Enchanted with his poem, I begged him to make up more, about other birds—an owl, a seagull, a pheasant, a swan! But his bolt was shot, he could not perform to order; he retired again into erudition and silence.

"Be a good girl; don't let them turn you into a robot," he said when I was sent off to boarding school in England; and that was the last time I saw him. His utter nonparticipation as a parent has, I daresay, played its part in forming my scepticism about the possibility of the Ideal, of George's Bubble.

Yoga turns over one's thoughts; like shaking and plumping a pillow or turning cheeses to ripen; up to the surface float all kinds of long-buried concepts and recollections, matured by keeping. Particularly this is so when practising the Cow—a static position, not very comfortable, not very interesting, but strengthening to hip and thigh bones (for one must begin to look ahead, think of old age; so very often the first definitive slip into decrepitude follows a fall and a broken hip. Sudden drastically reduced mobility: consequent sloth, inertia, relinquishment of social life, active occupations, and outside interests; consequent impaired health and mental energy, reduced attraction for friends; consequent solitude, loneliness, withdrawal into vacancy, misanthropy, senility. . . . The path is mapped out as clearly as *The Rake's Progress*).

"The trouble about *us*," said Elly, the last time I saw her, "is that we know too much. We've seen it all beforehand; had this kind of ghastly preview of death."

"Most people get some kind of preview when their parents die," I pointed out. "I daresay the average citizen has escorted one or the other parent into the grave."

"Maybe."

Our parentless, sibless state has formed a part of the strong bond between Elly, Chris, and myself; we have become each other's family, for good or ill; incest, forbidden degrees, sibling rivalry, the whole works.

Elly's parents were swept away to some gulag in Siberia; they may be alive, or they may be dead, she has no way of knowing, but since they were not a physically strong couple, he an astronomer, she a classical scholar, it was only realistic to assume that they must have perished long ago.

Elly and I came together in the first place through Greek and Latin; two years older than I, brilliant at school, an academic from fourteen, also a natural athlete, she was in a higher class, moved with a different group, and we might never have got to know each other. But however the rest of my education had been neglected, I had received an excellent grounding in the dead languages. From age six, Vanessa made me read aloud passages from the classics at mealtimes and my father was strict about pronunciation; he had an acute and precise ear. So Elly and I participated in bi-weekly advanced classical tuition together at the house of lame old Miss Crabbe, where we read aloud Horace and Plato; for all the good it otherwise did me we might as well have been learning petit point, but walking or cycling back to school after those hours with Elly, I got an earful twice a week of her pungent original thought, unquenchable wit, her incisive intelligence, and that probably taught me more than all Plato's pronouncements.

"Having a husband die—someone of your own generation—is more immediate than the death of a parent; you relate to it more," Elly went on.

"You're not kidding."

Hugh's deathbed. We were both there. Hugh, a skeleton caricature of what he had been only a year before, favoured us with a ghastly grin. He had a cassette of Salvatore Mondo's *Don Giovanni* playing at top volume, and he muttered something about Elvira and Anna; "All we need now is the Commendatore to come and drag me down into the fiery furnace."

He could speak only with the most painful difficulty, between labouring gasps for breath.

"Don't waste energy trying to converse," Elly admonished him.

"Ah'll bluddy well—waste ma bluddy energy—ony way ah see fit." He was travestying the Yorkshire accent which he had shed long ago at university.

"And I could bloody well do with a fiery furnace," he remarked after a while. "It'd make a nice change from drowning in one's own spit. A pig's way to die."

I thought of Dan, long ago on the train from Cornwall to Paddington, telling me so authoritatively, "Drowning's not a bad way to go. If I had any say in the matter, I reckon I'd choose it."

Prophetic utterance? Or just a plain statement of intention which I had missed? For he did allot himself his own decision in the matter, and he did choose drowning. But when it came to the final point, how are we to know that he did not regret his choice?

"One thing—Elly my dear," Hugh observed presently, "I won't have to put up with any longer—your nagging at me—to give up smoking. And *you'll* be—spared the—painful necessity of keeping after me. You can—relax."

"Oh you know me," said Elly. "I'll find somebody else to bully."

Their hands were tightly clasped. Her voice remained light and dry, though her face was grey with strain.

"Well, girls—this is it," announced Hugh some time later. He was holding my hand too. Time had ground along in bottom gear, unconscionably slow; one could not help being reminded of King Charles II. The bruises showed on my wrist for a week after. I was sad when they faded and the last trace vanished. "Not a thing to regret—" Hugh went on, "except—that ghastly east wing —on Charteris House—"

I don't care to recall his final moments. Death from lung cancer is undignified and hideous. All that can be said is that it makes the transition from living to nonliving, nonsuffering, *purely* a relief; nobody could wish the patient to endure even a single extra second of such gasping torture. But, in consequence, the moment of change is rendered even more striking, more mysterious; one instant the victim is at full stretch, every muscle braced, every effort bent on the struggle to survive; the next, silent, inert, *departed*; the onlookers are like friends standing by an airstrip when the plane has flown; there is the same atmosphere of speed, shock, anticlimax, the cessation of noise, the vacuum of incredulity.

My radio music switches from Pachelbel to Mozart's Symphony Number 28, a small, meditative symphony, the genius just getting into his stride for Number 29, with the angelic slow movement, and then the incredible outburst of the 30's. The Mozart switches my thoughts, too, away from Hugh's last moments to quieter, domestic memories: Dan ecstatically discovering clarinet and bassoon concertos while I made omelets in the Covent Garden flat;

Elly bathing the twins to strains of *Figaro* or *Cosi* from the radio
in the bedroom at Thirsby; Hugh, like most Yorkshiremen, had a
passion for choral music and opera.

Radio news now: wholly depressing as always; some new ar-
tefact being launched into space with top froofra, the cost of
which, if spread about the world, would probably end hunger and
disease within a couple of years; new problems with the Arabs,
new cuts in social services, a batch of unfortunate customers
being held for ransom in a Spanish bank, signs that Asian flu may
be on the increase, and a millionaire's daughter kidnapped.

Yoga finished, I gladly switched off the melancholy stream.

This is the final day of the medical conference: a last buffet
lunch for the doctors, light, since many of the delegates will whip
away to catch noon planes; and then my staff can pack up their
knives, garlic, and pepper grinders. We always travel with those
basics, I'd like to bring vegetables as well; American vegetables always taste as if they have been grown on cotton wool; but that
would hurt the feelings of our hosts and entail a lot of complicated import permissions. Over here they are terrified of Colorado
beetle. Our superior technology carries plagues about the world
even more speedily than humans. Did you know that the phyllox-
era vine louse could not survive for the length of time it took a
sailing ship to cross the Atlantic? It required the advent of steam
to introduce this tiny but powerful agent into the vineyards of
Europe.

When the crab salad and quiches are consumed, I dispatch my
crew towards Los Angeles and a nonstop flight back to London.
Having myself no commitments at home for the next few days, I
have decided to remain out of England for a while. Regretting, to
some degree, that parting interview with Anthony, I feel more
comfortable at a safe distance away from him. Maybe I will go to
New York, spend a short time peacefully browsing in bookshops
and wandering in galleries. New York is a fine town for menu
browsing, too, and absorbing ideas; almost every ethnic variety of
eating place can be found in this compact area. Catering, as Cuisine Churchill often does, for international conferences, we are
sometimes called on for obscure dishes, the ragouts of Upper

Volta, flatbread of Anatolia, ice pudding as enjoyed in Herāt; recipe books are helpful and I have amassed a good library of these
in what used to be Aunt Thisbe's dining room, but direct experience is better still, and almost any exotic and out-of-the-way cuisine can be sampled in New York if one looks around a little. I
would stroll through the fabulous food markets, too, Balducci's,
Zabar's, Dean & Deluca; also visit my friends the old man and
Charley.

Having boarded the New York plane I settle by a window and
pull out a paperback: Wittgenstein, hoping to discourage neighbours. The plane is filling rather slowly, giving me cause to hope
that the two seats beside me will remain unoccupied. The medical symposium has been busy, purposeful, convivial; Brezhnev's
doctor never did divulge any details about his illustrious patient,
but he was quite communicative in other respects, and I have
gathered that the conference was a success; achieved at least part
of its purpose. I feel, comfortably, that I have in some degree
been responsible for this success, by keeping the delegates fed and
satisfied.

But now I want some peace and a lot of solitude. I have much
to think about.

When you put out most of your energy in love, in the form of
love—as I did during those four critical years—when you are so
powerfully involved with, and affected by, outside people and circumstances—then you are bound to lose much of your own
power, your *ens*.

Power gathers only in solitude.

Since Hugh's death, since the parting from Anthony, I have
spent my time in solitude and gathered power.

So it was like a breach in a dam when I first began to believe
that little Finn might still be alive.

Hope accumulates inside one willy-nilly, like honey in a cell;
hope for a fine summer, hope of some good outcome for us all,
for a cordial ending to the conference, even the small unimportant hope that the seat beside me will remain vacant.

For a considerable period I felt certain that I had given up
hope—like smoking, like starch, like sex. But now, curiously

enough, this belated unwelcome traveller who has come briskly down the aisle at the last possible moment and plunked himself down in the seat next to mine—curiously enough, he glances at me sidelong with that unmistakable, engaged, attentive potential, as if some current in me has suddenly come alive, some spark signalled to an equivalent spark in him. This has not happened to me for several years.

The hectic, jigging pre-takeoff music on the plane changes to "Jennifer," nostalgic lilting ballad of my teens, taking me back, throwing gleams of light into forgotten corners; can this be some kind of omen? Jen-nifer, Jen-nifer, where are you going to go to, Jennifer?

The man next to me gives off a homely domestic odour, clean freshly ironed laundry in a warm wicker basket, new rolls wrapped in a white napkin; he wears a brown tweed jacket and unassuming grey slacks; has gold-rimmed glasses, thick sandy-fair hair, well cut and cared for, good strong hands covered with reddish fur, long, bony un-English face; he inspects the dinner menu right away, pursing his lips in disapproval, then swiftly absorbs himself in the airline magazine. By this I instantly judge him to be a low-grade intelligence. (George would condemn this reaction as snobbery.)

I do my best to ignore him. I am occupying my topmost, superficial layer of thought with a conception for a casserole of chicken breasts, broad beans, water chestnuts, and leeks. One would simmer the chicken until a good deal of the natural juice had condensed, then add the lightly sautéed vegetables, and, shortly before serving, a *beurre blanc* of onions, butter, and white wine; a touch of Parmesan on top. Serve with a tomato salad, flavoured with tarragon . . .

I fell asleep.

After a while (I must have missed drinks) the airline meal arrived: a flat square of liver sausage, a dank portion of what they were pleased to call Boeuf Bordelaise, and a soggy lump of coconut cake, accompanied by a small cup of lukewarm brown liquid.

"Not quite so excellent as what you have just been regaling us with, madame," politely remarked my companion. "But may I have the pleasure of offering you a glass of wine to—as you say in English—*wash it down?*"

"You were at that conference?" Surprised, guilty, I realised that I had misjudged him.

"In the French delegation. Why should you notice one among so many? But I recognised you, of course, because of your reply to the toasts after the banquet. Allow me to congratulate you on your cuisine, madame. A Frenchwoman could hardly have done better."

"Thank you. And I admire that *hardly!* But one is obliged to employ the materials that are at hand."

"You did miracles," he said, smiling. He then formally introduced himself as Dr. Théodore Rabuse, a bacteriologist, and we began to have a most interesting conversation about whether extraterrestrial intelligences could, millions of years ago, have fired rockets to this globe from some other habitable planet way out in space, rockets containing bacteria, which then spawned and incubated in our warm and gooey oceans. "The sea must have resembled the best bouillon at that time," said Dr. Rabuse with enthusiasm. "And such organisms, full of amino acids and nucleic acids, would have settled in excellently. Giving rise, in the end, to us."

"But would there have *been* other planets at such an advanced stage of technological invention so many millions of years before we got going?"

"Oh, *mais certainement*, why not? Some ecologically favourable planets may have been formed as much as nine billion years ago. Whereas the arrival of such rockets to our own earth need not have occurred more than one billion years in the past."

"If you say so. . . . But what would be the object of sending such rockets?"

"To ensure the continuance of life."

"Well, if somebody did *that*, they were certainly long-term planners." I sighed. "Life . . . why do we esteem it so highly? Is it such a benefit?"

For some time I had thought but poorly of life. Is it really worth taking trouble to cultivate a plant that can be uprooted so very easily, snatched away so swiftly?

And yet of late, despite my doubts, I had found myself observing life: a clutch of starlings scrabbling and clinging to a wall where some dried grapes clustered; an old man painfully balancing himself on the pavement with his face upraised to catch the warmth of the sun; I suppose what I felt was love, admiration for the unquenchableness of this force.

"Most certainly life is a benefit," said my companion with energy. "Think of the monotony of a universe which contained nothing but stones and inanimate objects."

"No wars, no bloodshed, no tragedies . . . there'd still be plenty going on. There would be earthquakes and volcanoes and sunsets and the aurora borealis."

"But nobody to admire them."

"Perhaps a machine could be invented to do so. Suppose you make a machine that can think," I said idly, "will it have moral problems?"

Rabuse gave me a severe look and said, "Life is what provides the appreciation—and the surprises."

"I've had enough surprises. For a lifetime." And, even as I said that, I knew that it was not true.

Then, for some reason, we began talking about the novels of Ivy Compton-Burnett.

"I do not read much English fiction," remarked my companion. "Indeed, not much fiction at all. One's work is cut out keeping abreast of facts. But Compton-Burnett I do read. That lady is a prodigy. My English friends assure me that life in your families is not really conducted in this wild torrent of murder, incest, rape, and betrayal; but what is your opinion on the matter?"

"Well," I answered slowly, "I suppose I am hardly an average example of English upbringing; my parents were archaeologists, I was reared on various earthworks around the Mediterranean . . . but yes, thinking it over, I would say hers was a fairly true picture. Of intention, if not execution."

I thought of Dan's hate for his mother, his mother's detestation, first of Ingrid, then of me. Concealment, betrayal, ambush.

"*Tiens!* You are honest, madame." Rabuse looked at me almost with affection. "How glad I am that I was born French."

When you are lonely, recognition from a stranger can assume undue importance. I have, on occasion, been depressed for a whole morning because I felt the postman had neglected me by not bringing me his tribute of mail. When inanimate objects cooperate—when the record player shines its little red eye for me, I feel kindly towards it. The eye shines only about once a week; electricity is perverse and capricious, like human nature.

Now, accordingly, I regarded Dr. Rabuse with a certain caution, and, after we had talked about Ivy C-B some more and quoted our favourite scenes, I politely disengaged myself from the conversation and returned to Wittgenstein. The doctor brought out and read the typed proceedings of some *societée;* and later the movie, which neither of us watched, provided a natural barrier.

I was mildly surprised, therefore, when, as we circled over New York, waiting to land, my neighbour suddenly remarked, "You mentioned that you proposed spending a few days' vacation in New York, madame. But I am wondering if I can interest you in a small proposition—if you would consider passing your *vacances* in France, rather? *Excusez-moi*"—since I must have looked a little startled—"I do not make sexual propositions to young ladies—however charming—in planes. My proposal is wholly practical. By means of it you would obtain—if you wished it—a free plane ride to France; and I should give myself the pleasure of introducing you to some of the lesser-known gastronomic delights of Brittany."

He explained that in order to cover part of his fare to Nevada he had accepted a professional commission for the return journey: from New York to Quimper he would travel as the medical attendant of a semiparalysed businessman on a private ambulance plane. (He had studied straight medicine before specialising in bacteriology.)

"It is part of the arrangement that a nurse accompanies me. But I have learned, while in Mitchison, that the nurse I hired has appendicitis; would it amuse you to take her place?"

"But—good heavens—I'm not a nurse."

"Oh, that is pure formality. The man is not really sick. There is no occasion for a veritable nurse. And if I vouch for you, no one will question. I know both pilots well."

He had done this several times before, it seemed.

"The man that I am to accompany—Sir Bert Wilder, another English person—he will amuse you, I believe. He is a millionaire —if you decide to accept the plan, I will give you his history. I believe you would find the experience a stimulating one. But you must decide for yourself, naturally."

Certainly I was intrigued.

"When would you be leaving?"

"Tomorrow evening—not late. So you would have one day in New York."

Long ago I had a maxim to the effect that one should go where the wind blows, never reject the odd tidbits that life once in a way holds out. Recently my maxim had fallen into desuetude simply because life wasn't offering any tidbits. On this occasion I did feel some caution. Was it really sensible to get involved with Dr. Rabuse and a paralysed millionaire? Wouldn't it be wiser to say no, thank you? Already I had plenty to worry about: the anonymous letters, the verbal message, the huge question of little Finn, my resumed, if hostile, dialogue with Anthony. But perhaps, I decided, it would be beneficial, help me to keep matters in proportion, if I were equipped with a counterdistraction.

So in the end I agreed to his proposal.

"Very good," observed my companion matter-of-factly, as if he had never been in any serious doubt that I would let slip such an opportunity. "Then I will look forward to seeing you tomorrow at six-thirty," and he gave me instructions as to place. "Or, if you prefer, a limousine can be sent to pick you up. Where will you be staying?"

"With friends." I gave him the address, and, as our plane had now landed, we parted in the most prosaic manner, like old business associates. I almost began to feel I must have been mistaken about that first sense of recognition and response.

Next evening the limousine arrived, dead on time, and whisked me through the evening rush to a select enclosure of the airport which might have been marked *Millionaires Only*. Dr. Rabuse was there already, efficiently superintending the removal of a prone man on a stretcher out of a private ambulance and into a smallish jet plane. It looked a highly uncomfortable process; the patient had to be inserted through the door hole feet first and head down.

"Is this all your baggage?" With approval, Rabuse observed my one small bag.

"I sent the rest home with my crew."

"*Très bien*. Let us embark, if you please. You first. Kindly sit in the rear seat."

He took the seat in front of me and, with amazingly little fuss or ceremony, the door was shut and the plane was airborne.

"Now I make introductions," said the doctor cheerfully. He twiddled his seat round. "Sir Bert Wilder—this is Madame—or is it Mademoiselle?—Churchill, who prepares delicious banquets for conferences."

"Always go for the steak, myself," said the tycoon.

Never having met a millionaire at close quarters I had not known what to expect, but Sir Bert was not it. He had a weathered, beaky, lively Cockney face with darting shrewd brown eyes; in his slightly receding brow were about a million wrinkles, which seemed to have been created not by care but by vivacity. His face was never at rest for a moment. Almost at once he ordered Rabuse to change seats with me, so that he could tell me about himself, and then with hardly a pause for breath, I had the whole story: how his trucking company had started with a hand barrow in Brixton Market, risen to a Ford van, he had made his first million before he was eighteen. "While you were still in your cradle, young lady." His accent was a rich mix of Bermondsey and Brooklyn. He had acquired several American transport companies, and now spent a large portion of his time in Elizabeth, New Jersey. "It was there I got shot and paralysed; in a nursing home I was, for eight months, but wotthehell, it makes getting about a lot easier. I just sit in a wheelchair and let other people do the pushing."

"But do you *have* to get about so much, if you have all those millions? Couldn't you sit still in one place, now, and just let the money roll in?"

"Oh no, ducks, you haven't got the idea *at* all."

When he explained the cause and meaning of his nonstop life-style, I was appalled.

"You really mean to tell me that you daren't stop in one place for longer than *three days*? And that you never know where you will be going next?"

"That's right. It's all worked out by computer, love," he said, enjoying my thunderstruck horror.

"But—for heaven's sake—you said you've a wife and six children—when do you get to see them?"

How could those children ever have been conceived, let alone born? I wondered.

"Oh, we meet up here and there."

"Do they have to keep moving too?"

"You bet your sweet life they do! We never know when we're going to cross over. I've the château in Brittany—Plouhaix, you'll like it—another in the south, I forget where exactly—a *castello* near Florence, we called one of the girls Flo—a chalet near Grenoble, a ranch in Iowa—or is it Idaho? I always get those two mixed—and a seaside place in Santa Barbara. Those are the main ones. So we keep ringing the changes."

"All just because of the chance of kidnapping?"

"It's no chance, ducks. It's a dead certainty." His lively face became serious for a moment. "How d'you think I got me this bullet in my spine? Once they almost did snatch little Min—she's my youngest—but the security boys arrived just in time. And, last summer, my wife and I and two of the kids were staying at the flat in Menton—oh yes, forgot to mention that one—we found a note slipped under the door: 'Don't think you're safe, we'll get you in the end.' Somebody managed to get into the building past three security doors and two armed guards."

"Good God."

I mulled over his story for a while, then said, "I couldn't endure to live like that. How do the children get educated?"

"Tutors. Governesses."

"But when they are grown—want to go to college—marry? Do they always have to be protected?"

"Always. Unless they go over on the other side. Like Patty Hearst."

"I'd rather give away all my money. Every penny."

"Wouldn't wash," he said at once. "Don't think we haven't considered it. But that money's going to be still *somewhere*, at somebody's disposal, isn't it? And even if we haven't got it in our pockets, they'd still come after us, and use us to prise it out of the ones that have got it."

"Couldn't you somehow tie it up—make a trust—?"

"Ducky," he said, "I've got the best lawyers in three continents. If they can't find a way out, you can be sure there's not one to be found."

"Then I'd commit suicide."

"Ah, you're just a silly girl. Suicide? All eight of us? And Jed and Tina's both married—that makes ten—grandchildren on the way, too," he said proudly. "No; you just learn to live as best you can. It's a funny old life. Now I enjoy collecting pictures when I've the time, that's *my* little hobby, and Rose, Rosie's my missis, she's crazy about gardens, gets herself right out there grubbing in the dirt, wherever she is, only of course she always has to have a security man and a guard dog with her. We've got some terrific guard dogs at Plouhaix," he told me, "half a dozen of the beggars —tear out your throat in fifteen seconds flat. There's only one chap as can handle them. They know his voice."

"How very convenient," I said faintly.

"I'll show you my pictures—got lots at Plouhaix. Like to know what you think of 'em, an educated young lady like you. I bet you've been to a lot of museums and know what's good and what's bad.

"Now, if you won't be offended, dear, I'd best do some phoning. Just lying on my back all the way over won't get the bread baked." And he began talking to Algiers, Ābādān, Bombay, and Lima.

Dr. Rabuse presently supplied me with a hamburger (not, to

be honest, one of the best I have eaten—but the champagne that accompanied it could not be faulted); then, as it was growing late, and I had put in a busy day in New York, I asked if there would be any objection to my taking a nap.

"Naturally not, not the least in the world." We changed places again, and Rabuse showed me how to tip my seat.

"But what about him?" indicating Sir Bert. "Will you be wanting help with him—bedpans and so forth?"

He shook his head, passing me a downy Angora rug.

"I can deal with all. Sleep while you may, we reach Quimper at 6 A.M."

So I slept, briefly and fitfully. And my dreams were grievingly full of the other Rose, Anthony's Rosie, who had also been crazy about gardening, able to charm out of the soil delicate rare mysterious flowers that were the envy and wonder of all her friends. She knew all the horticultural arts—grafted slips, budded roses, had merely to breathe on a leaf and it would take root. "Sure, it's just a knack," she would say bashfully. Rosamund O'Connor Roche, killed when she was twenty-four by a motorcyclist skidding on a patch of oil.

"Look after my old Anto for me, Clytie, won't you *please?*" she whispered to me, lying in the emergency ward where they had rushed her and were doing all they desperately could.

But how in the world was I supposed to do that when he hated me worse than poison and had made a will blackening my name?

While we watched the careful process of Sir Bert being extracted and loaded on to the private ambulance at Quimper Airport, and shivered in the predawn chills and mists, Dr. Rabuse politely inquired how I had amused myself during my day in New York. I told him about the art shows—the Magritte, Burra, Morandi, Klimt—the room full of earth, the hundred photographs of a tomato, taken at all stages from green to red, the upside-down tree, the giant toothbrushes.

"Tell Sir Bert, he will like to hear about that. He never gets enough art talk."

We had been invited to the château for breakfast, to see the millionaire installed among his next relay of guards and attendants. Our limousine followed behind the ambulance, and I noticed a couple more large cars unobtrusively draw in, ahead and behind, as the cortège moved away.

While we drove, I told Rabuse about the old man and Charley, whom I visit, if possible, when in Manhattan. They live six floors up, in a huge room that goes from side to side of a ramshackle building. The room is a bookshop, crisscrossed with high, close-set shelves of tippling, sliding dusty volumes; Charley is a massive tabby who sleeps all day on a windowsill in a patch of sunshine, while his master, sternly ignoring the customers (if any), listens to erudite radio talks.

"This time it was Frank O'Connor, talking about James Joyce's *Ulysses*. Charley has never been out of that room in his life. He was born there. But the landlord is going to sell the building; the new owner will probably pull it down and throw up something six times as high. Then the old man and Charley will have to move miles away to the suburbs, they'd never find anything else they could afford in the city. I can't bear the idea. They belong in the middle of Manhattan. But each time I return, I'm amazed to find them still there."

"You resist," said Dr. Rabuse gently, "you resist the onward movement of life."

"No. No, I'm grateful, really, that they had such a run of luck. But if only it could last a little longer!"

"For their sake—or for yours? Who knows, Charley may enjoy life in the suburbs. Now, here is Plouhaix."

We had long left the environs of Quimper and had been whizzing through a sizable forest, the road straight as a rule. At the point we had now reached, the forest retreated on either side, leaving a grassy clearing in a huge natural basin; exactly in its centre, amid formal gardens, lay a fairy tale château, pinnacled and machicolated, with dozens of those absurd little pointed towers like inverted ice-cream cones that the French love. It stood pearl-white amid the forest glades, and a late, pale moon hung above it like a signature on a Japanese print.

"Oh . . . what a perfectly ravishing place!"

"Very convenient, it used to be, when Sir Bert first bought it. Just an hour from London in the jet, and there's so much open space around, you can see people coming long before they get near. But now, of course, there are such sophisticated long-range weapons that it's a bit vulnerable—things can be fired from the middle of the forest."

We entered the grounds through a pair of electronically operated wrought-iron gates fourteen feet high, and drove past the mathematically laid-out gardens, past a fountain that looked like and probably was a Bernini, and a lot of other classical and semiclassical statuary. Several huge Alsatian dogs were loping purposefully about among the box hedges; they stared at us hard with their pale mad eyes making me glad that I was in the car and not on foot. By now Plouhaix wore, for me, a much less fairy tale aspect; or, at least, the fairy tale had changed from Perrault to Grimm.

Through another gate; the ambulance had already pulled up outside the main entrance, and the owner of Plouhaix was bundled inside faster than the three-card trick. I was reminded of those cakes that you mix with hot ingredients—adding soda bicarb and flour to melted butter and sugar—which have to be almost hurled into the oven.

We, too, followed inside quite expeditiously. For myself the thought of sharpshooters lurking in those misty reaches of Druidical woodland, with their telescopic lenses trained on the front door, was enough to get me through it with less than dignified speed. After all, they weren't to know that I was a total stranger; I might be Sir Bert's newest daughter-in-law, or his current mistress. I began to be sorry that I had ever embarked on this *outré* excursion.

The interior was worth seeing, though. We were immediately in a circular vestibule, floored with lucent green marble. The walls were a darker green, their gilded cornices and woodwork all carved in garlandries of leaves and fruit and flowers; round-arched niches held antique gilt wooden figures of dryads and fauns and satyrs; somebody—surely not Sir Bert?—had had the notion of bringing the forest right into the château. Above us a fantastically

elaborate art-nouveau candelabrum poured down green-and-blue
Tiffany convolutions like a frozen cascade.

The master of the house, already shunted into a wheelchair,
had spun himself across to a gilt telephone in a niche and was on
the line to Hamburg. People were bustling about with luggage,
portfolios, and bundles of papers. I pounced on an elderly bonne
and asked to be directed to a loo.

"*Mais oui, mademoiselle, suivez-moi—*" She escorted me down
one of the passages that radiated like the spokes of a wheel, and
into a sumptuous flowery blue boudoir, which must have faced
east, for sunshine flooded in; it was furnished with gold taps, marble basins, Venetian glass powder bowls, the whole works. There
was also a divinely comfortable-looking article—a fauteuil or
chaise longue, I wouldn't know, but anyway of a baroque eighteenth-century fashion with blue velvet ruchings and cushions,
tucks, rucks, pouncing and quilling. When I had splashed, powdered, and cologned myself, I was irresistibly drawn to this inviting couch. I thought, Well, I'll just stretch out for five minutes, it
was a short disturbed night, I'll meditate a little in a recumbent
position . . .

When I next woke I realised at once that some considerable
time must have elapsed. The light was totally different; my opulent refuge now lay in shade. Yawning, I stood up, splashed on
yet more cologne, and then, assailed by conscience, hurried back
to the entrance hall.

Dead silence reigned there. Not a soul to be seen.

"Hullo?" I called rather nervously. "*Allo? Allo? Est-ce-qu'il y a
du monde par ici?*"

Nobody replied, and I began roaming about, upstairs and
down, into a magnificent library, dark brown panelling, gilt, and
leather; a banqueting hall which could easily have accommodated
the whole body of the recent medical conference in Mitchison;
upstairs I found various reception rooms furnished with great
Louis Quinze elegance in striped satin, marquetry, formality and
discomfort; nobody seemed to be anywhere.

I began to feel like a character out of the *Sleeping Beauty*, or
was it *La Belle et la Bête*? Would ghostly hands holding fruit

bowls drift out of the walls? Or, on a more probable level, had Sir
Bert and his entire entourage been kidnapped while I slept? Was
I, in my turn, liable to be coshed, drugged, and whisked off to a
cellar in Venezuela? Or did the millionaire and his staff inhabit
some remoter, humbler region of the château?

I descended the gracefully curving stair again and stood
thoughtfully gazing out through the two huge gilt-garlanded
plate-glass, bulletproof, I hoped, inner entrance doors. Beyond the
open outer doors, beyond a flight of steps, half an acre of
gravelled driveway, and a stone basin of water, lay exquisitely
trimmed lawns, drenched in sunshine. Who kept the grass
mown? Phantom gardeners? Were there guard dogs about? Dare
I venture outside? Or was I a prisoner in this place and likely to
starve to death? I began to feel hollow with hunger. My watch,
which had stopped for lack of winding, said noon, but plainly it
was much later than that by European time. The light was
golden. The shadows of the clipped box bushes stretched length-
ily over the grass.

"Miss Churchill! *Attendez!* For the love of God, don't go out!"

A shout from behind spun me round. There was Rabuse,
approaching at a run along one of the radiating passages. "Thank
heaven I caught you," he panted, grabbing my arm. "It is death
to go out there."

"Don't worry, I wasn't planning to; I rather thought it might
be."

"Come back; come this way." As if still mistrusting my intentions, he began dragging me in the direction from which he had
come.

"Where is everybody? I'm very sorry I fell asleep."

"They are all gone. It happened while you slept."

"*Gone?* The whole shebang? What in the world happened?"

"I will tell you. But first—you must be hungry. I was about to
prepare myself a snack."

By now we had arrived in a splendid red-floored kitchen, larger
than that of the Ritz, equipped with half a dozen cooking stoves,
several refrigerators the size of bathrooms, chopping blocks made
from entire tree trunks, and whole walls festooned with copper

pans. Judging by the ingredients Rabuse had assembled on a table, he was about to make himself an omelet, but my hunger demanded something more substantial.

"Why don't you let me cook?" I suggested. "Then you can tell me what has been going on."

"A good idea," he said, "but first I will find us some wine," and he disappeared down a flight of stone steps to a cellar while I investigated the food supply.

There were vaultlike freezers packed with steaks, legs of wild boar, turkeys, sides of beef, and haunches of venison. I started a hot country terrine of salt pork and chopped beef, but since I don't really approve of eating meat straight out of the freezer I searched farther, and, discovering a well-stocked game larder, selected a pheasant which seemed about right for roasting. I would have preferred a salmis, but could find no truffles, so decided we must make do with country cabbage salad, garnished by strips of bacon, brussels sprouts, potato straw cake with carrots tucked in its interior, and a dessert of cheese and fruit; there was a whole cold-store filled with cheeses, and another containing magnificent apples and pears, presumably off the estate.

Meanwhile the doctor had found a light dry Chablis and a beautiful red Graves, 1975; he fetched up several bottles of each. The cellar, he said, seemed a bit of a muddle; Sir Bert had no interest in wine, he preferred Worthington, whatever *that* was.

"So what happened?" I demanded again, while I was plucking the pheasant and we were sampling the Chablis.

"The guard-dog handler had a heart attack."

"Good God! Did he die?"

"No, fortunately, it was not a severe attack, but it was necessary to take him into hospital. Sir Bert went with him; it is too risky for Sir Bert to remain here without an ambulance and lacking the only person the dogs will obey; consequently he has gone with his staff to the other château, near Albi."

"But what about us?" I demanded with some indignation, taking out my terrine to inspect it, and sliding a frozen baguette into the oven. "Are we simply left here for the dogs to gobble?"

"No, no, in due course a veterinarian will arrive who will shoot them with drugged darts."

"What happens to the poor beasts then? Are they destroyed? Or do they have to be kept under sedation till the handler has recovered?"

"God knows. *Ce n'est pas mon affaire,*" said Rabuse rather callously. "But the vet cannot come until tomorrow morning, so until then we are prisoners."

He seemed, I thought, not too displeased with this state of affairs.

But I felt somewhat abused. "Suppose I suffered from claustrophobia? Or had an urgent appointment in England?" I felt I should have been woken earlier and given the option of leaving with the millionaire and his staff. But Rabuse said placidly, "I knew you had no appointment. Whereas I must deliver a lecture in Paris tomorrow night, and had no wish to travel south."

"Suppose I had fancied a trip to Albi?"

"You are pleased to tease, madame. Did I not promise to introduce you to some Breton delicacies? Tomorrow morning we will go on a little tour of the countryside."

I gave up the game. In fact I was content enough to remain in the château with this calm, friendly disposed character; true, it was frustrating not to be able to walk outside and explore the gardens and forest, the one full of man-eating dogs, the other of kidnappers equipped with all the latest weapons; but our imprisonment would not be of long duration. No doubt there was plenty of entertainment to be found within the château; I had hardly investigated more than a twentieth of its possibilities.

"May one telephone? I would like to tell my staff where I have got to. Is that possible?"

"*Mais oui, madame, naturellement.*"

"Do call me Clytie, won't you?"

"Cligh—tee," he repeated carefully; his pronunciation made it sound extremely French—a long diphthong on the first syllable, a short crisp little vowel on the second. "That is a charming name —what does it mean, may one ask?"

"Oh, Clytie was a Greek nymph, a water nymph I think, who fell in love with the sun god, Apollo."

"And?"

"No good came of it. He knew that if he made love to her she would burn up, evaporate—like Semele, you know, who had a thing with Zeus—so he never even approached her. And she pined for him all her life, watching his chariot travel across the sky, so in the end she turned into a sunflower, or a heliotrope, I forget which."

"*Un tournesol!* A charming tale to match the name. Are you then like your namesake—always yearning for the unattainable?"

The unattainable. Dead, gone, vanished, lost. Lost.

"I suppose I am, in a way."

I spread my hands on the beautiful solidity of the wooden block. Ran my fingers through the softness of the feathers.

"Ah," he said thoughtfully. "But to return to your question, yes, certainly you may telephone—to anywhere in the world, if you wish."

His words gave me a sudden mad urge to phone my mother. So often—when she was alive—she would be in some unattainable spot: Pernambuco; Tasmania; Tashkent; Sunrise, Alaska; Samarkand; even if I had a phone number for her, I could never afford to make the call; so my one piece of self-indulgence if staying with rich benevolent friends was to phone her and have a good gossip.

If I had her number, of course.

"Hey, Vanessa, just listen to this, will you—I'm shut up in a château with a French bacteriologist."

There would be a great deal to catch up on. She had died eight years ago; it was with her legacy that I had been able to buy Watch Cottage. Oh, what a lot had happened to me since then. George. Hugh. Anthony. And Rosie. And the possible resurrection of little Finn.

"Thanks," I said, and sped to the nearest telephone.

My staff were relieved to hear where I had got to. "We'd discovered already that you had left New York; your lawyer has been trying to contact you."

"My *lawyer?*"

"Mr. Roche."

"Does he want me to call him?"

"Yes he does. His number is Affton Wells . . ."

"I know it, thanks."

Some numbers you never forget.

I called Anthony. By now it was well after work hours, there was no reply from his office number. So I tried the house in Hanover Crescent. I had not called that number since Rosie died.

The phone was answered by a shrill, cracked elderly voice. My heart sank, knowing who it must be.

"May I speak to Mr. Roche, please?"

"Who is that?" Suspicious, surly. Not many ladies called Anthony, I guessed, unless they were ladies of considerable temerity and tenacity.

"Clytie Churchill."

"Ugh!" She really said it. Her grunt expressed utter disgust. "Hold on," she growled after a moment. I half expected her to slam down the receiver, but when a longish pause had elapsed, Anthony came on the line.

". . . Anthony? Clytie Churchill here. I believe you wanted to get in touch with me?"

"Oh. Yes. Where in the world did you get to? Are you back in England?"

His voice was brusque, as if I had interrupted him in the middle of reading some lengthy law report.

"No, I'm not in England. I'm at a château in Brittany."

I thought of mentioning that I was a prisoner, and decided not; even the château seemed to incur his disapproval; he said, "In *Brittany?* Why there?" sounding irritable. "I thought you were coming back to England after the conference?"

"I probably shall tomorrow. What did you want to talk about?"

My heart was banging ungovernably against my ribs. "There— there hasn't been—been any news—you haven't made any discovery about Dan's son?"

He said rather cagily, "Well, there's no cause to get excited, but—fairly coincidentally—I have had some contact with Ingrid Christ's family."

"*Really?*" This news certainly did surprise me. "How did that come about?"

"Through Caspar Monk," he said. "Working away on his biography, managed to track down a stepsister living on some out-of-the-way island in the Baltic. So the main reason why I've needed to get in touch with you is because this stepsister, Mrs. Olafson, holds that she has a better claim than you do to be considered the owner of the copyrights; or, anyway, an equal claim."

"Is that all?" I was bitterly disappointed. "I don't give a damn who has the copyrights. She's welcome to them if she wants them —just so long as she doesn't try to hinder publication of the biography, or the poems."

"I don't gather that she has any intention of that kind. But she is planning a visit to England shortly, hoping to collect the papers from you. You may lose quite a bit of money on it, you know," said Anthony disapprovingly.

"I don't care. Monk has copies of the papers. But the originals are at Watch Cottage. I'll be willing to see the stepsister, of course, tell her."

Though I was not impressed by the fact that this Mrs. Olafson, who had left her stepsister's papers to the mercy of providence for thirteen years without troubling as to what had become of them, became interested only when she began to realise that there might be profit to be made.

"I'll see her, if she thinks it will be any use," I repeated. "And I'll hand the papers over to you, if you wish."

"No, you don't have to do that," he said hastily. "I'll give her your address, so long as you don't object."

"Very well." Very well, if that's the way you want it, you hostile bastard. "I'll be in touch then," I said coldly. "You have no further theory about those anonymous letters?"

"Yes, I do have a theory." His voice was full of legal caution. "But I won't discuss it over the phone. It can wait till you get back. When will that be? And do you have a telephone number where you are?"

I gave him the French exchange and number, adding, "It's Sir Bert Wilder's place—one of them."

"*Who?*"

"Sir Bert Wilder."

"I thought that was what you said. The container trucks millionaire? How in the world do you come to be there?"

"Oh, Sir Bert isn't here, he left this morning. I'm just staying in his house."

"With a friend, I assume," said Anthony unforgivably.

"Excuse me, I have to go and take my pheasant out of the oven. Goodbye, Anthony."

"Your telephone call seems to have distressed you, madame," remarked Dr. Rabuse, after I had returned to the kitchen and began rather hastily sweeping pheasant feathers and brussels sprouts shards into a refuse bag.

We had regressed, I noticed, to formal terms again; Rabuse was really an observant companion, sensitive to one's moods, adapting instantly. He added with polite solicitude, "I hope nobody is in anxiety about your presence here? You will come to no harm in this place, I give you my assurance."

"Oh no, it isn't that. Not that at all . . ."

I poked the bird, tested the straw potato cake, strained the sprouts, and transferred them to a handsome Limoges dish, gathering the last of the pale green globules out of the colander with my fingers, taking comfort from their soft springy warmth.

I do so many things with my fingers now. Probably in reaction against the restrictions of childhood. I can remember Vanessa saying so often, "Don't touch that, sweetie. It's certain to be filthy. Crawling with flies. All the dogs of Arabia have probably shat on it." I suppose she had to be constantly on the alert against dysentery, enteric, cholera, diphtheria, bubonic . . . I suppose my survival at all was quite a triumph. And my father, of course, did not survive. He died, I realised later, quite young; in his early fifties.

Sometimes I feel myself moving towards her identity. She used to sit, sometimes, with a fixed, distant look in her eyes, staring far away into space. I can feel the same expression on my own face. Why did it never occur to me to ask her what she was thinking? Why, when we are young, do we pay so little heed to the older generation?

Anxious to steer the conversation away from my telephone call, I remarked, "Has it ever occurred to you what a lot of tactile pleasures women have, that most men miss? Or indeed, the majority of people; we use our hands so little, now that most food comes in packages. . . . But consider the pleasure of peeling oranges, testing fruit for ripeness, scooping broad beans out of those furry resistant pods; or stripping the peel from tomatoes after you have dipped them in hot water, or kneading soft springy bread dough, or groping about in a warm potage to get out the bones—? These activities are so therapeutic, so atavistic, but how many people benefit by them nowadays? It is all done by machinery."

He replied rather self-righteously, "Frenchmen probably experience such pleasures more than males of other races."

"I wonder? There are supermarkets in France, too."

Having cleared a space on the table I set my terrine there and said formally, "*Monsieur est servi.*"

He tasted the terrine, raised his glass to me in compliment, then, eating vigorously, went on, between mouthfuls, "On the whole, however, I am inclined to agree with your thesis; particularly in respect of the two sexes. Men, nowadays, lead sensually deprived lives compared with those of women. A man goes each day to his place of business and does his work—commerce, research, journalism, medicine, industry, whatever it be. He has his hobby, too, plays golf, attends the races, goes sailing. But, apart from that, and from a certain amount of sexual activity, he does not employ his physical mechanism at all. Whereas women, I have observed—even professional women with successful careers —women still contrive to find time for practising a far more varied range of skills. For instance you, madame . . . of course your particular profession is a continual therapy in itself, but in addition to that I am prepared to predict that your day-to-day life will contain a whole gamut of most divergent activities, am I not right?"

"Heavens, yes: painting, upholstering, plastering, making mayonnaise, chopping wood—soldering—plumbing—carpentry; besides grappling with various hateful machines, motor mowers, photocopiers, typewriters, blenders, sewing, recording, and washing machines. And it is true that many men whom I know—whom I have known—don't possess these skills, don't seem to want them; it's really perplexing; as if they preferred to direct their current into one channel only, or at the most two or three? But why, why canalise their activities so? It can't be natural? Primitive man must surely have had a whole repertory of different skills?"

"I doubt it. When you use the term 'primitive man' you think already, perhaps, of the farmer, the herdsman; but our earliest ancestor, the hunter, had one skill and one only. Have you heard the legend of St. Julien the Hospitaller? He had a mad lust to kill; that was his driving force. He is the basic man in all, perhaps; remove that and you remove the mainspring."

"Well no one *has* removed it," I argued. "That's why we are all in such a mess," removing the terrine, and replacing it by the pheasant. Dr. Rabuse fetched the vegetables from the back of the great brass-plated cooker, brought the red wine, which he had opened earlier, and poured glasses for both of us, continuing to talk as he did so.

"There are many who will say, of course, that, by thus concentrating on one skill, man achieves a higher degree of expertise, of grasp, than woman, with her diffused range of activities, can ever hope to reach. Where is your female Galileo, your female Einstein, Leonardo—?"

"You can't bring *him* in; if ever there was a jack-of-all-trades—"

"Okay, I am not playing competitions, I try to prove a point. Shakespeare, Ibsen, Tolstoy?"

"Oh, I daresay you are right. I am not a feminist. Actually I believe that feminism is a commercial racket. Have you noticed how, whenever inflation becomes severe, or there is an industrial crisis, the people who organise industry invent a new group, and then create a new market to cater for it? First it was teenagers—then various ethnic clans who suddenly had special needs—then the cult groups—then athletes—then vegetarians and health food coteries—then women. There are women's book shops now, and women's food shops, even women's banks—as if females hadn't existed before the end of the seventies. I'd be ashamed to go into a women's book shop!"

By now I had talked myself back into a more cheerful frame of mind; the dark cloud that Anthony had power to throw over my spirits lifted and drifted away.

Rabuse, who had appeared somewhat pensive at the start of the meal, began to relax. His face, for a Frenchman, was not expressive; heavy, rather sculptured lids often concealed his large dark brown, well-set eyes; when the lids did flash up the effect was quite startling, as if two targets had been revealed. His mouth, a trifle thin and severe when at rest, pursed into a magisterial line, could be forbidding; though it had an endearing habit of twitching rapidly two or three times when something amused him. It twitched now. He said, "You keep asking if I have noticed this or that? One thing in my experience I *have* observed is that when a man and woman begin to take stock of each other sexually, they very frequently embark on this kind of discussion, busying themselves with generalities, circling round the real object without touching it."

I was brought up short by his simple directness. Making coffee I asked, "Are we taking stock?"

"We would be highly unnatural if we did not," he said, carefully cutting himself a small wedge of Brie. "Why do you suppose I suggested your coming to France? Because I felt a compatibility between us. Not for life, perhaps," he added quickly—I must have looked disconcerted—"but for a pleasant interlude, an idyll, perhaps, leading on, as such passages often do, to a valuable friendship. Did you not feel an affinity between us, almost from the first? You are an honest person. Come, I am sure that you did! And what could be more natural than such reckoning now, situated romantically as we are?"

"Well yes—perhaps—"

"You seem doubtful, nevertheless? And yet you are a person of maturity; you have been married? Have had lovers, several perhaps?"

"Fourteen or fifteen."

If he could be honest, so could I. He took my answer calmly.

"Among so many, none pleased you? Your heart was not touched by any one of them?"

"Oh, but it was; it was."

Suddenly a most appalling wind of desolation swept through me. My very vitals seemed to freeze with sorrow. I said, "If you draw that conclusion, you couldn't be more mistaken. There were three—" And then stopped, absolutely unable to proceed any further. My throat had seized up; my tongue clove to my palate. I put my elbows on the table and pressed my palms over my eyeballs.

After a moment his voice came, quiet and kind.

"Shall I tell you why I am a bacteriologist? It is because, twenty years ago, when I was still going through my medical training, I, too, loved somebody. She was a young nurse, halfway through her own training in the hospital where I worked, in Toulon. She was a serious, devoted girl, most dedicated to her job; good as bread. She caught a rare tropical disease from a sailor in one of the wards. He died, horribly, and Lucienne died too; everybody was able to predict the course of her disease, which was horrible—but nobody could do anything to avert its end."

"Ah, I see. You have been there too." I spoke muffled through my hands.

"Yes. I have been there too." He added, after a pause, "For a long time I was there. Like a badger in its burrow when the entrance has been blocked. I did not think I would ever love again. Certainly never to marry. I am a religious man, a Catholic. I take the marriage vows very seriously. Ah, you look up? You are not Catholic yourself, I am certain. One of your lovers, perhaps? You do not like Catholics?"

"It isn't a case of liking or disliking. I respect them—

profoundly. I find them hard to take. It is another dimension. All that mystery, going on behind the wall—about which one knows *nothing*. Somebody looks through a grille from time to time. A few words are exchanged. And then—suddenly—some emanation. A lightning flash. A rattle of thunder. And somebody's lamed, hurt, killed. Like the shot from the forest."

"The Act of God?" He smiled, taking off his gold-rimmed glasses to rub his eyes; without the spectacles his face looked younger, less magisterial. "It is a reflection of our attitude to God, is it not, that His acts must always be unpleasant ones?"

"But you did, in the end, love again?" I suggested, wishing to get away from God.

"Not in the same way. Ever. A benign, mild day in winter. Never the heat of July."

The telephone rang. Rabuse moved unhurriedly to answer it, observing, "Whoever calls, it is most unlikely that we can do anything for them. Unless it is the vet."

As he picked up the receiver (copper, to match the kitchenware) I had a sudden irrational nutty hope that it would be Anthony calling back with news. News of what? The relief of Mafeking? The taking of Lucknow. Mons. Hiroshima. The news they brought from Ghent to Aix.

> *Where were they rushing to, Paul Revere, Mazeppa?*
> *Mankind recurrently makes these headlong mistakes,*

Ingrid Christ said, in a poem called *Tidings*.

"*Ah, oui?*" cried Rabuse cordially into the phone. "Yes, certainly I will, if that is your wish. *Bien sûr, monsieur*; the teapot—the pyjamas—the papers in a red leather portfolio." He repeated a string of numbers slowly and carefully. "No, I will not write them down. Mademoiselle Churchill will help me to remember them. *Au 'voir. Dormez bien, monsieur.* Yes, I will. And I will ask her to give you her opinion."

He put back the receiver, smiling broadly.

"That was Sir Bert. He has left behind him his favourite pyjamas, which have in the breast pocket a little poem that he was committing to memory. And his wife wishes for a teapot he promised to bring from here and forgot in the haste of departure. It seems he found her, staying there at Château d'Oix, so there has been a joyful reunion. The misfortune has been for them a blessing. They are a very devoted couple."

"And what was the third thing he wanted?"

"The papers from the safe. I had better get them directly while I remember the combination."

"He seems a very trusting man. We could make off with all his valuables. Or pass on the combination number to thieves."

"The combination number is changed automatically every day."

We went upstairs into the magnificent library. Rabuse pressed a button and shutters clattered down across the row of black windows. "No need to advertise where the safe is," he remarked.

"You forget: the only creatures outside those windows are man-eating Alsatians."

"*You* forget: for all we know the United Arab Haulage Employers' Federation, or the Policy Committee of the International Truckdrivers' League have spies up in those woods with radio-telescopes trained on our every move."

Sir Bert's safe, traditionally, was behind a gilded row of fake leatherbound volumes, the collected works of Angela Brazil, I was delighted to notice. Apart from the red leather portfolio, it contained little: a few packets of seeds, a diamond tiara wrapped in a chamois cloth, a hunk of gold, a packet of orange spice tea, and what looked like a folio Shakespeare.

"How are you supposed to dispatch the things to him?" I asked, as, after taking out the portfolio, Rabuse swung the heavy door and it clicked back into place.

"I must leave them with the steward tomorrow; he sends a courier to Quimper and they are flown down. Sir Bert will receive them by noon."

I was curious to know what poem the millionaire was in process of learning, and when we went to find his pyjamas—a plain blue cotton M&S pair flung carelessly over a half-acre bed covered by what looked like one of the Cluny tapestries—I investigated the breast pocket and found a slip of paper containing a dozen handwritten lines.

"Heaven, you say, will be a field in April . . ."

Odd that Sir Bert had chosen that poem. George used to quote it too.

"But I, being older, sadder, Having not you, nor aught save thought of you . . ."

"Who is the author?" inquired Rabuse, as I tucked the slip back, and folded the jacket.

"An American poet, Conrad Aiken."

"I regret, I know very little poetry. I have not the ear for it."

"Don't apologise. You have been busy collecting facts, and reading the works of Ivy Compton-Burnett. One can't do everything."

He packed pyjamas, portfolio, and the teapot, which we had brought from the kitchen—it was a plain green Denbigh-ware one —into a Gucci case which we found in a closet. Then he said, "Sir Bert especially requested that I show you his collection of paintings. He wishes to know your opinion of them. He thinks you are a very nice, sympathetic young lady. Hopes to see you again. And he wants you to telephone him sometime and talk about the pictures, tell him if there are any others you think he should buy—reversing the charge, of course."

"Where are these pictures?" I asked rather apprehensively.

"In the gallery."

We traversed various corridors and came to a room about seventy feet long by twenty wide, hung with natural creamy tussore, illuminated by overhead track lights, and floored with sisal matting. It seemed almost monastically severe compared to the other furnishings at Plouhaix. Rabuse turned on lights and operated shutters as he had in the library, and I wandered along looking at the pictures, which hung on the back wall. There were a lot of them.

Sir Bert, I discovered, collected pictures of houses. That seemed to be the connecting link. Some of the paintings were basically landscapes, some had figures in the foreground, but always there would be a building somewhere in the composition. Was this, I wondered, because the millionaire owned so many domiciles already that he liked, as it were, to extend the number in reproductions? Or were his hunted life and continual insecurity thus manifest in a never-ending search for the perfect dwelling?

His collection ranged from townscapes by Canaletto and Guardi and Belotto, through tidy Gainsborough country seats with proud owners in the foreground, to Paris suburbs by Utrillo, and romantic ruins by Samuel Palmer, and American mansions by John Henry Hall, and street frontages by Hopper, and wrapped mysterious edifices by Christo, and wild sinister structures by Piranesi. There was even a little oil painting which I viewed with a curious pang, for it was signed H. H. Herdman and I had last seen it at Hugh's show in 1974. "Haunted House" Hugh had called it; he liked painting haunted houses, or so he said. He had been disappointed when I told him there was no ghost in Watch Cottage.

Standing there, in the large, rather aseptic gallery, I was suddenly overcome by homesickness and wondered what the devil I was doing here in this spooky château besieged by man-eating dogs, and why I wasn't at home in bed. What had possessed me to come to such an unchancy spot? I asked myself. Never mind, I would go straight home tomorrow; by this time tomorrow night I would be in my own cosy kitchen, scrambling eggs and committing my chicken and water-chestnut casserole to posterity via the tape recorder, with the owls hooting on the Castle Mound outside my window.

I said, sincerely, that it was a very interesting collection. Rabuse must have detected a note of reserve in my voice, for he switched off the lights and escorted me expeditiously back to the library, where he set a match to a log fire which was already laid, and brought out a bottle of Courvoisier and glasses from a cupboard behind some more fake books.

Then he said briskly, "Shall we go to bed together or shall we talk?"

"Dr. Rabuse—Théo—I hope . . . I hope you won't feel that I have encouraged you to cherish expectations which I never intended to gratify—"

"My dear girl! Do I seem such an unreasonable man?"

"I don't think I'm ready to go to bed with you yet. If ever."

"Please don't look so troubled! We shall converse, instead. It will be a different kind of pleasure, that is all. The good is the enemy of the best. Who said that?"

"Plato, probably."

"And who shall decide which is good and which is best?"

"The question—the real question, is . . . Of course we could just spend a night together and go our separate ways. But I think you were right. There does seem to be an affinity between us. We might not want to leave it at that."

Was I being honest? I thought of Anthony, smouldering back in England, like a time fuse. Must he stand forever between me and all human contact? I went on, "You'll think me crazily superstitious, I daresay, being a cool sceptical Frenchman—"

"Who says that I am cool and sceptical?"

"—but men that I—that I come to love, so often die miserably."

"*Quoi donc?* So often? *How* often?"

"Three that I loved all died. And a fourth—with whom I had been briefly involved—whom I liked and respected."

"These were natural deaths? Not through your agency? You are not telling me that you are a kind of Lucrezia Borgia, who has each lover assassinated by his successor?"

"No, no! One drowned, accidentally. One committed suicide by drowning. Two became ill and—and just died. And two very dear women friends were killed—in horrible needless accidents—"

"So?" he said, looking at me acutely, "you believe that you are a bad-luck bringer? That you cause death by your fatal proximity?"

"No, not really. That would be too self-important, wouldn't it? Only—" I covered my face with my hands again, rubbed furiously at my forehead, then looked up at him. "Don't you see, I just couldn't bear to have it happen any more? I've had as much as I can take. Of loving people—investing in them—and then losing them—"

Unexpectedly he quoted:

> "*I always think as they do what they please*
> *Of Tom Dick and Harry who were tall as trees*
> *But most I think when I'm by their side*
> *Of little Willy Wee who downed and died.*"

I stared at him.

"How extraordinary. You picked those words right out of my mind. I thought you said you hadn't an ear for poetry?"

"Lucienne, long ago, introduced me to Dylan Thomas's work. Sometimes I read him again, in memory of her."

I wondered if he had ever gone to bed with his Lucienne. Probably not.

He laid another log with care across the briskly burning fire, and said, "Four of the men you have cohabited with are now dead? From a total of fifteen? Statistically, that is not significant. Eleven are still alive. Moreover, men's expectation of life is less than that of women. This is a fact to which women must resign themselves."

"It's easy to say that! Three of those four were men that I loved *deeply*; and—and in perpetuity. I love them still. I always shall."

"Therefore you loved them with more than the body?" His tone was measured, judicious.

"With much more than the body. But with the body, too, of course."

Our talk had summoned them. I felt their physical presence like ghosts around the hearth: George, slight, sallow, shrewd, smiling, the slanted cigarette between his fingers; Dan, agile, wary, faulty, touching, nervously pushing the dark hair back from his brow, hunting for a way out of whatever predicament he had got himself into; Hugh, massive and vigorous, in country corduroys and tweed jacket with leather-patched sleeves. Seated in an armchair at rest, Hugh was like one of his own monumental bits of statuary. He had invincible faith in his own health and strength. "Nothing is ever going to happen to old Hugh," he used to say comfortably, reassuringly. I liked to sit on the floor curled between his knees, leaning back against him; it was like leaning against a tree. When told of his illness, he was at first stunned, disbelieving; then in shock; then raging. He was not a believer in any kind of religion, all of which he dismissed as superstitious twaddle. His forbears had been Quakers but he had shed all beliefs at university. After learning that his death was inevitable, however, he began to believe in some kind of malign, actively hostile providence. Gaunt, savage, rebellious against his pillows, he was Prometheus, resigned to nothing, outraged at the injustice that had overtaken him. Only for Elly's sake had he thrown a pretence of civilised behaviour over his extinction.

"I love them still," I repeated. And another who isn't dead. Anthony, who hates me.

Rabuse said, "Indubitably, in a better world, they are glad to know of your love. But you, not being a Catholic, do not have faith in a life after this one?"

"No, none. They are just irrecoverably gone. And when I am dead—with all the others who loved them, who remember them now—then they will be even more lost in the past. No trace will be left of them at all."

Except Hugh's pictures, I thought of "Haunted House."

"It is so sad for nonbelievers," sighed Rabuse. "To lose that comfort, of knowing that you will at last be reunited with your dear ones. As I with my Lucienne."

I studied him, really puzzled. Here was the wall again; the wall I had so often encountered between me and Anthony. What an odd, what an extraordinary confidence to have. It certainly must condition one's attitude to the opportunities of this life. It quite evidently did.

Yet Rabuse seemed an intelligent man, a questioner, a sceptic. And so had Anthony been.

"That's so simplistic!" I said. "Even if some part of the spirit did linger, how could there be any kind of real reunion? It's a creed of children, of savages: a kind of celestial picnic, with old Granny coming back, and little Paul who died young; everybody meeting again round the campfire." I shook my head. "It makes

no sense to me. And it wouldn't work for me. Dan, for instance"
—I couldn't help smiling at the thought—"my husband probably
wouldn't be allowed into heaven at all. He was far too shifty and
self-interested."

"Yet you loved him."

"Oh yes. Oh yes. I did."

"Tell me about him. Tell about them all."

4

How well could I have spared for thee, young swain,
Anow of such as for their bellies sake
Creep and intrude, and climb into the fold?

After Dan's death I went wild for several years. Elly was up in York with her Hugh, knee-deep in domesticity and languages; Chris was taking a Ph.D. in psychology, working part time, and soon married to George; I went really wild. My father, brought up a Baptist, would have called it weakness of the moral fibre. A degenerative disease. Leukemia of the spirit. Twice I had been violently dashed down by life, told in no uncertain terms where I got off; I began to feel there must be something poisoned about me which brought on these misfortunes. Or else that I had no real existence—apart from maybe cooking meals for other people. I was just a kind of nonexistent point where other people's lives intersected. Or why would they use me so? For a couple of years I made no attempt to see Chris and Elly; I felt that if I were indeed a bad-luck agent, I had no business to contaminate their lives. They were healthy, sound, hard-working, rational, getting on with their avocations; let them stay that way, uninfected by me.

I had various short-lived affairs; with Flagellant Reggie, and a sad, kind man suffering from a most unfortunate glandular disability; "*uber gor, uber gornischt,*" he used to say about it resignedly; then a short Lesbian interlude with two sisters who kept a bookshop; I liked their taste in literature, we had many a comfortable conversation about the works of Wilkie Collins and Sarah

Grand, but I couldn't stand their messy lifestyle: unwashed dishes everywhere, dead flowers reeking in stagnant water, cigarette butts squashed in the jam, bloodstained tights soaking in the kitchen sink, and one of them dashed off late to the bookshop one day leaving an overturned electric bar fire lying on its face, burning a hole clean through a rather nice little Persian rug Vanessa had given me for my twenty-first birthday, and into the floorboards beneath; it never even occurred to her to apologise about the rug, to her it seemed of no importance. So I disengaged myself from Cammie and Gilda, but remained on friendly terms. I see them still. Then there was Lionel, whose wife had just died; all he wanted was to use me as a sexual outlet while talking about her and he couldn't understand why I regarded this as dishonest dealing; "It isn't as if you don't come on yourself, you get your kicks out of it too," he said injuredly, "so what's the fuss about?" We get what we can out of each other, I suppose; I went on seeing him for a while, he thought my beef stews were wonderful, which made a kind of bond, but it became too lugubrious when I realised that he was *never* going to stop talking about Hermione. No doubt my own attitude was equally fraudulent.

Simultaneously there was Arthur the stockbroker, who didn't really want a lover at all; what he wanted was somebody to talk to on the telephone for about two hours every night from eleven to one while he masturbated; his talk was so interesting and remarkable that for a year or more I acquiesced in this nutty arrangement; we hardly ever met, for he was busy in the stock exchange by day and in the evenings gave lectures at L.S.E. on monetary theory; he invested a bit of cash for me and quadrupled it, which was about the only solid benefit I derived from him, except a lot of erudite information on all kinds of topics and a box of Mahler records I rarely listen to; he worshipped Mahler and liked to put them on if he ever came round to dinner.

He was a finicky eater but enjoyed my soufflés; he said you could hardly ever get a decent soufflé in a restaurant. At last I was invited to cater for a booksellers' conference in Stockholm (Cammie and Gilda gave me this break, for which I was proportionately grateful); it made a good opportunity to detach myself from Arthur. I simply didn't phone him after I got back from Stockholm, and, a couple of weeks later, removed myself to a new address and so out of his ken. If he can be said to have had a ken. Recently I read in the papers that he has been appointed Economic Adviser to the Department of Trade and Industry. Who, I wonder, is the recipient of his midnight wit and erudition now?

Then there was a man who owned a fish-finger factory, and a journalist from a news agency, and a brigadier, and a gay actor who wanted a change.

Three years went by in this hit-or-miss fashion. I sank into a depression, used to wake every morning bathed in tears, daylight broke on me with the hideous clang of the get-up bell which had been wielded by the matron at my expensive boarding school. In four years' schooling I never became reconciled to that bell. After the Mediterranean mornings of childhood with Vanessa, waking among olive groves or on silvery beaches, the reality of brass bell, iron bedsteads, clanking cubicle curtains, enamel jugs, and two hundred unfriendly, uncaring people close at hand was no reality, but, just simply, hell.

I used to argue with Anthony about hell. Anybody can invent hell, I said, there's no trick to that, hell is the quintessence of our own worst experiences and our worst fears; if God were really up there, all-knowing and all-loving, why should He see the need for any such arrangement?

"We're supposed to be His *children?*" I said indignantly to Anthony. "You don't send your children to *hell?*" But Anthony said I was just an ignorant little heathen.

I didn't go to a psychiatrist for my depression. It never occurred to me that was what it was. I simply thought I was unhappy. Giving something a name with a capital letter doesn't necessarily help. One year my back gave me agonizing pain; I could hardly crawl out of bed in the morning, and had to shuffle around bent double while I brushed my teeth and percolated the coffee. Then I developed an excruciatingly tender lump on the sole of my foot, so that for about eight months I walked with a limp, particularly during the first half of the day, until I got used to the pain. Slowly the infection proceeded along its course and finally removed itself from my foot in the form of a hard circular hunk, like a knot coming out of a wooden plank; that was quite an exciting and interesting period. Some time afterwards, thumbing through a dictionary of symptoms that George's firm had published, I learned that my afflictions had been, respectively, a slipped disc and a plantar wart, or verucca, and not, as I had assumed, merely manifestations of my noxious condition or the malevolence of providence, sent to me like Job's boils. I could have gone to a doctor about them. But would the doctor have cured me any faster than time had done? These experiences confirmed my feeling that doctors can't do much for us except sometimes provide an ear to listen to our yells when the anguish becomes unbearable. And perhaps the verucca and the slipped disc *were* part of my state; one may be more prone to succumb to such ills when in a state of general misery and debility. No doubt the wart was acquired from one of my bedfellows and the slipped disc due to extramural activity. I was lucky to have escaped athlete's foot and syphilis.

Work was what kept me going. I clung grimly to Daisy Dairy Products (which I returned to after Dan's death) and rose to be a director of that undistinguished firm; I wrote two more recipe books, *Know Your Onions*, and *Cheese Please*. I also rewrote my novel, *The Last Cup of Coffee in the World*, and found a firm of publishers willing to take a chance on it; they threw their money away, for it received terrible reviews and finally extinguished my hopes of a literary career.

Instead, I began planning my own business, some kind of catering agency.

At that time I had quite given up entertaining expectations from *people*; oh yes, I had wholly relinquished all that side of life. People, so far as I could see, were completely unable to provide any emotional sustenance for each other; the best thing we could do for our fellow creatures, I thought, was to leave them in peace.

Then Vanessa died. Believe it or not, I heard the news on the 8 A.M. Third Programme radio bulletin, after a summary of the unresolved disputes at the Labour Party Conference in Blackpool. "The distinguished archaeologist Vanessa Raintree Churchill died yesterday of snakebite in Godwit, Western Australia. Professor Churchill is best known for her theories on Minoan culture and her recent book on Tasmanian pre-aborigine civilisation . . ."

Oh, the strange, piercing numbing shock of hearing one's own parent thus drafted into infinity by the impersonal voice of mass information. Mercifully I was in bed with some fellow at the time, I now forget who it was. Males absolutely hate to stay the whole night, they long to pad off home to their own lair at 3 A.M. once the urge has been allayed, whereas females yearn for the comfort of another head on the pillow when dawn breaks, the pseudodomesticity of company over the coffee mugs and breakfast conversation. Well, that time I had been lucky. I could turn and weep in his arms, whoever he was. And how impressed Dan would have been, I thought sourly in the midst of my anguish; to hear one's own mother's death announced on the eight o'clock news would certainly gratify his sense of chic. So then, rendered more accessible to grief by the loss of Vanessa, tough, gay, workmanlike little monkey of a woman, who should have survived to the age of eighty if heredity had played any part in the business, I had to mourn again for Dan, five years dead and long out of the world's mind. Who remembered Dan now—except possibly his mother, with whom I had long since lost touch? But Vanessa, at least, would be remembered for her writings and her discoveries.

Indeed there was some kind of suggestion that her ashes, flown back from Perth in a plastic box, should be interred in the Abbey.

But Thisbe scouted any such notion. She and I were the sole survivors, and met to discuss the question. Thisbe always does me good; she is so direct, abrasive, unimpressed by what she calls fogrum: that is, any kind of self-importance, pomposity, hypocrisy. The elder of the two sisters by nineteen years, she was now in her seventies, but still took a keen and critical interest in world affairs; she ran an agency which raised money for Spanish Civil War refugees (all now at an advanced age, poor things, living in the south of France as best they could); she belongs to Amnesty International and PEN and EXIT and goes to all their meetings; she was an early Social Democrat, and an avant-garde theatregoer, and writes formidable learned reviews for literary quarterlies. Thisbe listens to people. That is her strength, that is why she will live to be a hundred. She takes in all that she hears, reflects on it, makes use of it. She has no preconceived ideas, and will pay as much heed to a fifteen-year-old as to a cabinet minister.

"Are *those* the ashes? In that thing?" she demanded suspiciously. "There seem to be rather a *quantity* of them. I suppose they didn't cremate some kangaroo by mistake? Or chuck in the snake that bit her as well?"

Thisbe has a deep authoritative voice, and a slow, spontaneous grating laugh that sounds like the whirring of an old hand egg-beater. She and Vanessa, like me, inherited the undersized physique of the Raintree family (Grandpa Raintree was only four foot six); but where Vanessa and I are thin as monkeys, Thisbe is stocky, square set, with legs straight up and down like logs, and a powerful presence. She is a kind of lighthouse in my life, turning her unsparing beam on me from time to time. Curiously enough, I have never felt she disapproved of me.

"I suppose, if you consider the size of a human body, it must produce at least two or three pounds of ashes?" I suggested.

"What about this Abbey nonsense? You don't want it, do you?"

"Heavens, no! It would mean we'd have to keep going to pay our respects—like Buckingham Palace garden parties."

"Except no tea and cucumber sandwiches would be served," said Thisbe, who has attended several of those. "Well then, you write a civil note to this fool of a dean and tell him no. What *shall* we do with the ashes? Drop them in the Thames? Vanessa wouldn't have wanted a lot of fuss."

In the end, we did drop them in the Thames. But we drove to Oxford, one of Vanessa's favourite towns, and scattered the ashes in Dames' Delight, among the pale yellow willow leaves of autumn; there would be time for them to settle before next summer's divers plunged into the cold, mist-exuding river water. Vanessa always adored swimming, she would hurl herself in off any beach, reckless of sharks, rocks, or currents; it did seem ironic that she should have ended up in the middle of a huge, sandy continent.

"*You* look very white and peaked," Thisbe said, surveying me censoriously over lunch at the Mitre. "Vanessa's death can't have hit you that hard, you hardly saw one another more than twice every five years. What's the matter? Work not going well?"

"Work's going fine," I said with truth. "I'm hoping to set up my own little firm soon. Catering for meetings and conferences."

"Sounds an excellent plan," Thisbe pronounced. "Very probably half the stupid political disagreements in the world would never have occurred if the delegates hadn't been suffering from jet-lag and indigestion."

"That's what I think."

"Well if work's not the problem, what is it then? Boyfriend trouble?"

Thisbe's own emotional life is something about which she is entirely reticent.

She was married once, for a brief period, long ago. "It was a *disastrous* mistake," is the only comment I ever heard her vouchsafe about her single essay into matrimony. She has many close and valued friends, of both sexes, but which, if any, have been admitted to greater intimacy remains her secret. Even Vanessa, her own sister, hadn't known.

I sighed. "No. Not particularly."

The behaviour of bedfellows affected me less, at that time, than the doings of my colleagues at work.

"Where are you living now?" Thisbe asked. "Still that terrible little place by Hammersmith Bridge? I'm not coming all the way out there to see you, not even to eat your cooking."

I had moved over the river, since the Putney days, so as to save time and bus fares, but I found it impossible to take much interest in my surroundings; any room, any bed, would do, so it was private and quiet.

"You can come and use part of my place if you like," said Thisbe. Her long sardonic upper lip drew down over her large well-cared-for teeth; she snorted. "The wretched Georgian Society has run out of funds; they are going to close down. So my three front rooms will be free."

The rent of Thisbe's enormous flat in Ordnance Mansions is paid out of a trust set up for her when Great-grandpa Raintree died at an advanced age; he was a Quaker who made a lot of money out of processed cheese. The money was divided between his two granddaughters. Vanessa spent all hers on excavation, Thisbe gave most of hers away to good causes. But the flat is hers for life at a peppercorn rent.

"Of course," she said, "you'd have no security; if I die you'll be out; but in the meantime they are big convenient rooms. And you could be as private as you like; I live in the back with twenty feet of corridor in between."

"Are there restrictions about use? Could I run a business from there?"

"No reason why not," said Thisbe. "No one's complained about the Georgian Society."

She spooned up the last of her crème caramel and glared round the Mitre dining room. "This place is going to the dogs. Don't tell me that pudding didn't come out of a packet. At least if you come and live in Victoria Street I'll have the chance of a decent Charlotte Russe once in a while."

"Well . . ." I said. "I'll think about it."

Thisbe is not the easiest person to get along with; she has an astringent tongue, never considers other people's feelings, and, believing herself justified by the amount of public good she does, is completely self-oriented in all her activities. I was not concerned that she might object to my lifestyle or companions, but I did wonder whether she might try to organise me more than I was prepared to stand for.

"I'll have to consider my finances," I said cautiously.

"Don't leave it too long," said Thisbe. "I might change my mind."

A couple of days later, quite by accident, I ran into Elly and Chris.

At that time I was going round with a thoroughly unsavoury

character called Enrico Perzetti. It was in connection with olive oil that I had first come across him; he was able to get me very good oil, in bulk, at most advantageous prices. It soon became apparent to me that this must be through connections with gangland, and after a while I judged it prudent to go elsewhere for my oil, not wishing to be charged with receiving stolen goods; but in the meantime I found Rico very amusing company, and he, for some reason, was much taken by me, temporarily at least; like many gangsters he was a great snob, impressed by the fact that I was Vanessa's daughter and Thisbe's niece. Strangely enough, he had encountered Thisbe on a TV programme called "Meet Your Neighbour," where he was being interviewed about crime in Soho and she about her Fabian past; she had somehow managed to impress him to his roots. "You can always tell real class," he said admiringly. "She isn't your average movie-queen dowager, all pearls and blue rinse, but the genuine article." If he hoped that I would later develop into the same article he had a long time to wait but meantime he was tickled to death by my involvement with him, and liked to take me to what he called snob joints.

Rico studied to appear as much like a gangster as possible and certainly looked the part, being large, black-haired, exuberant, fat for his age, which was thirty-five, with a pale face, small twinkling black eyes, given to pink silk shirts and loosely knotted Guards ties, sharp footwear, black leather jackets with shiny studs, and camel car coats. He was of course very rich and though the snob joints were not happy with his appearance and manners, they put up with him patiently and politely. So one night, dining at the Ritz, whom should we see at the next table but Elly and Chris and their respective husbands Hugh and George. That gave me a guilty pang for I, too, had been invited to the party—it was Elly and Hugh's eighth wedding anniversary—but had declined, giving as my excuse that I had arranged to meet a business associate. Now here was my associate revealed as the Tough Boy of Brewer Street, but my friends were very nice about it and suggested that we join them. This delighted Rico—he always enjoyed launching into new circles, and here were an architect-sculptor married to a language professor, and a publisher married to a social psychologist, so the pasturage was rich indeed. Rico, when he chose, could employ formidable sulks and rages, but he could also be great fun, and that evening he fairly crackled with joviality; his un-buttoned form of humour dismantled various barriers, and by the time we all parted I was on much easier and more jokey terms with Hugh and George, whom, up to now, I had treated with somewhat edgy wariness, doubtful whether they deserved the privilege of being married to my greatest friends. After Enrico had persuaded us all on to a hair-raising nightclub called the Soft Touch, which everybody thought frightful, the barriers were just about down to ground level. It was certainly a more successful oc-casion than my dreadful wedding lunch.

Next day Elly phoned me. She and Hugh were spending a few days in London. Hugh was taking time off from architecting to oversee a show of his sculptures and paintings, which was about to open at a gallery in Dover Street. During the previous evening I had discovered from Elly that he had invested a lot of hope in this show, which was his first major one; though a reasonably suc-cessful architect he was becoming deadly bored with plans for high-rise blocks and textile factories and comprehensive schools shaped like chunks of processed cheese; he wanted more time to do his own thing.

Elly did not mince matters. "Come and have lunch with me. I want to scold you."

I'm very fond of Elly, so I went. Eight years of marriage had been very good for Elly; had given her a golden bloom and glow. She looks like Pontormo's "Portrait of a Lady," the one in Frank-furt; she has classically regular features, straight nose, wide gen-erous mouth, and beautiful shallow brows over heavy-lidded eyes; her massive coil of gold-brown hair is drawn round the back of her head in a bulky coronet; you would expect blue eyes with the gold-fair colouring, but, improbably, they are brown, which adds startling intelligence and edge to her face. She walks and sits very upright, and makes impressive play with long, beautiful tapering hands. I could see that Rico had been knocked for six by her ap-pearance. Her sons, unidentical twins, are unlike each other but both of them, somehow, like her; most un-English-looking little boys, despite their fairness. She loathed sending them away to boarding school, but Hugh insisted; it was the single point of dissension in their otherwise wholly harmonious union.

Over lunch she opened up with all her batteries.

"Clytie! How *can* you be seen *anywhere* with that ghastly *cad?*"

Elly learned her English at age fifteen, and thoroughly; she speaks it with a fluency and upper-crust accent unequalled by any duchess; and she prefers to use the vocabulary of duchesses.

"Enrico's interesting and he's fun," I said defensively.

"Hugh and I couldn't *stand* the way he was wrapping himself all round you like flypaper—Hugh said it made him want to push the chap's teeth down his throat. You aren't serious about him, are you?"

"Good God, no, Elly, of course not. I told you—he's a business connection."

"You are becoming hopelessly undiscriminating," she scolded. "Last time I saw you, you had that appalling redheaded pansy in tow, the composer, or whatever he *said* he was—now it's an obvious crook—why can't you ever come up with someone decent?"

It's too much of a risk, I thought. But I said, "Oh, have a heart, Elly, I'm busy; I'm working very hard. I don't have time to pick and choose. I just take what comes. It's all very well for you to talk—"

Elly and Hugh met and married at York University, where she now continued to teach. Most of his architectural work was done in the north of England; they lived in a dear little Georgian-brick town called Thirsby, not far from the North Sea.

"Come round and see Hugh's show," she said. "I haven't nearly finished with you yet."

I didn't really have much time, but I was curious to see Hugh's show. On the face of it, he seemed so unlike anyone's blueprint for an artist: a Yorkshireman, tall, rangy, redheaded, nihilistic, blue-eyed, bony-faced, and fond of watching football; so where did romance and imagination come into play? And I had heard from Elly that he had a wild romantic streak.

It came in a very secretive way, I discovered; the sculptures, which were simply titled "Other Women," with numbers, consisted of stone blocks, cut so as to suggest draperies covering unguessable objects, which seemed to be partly round and partly spiky—as if both human bodies and machinery were concealed under the granite shrouds. The paintings were mostly northern industrial landscapes, bonily structured in clear dark colours; very dispassionate pictures, they were.

Hugh, there in the gallery already, was being rather childishly contentious, which meant, as I discovered when I knew him better, that he was trying to cover up a bad attack of nerves. Businesslike and confident in his profession, about these personal works he was profoundly diffident and lacking in calm. But the show seemed, I thought, to have got off to a good start; the gallery owner looked complacent and there had been an excellent notice that morning in the *Guardian*. Several items had red stickers. And there was quite a crowd in the gallery.

After a while Elly dragged us both away to tea in Brown's Hotel, which always makes me nostalgic because it is where Vanessa used to put up, latterly, on her brief rare visits to her native shore.

"We're driving home to Thirsby tonight; why don't you come along with us and stay for the weekend?" Elly suggested, pouring tea with a competent nonchalance which instantly revealed to me that the whole manoeuvre had been planned.

"I can't, I'm cooking a banquet tomorrow—it's Thisbe's birthday, I'm taking her to Sadler's Wells—I have a date to go to Kew with a client—"

All kinds of excellent excuses leapt to mind, but in the end I said, "All right. Thanks. I'd like to."

"But don't think you're going to marry me off to some Yorkshire squire," I snarled later at Elly, when we were waiting for Hugh to bring the car from its underground place of stowage, "for I can't stand country bumpkins and have no intention of ever leaving London."

How firmly one makes such assertions and how queer it is to remember them later.

"I haven't the least intention of thrusting country bumpkins at you," said Elly coldly. "For a start, we don't know any. I just wish to remind you of the pleasures of being among intelligent, civilised people—something you seem, temporarily, to have forgotten."

"Right, girls," said Hugh, coming back with the car, which was big, efficient, and comfortable—just like him, I thought—"Hop in."

So I went up to Thirsby with them. And that was the first of many weekends during the autumn and winter. We walked on the moors, I played chess with Hugh, sang duets with him to Elly's accompaniment, watched football with him (which I enjoy), and talked endlessly.

One Sunday afternoon Elly said she had students' papers to correct and would I take Hugh for a walk, so we drove half an hour to the nearest beach and walked through the sand dunes. A spectacular winter sunset was building up—layers of sulphur yellow, aniline green, and crimson lake to westwards, while across the whole eastern half of the sky a thunderous plum-pink afterglow hung on cumulus cloud and was reflected below in the churning grey North Sea.

"Storm coming," said Hugh. "Better not walk too far down the beach; tide comes in here like a race."

It was a huge flat beach; wide enough for Ozymandias, King of Kings. We walked fast in the shrill wind, talking easily as was our habit now—of books, music, his work, mine, his boys at school, how to plant cabbages. There was always plenty to talk about with Hugh.

A man in breeches passed us, running. "Lost a grey colt," he panted. "Nervous young 'un—threw me and got away. You see him?"

No, we called, but we'd keep a lookout. "They bring them here for training gallops," Hugh said. "Salt water's supposed to be good for their legs."

The wind sang even shriller and sharper; by mutual consent we turned back into the shelter of the dunes, which had been tossed by autumn gales into wild crisscrossing curves crowned by tussocks and swatches of pale sea grass, now coloured pink and lavender by the sunset. Their shadows fell in beautiful cups and hoops and loops, black as velvet ribbon. Suddenly, as we scrambled along a narrow canyon between two steep slopes, we heard a thunder of hoofs. Hugh shouted, "Look out!" and flung me sideways against the sandy rampart. Directly confronting us, head-on, eyes wild, snowy mane and tail tossed high and heraldic like some Valkyrie's ghostly mount, the white colt came at a lunatic speed —was past—was gone—all in the space of a couple of heartbeats, while Hugh protected my body with his.

"God, that was close!" I gasped, scrambling to my feet and spitting sand out of my mouth. "Thanks for—"

"Look at him! *Look* at him!" Hugh pulled me round, his arm on my waist; together we watched the frantic animal bolt over the huge beach, growing tiny in the distance like a white blown leaf, taking a spectacular curve, into the water, out of it again, his tail and mane streaming, his coat flashing against the grey of the swell. As if chased by invisible demons he careered towards a headland which created the north end of the bay.

"If he goes past that he's done for," said Hugh. "There are quicksands in the river mouth—"

We saw the man, the rider, a speck in the distance, follow, running at top speed along the line the colt had taken, then slow to a walk and turn, defeated, inland towards the dunes.

The whole experience was so dramatic, so portentous, so disturbing, that we had no words, no wish to discuss it. Silently, hand in hand, we turned and began the slow sandy trudge back to where Hugh had left his car.

The weather was worsening. Angry little pellets of sleet stung and bit our faces as we ran from car to house. I laid and lit the fire in the comfortable untidy sitting room. Elly came stretching from her study and offered sherry or whisky; Hugh coughed a bit, for the illness had already taken root in him, though we did not know that yet.

"You two look as if you had seen an angel with a flaming sword," said Elly.

So it started, between me and Hugh.

I went back to London and told Aunt Thisbe that I would sublet her three front rooms with k and b. This proved an excellent arrangement, as Thisbe is wholly self-sufficient, and, like Elly and Hugh, thoroughly civilised. I went my way, she went hers, we had our own visitors independently, we did not patrol one another's activities, but met at friendly and informal intervals; my various bits of business flourished and soon I felt confident enough to establish Cuisine Churchill. For the legal work relating to this, I employed the advice and services of Dan's erstwhile friend and lawyer, Anthony Roche.

Anthony had chambers in Lincolns Inn when first I reopened my acquaintance with him; but he had just been offered a partnership in his home town of Affton Wells, and during the process of our dealings he moved back there; he still came up to London several times a week, but I fell into the habit of seeing him at his office in Affton. Living, as I did, within a stone's throw of Victoria Station, it was easy for me to get on a train to Sussex, the trip took under an hour, his office in Affton was five minutes' walk from the station, and I found the double journey, on comfortable, uncrowded trains, easier than getting across London, and a perfect interlude for uninterrupted planning, paperwork, and creative thinking. I always get my best ideas on trains.

One day, after I had left Anthony's office in Monmouth Street, and still had half an hour before the next London train, I took a fancy to climb the short steep length of Watch Hill for a nostalgic look at Dan's old home. Visiting Affton gave me a strange, painful pleasure; the whole place was numinous, full of attraction and awe. Each time I returned there, I was teased yet again by those two baffling questions: why had Dan left, why had he brought me back? The questions had a mysterious importance for me; Dan had somehow come to represent a turning point in my life. He and his mother and the unknown Ingrid, minor or random figures in the whole scheme of things, perhaps, had taken on for me a strange significance, like distant, unidentified objects in a misty landscape.

The footway of Watch Hill is cobbled, with two brick strips, carriage-wheel distance apart, down the centre of the street; though who in creation would be so crazy as to take a carriage up that breakneck slope I can't imagine. Horses must have been stronger in the seventeenth century. I carefully avoided the brick strips, for it was a grey, freezing January day, and the clean red bricks were neatly cased in ice.

On each side, the little old houses looked shut and secretive; those with creeper-covered frontages were brown, dry, wrinkled, like sleeping mummies. High up here, far from the crowded shopping streets, it was coldly quiet; the castle hung overhead on its mound; down beyond the town's outskirts the marsh stretched away into mist, flat, and seamed with dykes. Poor Dan, I thought; whatever his ambitions, surely he must have hated to sell the house where he was born; and what kind of persuasion can he have exerted on his mother to drag her away to an ugly London suburb, for that ill-advised ménage-à-trois with Ingrid? What in the wide world gave him the idea that it would ever work, even for a month? Dan had a terrifying gift of persuasion, he could sell a deep-freeze to an Eskimo, but that time his gift betrayed him. Why, why did he do it? Was it because he guessed, right from the start, that Ingrid was going to need special care? Or, in spite of hating his mother, was he still attached to her by ties too strong to break?

What had happened to Mrs. Suter? I wondered, toiling up the hill, which she must have climbed so often with shopping basket or umbrella, pushing pram or holding child's hand. Where was she now? Maybe, like my own mother, she had died. Twice a year I dutifully sent her Christmas and birthday cards, with five-pound Boots gift tokens enclosed; I never received any acknowledgement. For all I knew the postman pocketed the tokens; I didn't greatly care. Mrs. Suter had hardly regarded me as a person, I had come to realise after Dan's death. She never once addressed me by my name; to her I was merely "you," "her." "Does she take sugar in tea?" I remember her saying to Dan in my presence, as if I were deaf or speechless. For her I was merely an extension of Ingrid, a most unwelcome one. And I suppose my sending the gift tokens was a kind of propitiation; as one leaves a shred of cloth at the shrine of an evil spirit.

Pausing for breath, looking up to the top of the street, I saw that Watch Cottage was for sale. Four different house-agents' boards proclaimed the fact: sure sign that there is something badly wrong with a house. In this case, it was neglected dry-rot and woodworm in the panelling; the elderly recluse who had bought it from Mrs. Suter in 1965 had never mended a leak or laid on a brushful of paint during his nine-odd years of occupation; and when the police finally broke in, alerted by the line of milk bottles on the step, to find him dead in his armchair, the house was in a scandalous state; since when the price had been coming down, leap by leap.

I simply couldn't resist it.

Aunt Thisbe was aghast.

"Use up Vanessa's legacy on that little *tumbledown hovel?* An hour from town, and it isn't even in the *country?* If you are going to buy something outside London, you might at least find something with grass and trees."

"There's a pear tree in the garden. And the view extends over twenty miles."

"Tschah! Besides, what about your neighbours? The society in a provincial university town will be deadly. I've heard stories about that Cinque Ports University—"

Thisbe is never willingly out of earshot of Big Ben; she can see the Palace of Westminster from her bathroom window. Her real fear, of course, was that I meant to give up the rooms in Ordnance Mansions and that she would be put to the bother of finding another tenant; when I reassured her that I intended to do no such thing, that I could afford to keep the flat as office and pied-à-terre, she became partway reconciled to my plans.

"Anyway," I said, "I shan't mix with the town society. I'll be coming up to London most of the week, and seeing my friends there."

"And *that's* not a satisfactory way of life," said Thisbe. "You're never properly integrated at either end."

In a way, she was right. In a way, that was the cause of what happened.

Anthony Roche had plenty of objections when I asked him to act for me over the purchase of Watch Cottage. He pointed out firstly that it was in a run-down, slummy quarter of the town.

"God alone knows who you'd have next door," he said, echoing Thisbe but in a different vein. "Drunken old-age pensioners, probably, that you'd be continually rescuing. There's no garage—nowhere to put a car—I doubt if there's a rubbish collection; you'll probably have to carry your bin to the bottom of the hill—heaven knows if there are drains, even—the house is a total mess—"

"Don't you want me to come and live in Affton, Anthony?"

He gave me a strange look. I remembered it four years later when he and I were in St. Malo, eating oysters, and the man at the next table, also eating oysters, went into a convulsion and toppled sideways off his chair, dead when he hit the floor. It turned out subsequently that he had some heart trouble, his death was nothing to do with the oysters, but at the time I could see that Anthony anticipated immediate death for us both, and his would be without the benefit of confession and repentance.

What a simplification *that* would have been!

Where Anthony was reluctant, Rosie Roche was enchanted. She came along with Anthony one afternoon and explored the house, bubbling with irrepressible enthusiasm.

"Oh, what a marvellous time you're going to have! You must put all the panelling back just as it was before—it's so cosy and warm. And the heavenly little paved yard at the back—you should have lavender and sweet-smelling shrubs there; I shall start striking cuttings for you right away. You'll be able to eat all your meals out here in the summer, it'll be a regular sun trap. And, look, you can climb out on the roof between the gables and see the whole of Affton. You can see our house, we'll be able to signal to each other! And the attic! Perfect for nurseries! You've got to buy the house, Clytie, I shall never forgive you if you don't. It will be such fun to have you for a neighbour!"

Anthony and Rose lived in Hanover Crescent, the respectable part of town; they had a dignified Queen Anne house with a pie-wedge-shaped garden, which Rosie had already transformed into a bower. I used to go back there for lunch with Rosie after my visits to the empty cottage. She and I became dear friends. She was like some exquisite little water bird, blue eyes, brown hair, soft County Clare voice, and an infectious bubbling laugh. Anthony fondly called her his bird-wit, but she had a shrewd earthy intelligence of her own, removed and different from his cold and formidable cleverness. She had courage, too; early in our friendship she told me about the malformation of the womb which was going to make it terribly difficult and dangerous for her to undergo childbirth.

"Father McNalty said I'd better have a hysterectomy—even the Pope wouldn't say no, considering the circumstances—but I don't want to. *I* think that would be cheating Anthony. And anyway, I *want* children—lots and lots of them. Adopting isn't a bit the same. After the first it'll be all right, I've no doubt. I'm just going to leave it to God—that's much the best way. I'm sure He'll look after me." (And of course, He did.) "Now, Clytie, you must grow pinks between these paving stones, and camomile; I'm going down to the flower market this afternoon, I'll buy you some roots, you can't start too soon."

For, despite Anthony's demurrings, I had gone ahead and made an offer for the house, which was instantly, gladly snapped up by old Murgatroyd's executors; they were plainly terrified they'd never get the place off their hands. Nevertheless Anthony, once he was grudgingly engaged in the business, managed to beat them down by another eighteen hundred; he pointed out that there were no drains to speak of and the dining room floor would all have to come out.

"That doesn't matter," I said, "I'm going to have the kitchen and dining room thrown into one."

"You'll be spending a fortune on the place. For the same money you could buy a decent substantial house."

"But I love Watch Cottage. It has all the charm in the world."

"Charm," said Anthony dourly. Fine for him to sneer at charm, I thought, who married the most charming creature in Ireland. "Don't you catch cold in this coffin of a place, Rosie Bawn," he admonished his wife, who was flitting about the empty rooms, measuring windows.

"I wonder, now, if there'll be a ghost in the place?" she speculated. "Maybe you'll find old Murgatroyd sitting by your fire one evening. He was a dear old thing; I used to see him in the Upper Severals, sometimes, taking a glass of the mineral water."

Everybody was a dear old thing to Rosie.

I never saw the ghost of old Murgatroyd; but, even before I moved in, having put in hand the minimum needful alterations and promised myself more as time went by, I began to be troubled by the thought, the apparition, of Mrs. Suter. Never of Dan; this had been his birthplace, his childhood home, and I loved it for him as well as for myself; I thought it would make him happy to know that I was here, inhabiting the house, keeping it warm and cherished. But Mrs. Suter had left it angrily, reluctantly; now I began to feel acutely sorry for her, I thought she had had a rotten deal. Now I could not help remembering more and more of those curt, grim remarks she had occasionally let drop, hoping to sting Dan's somnolent conscience, about the plants she had tended, the birds she had fed in the yard, gulls that came up from the shore in windy weather, blue tits and robins, the nightingales that were supposed to sing in May among the castle thorn trees.

I began to dream about Mrs. Suter; night after night she grumbled and muttered through my hours of sleep like one of the Erinnyes, always limping at my shoulder. "You forgot my birthday again!" she would say. "At least Ingrid never did that." Or she would address me as Ingrid, as if my own existence had escaped her attention. I began to feel like a criminal, an interloper, an impostor.

At last, with utter reluctance, I sat down and wrote to Mrs. Suter at the Dodman's End address. It was like automatic writing; my hand put down the words while I watched it.

I had recently been lucky enough, I wrote, to be able to purchase Watch Cottage. I knew how fond she had been of the house; as she knew, it contained ample space for two people to live there and not be on top of one another. Would she like to return to Affton and occupy part of the house? We could lead separate lives and not disturb each other; I went to London almost every day for my business, was away frequently; it seemed a waste that she should not be there as well, making use of the place. I could well understand why she had loved it so. I would ask no more rent than whatever she was paying now, and she could bring her own furniture if she wished. I trembled as I wrote, remembering the hideous grey and brown moquette, the molasses-coloured machine-carved bulbous dining table and rexine-covered chairs; but, poor woman . . . She must still, surely, I wrote, have friends in Affton, etc., etc. Though I did remember Dan saying that his mother never made friends, she deeply suspected any overtures from neighbours. "Nosy. They just want to find out about us," she said. She had had only one close friend, a nurse who had moved away to Norfolk years ago.

Sick with horror, I posted my letter, waited a week, two weeks, three weeks, a month, wondering in agony what could have possessed me to do such a masochistic thing. I never told Anthony about it. I could imagine his outrage. "Without even any form of legal agreement? Are you clean demented?"

Mrs. Suter never answered. So I had no need to confess my folly to Anthony. And no means of discovering whether she had ever received my letter. I feared, I hoped, that it might never have reached her. And I did not write again. I did not want to push my luck.

Sometimes, at midnight, I wondered: had the news that I, whom she had angrily thrust out of her life, whom she detested and despised, had now reached a position when I could offer her own home to her again—had that news made her so angry that she could not even bring herself to reply?

Whatever the reason for her silence, my transitory feeling of guilt seemed to have been absolved by sending the letter; Mrs. Suter ceased to haunt my dreams; such ghosts as came to inhabit the cottage were not hers; and she slipped out of my thoughts again. Work had begun to absorb more and more of my time; and what time remained over from work was almost wholly given over to Hugh and George.

5

The white Pink, and the Pansy freakt with jet
The glowing Violet
The Musk-rose and the well-attired Woodbine . . .

I thought I would give a housewarming party for Watch Cottage.
As a rule I detest parties. In the course of work, I see too many. A
party is a lowest-common-denominator occasion, during which everybody says the minimum the maximum number of times—
shouts it, straining larynx and patience, to an auditor who hears
only half, because of the background row, and anyway probably
isn't interested in the other half.

Hell—if Anthony is right about the existence of hell—will be a
continuous party, so far as I am concerned.

But still, my Watch Cottage housewarming was going to be a
very different affair.

The little house was blossoming under my attentions. White
paint and new carpentry made the delightfully shaped rooms
light and trim. Hugh gave me expert advice gratis, and Anthony
put me on to the reliable firm of builders who had redecorated
his offices in Affton. Anthony and I were good friends in those
days. And Rosie was part of everything that happened, everything
I chose and planned and did. Under her tutelage, with her help, I
even made my own curtains, a thing I would never otherwise
have dreamed of attempting. I'd have gone straight to Heals. But
Rosie ran around with her tape measure, lured me into drapers'
shops, bought yards and yards of stuff I'd never heard of, with

slotted curtain tape, and little plastic hooks to slot into the slots; we spent whole afternoons in her sunny sitting room, at the big round rosewood table inherited from some great-aunt in County Clare, peacefully cutting out and sewing seams on an aged wilful Singer machine. I can still see her shining nut-brown head bent over the piled material as she instructed me: "You must always make sure that the curtains are cut longways in the fabric, Clytie, never crossways; they hang better so."

I had no idea there was a longways or a crossways in fabric; I have always loathed anything to do with sewing, needles, or thread. Except during that period.

Anthony would come home at teatime, big and energetic, stamping into the room with its tranquil view across Rosie's triangular fragrant garden; he would cast a censorious eye over the billowing mounds of cotton, chintz, and furnishing tweed. "You're certain you aren't overdoing it, acushla?"

Rosie was pregnant, to everybody's joy and terror. But she herself, serenely aglow, kept repeating with obvious truth that she had never felt better, that it was the best time yet, the happiest time of her life. An elderly nurse, who had looked after Anthony and his sister Helena when they were young, was fetched back to Affton from Helena's children in Kings Lynn, established in Hanover Crescent, and did her best to prevent (in the biblical sense of the word) Rosie's every action, but Rosie bought a padded basket chair, set it by the bay window in the kitchen, and kept her at arms' length by saying, "Oh, do go and read, nurse dear; I've put the *Catholic Herald* by your chair. You'll have plenty enough to do when the baby's born, indeed you will!"

Nurse Kelly, alas, hated me; first, I was a godless heathen; secondly, she was a native of Affton Wells, whereas I was an incomer; thirdly, she would have liked Rose all to herself. But Rosie was bursting with energy, she could not be confined; she had become involved with various activities in Affton, library committees and drama groups and swimming-pool funds. She had an instantly subjugating effect on people, even the most resistant. I had thought it possible that she, Elly, and Chris might not have a ot in common, they so deeply absorbed in their professional lives, Elly so Teutonic in her efficiency, Chris so wry and disillusioned, Rosie such a delightful butterfly; they had not met since that terrible wedding party; but of course in ten minutes she had them twined round her little finger, eating out of her hand.

I can remember a Saturday when the three of us came down to Affton by train, Elly, Chris, and I; Elly and Hugh were in London for the weekend, going to hear Salvatore Mondo in *Don Giovanni* at Sadler's Wells that evening; Elly had said it was high time she saw my house so that she could decide what to give me for a moving-in present, Chris said she'd like to come along, too, and it turned into a memorably lighthearted excursion. In the train, on the way down to Affton, we played Word and Question, that intellectual game out of *What Katy Did at School*; and Chris produced an instructive triplet (in answer to the question "Who bent the Housemaid's Knee?"):

> *The use of the synovial is the kneecap to anoint*
> *The function of the fluid is to lubricate the joint;*
> *It has no other purpose and it has no other point,*

which, for some reason, has remained in my head to this day. Sitting in the train, I thought how much I loved my friends, how lucky I was, what a singular and particular pleasure it was to be with them in this carefree manner.

Where, then, were George and Hugh? Playing squash, I imagine. They nearly always got together for games of squash when Hugh came to London. Where was Anthony that day? I don't remember. Not at his house, certainly; I think he had said he was going off to visit an elderly client who wished to revise a will. We took Rosie out to lunch at the Monmouth Hotel, and toasted Rosie's baby in champagne. She would only take a sip, she said champagne might be bad for little Philomena.

"How can you be sure it will turn out to be a girl?" said Chris, sceptical.

"Oh, I'm quite, quite positive." Rosie beamed at us all. "Philomena Antonia Rosamund Roche, she's going to be, and you must all be her godmothers."

"But two of us are heathens," I pointed out. "And Elly isn't a Catholic."

"Well then—you poor misled heretics," said Rosie, "you must be her Lifemothers."

"That we will." And we discussed the ways in which Lifemothers ought to serve, instruct, and be of use to their Lifechild.

"Teach her chess, and a lot of poetry, when she's three," said Chris. "So her head is well stocked and she needn't ever be bored."

"How to converse with the male sex when she's four," said Elly. "So she need never feel at a loss, but can apply her mind to more important matters."

"Teach her how to enjoy playing games," I said. Not having learned that, it seemed important to me. "And how to enjoy music and art and cookery."

"Political economy at six," said Chris. "I'll take care of that."

Elly: "I'll look after her languages. A girl can't have too many. Then she can travel wherever she likes on her own, see the world, form her own judgements."

"Basic grounding in psychology at eight." Chris again. "So she can understand why people act the way they do."

"At this rate," said Rosie, "she'll have her education all behind her by the age of ten."

"Her *basic* education," corrected Chris. "Then she can *really* begin learning, which is, after all, the chief and only pleasure in life."

"Ah, what nonsense you all talk!" cried Rosie, delighted. "Why, and indeed, life's so full of pleasures that I just keep skipping from one to the next. Come on, now, let you, the lot of ye! Let's go up to Clytie's house and hang the curtains."

"*You* aren't going to hang any curtains, don't think it," said Elly severely.

We were all very firm with Rosie, she was our child, our younger sister, our darling.

Up at Watch Cottage, she was established as overseer in a cushioned armchair, from which she bossed us while we hung

the curtains and Elly and Chris explored my house, which neither of them had visited before.

"You were quite right to buy it, Clytie," pronounced Chris.
"And you may expect George and me for every weekend from
May till September. George and Anthony can play tennis down
on the Severals, you and I will take Rosie and her baby to the
beach."

"Ah, but you should come here in winter too," I said, "when
there's snow on the marsh. I came in February when the house
was empty and damp and freezing, and I could have stayed by
that upstairs window all day, just looking out."

It was March now. Purple and white crocuses were still flower-
ing in the little courtyard at the back, and my big L-shaped
kitchen, which now had sun in the morning as well, became
filled, at this time of day, with a wonderful, reflected glowing
light thrown off the wall of an old cream-painted garden shed at
one side of the court.

"Next spring you must have pink hyacinths out there too," said
Rosie contentedly. "I'll get you some bulbs in September."

I wondered about Dan and Mrs. Suter. Had he kept bats, balls,
bows and arrows out in that shed? Had she given him his tea in
this room, when he came home from school, with the creamy
light pouring in over the kitchen table? Over the bread and
marge, and the tinned peas? Had Mrs. Suter, more than ten years
ago, planted those white and purple crocuses? Oh, Dan, poor
Dan, why did you ever drag your mother out of this peaceful
haven?

Plucking my thoughts away from such a sad, unprofitable
strain, I began to plan my housewarming party. I would have it
on May 1, which was a Saturday. Not a big party, just the people
I liked best. My devoted staff from Cuisine Churchill. For once I
would do all the cooking, and they, the hard-working dears,
would idly sit and graciously receive. All the food, I decided,
would be served and eaten here in the spacious kitchen, with the
solid old kitchen table pushed back against the inner wall. Drinks
upstairs in the pretty panelled sitting room with Rosie's classic

white curtains framing the huge view of dusky marsh and distant twinkle of isolated marsh hamlets. Glow of firelight and sparkle of wine, and all my favourite people assembled: Aunt Thisbe, if she could be persuaded to travel out of London; and my three friends and their husbands; or, to put it in a different way, Anthony and Rose and my two lovers and their wives, I thought with a sudden chill, a queer premonitory shiver.

"This house still feels damp," said Elly at the same instant. "You ought to turn the heat on at least a week before you move in, Clytie. Damp plaster—it takes forever to dry. Come along, we'd better leave, Rosie shouldn't get cold."

"No, and I promised Nurse that we'd all be home to tea by half-past four," said Rose. "She'll be after me with an axe if I'm late; she's expecting you all to eat crumpets and Sally Lunn."

"After that lunch? God help us."

I did manage to persuade Aunt Thisbe to come and look at the house before I moved in. Fortunately for me, there was an aged and famous Fabian lady, Anastasia Martineau, who lived in Saddlers Row, near the Upper Severals. She and Thisbe had been undergraduates together at Girton in World War I and seldom found time to correspond; Thisbe is of the generation that cannot chat on the telephone; only life-and-death information can be exchanged via that medium; so she was pleased to have an opportunity to visit her chum. I drove her down, along with a load of books and papers which I intended to put in my new shelves.

I left her with Miss Martineau for a couple of hours while I stowed the books in their new places, then collected her again and took her up to Watch Cottage, where I had a picnic lunch laid out in the kitchen.

"Hm," said Thisbe, long lip, long eyelids drawn severely down. She stomped about the house on her solid treelike legs (in grey-and-fawn clocked woollen stockings) critically appraising my arrangements. Thisbe's clothes are of unchanging uniformity bought from Harrods: handsome youthfully tailored cotton shirts in checks or stripes, long classic skirts with a bit of pleat, made of durable tweeds in shades of black or dark brown; laced shoes from

Charles Baber, and a tasselled, leather-capped walking stick. She would, and does, wear the same clothes for a Buck House tea party or an alpine excursion, seeing no occasion to vary such a practical ensemble.

"Hmn," she said. "All this matchboard panelling . . . I know *you*, Tuesday. You won't be able to resist putting up postcards, sticking in drawing pins—"

"No, that's what I particularly love. I shall have postcards everywhere."

"Very low ceilings," pronounced Aunt Thisbe.

"Makes it easy to change light bulbs."

All the ceilings in Ordnance Mansions are eighteen feet high; changing light bulbs is a job for a steeplejack.

"Curved stairs; I always consider those *particularly* dangerous."

"But don't you think they are ravishingly pretty? The balustrade is William IV."

"All I can say is, don't expect *me* to come and stay here. I have no wish to break my neck."

"Then it's lucky there's such a good train service from Victoria. You can come down for the day."

"I have heard from Jock Caversham" (he was her M.P.) "that all these services are going to be drastically cut. . . . My dear," she said disapprovingly, "what a lot of *birds* you have here." We were in the sitting room. The birds were singing their heads off outside, in the pear tree, and the blackthorn bushes on the Castle Mound. "I thought this was supposed to be a town?" Thisbe grumbled.

When she had inspected the two bedrooms, the third room, unfurnished, which might have been Mrs. Suter's sitting room, and the attic, now lit by a huge skylight, which was to be my study, she said grudgingly, "Well, I suppose Vanessa would have been over the moon about it too. It is just the kind of picturesque, ramshackle dwelling that would have taken her fancy, if ever she had decided to stop gadding about and settle down in England."

Thisbe's voice washed its hands of us and our vagaries.

"So she would," I said, pleased. "She can have an imaginary

room here. I'll allot her the empty one." Vanessa would be much better company than Mrs. Suter.

"Don't talk in that childishly fanciful way, Tuesday. It is tempting providence," said Aunt Thisbe, showing a certain inconsistency, I thought.

She inspected a pile of papers lying unsorted on my desk, and read aloud:

> *"My tide-green bed I shared with seven lovers,*
> *From three of them lighthearted took my leave,*
> *But four I grieve."*

Her tone mingled disgust with astonishment. "What, in the world's name, is this, Clytie? *Don't* tell me that you have taken to writing *poetry?*"

There could hardly have been more censure in her tone if she had said pornography. Not that Thisbe disapproves of poetry in itself; only as a profession.

"No, no, that's some papers I just got out of store. Ingrid Christ's unpublished poems."

"Ah; dear me, yes. That poor unfortunate creature. A sad, wasteful business. Her making an end to herself was due to some inadequacy in her upbringing, no doubt. Which is odd, when you think about it, because the Scandinavians are usually so rational and practical."

> *"Alas,"* she read, *"our dead are mourned in hieroglyphics,*
> *The house thus seen through branches is a lake,*
> *Which laps their wake.*
>
> *A final line is loosed, the snaking ripple*
> *That constitutes the only ship-to-shore*
> *Of nevermore.*

"There is something slightly anaemic about this verse, don't you find?" She looked at other manuscripts and added fairly, "But I believe that some quite reputable people are coming to think quite highly of her. James Montfaucon was speaking of her the other day at the Foyles' luncheon. He said he believed that her work was ready for reappraisal."

"Really? You mean she's due for a comeback? That's splendid," I said, thinking how pleased Dan would be. I must put the unpublished work in order and try it on a publisher.

"Not a *comeback*, Tuesday! Please avoid such disgusting readymade phrases when talking to me!"

"Is anybody about?" called a voice from downstairs. "I've just toiled up your terrible hill, and I'm not coming any higher, I can tell you, till I've had a sit-down."

It was Rosie, whom I had invited to come and share our picnic.

She produced, chuckling, a bottle of sherry. "I had to smuggle it out under my maternity smock; Nurse would have been down on me like a ton of bricks. Alcohol! And carrying it up the hill, furthermore! I'm hardly allowed to pick up a handkerchief if I drop it, these days."

Despite this restricted life, Rosie looked blooming. Her complexion had that angelic prismatic glow seldom seen except in pregnant women and children under eight. Her huge blue eyes were full of light.

Aunt Thisbe, of course, fell in love with her on the spot.

"Why, pray, have you never introduced me to this enchanting little creature before?" she demanded of me, when Rosie, having rested, had come upstairs to inspect her white curtains and get the benefit of the view.

"Well you could have met her five years ago, Aunt Thisbe, if you had chosen to come to my wedding."

"Och, that terrifying party," said Rosie. "How scared of you all I was!"

Thisbe sniffed. "Don't mention that ill-starred occasion to me, if you please."

"No sherry for me, thank you," said Rosie.

"I should think not indeed." Thisbe gave her a fond, protecting, admonishing look. "When is your baby due?"

"Oh, in about three weeks. So I'll be able to bring her to Clytie's housewarming."

I went downstairs to find fruit juice for Rosie, feeling rather
sorry myself that I had recalled the subject of my wedding. That
harrowing party! If I remembered Dan in this house, I preferred
to think of him as a boy, a child, not as the reckless, misdirected
character I had rashly agreed to marry.

Suddenly Watch Cottage, empty, sunlit as it was, did seem full
of ghosts. Vanessa, bless her, how she would have loved this
house that she had, in a manner of speaking, given to me; what a
pity that she couldn't be here to share our picnic. And Dan, and
his mother (who, for all I knew to the contrary, was still nursing
her grievance somewhere), and poor Ingrid Christ, and the
friends I had lost, so long ago, before I knew Dan. What a lot of
people are dead, I thought, shivering a little, as I took a bottle of
apple juice from a box in the stone-cold pantry.

Having brought the parcel of Ingrid's poems out of store, I had
been reading them at odd moments, and some had struck me
forcibly and lingered in my mind. I began to feel that I knew
Ingrid quite well; better, in many ways, than I had ever known
Dan.

> *Death is easy,*
> *but dying is no joke;*
> *death is clear,*
> *but dying is a step in the dark;*
>
> *death is peaceful*
> *but dying is the point of the knife;*
> *death is a moment,*
> *but dying is the whole of life.*

How had Ingrid Christ known *that?* With such certainty?

She had studied the subject of death as if for a doctoral dis-
sertation.

I ran upstairs with the glasses and bottle of juice, almost trip-
ping on the top step.

"There, what did I tell you?" said Thisbe. "Curved stairs are
certainly dangerous."

"Fortunately there isn't a single thing I can do to change them.

They are protected." I loved the oval twirl of the banister rail and the little gallery above the entrance hall.

After we had lunched, and I had tidied up, I fetched my car, which I had left parked round the corner in Bastion Street, locked up the house, and drove Rosie home to Hanover Crescent. She invited us in for a cup of tea. Anthony, who had gone to Hastings to see a client, would, she said, be home on the five-thirty train, and would be bitterly disappointed if he missed Aunt Thisbe. I had introduced my aunt to Anthony when her aged lawyer retired and she became dissatisfied with his successor; since then, Anthony had handled several affairs for her; she had a considerable respect for him, manifested in her usual tart, chiding way.

"But I really ought to get back to town," she said doubtfully, glancing at her sturdy no-nonsense wristwatch. "I am attending a dinner of the Humanist Society at eight—"

"There's lots of time, Aunt Thisbe. I can easily get you back by then—"

We were standing clustered round the shallow brick steps of Number Eight, Hanover Crescent. Nurse Kelly, hearing the car stop, had opened the front door and come out to cluck over Rosie and order her to go in at once and sit down.

A motorcyclist shot round the corner into the Crescent, accelerated wildly, skidded, with a shriek of tires, on something in the road (a patch of oil, it was later ascertained), flew clean across the semicircular bed of roses that stretched in front of the houses, and struck Rosie full in the back, throwing her violently forward onto her own doorstep. Motorcycle and rider spun in different directions. Rosie lay still.

Nurse Kelly began to scream—an eerie, high-pitched, banshee wail. Thisbe, her face white as lint, dropped on her knees by Rose. I flew to the phone in Anthony's front hall. My slippery hands could hardly hold the receiver.

"An ambulance *quickly*—for God's sake—as quickly as you can—"

We didn't dare touch Rosie, who lay moaning faintly. The cyclist, poor wretch, was unquestionably dead; he lay doubled over with his head under him, against the wall where he had been flung. The wheels of his bike were still turning.

Nurse Kelly began to upbraid me in a choked, raging whisper.

"If *you* hadn't been here—always wheedling her up to that house of yours—she'd never, *never* have gone out—it's all *your* fault! Oh, blessed saints above, how will I ever have the heart to tell Mr. Anthony when he comes home—and he due any minute—"

"Quiet, my good woman, pull yourself together," said Aunt Thisbe in her most authoritative manner. "Here comes the ambulance now. They'll do the very best they can. And Mrs. Roche might have stepped outside for any number of reasons—to post a letter for instance—"

"*I'd* have done it for her—she never needed to lift a *finger*. If it weren't for *that* one—"

From streaming eyes she threw me an implacable glance, then rushed to the door of the ambulance.

"I'll go along with the poor blessed lamb—"

"No," said Thisbe commandingly. "You will *not*. You'll be needed to stay here and look after her husband. Miss Churchill can go in the ambulance. Now, for heaven's sake, take a hold on yourself; go and put on the kettle, so as to have a cup of tea waiting for Mr. Roche—"

As Thisbe said to me later, "The poor unfortunate woman was giving off such ghastly vibrations of hate and panic and vindictiveness that I thought it would be quite *wrong* to allow her to travel with little Mrs. Roche. If there had been the slightest chance of recovery, she might have impeded it. And who wants to die in the middle of a cloud of stupid rage?"

Such an idea was uncharacteristic of Aunt Thisbe. In somebody else she might have considered the notion as sentimental and fanciful. And her decisive act did me a certain amount of harm, I suppose, for Nurse Kelly never forgave the fact that she had been, as she felt, rudely and arbitrarily debarred from accompanying her charge on that last journey.

But I agreed with Thisbe. I did not think that Rosie, in her

hurt, critical state, should be enveloped by waves of fury and terror. Holding her small hand during the short ride (fortunately
there was a large new hospital only three blocks away), I poured
myself into sending her messages of assurance and love.

Perhaps she received them. She was certainly not afraid or
distressed. But she seemed puzzled. While, in the hospital, they
did their frantic best, with transfusions, oxygen, ice packs, injec-
tions, she murmured, "Where's Anto? Why isn't he—?"

"He's coming; just as fast as ever he can," I promised her.

But it wasn't quite fast enough. When he arrived, distraught,
trembling, wild-eyed, she had been gone for ten minutes. I gave
him her love, as she had asked me.

My housewarming party never took place. It would not have
been bearable. Indeed, three months passed before I could even
bring myself to pass a night in Watch Cottage; the place seemed
so imbued with Rosie and her unborn child that it wrung my
heart to step inside. I used to go down there, sometimes, fur-
tively, forlornly, and wander about, wondering if the sensible
thing wouldn't be to sell the house again? With capital gains tax
I would be sure to make a loss on it, but then wouldn't I be rid of
a haunting reminder, free to begin again somewhere else? But I
didn't want to begin again anywhere else, I couldn't bear to part
with the house, it would seem like burying Rose all over again,
slamming the door in her face, rejecting her.

In the end, Chris gave me a talking-to.

"Life has to go on," she said. "You're a survivor, remember?
It's the job of the survivors to keep things going for the others.
Maybe you can do some good to Anthony, just by being around
down there—take the poor devil out of himself a bit. And Rosie
would just have *hated* you to give up the little house because of
her. Think of all those curtains she sewed!"

"Yes I do."

"Besides," Chris said, "remember the living. We could do with
a few country weekends. George has been queer and mopey lately—
have you noticed? He spends far too much time in that bloody

Aqua room of his. It would do him a power of good to come down to Affton and walk on the downs, walk on the beach, get some sea air—"

"Yes, of course you're right."

Slowly then, little by little, I moved in, spending a night or so a week there, camping at first in a clutter of half-unpacked belongings, coming to terms with Rosie's death. And I was lonely; lonelier, I sometimes felt, than I had ever been in my life.

Ingrid's poems were a kind of company for me. I read a few more each time I came down.

> So, *waking day by day I find me*
> *Exiled again from my dark trance;*
> *Eve, Adam rise in me to battle,*
> *Pluck up their weapons and advance . . .*

Gradually, in the course of months, I pulled myself together and made some effort to turn the place into what I had planned. While Rosie—loving, laughing, teasing, admonishing—Rosie was with me every step of the way.

6

Were it not better done as others use
To sport with Amaryllis in the shade . . . ?

Hugh and George were excellent friends. They knew each other
merely through the external circumstance of being married respectively to Elly and Chris; on a superficial assessment they had
little in common, George a quiet, reflective, introverted businessman, a publisher, an exile from his native land, a man who
had suffered many wrongs and sorrows, a deep, intense, wry,
guarded, troubled man; and Hugh, energetic, buoyant, extrava-
gant in ideas, cheerful in nature, optimistic in outlook. Hugh was
essentially English; he didn't much like going abroad, had done
all the things Englishmen do, been to public school, spent time
in the Army, lived the life of a countryman; he fished, he shot,
enjoyed going to sheepdog tests and hunter trials. Without giving
two thoughts to the matter he sent his twin sons away to prepara-
tory school and then to public school, despite Elly's vehement
protests.

"But, Hugh, it's a barbarous system! At age seven? They'll be
miserably homesick, beaten, abused, probably grow up homosexual; how can they ever learn to be civilised?"

Civilised was Elly's main adjective of commendation.

"I learned, didn't I? I'm not a pansy, am I? Besides, there are
two of them, the little beggars can look after each other. Yes, yes,
yes, I know, I remember, I suffered agonies, despair, wrote to my
mother every week my first term threatening to hang myself—but

it's a wonderful system really, in the end it didn't do me any harm, I survived and grew up normal, didn't I? Look at me now!"

George, whose European background was not dissimilar to that of Elly also argued with Hugh about this, not, as he said, that he had any right to interfere; but simply because he disagreed with Hugh's point of view and thought it wrong, intellectually and morally. Anyway, George loved to argue. He had learned disputation as a boy, and was very good at it; outside of his profession, which was his passion, chess, squash, and argument were among his main pleasures. George and Chris kept up a continuous running discussion, which, like a river, carried along all the daily material of their lives and swept it into a vigorous pattern; if they were parted for so much as a day they wrote each other energetic letters carrying on the debate which was, of course, never resolved; they merely shifted, in the course of time, to new debating ground. It was extremely sad, I often thought, that they weren't able to have children; things had happened to George, in prison, before he managed to leave his native land, which rendered him sterile; yet, in a way, perhaps it was just as well; those children would have been a battlefield over which such continuous skirmishes must have been fought as might have scarred them for life.

In appearance, George looked like a retired partisan; he was slight, dark, sallow in complexion, with a high, narrow intellectual brow and upstanding shock of stiff dark hair; he had large quick sensitive dark eyes, rather yellow and bloodshot as to the whites; fingers thin, skilful and stained with smoking; narrow mobile satirical mouth, small dark moustache; his face was seamed with crescent-shaped wrinkles, under the eyes, under the pouch of the cheek; for an instant, on first meeting him, one thought they must be the after-scars of some tribal ritual, duelling scars maybe, but no, they were wrinkles; his leg and shoulder muscles had suffered as a result of something else that had been done to him, so that his walk and his gestures were odd and stiff, he tended to move all of a piece, his back flat as a board, instead of limb by limb and freely; despite that, he enjoyed playing squash and tennis, and was good at both. He spoke idiomatic, incisive English, which he had acquired in two years flat, with a slight, soft, hissing accent which made his mildest remarks come out with vehement intensity; he knew, also, French, German, Italian, Hebrew, and Russian; he was deeply read in European literature, and had a law degree which was no use to him in England. He had decided, rather than retrain in English law, to take up publishing instead, and during the course of six years, succeeded in establishing and consolidating his own firm, which produced scientific, legal, and medical textbooks, plays, poetry, and translations of European classics. Politically, he was a left-wing Social Democrat and in a state of continuous despair about what was happening to the world; he said, sometimes, that it was a relief not to have the ability to procreate, because he would have felt guilty as hell about launching children into such a setup; and Chris seemed to agree with him there; it was one of the few points which they did not dispute. Nonetheless I thought it tragic that they could have no children, a couple endowed with such intelligence, warmth, and honour. George, dynamic, innovative in thought, large-hearted, seemed the material on which dynasties are founded.

He had his oddities, though, for one so versed in logic.

One of the things he had brought from Eastern Europe was the blueprint for a game invented by a friend of his who had vanished.

George spent a good deal of time and energy trying to patent the invention and interest some manufacturer in producing the game, which he called Aquajoust; but he had no success. At the time when he was trying, manufacturers thought the game too expensive and complicated. In a worse recession, he might have done better; people seem prepared to buy any expensive nonsense then.

Failing a commercial market, George himself constructed a model of the game. It could be an heirloom for Hugh's sons, he said.

Chris and George owned a house in Highgate, jointly bought when George's firm started to prosper and Chris, to her exasperation, was appointed to a well-paid position administering a psychiatric social welfare department in a huge north London hospital. Chris would at all times prefer to be out in the arena, to be the underdog fighting bureaucracy. She hated being a bureaucrat herself, but could not help seeing that she was the best person for the job.

One whole room of their house was given over to the Aquajoust game, which required a large tank of water, on the surface of which little radio-controlled boats dashed around.

"He's *besotted* over it," Chris said to me. "It's childish—obsessional—nutty—idiotic."

She said all this to George too. But she was entirely tolerant of his use of the room for that purpose; it filled a need for him, I daresay she could see, like Dr. Manette's little shoemaking kit in A *Tale of Two Cities*. There were black gulfs in George's past, of which he spoke to no one. He was entitled to his therapeutic oddities.

Aquajoust was an occupation that violently divided the sexes. Few females saw any point in it at all; few males were able to resist it. And, once hooked, they could spend unconscionable periods of time in the room, guiding the little ships around, eagerly sinking each other's navies. Hugh, strangely, was not of this fraternity; he found the game too static and fiddling. Dan, I was sure, would have adored it. Water, mother of us all.

George, at any time, was happy to spend a couple of hours in his Aquajoust room, making minute alterations to the system, repairing boats, thinking of new rules and permutations, or just, as Chris said, brooding over his tank of green water, his mind far away in some other dimension. And this seemed oddly incongruous with his otherwise wholly practical makeup.

"It's not natural for an adult," Chris said to me.

"It seems natural to George," I pointed out mildly.

I used to spend weekends at the house in Highgate, and while George pondered in his tank room, reliving lost causes maybe, Chris and I went for walks on the heath. This was before I acquired Watch Cottage. Occasionally George would persuade me in for a game, but I don't really enjoy games. I can see their psychological value, but they are not for me; presumably because, when I was a child, Vanessa and my father were too busy with their excavations ever to play with me, and I never learned the art.

"I'm a serious person," I once said, absently but truthfully, to a man I was in bed with at the time, and I could see a wary, calculating look close over his face as he worked out how fast he would be able to extricate himself from any further involvement with me.

Instead of the Aquajoust game, Hugh and George played tennis and squash. George published a small architectural textbook Hugh had written, which sold very well; Elly and the boys still receive royalties from it.

Often in the summer the two couples, George and Chris, Elly and Hugh, would rent a holiday house together, in Provence, Umbria, Arran, Cornwall, as finances ran. Hugh preferred the ones that were on English soil. Sometimes I went along for a week or so. Hugh and Elly's twins were babies at first, then toddlers, then two independent small fair-haired boys. Sometimes they made me think of little Finn, drowned.

I suppose George and I began to love each other by infinitesimal degrees over a long period of time without being much aware of the fact. I always found his face deeply satisfying. It was like a map of human achievement. One felt, seeing him, that here was a successful product of the human race; a real *oeuvre*. He had the quality of Rembrandt's self-portraits.

The culmination, when it came, was sudden enough. It happened on a rainy day in May; May 20 is Chris's birthday and I was in Museum Street, where I had been hunting for her present; she is fond of antique jewellery, which goes well with her rather severe good looks and classic style of dressing. I was pleased with the gift I had found for her: a pair of dangling chased silver earrings with peridots to pick out the green in her short-sighted grey eyes. When I came out of the jewellers the rain had increased to a slashing downpour; running head-down round a corner towards Bloomsbury Street and possible taxis I shaved too close to a wall and collided with a male form doing the same thing in the opposite direction. It proved to be George.

I said, "What a coincidence. I've just been buying a birthday present for your wife."

His jaw dropped. He said, "My God, how fortunate that you ran into me. As usual I had forgotten it totally."

George was in such constant active concern about the state of the world that these minor matters tended to pass him by. One could not help respecting his passionate preoccupation; but still it is pleasant to have one's birthday remembered.

"Advise me, now you have met me," he commanded. "What do you think she would like? A book? Bowlby? Levi-Strauss?"

"Oh, George, how can I possibly advise you? No, not Bowlby, she can buy him for herself. You must get something that she wouldn't buy."

"A piece of Scotch wool?" he said, glancing around in his usual stiff, harassed manner.

"N-no, I don't think so . . ."

In the end, guided by me, he did buy her a sweater, but not Scotch, a very beautiful Angora one of a dull faunish apricot colour; Chris loves subtle mysterious shades that are not one thing or the other, and has very little time to hunt for them herself, since she is obsessional at her job, seldom arrives at her office after nine, or leaves it before seven, or takes more than twenty minutes for lunch.

Then, as an afterthought, George proposed, "Why don't you come home with me now, and cook her birthday dinner? If you have no other engagement, that is," he added with scrupulous politeness. "I would suggest taking you both out, but Chris is going to be working late tonight, I know, and I know, also, that it will be a far better meal if you cook it, and in much more restful surroundings. In this way we can talk with greater comfort. It is a long time since we have seen you, Clytie."

That was in the period when I had bought Watch Cottage and was spending most of my spare time in Affton, superintending renovations.

"Chris will arrive home late and tired, wet also. It will be such a joy for her not to have to cook," finished George naïvely.

Men are extraordinary, I thought. Here is an intelligent one, sensitive as they come, warm-hearted, considerate; but does it ever occur to him to have the supper cooked and ready when Chris comes in? No. Cooking is the wife's province. George, of course, was a traditional European; his mother had done everything, plucked the goose, probably wrung its neck too, made strudel pastry, made everyone's clothes and cut their hair; that was what women did, and it will take five hundred years to forget it. George suffered in consequence; for Chris, though absent-mindedly acquiescing in this arrangement, is the world's worst cook. Totally uninterested in the whole process, anxious only to get through it in the minimum time, she cooks to provide sustenance, no more; and her most disastrous fault, as I know well from the days when I shared a flat with her, is her hatred of waste. *Her* conditioning has made her neurotically thrifty. To use up an overripe banana, she will mash it with egg and oatmeal, producing a batch of insipid little leathery cakes; then when these are rejected she shoves them back in the oven, renders them into crumbs, pours custard on the resulting mess, and calls it a trifle; that being left unfinished, she will . . . But enough. I could see why poor George's eyes brightened at the notion of my cooking the birthday feast.

I said, "All right. I will. That's a nice idea, George."

"I shall provide the ingredients, naturally," he said. "What shall we give her?"

"*Bifteck en croûte* is her favourite. And how about some caviare to start? And a savoury. Chris isn't much for desserts."

"That all sounds admirable."

"I'd better phone my office and tell them I won't be back."

We bought the materials for the meal in Soho, and took them up to Highgate by taxi. Their house is spacious, comfortable, early Edwardian, supplied by George with large well-cushioned chairs, Kelim rugs, impressionist paintings, and shelving for a million books; by Chris with Swedish wood, calm-coloured fabrics, and efficient central heating.

Prospecting in her basement kitchen I discovered various crucial deficiencies. Chris's kitchen was tidy, rational, fanatically clean; functional up to a point; she had a dishwasher but no garlic press, a blender but no cooking wine; the vinegar was of a most plebeian kind, there was no sharp kitchen knife, the most humble of my assistants would refuse to put up with hers for five minutes, I needed a really fine grater and a lot more butter—I had used all there was in five minutes making my pastry—and also some herbs.

"I will go out to get all those things," said George sadly, when I made known to him the inadequacies of his establishment.

"I can't think what you eat!" Then I took pity on him—he looked tired to death from his day at the office, and I knew he would far prefer to collapse in one of his huge armchairs with *The Times* and the *Economist*.

"Don't you worry, George, I want to choose a good knife anyway, you wouldn't know how. It can be another of your birthday presents to Chris. You can't even cut *cheese* with this. I can't think how I didn't notice it when I've been here before—"

"Well I will come and hold the umbrella and show you where the best shops are," he said honourably, for the downpour continued unabated.

Among the excellent shops of Highgate Village our purchases did not take long and we were finished and returning home, still well before the time when Chris might be expected, when we saw the burning car.

It was in a main shopping street, blazing vigorously. Flames and thick black smoke poured from the front. A ring of interested spectators had assembled at a respectful distance.

"In heaven's name," said George, who is all for action, "why does nobody do anything about this?"

"They've sent for the police," a woman told him.

"I mean, why not try to put it out. There is a fishmonger over there; they must have a hose."

"They've sent for the fire brigade," said the woman.

"My good madam, one does not always have to wait for authority to solve a problem."

She stared at him blankly.

At that moment a faint cry was heard from within the car.

"Good God! Do you mean to say there is somebody *inside* there?"

Nobody meant to say anything.

George let out some ancestral oath, pushed the bag of groceries into my arms, and tried the doors, which were locked. He said to a boy who was leaning on a bicycle, "Give me that!"

"Give you what?"

"The bicycle, idiot!" George whipped it from his grasp and, showing surprising muscle power for somebody with his slight physique, lifted the bike and dashed it against the rear window of the car, which was a two-door saloon, shattering the window completely. It collapsed into glittering nuts, a puff of oily black smoke came piling out, and another faint cry for help was heard.

Without more ado, George stepped on the fender, thrust his head and shoulders inside the gap, and withdrew after a moment, dragging the torso of a moaning, elderly woman.

"Give me a hand here, Clytie," he called.

But several helpers sheepishly now came forward; with a lot of frenzied pulling and effort they hauled the old lady out. She was gasping and crying, her face blackened by smoke, and bleeding from cuts probably made by broken glass; she was visibly in a state of shock.

"Does anybody have a car? She must be taken at once to hospital," said George authoritatively. Nobody responded, so he flagged down a taxi which was creeping by with inquisitive slowness.

None of the people around wished to dispute our right to take charge of the old girl so George told the driver to go to St. Phoebe's Hospital, which was the closest.

"Here—what about my bike?" called the boy sourly. It had a buckled wheel.

With a kind of snarl, George pulled a card from his pocket. "Give that to the police—if they ever arrive." Then we drove off. During the ride George muttered about *people*.

"We truly delude ourselves if we think we are any better than our ancestors in the Middle Ages who regarded it as a holiday treat to see an old lady burn to death in the marketplace."

"I wonder what happened to the driver?" I said.

The old lady had been in the back seat.

"Fell into a panic, doubtless, and ran away," said George. (That indeed as we discovered later was more or less what had happened; the driver was a girl, a young inexperienced social worker taking the old lady to be fitted for a pair of dentures; at the sight of flames coming from the bonnet she lost her cool, leapt out, and bolted for the nearest callbox, which was a long way off. But for George's speedy action, old Mrs. Luke would certainly have been fried to a crisp, since the car exploded shortly after we left the scene, and several minutes before the fire brigade arrived.)

At St. Phoebe's, George's patience was further tried. We would have done better to go to the Royal North London, where Chris carried plenty of clout; but naturally George had picked a hospital that was close at hand. Their Casualty Department left us and our protégée to cool our heels for two and a half hours before a dégagé young man in a white coat slopped some antiseptic and slapped some plaster over her cuts. To George's unbelieving horror and wrath he then refused to take her into a ward for the night.

"We're full up, we can't take cases like that. There's not much wrong with her, she's only got a bit of shock; she'll be quite all right at home."

"She has inhaled smoke, the inside of her mouth is all black, and probably her lungs also," George snapped.

The casualty officer peered inside her mouth in a sceptical manner, then said, "Well, make her gargle and rinse her mouth before she goes to bed and give her some hot sweet tea; she'll be all right."

And the little creep hurried away, twitching his stethoscope importantly.

Old Mrs. Luke, greatly distressed and confused by all that had taken place, was still crying and shivering almost as violently as when we had first rescued her. She seemed to have got it into her head that I was her granddaughter Millie. "You won't leave me,

Millie, will you?" she said. "Tom and those others don't care, but you won't leave me on my own for the night, will you?"

"Don't you worry, Granny, we'll look after you, we love you," I said, and gave her a hug to demonstrate good faith and bona fides. It was like hugging a bundle of broomsticks. She smelt of mothballs and burnt paint.

By cautious questioning and unobtrusive investigation of her shabby handbag, we had found her name and that she lived alone in a bed-sitter off Transom Way, by Eagle Grove. Her landlady's name, she divulged, was Moffat. Mrs. Moffat, when phoned, made plain her utter disinclination to play Florence Nightingale to her tenant.

George and I had been taking turns to call his number so as to catch Chris when she arrived home and inform her of our predicament. After the casualty officer had left us I did catch her, she having just arrived home.

"Bring the poor old thing here," she said at once. "We can keep her for the night, and tomorrow we'll think of some plan for her; or perhaps by then she'll be well enough to go home."

So in yet another taxi we carried Mrs. Luke back to the Davenports' house, washed her, rinsed out her mouth as best we could, gave her hot milk with honey in it, and one of the Valium pills that George took when his migraines became unbearable, inserted her into a capacious old brushed-nylon nightie of Chris's, and put her to bed. She held my hand until she fell asleep, which happened almost at once.

Then, light-headed with fatigue, we repaired to the basement kitchen and opened a bottle of champagne while I cooked the steak *en croûte*. Chris said that she couldn't remember a better birthday evening or nicer presents. She put on my earrings, which looked good with her plain black sweater, and after dinner we drank a lot of brandy and played George's favourite Stockhausen on the gramophone. Then I said I'd better take off for Ordnance Mansions; I had a heavy day tomorrow. Chris looked anxious.

"I hate to ask any more of you, Clytie, but suppose old Mrs. Luke wakes in the night and wants you. You were the one she really seemed to take a shine to. Could we possibly prevail on you to stay here?"

One ought to be prepared to follow through one's actions, I knew that. So in the end I agreed to stay. Chris said, "It's too bad we've only the one spare room. But the couch in George's study is perfectly comfortable; you remember it, Clytie, it's the one we had in Beaufort Street, big as a zeppelin. You've slept in it lots of times."

I had, and was quite prepared to do so again. George's study was a small upstairs snuggery next to the visitors' room where Mrs. Luke had been placed. We looked in on her, she was deep asleep, though occasionally she moaned and twitched. Then we all hugged each other good night on the landing—it seemed to have been a very long day. Then we went to bed. And in the small hours George came and joined me on the couch that was big as a zeppelin.

On moral grounds I could hardly raise objections. There, I hadn't a leg to stand on. My relationship with Hugh was already underway. Nor did I have any objections to George himself. Indeed I loved him and couldn't help being glad that our knowledge of each other had advanced by this step. In a way, it seemed inevitable. And I always feel so much more at ease with men when I have been to bed with them; after that there is no more need for fencing, caution, calculation, double entendres: "What will he think of that? Will he take it for an invitation—? What would he do if—? I wonder how—?"

Like my friend Chris, I prefer cards on the table.

But I did worry about her, and said so.

"You entirely underestimate her," said George, holding me tightly in the archaic dark. "Chris is a larger person than that."

"I hope you are right. Yes I suppose you are. But she, but she is vulnerable."

"Less than many," said George. And that, also, was true. "Now we will discuss Chris no longer," he said, "for that in itself is a kind of betrayal; but instead concentrate on each other."

And so the night received us. Making love with George was for me like being translated into another language, transported to another continent, another time; it was like being penetrated by history, embraced by the past. As he sank into me and gasped and cried out, I had a vision of huge empty plains, of travellers, migrants, moving on forever, searching for new realms to inhabit.

George was an intelligent man, an able, trained man. After his arrival in England he had accomplished, with startling speed, the basic essentials of what he had mapped out for himself, a decent profession, a good marriage; he had abandoned with grief and resignation his hope for children, and, after a dispassionate survey of the scene, his other ambition, that of a political career; I ask myself now if he did not begin to feel, subconsciously, that time was short, that any other exploratory voyages he wished to make must be undertaken without delay? For he was an explorer, he should have travelled further; he had the energy for it, the will, the imagination; it was only stamina that he lacked. That term as a political prisoner had, I believe, impaired him in some unguessed-at way, cut at the root of some vital function.

This is hindsight, of course.

In the morning I woke filled with guilt and despair—a not uncommon matutinal frame of mind. Three burdens lay on me heavy as lead: Chris, George, Mrs. Luke, in that order. My dearest friend, now possibly alienated, and two people of whom I knew no harm, towards whom I wished no ill, but for whom I passionately wished not to have to assume responsibility.

As it proved, I need not have troubled. Mrs. Luke was a chirpy old body; she woke up in full command of herself and slightly scandalised to think what trouble she had given us all; over the boiled egg that Chris insisted she eat in bed, she produced information about a married daughter in Ipswich who would be willing to have her to stay for a week or so, till her cuts were healed; it was arranged that I should take her with me to Aunt Thisbe's flat where Thisbe and her housekeeper, Mrs. Dalton, could keep an eye on her till the daughter came to pick her up.

So that was Mrs. Luke disposed of, without any Chinese necessity to look after her for the rest of our lives. And George went briskly away to his office, pausing only to remind me that the proofs of my new cookbook, *Unconsidered Trifles*, were due back on the twenty-seventh.

Which left only Chris, calmly stacking coffee cups in the dishwasher.

"Look, Chris, about me and George—"

She said, "Now listen, Clytie. It doesn't make the least difference. I'm not saying that in a slighting way—to put you down. In fact I'm happy for you and George. In a way it knits us all three closer. I have the firmest confidence in George's and my relationship. Nothing's going to disrupt that. Because we can't have children—because we met the way we did—because George is an exile—because—"

Because George is soon going to embark on a different kind of voyage? Because we are going to need each other's help and companionship more than ever?

We are survivors, Chris and I. Trees, our roots dug well into the ground, we know that our function is to provide a perch, a resting place, for the migrants who come and go.

"George and I are well grounded," she said again. "At first I used him as a father figure. I realise that now. I'd had enough of all those wets who used to rely on me. I wanted to do a bit of twining myself. It was easy for me, too; George makes a good father. He should have had six sons." She sighed. "But now I can stand on my own feet; we are steady with each other. And I'd much rather George loved you than some secretary; middle-aged men—specially in a foreign country—so often go off the rails, pick some little idiot. Look at Cordwainer." Cordwainer had been George's partner for a while; he was now having an affair with a bit-part TV actress, dumb as a day-old-chick.

"Don't be a snob, Chris."

"No, that's not what I mean," she said, genuinely perturbed at the accusation. "But if George were to fall in love with some girl just because she ignorantly admired him, I'd know there was something dreadfully wrong with him."

"Why should you imagine he would do any such thing? George is one of the most consciously activated people I have ever met."

"Yes," she said, "he's *too* conscious, in a way. The rest of us glide along like somnambulists, never noticing the bogs and the boa constrictors and the bomb craters and the sharks scraping their backs against the keel; George doesn't miss a single damn thing. How long can he go on like that? It'll be good for him to have a few larks with you, Clytie."

"Sure?"

"Sure. And come again soon." She gave me a light pat on the shoulder; we have never been in the habit of embracing one another. Then she smiled her full rueful smile. "Too bad you and George couldn't have a baby. He'd like that. And it would get you over grieving for little Finn."

I was really startled. I had no idea that she saw into me so clearly; or still had in mind the events of five years ago.

I said impulsively, "You've never thought of adopting—?"

Chris had always wanted children, I knew.

"Oh no. For George that wouldn't be the same thing at all. And I've got my hands full these days. Would you believe what those boneheaded idiots on the management committee have done *now—?*"

Chris went on her way, dismissing George, me, and Mrs. Luke from her busy mind; I took Mrs. Luke down to Aunt Thisbe and then organised a banquet for the Worshipful Company of Apron Makers. Catering seems an idle, frivolous way to make a livelihood, I sometimes think, remembering Chris and her department, George and his textbooks, Hugh building more and more schools, Elly lecturing on semantic relationships, Anthony guiding his clients through the mazes of the English legal system; all my friends are more soberly, worthily employed, more integrated with society, than I am. Yet people have to be fed; in the end I always console myself by coming back to that basic truth.

Two or three weeks later, Hugh came down to London on architectural business and spent the night with me. We went to a movie, Hugh liked Westerns, then wonderful roast beef at Simpson's, then back to bed.

Hugh had a lot of his own zappy sexual terms. The Maltese

Cross. The Mount of Mercy. The Mix and Mash. The Maharishi's Pyjamas. The Hormone Hoist.

Involved in the Maltese Cross, which achieves an excellent, if intricate, solution to the problems of our very disparate heights, he asked, "Do you do this with George?"

I was so astonished I nearly fell out of bed.

"You knew about me and George?"

"Certainly. He told me," said Hugh, calmly pulling me back into position.

"Really," I said, "men are extraordinary. Why did he do that?"

"Because he knew about me and you."

"He knew? George knew about us? How did he know?"

"It came up sometime," said Hugh. "I told him. Do pay attention, Clytie."

But my attention had been deflected. I could not give my whole mind to our friendly antics.

"You and George discuss me?"

"Not in a nasty way," said Hugh. "We don't disparage you. We love you, damn it."

"But I don't discuss you with Elly. Or George with Chris. Wouldn't dream of it!"

"Oh, females are full of these scruples and niceties. Why the hell don't you, if you feel like it? Neither George nor I would give a rap. In fact," he said, "I think I am insulted that you don't."

"We have more serious things to discuss," I told him snubbingly. "We don't waste our time together in idle gossip."

"Prig!" said Hugh, working his way into a more satisfactory position.

As we moved along, by carefully governed stages, to a well-organised climax—Hugh was a most efficient organiser—I had a sudden wild mathematical vision of possible permutations—Elly and George, Hugh and Chris, Elly and Chris and I, Hugh and George; why should I, all this time, have had the vague, solipsistic notion that I formed the central point of this pattern? How self-oriented, how egotistical we are, even when we believe ourselves to be quite humble and self-effacing. Perhaps there is a pattern that I can't see at all, with yet other characters—God?—the devil?—another dimension entirely; perhaps I am like those nee-dle-shaped characters in *Flatland*, who are unable to conceive of a cube.

Achieving a new, original idea is exhausting—like dragging some huge, heavy trunk down from the attic.

"Flaked you out, have I?" said Hugh in a self-congratulatory manner. Then he began to cough and rolled to the side of the bed.

"Are you all right, Hugh?"

"Of course I am. Just got a bit of a stitch. It's nothing. Nothing's ever wrong with old Hugh."

"Well," I said by and by, after some more thought, "do you talk about me with Elly? Make comparisons?"

"Certainly not!" He was indignant. "That wouldn't be cricket."

"*Cricket!* Oh, Hugh! That I should live to hear the day."

"Elly knows about us, of course." He lit a cigarette and added, "She's not in the least bothered. She had a bloke of her own for a while. Elly's a cool card."

"No, she's not *cool*, Hugh! How can you say such a thing? She feels life slipping away, that's all."

Later I remembered my remark.

I went on, "You and she married so young. She just wanted to experiment." I, too, had heard about the bloke, Dr. André Main-bocher, a visiting Canadian linguistics expert. He lasted no longer than the length of his visit. Elly had no intention of taking any step that would jeopardise the strength of her bond with Hugh, and she felt perfectly justifiable confidence in his lifelong attach-ment to her.

It was strange, it was sad, how, latterly, the course of those two men's lives ran parallel, although they were so disparate in charac-ter. I'm no palmist, but I bet if you had studied the hands of George and Hugh, you would have discovered a queer identity of design. Bats send out sonar patterns around them, don't they, like submarines, so in their blind flight they can avoid objects that lie across their flight path. I wonder if we do not have some similar unconscious apparatus that tells us, however faintly, what space of time still extends between us and the hour of our death? Someday, maybe, scientists will have it all clear (accidents excepted) like the sex of unborn babies; and, on the whole, I think that will make for a tidier approach to life and death, certainly as regards making final dispositions and sorting out one's more important relationships. In the meantime, it is left to blind instinct, which does the best job it can. And the shrewd and foresighted, like Aunt Thisbe, make provision for the future on the last sheet of loo paper.

One could feel at that time, in both Hugh and George, a kind of acceleration, a branching out, a diversification, as if they wanted to extend themselves, look about, waste no time, make hay while the sun shone, before night fell.

"Experiment?" said Hugh. "What was experimental about that fat Canuck? What highfalutin' nonsense you girls do talk." Then he looked at his watch. "Good Jesus, Clytie, it's nine-fifteen, and I have to be at County Hall by ten. Will you be a kind, darling creature, and scramble me some eggs while I shave?"

7

*Comes the blind Fury with th' abhorred shears
And slits the thin spun life.*

George telephoned me one day to ask, "How is Monk's *Shell-foundry* coming along? The printers want the galleys by the eighth of September."

I have always had a passion for sorting things into neat categories. Due, no doubt, to my having been brought up in such an untidy way on those Middle-Eastern digs. When my cookery books began to grow thicker and more serious, I took a course in card-indexing, because a really good index is vital to any recipe book and it is surprising how atrociously indexed some of them are; try looking for chestnut stuffing in that famous best seller, you know the one I refer to, and you will see what I mean.

George discovered that I was trained in the art of indexing—the subject came up, somehow, in conversation, I forget how; and one time when he was in a spot, needing some job done fast, and I was beset by cash-flow problems and wanted a lump sum, I did his fast job for him at top speed and he paid me handsomely. After that, from time to time, he tended to call on my services when something was urgent, or if his regular indexers were tied up. I enjoyed the change in work style; there is a kind of gritty satisfaction about nibbling through a text, systematically getting every point pinned down, attached to its separate little guide thread and marker peg. It soothes, settles the mind, is utterly different from the open-ended process of planning menus or inventing recipes.

George's publishing list, as I said before, included classics but almost no contemporary fiction. He did have just one live novelist, however, whose works were so dense, so packed with political, epistemological, demographic, geographical, and scientific information, that they hardly counted as novels or works of fiction at all; they required a small army of researchers to check all the information in them, sold magnificently, despite the high cost necessitated by their thousand-page bulk, received most respectful treatment by reviewers, and, because of the huge mass of matter and cast of characters (some invented, some real), were handled by George as if they were history rather than works of imagination, which meant that they were given full indexes. George said the extra cost was entirely justified; readers were happy to have the index, found it essential, in fact, for keeping track of events and characters.

The author's name was Caspar Monk, and he lived secluded in the Hebrides.

I had done the indexes for the second and subsequent novels (they were to be a series of six), then gone back to the first, originally issued without an index, and done that one, too, so by now I had a comprehensive knowledge of Monk's books. George automatically sent me each massive bundle when it reached proof stage. The work constituted a kind of hobby for me, like embroidery. I plodded through twenty pages a night, and they settled my mental processes for sleep, the way eggshells are supposed to clear coffee.

So when George asked me how *Shellfoundry* was coming, I was able to tell him that I had another sixty pages to go, three nights' work.

"Very good," said George. "Do you care to have lunch on Thursday and deliver the manuscript?"

"I have a Weavers' Week coming up—" I began cautiously, but George went on, "And meet the author, who is making one of his rare trips south?"

Curiosity, of course, is my major trait, so I said I would come. "Where, George?"

"Bones, in Charlotte Street. Monk eats nothing but fish. One o'clock."

I said I would be there.

"By the way," he said, "do you want the foul matter from *Unconsidered Trifles*?"

Foul matter is a publishers' term for corrected copy that has been dealt with and is no longer in use: worked-over typescript and proofs.

I said, "No thanks, throw it out."

Major writers, I assume, keep all that stuff, and some minor ones, too, perhaps, in hopes of irresistible offers from midwestern universities or literary libraries; but I have never cherished any such fantasies.

I can't attach too much importance to *things*; doubtless because I was reared with so few possessions. Vanessa had hardly any, except a very reliable watch and a compass. For toys I had to make do with sticks and stones and the sky, better and bigger than any TV screen. Because of this, what some might call childhood deprivation, I've never been able to acquire the right respectful attitude towards belongings. With a kind of inept, hopeless awe, I admire other people's Waterford decanters, Balmain suits, Charles Rennie Mackintosh chairs, Morris wallpapers, first editions, herbacious borders that show the effect of unceasing years of care, velvet lawns, vintage port—but without having the least wish to own such things myself. Attention to objects: it is a faculty that I simply lack. Cammie Packer burning a hole in my little Shiraz rug seemed to extinguish that faculty once and for all. I never replaced the rug; I decided that precious possessions are too much of a liability. It's sufficient of a bother getting one's own organism from hurdle to hurdle without a lot of other extraneous clobber to lug through the eye of the needle. Food is different: you take a lot of trouble over it, and then in twenty minutes it's all eaten up; there's something highly satisfactory about that—like beautiful pictures chalked on the pavement.

Mind you, there are plenty of people I really respect who manage to treat their belongings with consideration. I can see it's a point of view. We live in a gracious world, why not honour its features? Rosie could take an hour's careful thought deciding between two shrubs or two swatches of curtain material. Elly (when she has the time) can immerse herself in *Vogue* and *Harpers*, planning her wardrobe, and then looks superb wearing it. Even Chris, the obsessional worker, has a healthy respect for her hair and skin and will, every once in a while, devote much serious consideration to the choice of cosmetics and shampoos. Dan was an exorbitantly slow browser over menus, attaching as much importance, it seemed, to the selection of what he was going to have for lunch as Noah to the passengers of the Ark.

Importance: that seems to be the key word. If you don't consider your own entity of much consequence, then the choice of your accessories won't weigh on you too heavily. I can't, myself, feel that I have priority over my surroundings.

What about Watch Cottage? Well, that was . . . a divergence.

Houses aren't just for us, after all; they belong to posterity as well.

"Throw out the old copy," I told George. "I don't want it."

Foul matter. Who needs it? You might as well keep all your old appointment books, mail order catalogues, nail clippings, laddered tights, broken eggshells, bits of lemon peel. Some people do, of course, and just as well, or history would never get put together. But I'm not one of those. History will have to get along without my help. Life, memory, is enough foul matter for me.

On Thursday, at Bones Fish Restaurant, I studied Caspar Monk with the deepest interest. Here, I could see at once, was a case of total self-importance, justified, no doubt.

Monk was a tall, bonily thin, narrow-headed man with yellow-grey hair, muddy grey eyes, and a muddy grey complexion. His origins were part Scots, part Scandinavian, and his accent was a smoothed-off Glasgow. He spoke very slowly and quietly—it was necessary to pay sharp attention in order to catch what he said; and he took more time and trouble fixing on what he was to eat than even Dan in his most prima donna mood. Monk suffered, we learned, from diabetes, hypoglycaemia, hypertension, and a number of other conditions requiring, so far as I could make out, mutually exclusive diets; he could take no salt, no pepper, no sugar, no fat, no fibre, no cholesterol, no acid, no wheat flour. I began to feel heartily sorry for his wife. But luckily he didn't have one, it turned out. In the end he settled for steamed Dover sole and a glass of skim milk; but the milk, when it arrived, was rejected because he detected a portion of a fly's leg floating in it.

"A glass of water?" George suggested rather hopelessly.

"My dear man, no. Thank-ee. I daren't drink London water. God knows how they adulterate it."

"Some Perrier?"

"Ech! Did ye not read that report on French mineral waters? They are all poison, pure poison."

To change the subject, which I was beginning to find highly tedious, and also to tease Caspar Monk a little because I had taken a dislike to him, I asked at what point it had dawned on him that he had accidentally changed the name of one of his vast pageant of characters, in midstream as it were, between Book One and Book Two, *Manforest* and *Haggardforge*. Nobody had spotted the mistake until both volumes were in print and Book Three well under way.

The slip seemed to me of slight importance—the character concerned was a minor one—but Monk took my question with passionate seriousness, as if Cordelia had changed to Cressida in Act III.

"*Most* unfortunate. Ech—a very great pity. I intend to insert an Author's Note about it at the beginning of *Shellfoundry*. And, of course, an erratum slip in each reprinting of *Haggardforge*. Readers should not be misled."

Fascinated by this religious attitude I went on drawing him out, discussing the relationships between his characters, his plots; comparing to other books in series, Trollope, Balzac, C. P. Snow, Anthony Powell, Shakespeare. His gravity was complete, he peevishly rejected an introduction of Dr. Dolittle into the conversation. Nor was he at all impressed by the fact that I knew the whole Caspar Monk *oeuvre* almost as intimately as he did him-

self, but took this as no more than his due, ponderously deliber-
ating on the responsibilities of his labour while he chomped on
his Dover sole and plain boiled potato.

I avoided the temptation of trying to catch George's eye. I
could tell, though, that he was glad of my company and support.
Compared with Monk's bony bulk George appeared slighter,
stiffer, frailer than ever; also he looked tired to death. As always
in fatigue his eastern Tartar looks became more pronounced, the
sickle-shaped pouches under eyes and cheeks more noticeable; his
eyes narrowed to slits in ennui, he looked as if his ancestors had
ridden on stubby ponies over blizzard-gusted steppes from the far,
far east, myriads of centuries ago, as if he hardly belonged to this
time and place. He seemed, I thought, unusually distrait and preoccupied, particularly in view of the fact that he was entertaining
one of his most prestigious and selling authors. He talked little
himself, took, for George, an unwontedly long time to decide on
grilled trout, then hardly touched it when it came.

I knew, of course, that he wouldn't enter with me into any
complicity of malice or amusement over Monk's humourless self-
importance, either then or afterwards. George had a kind of
sweetness and innocence, a directness; he never, ever, used his
own standards as a yardstick for judging those of others, he was
truly objective and dispassionate. *Compassionate.* George said
once that, being so much an exile himself, he understood that everybody is an exile in some way, from some territory they have
lost long ago. Each of us has his sequestrated Eden.

In the middle of this lunch with Caspar Monk, George did a
strange thing. He suddenly got up and left the restaurant, not in
haste, as if he had been taken ill or remembered some urgent
omission, but quite slowly and deliberately.

Monk was engaged in talking about the symbolism of the females in his character pattern, I remember. In the middle of it,
George pushed back his chair and, without glancing at Monk or
me, as if he had completely forgotten our existence, rose and
walked towards the door. At first I thought he must be going to
the Gents; then, amazed, glancing past Monk's shoulder, I saw

him take his coat from the stand, put it on, go through the door, and walk unhurriedly past the window down Charlotte Street. It was a shock, I must say. Irrational behaviour would always be the last thing one expected from George; in fact it was so utterly out of character that I spent some time trying to convince myself that I had to have forgotten some perfectly sensible explanation for his departure which he had previously given me.

After a while I turned my attention back to Monk, who, apparently unperturbed, was dissertating about how his books were a collage on reality; or perhaps reality was a collage on his work, it may have been that way round.

"And what has become of Mr. Davenport?" he inquired after a while, finally becoming aware of George's absence. "Was he taken unwell?"

"I—I think he must have been. It's exceedingly unlike him—"

Caspar Monk shrugged. He was plainly of the opinion that anybody so ill-advised as to reside in London must be likely to drop dead of stress at any moment. It seemed, I thought, an ungrateful attitude, since a large proportion of the people who published, bought, and read his work must live in the Wen or other capital cities. But I decided that it was no part of my duty to apologise for George; and luckily there was enough unconformity about Monk's own manners to prevent his taking exception to those of George.

Feeling some hostessly duties incumbent on me, however, I suggested dessert or coffee. Mr. Monk shudderingly rejected both, but was persuaded to eat a banana. Several were brought for his inspection. "One of nature's most hygienically packaged articles," he assured me, solemnly peeling and demolishing it while Emil, the head waiter, deadpan, placed an espresso coffee in front of me.

As I was tired of discussing his work, I then introduced the subject of Ingrid Christ. Had he, I demurely inquired, ever considered turning his talents to biography? If so, here might be a subject suitable for his attention: a serious, dedicated poet, alive during the span of years analysed so extensively in his novels; also there was the Scandinavian connection. To my surprise, he took this suggestion with the utmost seriousness and said he would think about it.

"I, too, must be on my way," he said then, glancing at a kind of portable grandfather watch on a thick cable which he wore across his Jaeger-waistcoated middle. "I have a press conference at three-thirty back at my hotel." *Otel*, he dropped the aitch in an upper-class way which Thisbe would have approved. He was in London, I knew, to receive the Benelux Literature Prize for his last book, *Warhaven*. "Ech, goodbye," he said to me vaguely, collecting his muffler, gloves, and umbrella. ". . . enjoyed our talk . . ." And he also departed, leaving Emil to present me with Bones' bill; but that was all right, I am an old friend of Harry Bone's and told him to put it on George's account.

I was increasingly worried about George, though, and telephoned his secretary as soon as I returned to my office.

"Mary? Has George come back from lunch?"

"Yes, he's here," she said, sounding surprised. "Did you want to speak to him?"

"Oh—well; yes, just for a moment then, if he's free."

George came on the line. He sounded just as usual. "Clytie? What is it?" His tone was a trifle brusque. He hated time wasted on personal calls during the working day, and I never called him at the office except on business. So I merely reminded him about Monk's erratum slip, and that he and Chris were to dine with Aunt Thisbe at Ordnance Mansions next week, thanked him for the lunch, and rang off.

I continued to be puzzled, though, and a little scared.

When George and Chris came to Ordnance Mansions, he brought back the folder full of Ingrid Christ's poems.

After moving into Watch Cottage, after Rosie's death, I had set myself to the task of putting the poems in order. I read them one by one, sorted them into chronological sequence, typed out all those that were handwritten, and made them, so far as I was able, into a codified unit. A few were dated, many were not. Sometimes there would be half a dozen versions of the same poem. Occasionally these were numbered, more often not. From internal knowledge—handwriting, style, even the paper they were written on—I tried to work out which were the later or final versions, and was interested to see how Ingrid clarified her own thoughts and diction as she moved forward. I had a very fraternal feeling towards her and her solitary struggles.

What an extraordinary occupation poetry is, when you stop to think about it—groping around in your own recesses for some hidden thing—how do you even know it is there, let alone what shape or form it will take?—then dragging it painfully out into the daylight. Why? And for whom? Who cares a damn about your struggles? Never mind the sessions of sweet silent thought; it was evident that Ingrid's creative processes were more in the nature of a bloody battle with a Giant Squid.

It struck me that the later unpublished body of her work was far superior to the poems in that first pair of slender volumes, *The Broken Anchor* and *The Rat Wife*. And the effect of all her poems, taken together, was by far more impressive in its impact than those scattered ones published in the *Paris Review* or the TLS; in fact the bulk of her work seemed to me like a *shout*, a shaman's shout, capable of shattering glass, causing deafness or mania or death in the hearer. Had Ingrid shouted thus at Dan? Was that her final bequest to him? A shout that continued to reverberate in his ears after she was gone, drawing him after her in the end, like Little Eyolf after the Rat Wife?

I was sure that Ingrid had not meant any harm or malice, however; she was just a single-minded creature, she felt—judging from her poetry—no animosity against any *person*; merely a sense of outrage against life itself, which had deposited her in the wrong body at the wrong point in history.

What in the world could Mrs. Suter have made of such a daughter-in-law, living in the same house? It would be like exposing her to radiation.

I had shown the poems to Chris, and discussed them with her. Poetry is not her bailiwick, she is too wry, dry, foursquare, and close-set to enjoy its leaps, ardors, and obliquities, but she did agree that they were impressive. A battler herself, Chris could appreciate the hours of discipline, of life-and-death engagement, that went into those packed blocks of words. After some consideration, she suggested that I show them to George. I had been shy about doing this. I didn't want to presume on our relationship, I'd thought of trying them on Faber or Chatto. But fortified by the encouragement of Chris, I did finally mention them to George, and he asked to see them.

He kept them for six months. This in itself was enough to startle and dismay. Rapidity was one of George's great professional assets; while other publishers hesitated, pondered, debated, George acted. His judgements were lightning quick, and he had total confidence in them, hitherto well justified. He could read any text, no matter how long, overnight, and have all its faults and values tabulated by next morning. He would be giving his yes or no, making his offer, before anybody else had got to Chapter Five. So it was unheard of for him to take six months, and boded ill for Ingrid, I thought, not realising that this was all part of a much larger pattern. I would not have dreamed of nagging or reminding him, but I was bothered about it. The sheer discourtesy of making anybody wait for such a period was so unlike George. He could not possibly have forgotten about them; I knew that.

Indecision is like sewage; it poisons your mind.

Aunt Thisbe's rooms at Ordnance Mansions resemble glowing caves. Entering them you do not think of style or period; you do not feel "An elderly woman lives here"; you are simply spellbound. The walls are painted in dark colours, bitter-chocolate-brown in the sitting room, indigo in the dining room-study, sooty emerald in her bedroom; ceilings, cornices, paintwork, and bookshelves are brilliant white. The rugs are oriental, also in rich ikon colours. Her furniture, inherited from Great-grandpa Raintree, is all eighteenth century and fanatically cared for, but generally hidden under sheaves of magazines, papers, books, letters, and proofs. She has an oval walnut dining table that is the exact colour of a clear peat brook and has the same shine. On the sitting room wall hangs a portrait of Great-great-uncle Joshua Raintree, who, in the eighteenth century, when the Society of Friends

was somewhat turned in on itself because Quakers were still excluded from public affairs, came in for a considerable amount of
obloquy among his colleagues because he published several pamphlets disputing against the doctrine of Quietism, which, he
argued, was a spineless creed, and flat contrary to the plan of God
for humans. Great-great-uncle Joshua, in his wig and brown velvet
jacket, looks a formidable old party, and also remarkably like
Aunt Thisbe with her long sardonic lip and hooded eye; drinking
sherry in that room I have often wondered what he would make
of us and our frippery ways, our idle flights of fancy and un-
directed conversation. I'm quite sure Great-great-uncle Joshua
never wasted ten minutes in his whole adult life.

Quietism tells you not to resist the devil, because resistance
upsets the contemplative part of the soul. "Fiddlestick!" one can
imagine Great-great-uncle Joshua saying, "I trust I have it in me
to resist the devil without putting too great a strain on the superior part of my soul."

Aunt Thisbe has a number of Joshua's writings, which are, of
course, long out of print, and she had suggested to George that
he use some of them in a religious anthology that Cordwainer
and Davenport were putting together. I assumed, therefore, that
the brown paper parcel which George brought in and laid on a
chair was some of the Raintree pamphlets. George, I thought,
still looked deathly tired; he had a kind of twitch in his temples
and was a bad, greyish colour. Every now and then he heaved a
deep unconscious sigh, as if he were carrying more weight than he
could bear; not physical weight, for he was thinner than ever.
Chris, too, looked pale; I had not seen her for several weeks and
wondered if she had been having a bad cold.

Thisbe's old cat, Oberon, came in. He is an immense Persian,
twenty years old. Because of his great age, inside the opulent
flowing coat of fur there is now only a frail skeleton of a cat. Pick
him up, and the surprise is startling; he feels light as a dead leaf.
He spends most of his time in a state of irresolution. Thisbe has a
glass door between sitting and dining room; Oberon will generally
be found on one side or the other, waiting for someone to let him
through. If you open the door another period of uncertainty

elapses before he will slowly rise and walk doubtfully into the other room, his face wearing that expression of cross preoccupation which is common to all Persians. On this occasion Chris noticed Oberon's shadow through the reeded glass (he has spent so many hours on that spot that I am sure his ghost will be there in a hundred years); she opened the door for him and, as usual, he hesitated for a considerable time, displeased at the sight of company. Chris gently picked him up and deposited him on the sofa beside George, from where he instantly and affrontedly jumped down. He went and stood beside Thisbe, trying to decide whether he wanted to climb up on to her lap.

"He takes longer and longer to make up his mind," said Thisbe, gently pulling out his handsome fawn-coloured ruff. "He's been sick lately and it slowed him up even more. I've known him sit for half an hour trying to decide whether to eat a sardine."

She settled Oberon, then went briskly back to the discussion that she was holding with George about which of the Raintree papers to use.

I caught a strange, painful, troubled expression on the face of Chris.

Mrs. Dalton, Thisbe's housekeeper, was dishing up a meal which we had put together earlier in the day of soup, salmon mousse, and a delicacy called Lingfield lemon pudding. I went into the kitchen to unmould the mousse, and Chris followed me.

"Do you notice anything odd about George?" she asked me at once.

"Well . . . he does look very tired . . ." I wondered whether to mention the lunch with Caspar Monk.

"He has developed this frightful sensitivity to noise. Every single sound seems to strike him like a blow. I don't know what to do about it. We went to Finchingfield for a weekend, I thought it would do him good to get out of London, but they were having a bell-ringing festival; we just had to come straight back. George couldn't stand the sound of the bells."

Unbidden, there came into my mind the recollection of a night I had spent with Hugh at the Holborn Hotel. As the crow flew, it proved to be very close to St. Faith's, the little church just across the road from Dan's Covent Garden loft. The sound of the bells came through the darkness with piercing familiarity. I endured the well-remembered quarter-chimes until halfway through the night, then, choked by anguish, despair, who knows what, I rose, dressed, left a note for the sleeping Hugh, and took a taxi back to Hammersmith. Hugh thought it most extraordinary behaviour.

Sometimes a black thought comes to me. Could my involvement with George and Hugh have helped, in some way, to shorten their lives? Or—never mind that piece of self-importance—was it, simply, in Great-great-uncle Joshua's terms, *wrong?* Wrong in an absolutely final manner—as five would be the wrong answer to twice two? Did I go to bed with them simply because of their connection with Chris and Elly—because they were appendages of my friends, whose vital essences, through envy, love, or jealousy, I wanted to absorb, suck out of them?

"I really came out to warn you," Chris added urgently. She took from me a basket of bread I had been about to carry into the dining room, intercepting me. "I'm afraid George has brought back Ingrid Christ's poems. He doesn't like them, he doesn't want to publish them, he's in a funny state about them—"

"Oh lord, don't worry about that!"

She seemed greatly in need of reassurance. I thought it rather cowardly of George just to bring the poems and leave them, as I assumed he meant to, instead of discussing his reasons for returning them. But none of that was Chris's fault, so I said consolingly, "After all, there was absolutely no obligation on him to take them; I only wish he hadn't kept them quite so long. I'll send them to Faber now, I think. Now, could you bring the butter and then that's everything—"

"No, it's just— Please don't be upset, Clytie. I just wanted to prepare you a bit—George simply isn't himself at the moment. Don't let him wound you."

"Don't let George wound me? How could he possibly?" I said, astonished, and then we all went into the dining room and Aunt Thisbe, who has a strong sense of social obligation, firmly switched the conversation to the new National Theatre production and kept it in that region through soup and mousse.

George was sitting in front of an early veneer grandfather clock, said to be of Sheraton's design; it had a gentle, measured tick, barely audible through the general talk, but I noticed him repeatedly half twist his stiff body round so as to listen to it with an irritable, preoccupied frown. He seemed to be eating very little and his participation in conversation was spasmodic, coming in short nervous gusts with intervals of silence between.

I had made the Lingfield lemon pudding with George in mind. He seldom ate desserts but relished anything with lemon in it, so I had resurrected this interesting delicacy, to create which, you wrap a pierced lemon in brown sugar and butter, enclose in a suet crust, and steam the whole affair. It looks unbelievably sinister and tastes sublime—a caramelized Garden of Eden. But George, when a plateful of the black and gooey confection was put before him, almost rose from his chair in horror.

"No—no—thank you. I don't want it—*no!*—"

Chris never eats desserts, and Thisbe is too polite to partake of a dish refused by her guests, so we nibbled a little cheese and left the table; Mrs. Dalton brought coffee in exquisite little vermilion Chinese cups. George suddenly picked up the fat brown parcel and handed it to me, saying, "Well: I've brought back your friend's poems, Clytie."

His tone startled me. It was aggressive, almost hostile. Aunt Thisbe looked up in alert surprise. Chris visibly flinched. I said, anxious to hurry the affair to its conclusion, "You mean Ingrid Christ? I didn't know her personally of course, she wasn't really my friend. Thank you for looking at them, George. And if you don't like them it doesn't—"

"I found them pestilential rubbish," he went on, his tone rising higher.

"I didn't mean to give you so much trouble—" I had been about to drop the package in some inconspicuous corner but, taking me unawares, he suddenly whipped it back from me again, opened it, and began delving among the contents.

"Rubbish, rubbish," he kept muttering. I felt a guilty Judas. Why had I disclaimed friendship with Ingrid Christ? For all intents and purposes I *was* her friend. But what I had meant

George to understand was that I had not pushed her poems on him because of our connection, but because I truly felt that they deserved attention.

George was muttering stray lines to himself as he rummaged untidily among the separate sheets, dropping some on the floor. I could see that all my careful arrangement had been totally upset. " 'Midnight; but soon the serpent tide comes knocking, with knuckles of sand . . .' *Fah!* 'Streetlamps have roots, perhaps . . .' *Foo!* Listen to this idiocy." He read:

> *"Evade the worst of nature's laws*
> *Exclude old Santa Pantaloon*
> *Cry quits! embrace the menopause*
>
> *Discard the warrior's bloodsoaked gauze*
> *Resign, the time is opportune,*
> *Hang out no sock for Santa Claus.*
>
> *Nail up the ancestral chest-of-drawers*
> *Draw sheets, now darkness talks at noon:*
> *Hang out no sock for Santa Claus*
> *Cry quits: embrace the menopause.*

In my opinion," said George, "that is just empty-headed, pestilential, disgusting *rubbish!*"

If we had been alone together I would have said, "Hey! Take it easy, George! No one said the girl was Emily Brontë. Keep your hair on," or words to that effect. But I was hamstrung by Aunt Thisbe's presence, the formality of the occasion, and Chris's look of distress. The moment was acutely embarrassing. Also, that was by no means one of Ingrid's best poems, I considered.

"Menopause: what a beautiful word that is," Aunt Thisbe said dreamily. "I am so glad that somebody has made use of it in verse at last; a villanelle, if I caught the form correctly? I always think it a pity that so little good *light* verse is written these days. Perhaps if poor Ingrid Christ had lived longer she would have contributed more to that genre—"

" 'Hang out no sock for Santa Claus,' " George repeated furiously. But, for some reason, he hung up on the word *Claus;* he repeated the hard syllable, "Ca, ca, ca," several times, rubbed his fingers up and down his forehead as if he were searching for something buried in his brain, then savagely crumpled the page and dropped it, and the whole folder with its contents, on the floor.

Talking at random I gabbled, "I don't think that's a very good one, but there is a theme in several of Ingrid Christ's poems which I find very sympathetic; she states it clearly in the one that begins, 'Night after night begins the serial dream'; the idea that our unconscious dream-life at night is as continuous as our day-time existence, only in a different dimension; so that death, if I take her rightly, is not a step into unknown territory but simply a continuation of another life that has been going on all the time concurrently. I think that's a very attractive concept. I wish I could believe it."

George said very quietly and distinctly, "The woman was a dangerous fool."

Then he walked straight out of Aunt Thisbe's flat, forgetting, apparently, that he had been wearing a topcoat when he arrived.

"Oh dear," said Aunt Thisbe simply to Chris. "I am afraid your husband does not seem to be quite well, my dear. No doubt he has been working much too hard."

Chris, desperately pale, her eyes full of tears, hardly knew whether to stay or go after George. She looked at me appealingly.

"Honestly, don't worry!" I refilled her coffee cup and shuffled the Ingrid Christ manuscript out of sight. "*Anyone* could see that George wasn't himself. You stay here awhile till he has got home and settled down and forgotten about it all."

I was trying to make light of George's behaviour, but I did not *feel* light about it; the whole affair was so completely uncharacteristic of George, or at least of any George that we knew.

"He's been—well, strange, at home lately; other people hardly seem to exist for him, in some ways he's quite childish, wanting things at *once*, and *exactly* his own way; and then, sometimes, that stammer, or lisp. And he has been forgetting things—"

"What kind of things?" asked Thisbe gently.

"We were talking about mothers, and he said, 'What's that

play of Shakespeare's where the hero's mother marries his uncle?' *Extraordinary* things like that, things you'd think he'd remember as long as he remembered his own name—"

A little cold silence fell, into which Thisbe said briskly, "My dear, don't you think he should be persuaded to see a doctor? It may be something quite straightforward, some glandular deficiency which could be put right very simply."

"The difficulty is that George is quite paranoid about doctors. He has *Cancer Ward* notions about them even when he is feeling thoroughly well and cheerful. He had some bad experiences with them in his own country—"

"Is there any possibility of your getting him away for a holiday? To the Canary Islands or some peaceful place where he could unwind?"

Chris looked miserable. "He's very hard to persuade. He has really been living for his work, these last two or three years, he hates going away. And unfortunately I have to go off myself next week to a social psychiatry conference in Zurich."

"No chance of persuading him to go too?"

"He'd rather be dragged over the Alps by his tongue!"

After an hour or so Chris took her leave, looking very despondent, apologising again for George's abruptness, though Aunt Thisbe repeated that it was not of the least consequence; "After all, he was very nice to me, about the Raintree papers!" and asking me, rather piteously, to keep an eye on George during her absence in Zurich, or at least phone him from time to time to make sure he was all right.

Aunt Thisbe shook her head when Chris had gone. "Poor thing; I am afraid that she is in for a very hard time."

"What do you think is the matter with him, Aunt Thisbe?" I asked fearfully. "Is he having a breakdown? He seems so antagonistic—so unlike himself—"

Miserably I rememberd that evening when we had rescued Mrs. Luke, when we had all hugged each other on the stairs. This George seemed a completely different person.

"I don't think he's having a breakdown," said Thisbe. "I think he's dying."

"*Aunt Thisbe!*"

"You forget how old I am," she went on gruffly. "I've seen that look on people's faces before—many times. Once you know, it is unmistakable. As if some other force were slowly but completely taking over. Before the meal, when you and Chris were in the kitchen—he leaned back as if he were exhausted, on the sofa, and shut his eyes; I saw it then on his face—"

"You saw—?"

"Death. Unequivocal. I don't think there's any use encouraging that poor girl to try dragging him to a doctor if he is so resistant to going. He knows, I suspect, all too well, in some latent part of him, what is going to happen."

"And that's why he is so angry with us. . . . Why did you suggest their going away for a holiday to the Canaries, then?"

"Oh, for her sake," said Aunt Thisbe sadly. "So that perhaps she might have a little halcyon time to look back on afterwards."

Chris went off to her conference, and I arranged to go and spend a couple of nights in the house at Highgate, to cook George meals and keep him company.

On the first evening when I arrived there at half-past seven, from a poetry festival for which I had provided the refreshments, I found the house in darkness.

Assuming that George was not home yet, I wandered around switching on lights, and was startled to death to find him sitting in complete darkness in the big untidy sitting room, apparently doing nothing, just sitting.

"George! I didn't realise you were there! What a fright you gave me."

His eyes slowly focused and found me. "Oh, hullo," he said vaguely. "Is it suppertime?"

"No, not yet; I just got here. Have you been home long?"

"Home? Long?" He accentuated the syllables loudly and thinly; he drew them out as if they were unfamiliar words from some long-lost archaic tongue.

"Were you at your office today?"

He picked up a handful of proofs which had been lying over

the arm of his chair, looked at them frowningly as if they were set in Chinese, and then said with slow bitterness, "I shall never be able to work again."

Aghast, horror-stricken, I hardly knew what to do. Getting some food into him seemed to have priority, so I made a nourishing soup and laced it with brandy. That he would eat, and it visibly had a good effect; his conversation became more normal, though he slurred his r's a good deal and misprounced his c's. He could talk on current affairs, we had a perfectly sensible discussion about whether England should remain in the European economic community and how this affected the publishing trade; he was able to argue about some problems that had come up in Caspar Monk's latest novel; but then, when I asked if Chris had managed to telephone him from Zurich, he said stumblingly, "Chris?" And, after a long pause, "Who is Chris?"

"Your wife. Chris," I repeated, with a terrible chill at the heart.

He laughed a little, formally, as if one of us had made a rather stupid joke. "Oh, *Chris*." Then, after a minute, he added fastidiously, "Do you know, she has lately begun to *smell* rather disagreeable. I have several times had occasion to mention it."

"Smell?" I repeated in anguish. George himself had a rather strange smell. I had noticed it immediately on entering. Like old, rusty iron.

"Yes. She smells of roast beef." His nostrils wrinkled in distaste. "And wet hair. If there is one thing I cannot stand, it is wet hair. You can't get it off your fingers." He rubbed his hands together querulously, and I thought of Chris's thick, lustrous hair, which, at George's insistence, she had grown long (when I first knew her she had a kind of boys' cut). Now she could sit on it, like the Empress Eugenia, and it was a terrible nuisance to her, requiring hours to dry when washed, needing to be groomed and cared for like some pedigreed animal.

Despite what Aunt Thisbe had said, I thought it would be dereliction of duty if I did not get a doctor to George and, when he had wandered back to the sitting room after his meal, I phoned Tom Cosgrove, a medical colleague of Chris's who had shared a holiday with them once in Provence and set George's broken wrist when he fell off a rock. Tom was an old friend and I thought his visit might be camouflaged as a social call.

I put the problem to him in a low tone, with the sitting room door closed.

"Well, I'll come," he said at once, "but actually Chris tried to call me in once before, and that was a dead loss. George just wouldn't play."

He arrived in fifteen minutes. I had made some coffee, and brought it and Tom into the room simultaneously, saying, "Here's Tom, come for coffee."

George gave us both a look of absolute exasperation.

"Why will you waste my time like this?" he said slowly and painfully. "When I have so little?"

He stood up, the stiffness of his neck and back even more apparent than usual.

"If you'll excuse me—" he muttered. "You two will have plenty to say to each other, no doubt—" and he brushed past us and went off to his Aqua room.

"Won't you even stay and have coffee with us?" I pleaded, but he replied, without looking round, "You make it necessary for me to lock myself in," and we heard the key turn in the lock.

"Oh, God. Now I've just made matters worse." I had been cut to the heart by the expression on George's face as he walked away from us—one of infinite loneliness and grief, impossible to forget. "I'm sorry to have brought you out on a fool's errand," I said miserably to Tom.

"Well, never mind. You did your best. I'll give you a sedative for him, and if you can slip it in, somehow, do; a good night's sleep is probably what he needs, he looks as if he hasn't slept properly for weeks and weeks."

This was true, but I felt it wasn't the root of the matter, only one of its symptoms.

Tom took his leave, kindly patting my shoulder and saying that he would phone Chris in Zurich; she had better come home as soon as she could get away from her conference.

The night passed somehow; I finally went to bed but not to

sleep. I wondered what was passing through George's mind, what strange solitudes he was inhabiting.

The sight of Ingrid Christ's poems had been a shock. George had a minute, graceful, cursive handwriting, and his proof corrections were a pleasure to the eye, particularly small, elegant, and clear, kept to a minimum as if he wished to avoid distracting the printers or defacing the text more than the absolute necessity.

And if a text had not been acquired by his firm, but was merely on offer, he would never have dreamed of marking it in any way. Very, very occasionally, if he noticed some particularly glaring discrepancy, or error of fact, he would clip to the page in question a pencilled comment on a separate slip of paper.

So it was startling, to say the least, to discover that my neat, carefully typed copies of Ingrid's poems had been almost obliterated, in some cases, by furious blue-pencil comments. The writing was recogniseably that of George, but much larger and untidier than was customary for him. The remarks recalled the vitriolic, semiliterate sort sometimes found in public library volumes: "This is feminist balderdash." "Contradicts statement made on p. 46." "Logic and syntax here both of a very low order." "Idiotic girl! How can she presume to make such a statement?" "Whom is she addressing here? The reader? Or God? If the former, he has a right to disagree; if the latter, He knows the answer already." That made me smile faintly, it sounded more like the George I knew; but the George I knew would never have committed such an unpardonable breach of manners as to write rude comments on somebody else's manuscript. Had the George I knew been merely a figure of my own imagination? Surely not? George was always severely restrained in his language, possibly because his English, though fluent, had been learned as an adult. A soft, vehement *damn* was the furthest extreme of swearing he ever allowed himself, apart from some occasional Slavic mutter under his breath. But here the blue pencil had run wild, four-letter words of the crudest were scattered thick as may petals up and down the margins. At first they made me furious, then terrified, then profoundly sad. I felt, looking at the defaced pages, that Aunt Thisbe was right. George knew that he was doomed, and reacting in rebellion, rage, or renunciation, he was cutting the painter, loosing the cord that bound him to shore.

Next day I came downstairs at seven and, going outside, looked through the window of the Aqua room. George was lying on the floor; at first, with dread, I thought he was dead, but when I tapped on the window he lifted his head, gazed at me in a puzzled way, then slowly climbed to his feet and made for the door.

I gave him a few minutes to get upstairs, then went to the kitchen and set about preparing breakfast. He came down presently, changed, shaved, and looking normal enough so that I was encouraged to think, momentarily, that his bad spell was over. But when I said, handing him toast and coffee, "Shall you be going to the office this morning, George?" he answered, "No; I told you. I shall never work again."

I waited a moment or two and then asked, "Why not, George?" trying to keep out of my voice any reproach, fear, criticism, or patronage, trying to express nothing more than the pure wish to know.

"How can I work when I am losing my will and my memory?" he answered in a cold, flat, dry tone. "I am ashamed to be seen by anyone. What I have done is totally gone from me. I am in space, empty space."

His eyes rested on the cup of hot coffee I had poured for him, the crisp thin toast spread with lemon marmalade, as if they were alien substances, of unfamiliar use; he pushed his chair back, stood, and walked away to the Aqua room, leaving the food untouched. I heard the click as he locked himself in once more.

Chris came back two days later, and from then on we took it in turn to stay with George, though when I say "with George" it gives a false impression, for at first nearly all his days and nights were spent locked up alone in the Aqua room, staring into the tank. All we could do was be in the house, hoping that, somehow, our good will, our love, our wish to share his suffering, would penetrate, if only in the slightest degree, his painful Trappish solitude.

By the fifth day he was very weak and with the help of Tom Cosgrove we finally managed to get him upstairs and into his bed; by that time he seemed indifferent to his surroundings; he submitted passively to the things we did.

Tom suggested taking him into hospital, into Intensive Care.

"Are you mad?" said Chris. "Don't you see, that would be the last indignity? He has given up. Why should we force drip feeding on him if he doesn't want it, drag him along if he doesn't want to be dragged?"

That morning she had brought him a *Times*, knowing that if his interest could be roused by anything it would be by the daily news. He had taken the paper readily enough, and run his eye up and down the columns, then jerked his head as if to clear his vision. Fumblingly he tried to pronounce a word; tried again, came to a stop. The look on his face was painful: a wincing fear, as if he were being, most unfairly, subjected to a test which everybody knew he was bound to fail. Again he tried to speak, but no clear speech came out; only incoherent mutterings, babblings, baby language. Chris, her eyes swimming in tears, took back the paper and softly read passages from it aloud; he listened with an intent, straining expression, but every now and then shook his head again, as if the whole situation were utterly hopeless. Curious brief twitches, tremors, kept passing over his face, like the air eddies that one sees over a field of grass.

"Even if we become adjusted to the concept of death," said Chris quietly and sadly to me that evening, "us two; even if we come to understand it, accept it, what use is that? What good are we, among the millions, billions of humans in the world, growing and dying like weeds?"

We were sitting in George's room, where he lay in his bed, lying and looking at nothing. We tried to be there as much as we could, and talk to each other, so that he might, perhaps, get some feeling of companionship from our voices.

"Well; how do we relate to each other at all—in the first

place?" I tried to be as objective as Chris. I said, "Do you think there was ever, at any time, an entity that was him, George? Or have all our dealings with him been merely intersections, like laser beams, lines making a nonexistent definition on a map, which is itself only a symbol, a bit of two-dimensional paper?"

We both looked at George. He did not move.

"People are the sum of what they have done," said Chris. "Aren't they? George created Cordwainer and Davenport; he published all those books; and he has done other things that we don't know about."

Despairingly I wondered if I were merely the sum total of all the meals I had ever planned or prepared; a grisly thought. What did I really know? Nothing. And there lay George, knowledge and wisdom locked inside him, a safe to which the combination has been lost.

"Knowledge," I said slowly, "is limitless—the extent of being, of facts, of isness—it stretches away around us in all directions to infinity. All we can hope is to reach out a little way into the area immediately beside us, and grasp a few facts, just a handful, like children with flying leaves . . ."

The twilight was falling fast. George lay against his pillows; his profile, severe and motionless, was a silhouette from a coin. Did he hear us? We had no means of telling.

"I suppose," said Chris, "if you achieve one thing—that makes it worth the effort. Make one discovery—pass one useful law—build one cathedral—or just carve one gargoyle—"

"*Si monumentum requiris, circumspice.* You think Wren built St. Paul's just to prove he existed? Why should one worry about proving that, really? Does it much matter—in the great sweep of time? After all, the only person who acknowledges the proof will be another person, just like yourself; what value is there in that? Someone staring at a stone, scratching his head. Wren? Sir Christopher Wren? Just a name. Even if it is remembered, what difference does that make?"

"You mean," said Chris—I could hear a faint smile in her voice —"who, in the year 2080 is going to remember that in 1980 Clytie Churchill invented a Bombe à la Clytie—?"

"But still I suppose one does care."

I thought of Aunt Thisbe. "Stranger . . . if I am dead when you read this, remember Thisbe Angela Churchill."

Thisbe amused herself by writing obituaries of all her friends. Not one had been left out. Every couple of years she revised them and brought them up to date. I used to write blurbs, sometimes, for books George published. When I was very poor he used to pay me ten pounds a blurb. Blurb writing was a kind of game, trying to see how many adjectives one could balance in one sentence without upsetting its gravity-defying equilibrium: "In this warm, perceptive, finely wrought biography, Mr. Higgins describes a tragi-comic life that never contrived to go in the right direction, a life of suffering, despair, erosion, and loss ending in a dramatic disintegration which yet contains the seeds of renunciation and hope. Mr. Higgins has never written better or with more powerful human perception." *The wild man went his weary way, to a strange and lonely pump,* as Lewis Carroll put it.

I turned to the bed and said clearly, "George. Are you hearing me? We shall remember you. You will be part of us. The things you did—the people you helped—they won't be lost or forgotten. You are knit into all of them. Remember old Mrs. Luke? Remember the burning car? Part of you is in her. She'll pass on that memory too. We are all woven into each other's fabric. But *we* shall remember you especially because we love you best."

I could hear his quick fluttering breath pause for a moment, then recommence. A faint sound came from him—acknowledgement? Or plea to be left in peace?

Chris said, "I'm going to read P and P."

She fetched *Pride and Prejudice,* George's favourite novel. He said he must have read it at least fifty times and there was always time for a fifty-first. If anything ratified the values of English literature, of civilisation, it was that book, he said.

Chris switched on the bedside lamp, angled it so that the light fell away from George's eyes, and began reading: "It is a truth universally acknowledged, that a single man in possession of a good fortune, must be in want of a wife . . ."

After she had read several chapters, I took over from her, and so we continued through the night. When dawn broke, we discovered that at some point during our reading, George had gone without saying goodbye; he had quietly slipped away and left us.

At the funeral—which was extremely well attended; Dan would have loved it; minor royalty was there, industry and art were well represented; even Caspar Monk had travelled down from the Hebrides for the ceremony—some high functionary from the Arts Council said to Chris how very said it was, George had been certain of a knighthood in a couple of years' time.

"What difference does it make," she said haughtily, "whether he was Sir George or just plain mister? Distinctions of that kind did not impress him in the least."

"You hurt that poor man's feelings," I told Chris later. "Try and take it easy. Relax. You have to be a survivor, too, remember? There's a long way to go yet."

"That's true," she said. "We have to last long enough to read Jane Austen to the next generation. Actually I'm going to endow a Davenport scholarship at London University."

"What subject?"

"Marine studies," said Chris. "The seacoast of Bohemia."

8

As killing as the canker to the Rose . . .
Or frost to flowers that their gay wardrop wear
When first the White thorn blows . . .

"You just permitted him to *die?*" said Rabuse. "Your friend, your lover? You made no effort to save him?"

His tone was censorious, not to say indignant; he placed a couple more logs on the library fire and, remaining on his feet, walked restlessly up and down the long library. I stayed curled in my armchair, listening to the soft crumbling of the red-hot logs and the flutter of the wind outside. It was very quiet in the Château Plouhaix. George would have liked it here, I thought.

"He preferred to die," I said after a while. "What conceivable right had we to stand in his way? I hope that, in similar circumstances, somebody else, other people, would show me the same consideration."

"But it was a waste. As you describe him—a man of great capacity, intelligence, discrimination, sensitivity—"

"But those qualities would have been no use to him if he had been constrained to live against his will. It would be like—like employing slave labour—"

"So what did he die of?" demanded Rabuse crossly.

"He died of death. You mean, what did it say on the doctor's certificate? Something to do with his heart, I believe."

"*Why* did he decide to die?"

"Chris and I have talked about that endlessly. She felt it was his disgust with the state of the world. He was quite realistic about his own personal part in it—how little that amounted to. He felt, too, that his best work was done—he had no children to follow him—his heart was less and less in what he was doing—he could not, being a realistic man, assign much value to his associates; it all began to seem pointless to him. And he had separated himself too far from the basic simplicities of life to derive pleasure from just breathing and looking at leaves and listening for the first lark in spring. . ."

"What about those poems by the woman who killed herself? You are not suggesting they had any supernatural effect on him?" Rabuse eyed me narrowly.

"Dear me!" I said. "For someone who is prepared to believe in all those saints and miracles, you display a pitiful lack of faith in mere cursing and witchcraft. . . . But no, I'm not suggesting that Ingrid put the evil eye on him. I think, though, that he felt she was poaching on his preserves. *He* was the expert. It would be like—when you had nearly finished your doctoral thesis—finding that somebody else had written a paper on exactly the same subject but from an opposing point of view. It would be fatiguing. Unsettling."

Several months went by before I could bring myself to type out Ingrid's poems again and put them back into order. For me, George's death was a terribly disabling event. He had been a point of reference in my life for eight years, my lover for three; my whole landscape changed with his loss. Somehow his going reopened the wound of Dan's death; I began to realise that grief all over again, at a deeper level.

Elly and Hugh took Chris away for a Mediterranean cruise. "We can all do with it," said Elly. "Chris looks like a living skeleton, I'm sick to death of students, and Hugh badly needs some sunshine and a proper rest."

"If I know anything about those cruises," grumbled Hugh, "it'll be more like a commando course than a rest. Up at six-thirty every day and on to some ghastly coach. I wish you were coming, too, Clytie, and then you and I could stay on board and relax in deck chairs while those two rush off on a sixty-mile drive to climb five hundred rock steps up to an acropolis."

"Well, I wish I could too. But, with the Commonwealth Conference coming up . . . And Mediterranean citadels are no novelty to me."

It was lonely when they were all gone, though; very lonely. Luckily I did have a lot of work on hand. And Chris had asked me to look after any questions that came up over the establishment of the George Davenport Marine Studies Foundation.

To my slight embarrassment—though I was touched too, naturally—I found George had left me some money, which was still being put through probate; this I decided to pass over to the foundation as I could think of no better use for it. I would ask Anthony to arrange it for me when the time came.

There was another minor but exasperating problem about which I wanted to consult Anthony. Some citizen of Affton Wells had lately taken to keeping pigs on the Castle Mound, behind my garden. At first it had been one or two pigs, inoffensive enough, but now it was nearer twenty. They grubbed and burrowed, ploughed up the grass into mud, trampled down the smaller thornbushes, and greatly impaired my outlook. Pigs are undecorative animals. If they had been goats or sheep or geese I would have felt much more tolerant. But they were muddy and unlovely and they were rapidly transforming the romantic, thorn-girt hillside into nothing more than a squalid patch of wasteland. Also, the pigs stank. Cows, sheep, horses, have a warm, breathing, likable animal fragrance; but pigs always smell unpleasant, even when kept in the most superior conditions. They make their own slum. The ancient Israelites were right to mistrust them.

I was busy and tired and sad, so the small extra burden of remembering to telephone Anthony's secretary and make an appointment began to take on a penitential weight; day followed day and I never managed to remember it at any practical time, only when I was in the train, or in bed at night, or making notes in somebody else's office.

While Rosie was alive, I often used to encounter Anthony on trains up or down to Affton; we used to have breakfast or drinks in the buffet car, and argue about novels; Anthony, surprisingly (at least it surprised *me*, for some reason), put in a good deal of rather solid fiction-reading on the train, he read French with facility and knocked off a lot of Balzac and Flaubert, Stendhal and Zola. He felt it his duty as well to whizz through the works of contemporary writers such as Greene, Burgess, or Waugh, but always returned with relief to the nineteenth century, and liked an audience on whom to unload his feeling that fiction was going to the dogs; I used to enjoy those arguments, and upheld the cause of modern novels with vigour even when, as sometimes happened, I half shared his opinions.

But since Rosie died our encounters had been very infrequent. I assumed that Anthony worked longer hours, travelled to town earlier on his London days, and came back later; it was a long time since I had run into him on the eight-fifteen or the five-forty-five.

When I am tired and faced with a whole set of uncongenial tasks, I have an automatic, almost unconscious habit of arranging them in order of unpleasantness, knocking off the most repugnant first, and so up the list.

Which would you least wish to do: write a letter of thanks for a book you found mawkish, clean out the pantry, make out your income tax return, pay all the bills, change the sheets on the guest bed, or wash your hair?

Just arranging things in order of unpreference can be quite salutary and instructive as to one's state of mind. Why would I rather do the tax than change the sheets? Why would I rather do almost anything than make an appointment to see Anthony Roche? Simply because I was not happy about the idea of possible litigation over the pigs? I delayed for some time and let things slide.

I received postcards from the Mediterranean: "Chris & Hugh look v. much better & browner," wrote Elly in her neat Germanic hand.

"This makes *Outward Bound* seem like a tea party in Cranford," wrote Chris.

From Hugh I had several highly characteristic letters. "The

girls are in their element sitting at the feet of Gamaliel every evening. All the classic authorities are on this boat, and we already do our crosswords in Linear B; by the time we get back we shall have reached Linear K. It is pleasant on the whole. . . . Elly is protecting her investment (me) for all she is worth; plugs me with vitamins, arranges me in the sun as if I were a green tomato. I feel more and more like some historic relic left over from a previous period."

Poor Hugh. The death of George had affected him more than he was ever likely to admit. With George he had been able to express opinions, emotions, that had no play in the company of other Englishmen. The friendship of intellectual George had been a deep satisfaction to him and he felt wretchedly deprived, now, I knew. "It's a shock, too," he said to me, when I saw them all off at Victoria, "if someone in your own age group goes off like that; you begin to look around and calculate and wonder how many more years you can reckon on yourself. Fifteen? Twenty?"

"I know," I said. "Is it really worth buying one of those enormous tins of floor polish from John Dron? Shall I be here long enough to use it all?"

"The last twenty years have gone in a flash so far as I'm concerned."

"We're so used to longevity now. In the nineteenth century they didn't take long life as their right in the way that we have come to."

"All this comfort is a mistake, I often think," said Hugh.

"Comfort?" I looked about at the clanging gloom and dirt of Victoria Station.

"Well," he said, "take mud. Tarred roads, Wellington boots, tiled kitchen floors. Even in civilised England these are all quite recent amenities, come in the last sixty years. Before that most people must have spent eight months of the year plodding about knee-deep in mud. Journeys were taken through mud. You hauled off your caked leather boots when you came indoors. You swept and scrubbed the mud off the brick floor, week in, week out. The sheer inconvenience of that, I reckon, must have been quite useful."

"What *can* you mean, Hugh?"

"It kept people's minds in the short term. Fetching buckets of water from the well; filling oil lamps, lighting fires, carrying out the ashes—they must have made quite handy distractions from all those big nasty insoluble problems like old age and illness and death that we still haven't got around to tackling. I'm not talking about the dignity of labour or any of that bosh; just about the way in which we occupy our time. It's all done so fast now, pop a frozen pizza in the oven, toss the drip-dries in the machine; leaves people with too much time on their hands."

"Well—if there are *enough* people with time on their hands, sitting around, perhaps they'll come up with solutions for some of those big nasty problems."

"It doesn't work like that," said Hugh. "Solutions are thrown up by one bloke working against the clock, not by thousands with time on their hands. All they create is more problems."

Then he hugged me and went off to the Mediterranean.

I remembered his words about mud, sitting in the train, late one Sunday afternoon, on my way up from Affton to London, carrying a big bunch of lilac for Aunt Thisbe. Spring that year was slow, cold, and grudging; the water lay in plough furrows in the fields, young crops sprouted from the water like rice. The country looked clogged, mist-shrouded, and heavy. I remembered Rosie, planning for pink hyacinths and lavender. She would not have liked this weather. Her baby would have been two by now. It's no pleasure taking small children for walks in the rain.

The train stopped at Marlbrook Halt, and a woman got into my otherwise empty compartment. She shook herself, smiled at me, and removed her handsome oiled-silk raincoat, flicking the water from it and hanging it from the rack.

"Weather for ducks!" she said. "What a weekend. Enough to make you emigrate."

"They always keep the worst weather for weekends," I agreed, and remembered how many sunny Sundays I used to spend with Dan, singing hymns in St. Martin's, then catching a train from Charing Cross into the country. Dan loved a good rousing hymn (having had much exposure to them in the Navy); particularly "For Those in Peril on the Sea." I wondered if he and Ferdi had sung it on *Valkyrie*, Ferdi accompanying Dan on the flute, as they used in Beaufort Street; had they arranged themselves a musical send-off as the boat went down?

My fellow passenger arranged herself comfortably opposite me. I noticed her clothes first, as any female would have, because they were so mouth-wateringly desirable without being in the least ostentatious: a dark brown velvet cord suit and dark gold silk shirt, tailored to an exact fit of her taper but well-rounded form. She wore beautiful knee boots and carried what looked like a crocodile handbag with gold clasps; her hair, dark, short, and glossy, had probably been cut and styled by Vidal himself. Her round, smiling face was familiar.

"Why," I said, "I know you of course, you're—"

"That's right," she said, smiling even more broadly. "Teddy Marshman, from the Monmouth. And I know you too; saw your programme on telly, couple of weeks ago, demonstrating how to make chicken à la Kiev. Though why bother, I always say, when you can get it from Marks and Sparks?"

I laughed. "And probably just as good, too, if the truth be told. Still, it's sometimes satisfying to do a thing oneself."

"Oh, don't I know! When my kids were young I used to make all their frocks by hand. Silly, really, when you can buy them just as good and twice as hard-wearing, but it's not the same."

"Let's see, what have you got—?"

"Three girls dear, Nadia, Varvara, and Tamara. Ten, twelve, and fourteen."

"You don't look it."

"Of course," she said, "I don't see them any more since the divorce. My hubby got custody. Very hostile he was—I can't get so much as a peep at them."

"You got divorced? I'm sorry—I didn't know. It's ages since I've been into the Monmouth."

Last time I was there, I thought, was that carefree girls' lunch with Elly, Chris, and Rosie. A long, long time ago. Had Teddy been there then? I couldn't recall.

Teddy, Mrs. Marshman, was the landlord's wife, and good as a blazing fire for drawing in custom, so friendly, cheerful, obliging, and calm was she, besides being sumptuous in appearance as any Renoir lady. Men came from miles around, it was reported, just to gaze; and she treated them all with the same good-humoured matter-of-factness, and this was just as well, for Geoff Marshman, the owner-landlord, was a black-haired, high-coloured man with a glowering eye, a small mean mouth, and, according to rumour, a deep and smouldering temper. So, I thought, in the end Teddy must have failed to keep one of the customers at arms' length, and it had led to trouble. Poor Teddy.

"Oh, you wouldn't have seen me, dear, even if you had been in the Monmouth. It's several years now. I expect you were abroad at the time Geoff and I split up; you travel a lot, don't you?"

It is always faintly disconcerting to find that comparative strangers know more about one than one does about them. Getting back to the subject of her, I said, "But that's dreadful, not being allowed to see your own daughters. Can't you get a lawyer to battle about it? Nowadays when everyone knows that mothers are so important, I'd have thought—"

An odd gleam of smile played over her face for a moment, just a dimple showing in each rounded cheek; but then she said, "No, it wouldn't do. I did discuss it with Anthony, but I decided it would only lead to trouble. Geoff, that's my husband, is so vindictive, you see; he'd be quite capable of putting detectives on me and stirring up a real stink. I miss the girls terribly, of course; I don't say I don't, but they're sensible little things, bless their hearts, they know their mum loves them still, and they'll be able to see me as soon as they're eighteen, Geoff can't stop them then. So in the meantime I leave them little messages and treats with Mum and Dad, and the kids get them when they go to see their granny and grandad; that's where I've been now. Mum and Dad have a council flat at Marlbrook. I come to visit them every second Sunday."

"It's lucky your husband will allow the girls to see their grandparents."

"Oh, he has to do that because Dad got Geoff his first job. And

Dad's a preacher in the Unitarian chapel; Geoff couldn't say *they* weren't respectable. In fact," she said cheerfully, "it's a real puzzle how they could have had *me!* But still they are very broad-minded about me. And I don't mean, 'They drink the champagne she sends them but they never can forgive'; I mean really broad-minded."

"Where are you living now?"

"Oh, London, dear, it's the only place really, isn't it? For someone like me, I mean. I could never go back to Affton. Or not," she corrected, "until I'm old and settled down. Maybe then I'll go back and give the council a lot of money for an old people's home. That'd be a joke, wouldn't it? The Teddy Marshman Home. That'd make Geoff really hopping."

"You're not married again, then?"

"No, love, nor likely to be."

I didn't like to ask about her job, since it seemed fairly evident what that was, but I asked about her flat and she said it was a very nice little convenient place in Hertford Street, W.1.

"Don't you miss the country?"

"No, it's queer, dear, I don't. And yet I've always been a country girl; grew up in Marlbrook; when I married Geoff and went to live at the Monmouth was the first time I'd ever slept where I couldn't hear cows and roosters. I often wonder a bit; my life has changed such a lot. The Monmouth, Geoff, the girls—a few years ago they were my whole world. Yet, now it's so different, I can't say I'm sorry; I have ever such an interesting time really. I meet all *kinds* of people; ones I couldn't even have *imagined* when I lived in Affton."

She told me about some of them: businessmen, politicians, actors, doctors. So how had this transmogrification come about, I wondered. What had been the catalysing agent?

"And there's one, you'd hardly believe me if I told you some of the things he gets up to, and yet he's ever so well known. If I told you his name you'd know it in a moment—"

For a flash I wondered if it could be my old acquaintance Arthur the stockbroker; did she but realise it, Teddy and I had more in common than she imagined.

"It keeps your mind alert, you know, it really does," she assured me. "The only bad part is not being able to see Naddy and Tammy and Varv."

It did seem bad to me. It seemed totally unfair that society should have been so lenient to me, and come down so heavily on poor Teddy. I tried to express some of this, but she said at once,

"Oh no, love, it's not society. It's my own silly fault for marrying a man like Geoff. I should have had better judgement; well, I *did* have, really, but I liked the idea of the life, you see? Running the Monmouth, I knew I could do that well. I just didn't reckon on Geoff's temper."

We were pulling into Victoria; Teddy buttoned herself back into her raincoat and then gave me an odd, measuring look, head tilted sideways, eyes narrowed.

"I'd have liked to talk to you a bit longer, love; if you wouldn't mind," she said. "I've got a favour to ask you; if I can screw up the nerve, that is. I'd best not invite you back to my place, you never know who's going to phone up; but would you mind if we went and had a quiet drink somewhere? Or are you very busy, or going on a date?" she ended, in a more diffident tone.

"No I'm not busy; I was just going home to cook myself an omelet." Puzzled, amused, curious, I wondered what the favour would turn out to be. Did she want to be taught how to make aphrodisiac snacks, or a Mickey Finn? "Listen, why don't you come round to my place? It's only a stone's throw from Victoria; we might just as well go there as into some pub where we shan't be able to hear each other."

"Honest? You really mean it? Well ta ever so, I'd like that very much, if you're sure."

As we mounted in the tiny, terrifying, creaky lift, which must have been installed at Ordnance Mansions in the 1880s, if not the 1870s, we both agreed that Sunday evening was the low point of the week.

Aunt Thisbe's end of the flat was in darkness; on Sundays she liked to go to evensong in the Abbey; so I put the fragrant nutmeg-smelling branches of lilac into a great grey Swedish glass tank in her bedroom and came back, followed by the grumbling

Oberon, to where I had left Teddy in my bed-sitter. I had three rooms, kitchen, which was of catering dimensions, office, and this room-of-all-work, with a divan, armchair, gas fire, and all the books I hadn't yet taken down to Watch Cottage. Teddy had found a book of Anthony's, a little handbook he had written called *The Law and You*, which Cordwainer and Davenport had published five years ago.

"What would you like to drink?"

She said she would have scotch and slimline ginger; shook her head at the nuts I offered.

"I have to watch it all the time, love; my mum's a regular dumpling. I'd get the same, soon as look at you."

Old Oberon, to my surprise, after the usual cautious and lengthy inspection and consideration, climbed up, leg by leg, onto her lap. Having him sit on one was an agonising ordeal, because he was so aged that he had lost the power of retracting his claws and sat nervously holding himself in position with every needle-sharp point embedded in one's thigh; but Teddy bore this with great good nature.

"He doesn't usually make friends with strangers. Do put him down if you don't want him," I urged. "I'm afraid he's likely to leave hairs all over your beautiful skirt."

"Doesn't matter. I've got one of those magic brushes; that'll get it off. Thin old boy, aren't you," she said, gently pulling his ears, and leaning down limberly to sniff at his fur. "Mmm! Don't cats smell yummy! I'd like to keep one, but some fellows don't like them."

She stroked Oberon along his bony spine, and a somewhat catarrhal purr could presently be heard.

"I remember when Anthony wrote this," said Teddy in a minute, turning *The Law and You* over to study the photograph of him on the back of the jacket. It was a good picture: head raised, eyes narrowed, three-quarter profile, the model of everyone's idea of a clever, acute lawyer.

Something had been fidgeting at the back of my mind, and now I remembered what it was.

"You mentioned Anthony before," I began slowly, "I wasn't—

didn't realise then that it was Anthony Roche you meant. Was he—did you have his advice over your divorce?"

She gave me a clear direct look.

"Oh no, dear. That wouldn't have been a bit sensible; me and Anthony having been friends, you see, before. No, he gave me the address of some lawyers in Chancery Lane. They did their best for me, but it wasn't no use, and I knew it wouldn't be."

I gazed at her fearfully, unable to frame any of the questions that seethed in my mind, but she went on calmly, "When Geoff divorced me, that wasn't on account of Anthony. Thank the good lord! That *would* have raised a dust! Struck off, would he have been, do you suppose? Or whatever they do to lawyers?"

"Only if it's a client," I said faintly. Teddy gave me a comradely grin, gently loosening Oberon's claws from her velvet skirt.

"Oh, I wasn't ever Anthony's client; you might say it was more the other way round. Dead keen on him I was myself, I won't deny. He's really *got* something, hasn't he? That damn-your-eyes look of his, and the way he suddenly frowns at you and then smiles; oh, I can tell you I pretty near busted my heart when he told me he wasn't coming to see me no more. That was when *she* died, of course; really changed him, that did, and you couldn't blame him. She meant the whole world to him really; the other was just a bit of fun-and-games."

"But—then, when was this?"

"Oh, before. Quite a long time ago, it seems," she sighed. "We were ever so careful. Geoff never knew a thing about me and Anthony. We used to meet in London; and then only in ever such quiet, out-of-the-way spots."

My whole world seemed to be loose on its foundations. That *Anthony*—the loving, utterly devoted husband—that *Anthony*—

"You see, what makes me miserable now," went on Teddy, leaning forward with such earnestness that she dislodged Oberon, who huffily scrambled off her lap, "what makes me feel so bad is that I know how miserable he is, and there's nothing I can do about it. He doesn't see me any more now. Ever. And I can't go after him. It wouldn't do, you can see that. Anyway, it wouldn't help. He never loved me. I wasn't such a fool as to think he did."

"Then—?"

"Oh well, I reckon it was because of her," Teddy explained. "Rosie. Delicate, she was. He used to talk about her such a lot, felt responsible for her, he did, more as if she was his daughter. He didn't want her to get pregnant, the doctors said it might kill her. And he's a Roman, they both were, took those things seriously." Teddy stopped and considered and then said, "I'm not against taking things seriously; some things you have to."

"So—when he was seeing you—you think that was just—"

"That's right. So as to keep him from plaguing Rosie too often."

I almost said drily, "I hope she was grateful," but stopped myself in time. Quite plainly there had been no cloud on the relationship of Rosie and Anthony; whether she knew, or didn't know, about Teddy Marshman was none of my business.

"But weren't you taking the most frantic risk? Both of you?"

"So far as I was concerned, it was worth it," said Teddy briefly. She took a swig of her ginger-and-whisky, then added reflectively, "For him—well—I dunno. He had to have somebody. And I was as good as the next."

I thought she was placing an unfairly low value on herself. I imagined that the majority of men would give their eyeteeth to have her speak of them as she spoke of Anthony. She leaned forward again.

"Do you know, I've waited, sometimes, for an hour, two hours, just to see him walk past the end of the road? I've watched, in Victoria, just to see him go through the barrier and get on the train to Affton. Sometimes I phone his number, just to hear him say hallo. Then I hang up. Oh, and he looks so thin, now! He's getting so grey on his temples! He's eating his heart out, anyone can tell that. And I can't do nothing for him. I believe he thinks her death was sent as a punishment on him."

"He *couldn't* think something so idiotic."

I took a gulp of my own drink, feeling quite dazed with all this knowledge. Then I recalled that Teddy had come with the intention of asking me to do her a favour. Did she—I flinched slightly at the thought—did she want me to carry some message for her to Anthony?

As if my thought had made itself heard, she gave me her clear look again and said quietly, "Of course it was you he always wanted. I knew that."

"I???"

"Don't you see? You and I do look alike. Since you've been on TV lots of my friends have commented on the likeness. Anthony did too. He often talked about you then. He said once if you put on a bit of weight, you and I could be sisters."

"Except that *you* are beautiful."

"A lot of that's just knowing about make-up, dear, and having good clothes. *You* don't dress to make the best of yourself, if you don't mind my saying so. No, he thought the world of you. You know how a man says a woman's name when he feels that way? Another girl can always tell." She glanced at a little gold watch shaped like a raspberry, set with brilliants. "Oh, my good lord! Ten to nine! I'd better put on my roller skates and roll away. Well—that's what I came to say, ducky. You won't take it the wrong way, will you? When I saw you sitting in the train, I thought, she doesn't look one to take offence. Why don't I try? I'd do anything for Anthony, I honestly would. But don't you tell him anything about this, mind! I'd curl up and die if he was to know I'd been saying these things to you—I would! This is to be just between us two, right?"

"Yes, of course. I don't—I really don't know exactly what it is you want me to do for Anthony—"

But of course I did know perfectly well. Teddy said, "Anything, dear, anything you did to cheer him up would be *something*. Wouldn't it?"

I said, "I'd very much like to see *you* again. Could you come round and have a meal here some evening?"

"Oh, I don't know, love." She looked very doubtful. "Don't you live with your aunt? *She* wouldn't want me around."

"On the contrary, I'm sure she'd like you very much."

"Well I dunno. We'll see."

"Give me a call, anyway. Here's my number." I handed her a little Cuisine Churchill card. Catering for All Occasions.

"Pretty, isn't it?" She eyed it with professional appraisement, then, beseechingly, "You *will* think over what I said?"

"Yes, of course I will. Only—" Only the strange thing is, I thought, I don't want to see him. I don't love Anthony. I can't say I dislike him—but oh, the reluctance, the doubt, the apprehension that I feel!

Teddy gave me a sudden anxious look. "You already got a bloke, maybe? A boyfriend? Someone who's going to get worried if you start seeing Anthony? I dunno why I didn't think of that. But your hubby died, didn't he? A long time ago?"

"No, no," I reassured her. "No one's going to be upset. I haven't a boyfriend."

Only Hugh, far away in the Mediterranean. And he's not mine.

I made my approaches to Anthony with as much hesitation, ignorance, and timidity as the first convict to the first kangaroo. Would he hurtle off into the distance, never to be seen again; or turn and kick me?

In truth, I was a coward. I just plain didn't fancy the situation. I had had a very particular feeling for Rosie—the innocent angel—and the thought that Anthony had already, in a manner of speaking, betrayed her, and with me, as far as intention went—if Teddy was to be believed—stuck in my craw. I didn't like it a bit. Never mind his high motives and all that; after all, Rosie *had* become pregnant in the end, anyway; she had *wanted* to. And it wasn't the pregnancy that killed her, so if Anthony was indulging in guilt feelings, they were wide of the mark. And if he believed his God had killed Rosie to punish Anthony for taking Teddy Marshman to bed, then I wanted no part of such a God, and thought the worse of Anthony for believing in Him. The whole thing was a nasty tangle, and I'd just as soon keep clear of it. Also, I didn't enjoy the feeling that I was already implicated, quite innocently. It is not generally my role to be wrongfully accused, so I suppose I felt it all the more unjust. Not that people were accusing me! If they had been, I could have turned and justified myself.

On the whole, I did believe Teddy. I had liked her a lot. And I felt confident in her honesty. After all, what axe had she to grind? The feeling in her voice when she spoke of Anthony was deep and genuine.

I wondered if Anthony knew of her present whereabouts, of the change in her situation. Did he keep up with Affton gossip, perhaps through Nurse Kelly, who still housekept for him?

Feeling I needed more briefing, I called Teddy and invited her round to a meal. She came, but reluctantly.

"It's not that I don't enjoy seeing you, duck, and this hotpot or whatever it is, is fabulous, but I think it's best if we don't meet. I just don't want the slightest chance of Anthony getting to know, and suspecting we've been putting our heads together. Men don't like to think they have to be managed. They do, of course, but you have to do it so they don't guess. That was where I went wrong with Geoff. I didn't take enough trouble. I'd know better now."

"Are you sorry? Would you go back if you could?"

She considered, and said seriously, "No. No, I wouldn't. Not that I didn't enjoy running the old Monmouth, and maybe one day I'll do something like that again—but you can't go back, really, can you? And I'd never stand living with Geoff again, even if he'd have me. He was too bossy. Just from pure bossiness! If you started to do something without asking him first, he'd want it all done differently, every time. Only to prove he knew best. It was like humouring a three-year-old in a temper tantrum. Took a lot out of you, really. I do enjoy having my own way now, I can tell you!"

"Why *do* men have to be managed?"

"They're delicate," said Teddy. "Like racehorses. Selected for speed, all long spindly legs and temperament. Temper, too. The way they're always quarrelling with each other! Women don't row like that. Women know they've got to get on with the job."

"So how did men get that way?"

"Just bred like it," said Teddy. "Faster and faster. Something's got to go. You gain something, you lose something. Think of those fancy breeds of dogs with no kneecaps and no eyesight and no sense of smell. Geoff used to keep King Charles spaniels. Horrible little beasts—lazy and delicate and bad-tempered."

I considered this view of society. On the whole it seemed to be a valid one.

"What can we do about men, then?"

"Don't ask *me*," said Teddy. "I'm no genius. Keep 'em fed, like you do, and humour them, I suppose. And tidy up the mess when they start throwing things."

I went back to our particular problem.

"Does Anthony know where you are living now?"

"Doesn't know if I'm still alive," said Teddy. "Or care, I daresay. We haven't met since just after she died. And through my divorce I kept well clear of him. Tell you the truth, didn't want Geoff sniffing in his direction. Now, I want to go on keeping clear of him. Like I said, I don't want my name coming up. So just forget I ever told you all this, will you? Forget you ever saw me."

"Easier said than done."

"Oh, go on! There's such a lot happening in your life. The TV shows, and you got to meet the Queen, didn't you, and all those Prime Ministers at the conference? Don't tell me there's any problem forgetting old Teddy!"

She snugged herself into a prune-coloured cape with gold clasps and stared into the mirror, carefully, professionally, inspecting her face, which looked as delectable as a peach gateau.

"Now, don't you go calling me again. You cheer up Anthony. That's your little job," said Teddy, and departed, waving a beautifully gloved hand.

But I didn't like this kind of manipulation, this calculation. I have done plenty of crazy, stupid things in my time, but at least they have been spontaneous, extempore. I would never have thought of trying to manage George, or Hugh, or Dan, or Rico, or Reggie the flagellant, or Arthur the stockbroker, or any of the rest. They had their ways, I had mine, and we respected one another's independence. I like honesty; I disliked the notion of keeping something concealed from Anthony. Something I knew about him that he didn't know I knew.

Still, I had given my word to Teddy. And, in any case, I thought, why am I flying into such a fidget? If he's all frozen up inside, as Teddy suggests, maybe I'll never get close enough for any of this to apply. And maybe that will be best.

I finally managed to catch him on the telephone one evening after work, and invited him round to lunch at Watch Cottage, saying I wanted to ask his professional advice.

"Can't you come to my office?" He sounded tired, brusque, wholly uninterested in me and my problems. "I've a terrible lot on hand just now."

"It's only five minutes' walk, Anthony, and I can have lunch waiting so you needn't waste any time." And it will be a better one than you usually get, I thought. "The point is, I want you to *see* the problem, which is right here, outside the window."

"Oh, very well." His acceptance was anything but gracious. I half thought he would fail to turn up. But he did arrive, rather late, and looking both tired and irritable. I had a frosted jug of drink waiting, vodka and cucumber, which Rose used to mix for him, and he drank a glass of it thirstily, without comment.

We sat in silence. I was in no hurry to unload my problem, and Anthony looked as if he could do with an insulating period of quiet. I thought what a disagreeable task, on the whole, lawyers and doctors have to perform: perpetually mending holes, attempting to put right people's stupid mistakes. Legal systems—we never realise what a spider's web surrounds us until we get entangled, infringe some bit of the code; we are like children playing hopscotch in a minefield.

It's easy to be a pioneer: to buzz off into the wilderness, abandon all your dismal old responsibilities, and projects that have gone wrong, to break ground in a new environment where nothing matters except keeping alive, making use of what comes to hand, extemporising. Anybody can enjoy that! You pinch land from the poor aborigines, and probably get a government grant as well. Maybe end your days in a blaze of glory as governor or viceroy of the captured territory. All that is pure fun. Enclosing new land is triumphant—but mending old walls is a bore. Few people enjoy dealing with recurrent problems, stopping in the same place and knowing that next year all the pipes will want mending. That's what lawyers and doctors do for us, when our affairs keep going out of order.

Is that why the world is in such a mess, I wondered. Because there are no unexplored bits left for people to go and be pioneers in?

Downstairs my kitchen tape recorder shouted, "Lunch ready in three minutes," and I told Anthony, "We eat in the kitchen for comfort and speed. Bring your drink, and the jug, if you want more. Or there's wine."

I had made a fish pie, remembering that it was Friday and that Anthony still chose to observe the fast, though restrictions for Catholics had been relaxed in this respect. Shrimp, turbot, and mushrooms were contained under a delicate buttery crust of mashed potato and accompanied by tomatoes grilled with fresh basil.

"Thank you for remembering my popish proclivities," said Anthony, and the atmosphere thawed a little.

"Garlic rolls ready now," gently reminded the tape recorder, and I removed them from the oven.

"That's an ingenious device you have there," Anthony observed. "I didn't know such things existed. Where did you get it?"

"I invented it, I think; had a man make it for me. It's an adaptation of an ordinary tape recorder and a kitchen timer. We use one in our office kitchen too. When you have a lot of cooking processes going on simultaneously, just one timing device that lets out a single ping isn't a lot of use. You can't tell if that means take out the bread or add more butter to the sauce or stir the jam. So we use these tape-timers, record our messages in advance as we need them. It can be very handy when two or three people are working together and perhaps going in and out; we can leave instructions for each other. Or, when I am by myself, I often use it for recording steps in a new recipe while I work. One can't write, one's hands are all greasy and covered with fish scales. You know," I added doubtfully, because it seemed probable that Anthony, a thoroughgoing prototype English male, who left culinary activities strictly to his womenfolk, did not know at all, "you know how, when you are cooking, you get some spur-of-the-moment idea; you toss in half an avocado that happens to be lying around, or the dregs of a bottle of port or a square of chocolate, or some chicken gravy; and then, later, you can't remember what it was that made the dish taste particularly delicious. Or particularly foul, of course, it can work in reverse. 'I'm putting orange peel in the scrambled eggs,' somebody records, and somebody else later adds, 'Well, never do it again, they tasted quite disgusting.'"

I ran to a halt, suspecting that I had sounded facetious and silly. But Anthony, continuing hungrily to fork up his fish pie, merely remarked, "You ought to take out a patent. Perhaps you'd make a fortune."

"Well if I ever decide to, I'll come to you for advice."

Silence fell again, a more relaxed silence this time. The day was a fine one; lozenges of sun came through the ell window. For some reason I thought of *We Are Seven*: Wordsworth's little cottage girl taking her little porringer to eat supper by the graves of her dead brother and sister. I peopled my comfortable kitchen with George, Rose, Dan, Ferdi Kundera, and Ingrid Christ. What a very different occasion this lunch would be if they were all here: Dan would instantly fling himself into literary argument with George, Rosie would distil heavenly kindness to Ferdi the foreigner; Ferdi would be humming bits of Telemann, George would go off to look at the bookshelves. And Ingrid Christ—what would she be doing? Reciting her poems into my kitchen recorder?

> *"My sea-green couch I shared with seven lovers,*
> *From three of them lighthearted took my leave,*
> *But four I grieve.*
>
> *Already, see, the boughs of May are gilding*
> *and strew a shroud along the tidy glade*
> *where they are laid . . ."*

Death has a whirlpool, suction effect; when people that you know die untimely, some part of you is pulled after them. Or part of them remains with you; Freud says, doesn't he, that you introject your dead friends and relations, haul them in and carry them inside you in the womb of your subconscious. I don't go along with Freud over hypotheses like penis envy (who would want one of *those*, for pete's sake, always going wrong at the crucial moment, the most inept bit of plumbing ever invented?); or about the Oedipus complex (Freud ought to have known my father), but he really hit the nail on the head in his essay on mourning and melancholia. Hardy carried his dead wives with him like knapsacks. We contain one another like a series of wooden babushkas, each inside the other, back, back, and back to the earliest ancestor of all.

Anthony declined cheese or dessert. He had lost weight, I noticed, and was smoking far too heavily.

I set coffee on to percolate, fixed the timer, and suggested we should move back upstairs to get the benefit of the view.

"What's this problem of yours, then?" inquired Anthony, without enthusiasm, walking over to put his dirty plate on the draining board.

"Right in front of you," I said. The window over the kitchen sink had a view up over the Castle Mound. At present there were some eighteen pigs to be seen, like fat black slugs, or outsize maggots, scooping and sloshing around on the muddy hillside among the relics of the tattered thorn trees.

I opened the window, and in came a reek of pig stench, which is sickly, like carrion gone sweet with decay.

"Feugh!" said Anthony. "Shut the window again quick, for heaven's sake."

"If it's like this now, in cool spring weather, what do you think it will be like in hot summer? Besides, see what they are doing to the hillside. It used to be so green and pretty. Now it looks like Vimy Ridge. I asked the police if it constituted a nuisance, but they said I'd have to get at least five other people to complain. And mine are the only windows that look this way. Though you'd think the people down the hill would be getting the smell. There must be some restriction about keeping pigs in a built-up area, surely?"

Anthony's face, I noticed, had, by now, assumed a withdrawn, cold, calculating expression.

"Unfortunately," he said—my heart dropped at his tone—"I know who has taken a lease of that land. Presumably the pigs belong to him—"

"Oh really, who is it?"

"It's Marshman, the landlord of the Monmouth Hotel. The land runs right down to the allotments at the back of the Monmouth car park."

"Oh, lord," I said, utterly dismayed. Such a possibility had never occurred to me. The width of Monmouth Street and the big trees along it tend to prevent one from noticing how sharply it curves. Geoffrey Marshman, husband of Teddy; yes, I could see that might be extremely awkward. My illicit knowledge about Anthony's affair with Mrs. Marshman seemed to clatter inside me like a pair of castanets. I almost expected the tape recorder to give out a banshee squawk, let out a poltergeist rap.

"He's a most difficult man, by all accounts," said Anthony. "Flies off the handle at the least thing. Bears grudges. Can be very unpleasant. Even if, legally, you had a good case, I think it might be decidedly ill-advised to take issue with him. Or at least, you should give it a great deal of careful thought first. He could make your position in the town quite nasty if he became your enemy; in his position, as landlord of the Monmouth, he's friendly with half the council."

Now I stood wrestling with conflicting impulses. The combative part of me naturally wished to shout, Like hell he could! Just let him try, that's all! Why should he be allowed to keep his filthy pigs practically in my backyard?

But I thought of Teddy Marshman, thought of Rosie, and stifled my outrage. Obviously the very last thing Anthony would wish was any action that might involve him personally in a collision with Geoffrey Marshman; however carefully that old connection had been concealed, there might, at the time, have been some hint, some suggestion; it would be like carrying a lighted taper into a coal mine, for me, with Anthony as my lawyer, to start litigation against the aggrieved husband. Indeed I wished heartily that I had never sought Anthony's advice on the subject; I felt I had left myself out on a limb.

How in the world, I wondered, looking at Anthony's arrogant, frowning face, how *could* you have been so crazily reckless as to embark on an affair with the wife of a man like that? In your own hometown? And you a lawyer? Then it struck me what a triumph of efficiency, not to say duplicity, the participants had achieved, in that the secret *had* been kept, apparently with total success. When Marshman divorced his wife, the corespondent named had been an insurance salesman from Leeds. Teddy, it seemed, had become careless at covering her tracks, once Anthony had gone. Or perhaps, once Anthony had gone, she no longer cared.

Old Miss Crutchley next door, a fervent reader of the Affton *Gazette*, and my landline to the town gossip, had told me a few of the details.

"Used to stay at the White Rock Hotel in Hastings they did, bold as brass! And she a mother of three little girls. Geoff Marshman was so mad, they say, he went after her with a carving knife."

Perhaps the salesman from Leeds had been Teddy's way of escape from an intolerable situation. Did Anthony ever think of her now? Ask himself what had become of her? Miss her?

I thought of Teddy saying, "He used to talk about you. Another girl can always tell." I could see no manifestation in him now of that feeling, and, on the whole, I was relieved. If he had once nourished some kind of fancy for me, it probably petered out, as such fancies do from lack of nourishment, at the time of Rosie's death. Which set me free—did it not?—from any responsibility for his well-being.

"Coffee coming up," reminded the tape, and I put the pot on a tray with cups and said to Anthony, "Forget the pigs. Don't give them another thought. Of course I'd no idea they belonged to

Marshman. I've heard he's a most bloody-minded man. I certainly don't want to raise a lot of dust trying to prove that he's committing a nuisance. I'll try to learn to love them."

Of course I had no such intention, but my main aim, now, was to keep Anthony out of the affair.

"Bring the sugar if you want any," I said, and mounted the stairs thinking that I would try the Conservation Society, the Historical Society, the Botanical Society—there must be some group of people in town who found the pigs as objectionable as I did. First, though, I would write a polite, straightforward letter to Marshman himself—it did no harm to begin directly; only if that failed would I apply deviousness and diplomacy.

Upstairs in the drawing room I poured coffee and remembered Rosie sitting, drinking apple juice and talking to Aunt Thisbe, in the chair where Anthony now sat. Why couldn't I tell Anthony how miserably I still missed Rosie, how desperately sorry for him I felt, how I pined for George, what a perilous lonely affair life seemed to me, every one of us cast away, swimming solitary, struggling for survival among huge breakers in a stormy sea? Why couldn't Anthony and I condole with one another, offer consolation to each other, instead of sitting and exchanging stiff conversation like strangers?

I wished that we were in a hayfield somewhere, far from human habitation. Conversation is always so much easier in a hayfield.

Anthony glanced at his watch.

"Oh, there's another thing," I said, and told him about George's will, and how I wanted the money he had given me added to Chris's Marine Studies Foundation. Anthony seemed mildly surprised that George had left me a bequest, but made a couple of notes and said he would deal with the matter. Then he rose to go and I did not try to detain him.

At the front door he thanked me politely for the delicious lunch.

"Come again, any time," I told him. "I'm nearly always here on Fridays. You know you're always welcome."

"No, it's kind of you, but I'd better not," he said. "People talk, you know. Gossip gets around amazingly fast in a town like this; you'd be surprised. We both of us have positions to consider. Well, you may not mind, perhaps—though you ought; but I can't afford to get talked about in that way. Too bad, but there it is."

The smile with which he concluded this brief lecture was a mere flicker; it hardly reached his cheekbones, let alone his eyes. Then he made a kind of saluting gesture and walked off down the steep hill, avoiding the gaze through lace curtains of inquisitive, censorious neighbours, left, right, eyes straight ahead; and left me speechless, quite at a loss, on the doorstep.

9

That strain I heard was of a higher mood . . .

How little I personally know of the wisdom of the ages. What a tiny fraction of all that garnered lore has been inherited by me. Sometimes I feel an ignorant worm as I scurry through a library on my way to Literature or Domestic Economy and realise the immensity, the sheer bulk, of Science, Art, Philosophy, Theology, Foreign Languages, and all those other disciplines unread to right and left; envisage all the other libraries in the world, the languages, alive and dead, that are unplumbed enigmas so far as I am concerned, the histories and ethnologies in which I am utterly unlearned, the unfamiliar arts, the unopened classics. Somehow, it is true, I manage to coast along without the benefit of all this knowledge; read a few books, hold a few conversations, cook a few meals. So where does wisdom actually come in? How is it acquired? Who uses it, and for what purpose?

These thoughts returned to me as I knelt among George's books, helping Chris to crate them up. *Si monumentum requiris, circumspice*, I thought, bundling up Latin, Greek, Hindu, Hebrew, Dante, Cervantes, Villon, Montaigne, Bacon, Heidegger, Goethe, Icelandic sagas, Levi-Strauss, Beowulf, Plutarch, and Darwin. The lightest reading in the heap appeared to be the novels of Flaubert and Henry James. And, of course, Jane Austen. Chris was donating the lot to London University Library; she had her own books in her own study. She planned to divide the house and rent out a self-contained portion.

Dealing with a dead person's belongings is a dreadful task. I had been let off lightly, I now realised, by Dan, with his camp bed and tin trunk of papers.

Elly and I had urged Chris to wait a while, not to rush at the business; intangible strings within one slowly begin to unloose, after varying periods of time have elapsed. Now, the inner voice murmurs, now the clothes can go; now the collection of shells and pine cones; now the books, now the letters . . . Now the guitar.

But Chris would not wait and be governed by such natural laws; rushing at grief in a hurried, abortive attempt to expel the grisly phenomenon, to be done with it, put it behind her, turn her mind away, she let herself in for a peck of trouble later.

I thought there was something odd, strained, about her when I arrived at the Highgate house to help deal with George's things. For a start, she had cooked me an elaborate lunch, not at all a customary thing for Chris to do; secondly, the house, or at least the kitchen, was in a state of frigid, unnatural cleanliness. Chris always did have a kind of demonic, obsessional tidiness; she lays objects in systems of mysterious order, understood only by her, tomatoes arranged in lines, four teaspoons marshalled on either side of a candlestick, pencils under the clock, scissors inside an old glove. Everything seems neat, disciplined, and clean at first sight; it is only when you look closer that you notice the coating of dust, the lack of any rational plan.

But on this occasion the place really did seem clean by anyone's standards, and Chris herself, thin, brown, and tense, was discernibly a little drunk.

During lunch she behaved in an extremely distrait manner and, after the meal, began to peck about in a hopeless way among the mammoth stacks of George's gramophone records, all those piles of music that he used to love, dumb now, locked up, turned to mere sculptural forms; Chris hardly ever listens to music when she is by herself, she said she would keep just a few and give the rest away. But I could see that, at this rate, months might go by while she tried to make up her mind.

"Why don't you leave it a while, Chris?"

"Because I want this room clear."

"Well, then, why don't you go through the piles systematically—"

"Don't hurry me!" she snapped. "I have to do it in my own way."

"Of course. I only thought—"

"Well, don't think here! Go and do your bloody thinking in the kitchen. At least *that's* civilised enough for you. It should be. I sweated my guts out this morning cleaning it up to your standards of housewifely perfection."

"*Chris!* For heaven's sake!"

Now I understood her feverish state of exhaustion. I was aghast.

I have sometimes felt the need to make sure that my house is looking its best for someone—haven't we all? But to think that anybody—let alone my best friend—would feel it needful to do so for *me* was a shock, a horrible one.

"You shouldn't have wasted your time—and shopping and cooking that lunch too—"

"Well you were coming to help me with this vile job, weren't you? It was the least I could do," said Chris tremblingly, and burst into tears.

I threaded my way among the canyons of records and hugged her, smearing her face with grime.

"You are a total idiot! What do I care if your kitchen is inches deep in grease, if you prefer it that way? I lived with you, didn't I? My housewifely standards never seemed to bother you in Beaufort Street."

But it was true that many of her habits, then, had driven me to a point of suppressed frenzy. "I'll just leave these to soak," she used to say hopefully, late at night, putting an immense, unco-ordinated pile of dirty dishes and pots and pans into the kitchen sink, immersing them in cold water, which would do no good at all, then going off to bed. Who would ultimately wash that lot I always knew full well, even if it had been Chris and her friends who had eaten off them. Once in a while, Chris would languidly pass a carpet sweeper back and forth across the sitting room rug;

that was about the extent of her housework. Did this, I now wondered, continuing to hug and comfort her, did this aspect of our life in Beaufort Street play any part in my precipitate marriage to orderly shipshape Dan with his tin trunk and deck chair? I could love Chris more comfortably from a distance where her intellect shone clear and her personal idiosyncrasies (such as that of leaving the communal sitting room continually festooned with damp underwear) were of no consequence.

"Stop crying now, it doesn't help. Plugs up your nasal passages. Come along back to your dazzling kitchen and let's have some brandy, and then we'll absolutely tear into those records and get the job done. I brought my car, I can take them round to the centre."

"Okay," said Chris, sniffing. But over the coffee and brandy she returned obsessively to the subject.

"George thought I was a slut, too."

"He did not!"

"Yes he did—because he came from one of those European traditions where the women are always thrashing the feather bed out of the window. He thought all English habits were pretty squalid, as a matter of fact. George and I," said Chris, "suffered from the tip-of-the-iceberg syndrome."

"Hnh?"

"Oh, you know: you meet a representative of some other group —French or Chinese or musicians or cooks—you fall in love with them because their qualities seem interestingly different from yours; you aren't aware that what seem individual traits to you are really characteristic of the whole group. You think the things they say are charmingly sweet and funny, not realising that whole populations of huge geographical areas talk that way. It's like buying some wonderful novelty in a market—and then you go on and realise that there are dozens of others on all the other stalls, just the same as yours—sometimes it takes years to find out—"

"Oh, come off it, Chris! I see what you mean, up to a point, but, damn it, you and George loved each other devotedly. He thought you were one of nature's prodigies, he used to talk of your intellect in a tone of wondering reverence, as if, as if he had picked up a priceless pearl lying in the middle of a public right-of-way—"

"Yes, but then at the end," she said, gulping, "his *real* feelings came out. He wouldn't let me come near him at one point; said my feet had a horrible smell of wet felt—"

"Oh, Chris! You know he wasn't normal for those last months—"

I thought how couples so often seem, at the start, to open out each other's lives, then later they narrow again as each retreats to his own sphere, blocking the other's exits.

Chris said, "George used to *look* at me in a devastatingly awful way, with his eyes narrowed, saying nothing. I couldn't stand it at one point, I left him for a bit—"

"I never knew that!"

"Oh," she said, sniffing, "it was only for three weeks. But I couldn't bear to be away from him so I came back again. And what frightened me was that he honestly didn't seem to notice that I'd been gone." Her eyes swam with tears again, they looked huge, like great grey precious stones. Angrily she took off her glasses. She had on several occasions tried contact lenses but had too many mishaps with them, flushing them down the john, letting the vacuum suck them up, dropping them in the soup. She always returned to spectacles. "George led a ghost life for the last six months," she said, rubbing at her thick lenses. "He had no firsthand experience at all. He read no books, went to no plays—only read reviews. Didn't meet people; only talked to them on the phone. Read news digests, not even the papers. I asked why, he said he knew enough about the world, knew his friends too well, they had no surprises left for him."

"He knew that time was getting short."

"He took longer and longer to make up his mind about anything."

"Like old Oberon."

I thought of the old cat's shadow, behind the glass door. Did the shadow of George linger somewhere about this house, still trying to decide what to take with him, what to leave behind?

"He'd start for the office sometimes, in the mornings, then come home again and go to bed. No reason given. Next day he'd go off just as usual. I asked him once if he felt ill, and he flew into a rage. Told me not to ask stupid questions."

"Of course he was ill."

But I spared a shade of sympathy for George. I knew how fatally inept Chris could be when in the presence of illness. She would come and stand uneasily in the door, as far from the bed as possible, while the sufferer tossed with raging flu or lay crippled with migraine; unimaginative, well-meaning, intelligent, but baffled, she would ask, "Is there anything you want?" in a tone expecting the answer no, hoping that the illness would go away of its own accord.

Perhaps it was as well they never had children. Though I remembered, with a pang, the occasion when George had told me about that.

"I am sterile, you see, Clytie. Too bad, eh? There will never be a tribe of little Georges to play with the Aqua game. When I first informed Chris of this, poor girl, she cried all night."

His face had worn a strange, recollecting, meditative smile which, at the time, had troubled me deeply. Had he, I sometimes wondered, felt, always, basically unsure of Chris, felt that in the tidy, unromantic, professionally arranged process of their marriage, she, the essence of her, had somehow escaped him, was only to be pinned down by such a thrust as he had dealt her with this piece of news?

When we had finished sorting the gramophone records and I'd taken a load round to the old people's centre, we went on to papers. Here, sifting through a huge disordered heap in George's study, I came across an Ingrid Christ poem called *Sleigh-ride*. I had noticed its absence when he returned the poems, but had a carbon and so merely replaced it. Now I wondered if George's retaining it was accident or intention. It was an early poem, too abrupt, I thought.

"She certainly was obsessed with death, that girl," said Chris, reading it over my shoulder.

> *Now we are off*
> *streaking downhill*
> *the going will*
> *be rough*
>
> *Tumble aside*
> *die now? or wait,*
> *to terminate*
> *the ride?*
>
> *No time for breath*
> *no stopping place.*
> *End of the race*
> *is death.*

"Well, I suppose we all have our manic depressive side."

"But she was a *woman*," objected Chris, as if females ought to be above such frailties.

"So what? There have been female suicides."

"Precious few, compared with males. Just as well, too," said Chris, stuffing an armful of old envelopes into the sack we were using for wastepaper. "If *we* weren't around to look after the male sex, they'd hardly survive long enough to procreate. That's the trouble, Clytie; we know it and they know it. We *don't need them.* Oh, I know, they used to be hunters and so on, but that's long gone by. Do you suppose men will become a luxury the human race will decide it can't afford? Once sperm banks are established, maybe the poor things will all be castrated after the optimum age of potency; that would soon put a stop to wars, wouldn't it?"

"You ought to be writing science fiction," I said, but her tone comforted me; it was like the firm gritty feel of third gear under one's hand when driving; you know you can take corners with beautiful precision and there's no chance of going out of control. I felt she had begun finding her way back to normal, though there might be a long way yet to go. Her views recalled Teddy

Marshman; I thought they'd enjoy each other's company and wondered if it would be possible to arrange a meeting.

"What's become of Anthony Roche?" Chris inquired out of the blue. She has always been able to intercept my thought in this disconcerting way. "Do you see him much since his wife died? Are you managing to cheer him at all?"

"No, I hardly see him. He's very elusive. I don't think I can do anything for him."

We went upstairs to deal with George's clothes; his funny foreign checked jackets, pink-striped shirts, exotic ties, saddle shoes, and trousers, which, even when their provenance was unquestionably Marks & Spencer, seemed to take on a Magyar look as soon as George wore them. During all his ten years in England he had never assimilated in the least, nor even troubled to assume protective colouring; he simply learned his way about. I noticed Chris bury her face in the jacket he wore most often; then she briskly bundled it up with the others.

"Perhaps domiciles aren't really important?" she said.

"I think they are to us."

"Nest building. I couldn't bear to leave this house, I must say."

"I couldn't bear to leave Watch Cottage."

"You'd better watch out that it doesn't start invading your persona like Shadie Nooke, or whatever Enid Blyton's house was called. I saw you on that revolting TV interview where the chap was being so coy about your kitchen and all its gadgets and cracking little boyish jokes into the tape recorder."

"Oh, God. I hoped none of my friends had seen that."

"Better your friends than your enemies," said Chris.

"Enemies?" I was startled. "Have I got any?"

"Oh, be your age, Clytie! Any successful person has enemies. Vanquished rivals. Sacked employees. People about whose rotten work you have been regrettably honest. I know three or four who'd like to murder me," said Chris with satisfaction, and recounted her latest skirmish with the Management Board. She seemed to have taken another step towards recovery.

But still, when it was time for me to go, I hated the thought of leaving her alone in that big, hollow house.

"Why don't you come down to Affton this weekend, Chris? You could do me a favour—drive down old Thisbe. She's coming to lunch on Friday with her chum, Asta Martineau. If you don't fancy the thought of lunch with the old girls you could drop Thisbe and take a picnic to the beach and come back later."

"Well, I'll think about it. Let you know in a couple of days." But she seemed quite attracted by the suggestion. She had taken three weeks' extra leave in order to arrange her affairs. "I'd like to see old Thisbe. I haven't seen her since that evening with George . . ."

"Don't wait too long to make up your mind," I said quickly. "Thisbe likes to have her plans established well in advance."

Again the shadow of George hovered near, and I went on, "Chris: maybe you should think of marrying again? You're only thirty-three."

"Another go at the Evelyn Farmer Agency?" She smiled, a small austere smile. "Or do you plan to marry me off to Anthony Roche?"

"Catholics are too complicated."

"Anyway"—she inflated her lungs in a great yawning sigh—"the answer is no. It's just too exhausting. I couldn't—just couldn't—go through all that again. I feel older than Machu Picchu as it is. I really put my heart into George. You know that."

"Yes, I do know that," I said gently, and went out to the car with a bundle of throw-away stuff I was taking to old Miss Crutchley for one of her perennial Congregational Church jumble sales.

On Wednesday Chris telephoned to say that she would bring Thisbe down on Friday but would leave the old ladies to enjoy their time together and take herself off to the beach as I suggested, arriving back at teatime.

The old ladies saw each other rarely enough so that my own main aim, also, was to leave them in peace together as much as possible, and, when in their company, to act as a kind of backstop, lobbing back balls that had gone astray. Though peace, of course, is hardly the right descriptive word; they generally went for each other tooth and claw. Thisbe considered herself a Liberal; Asta Martineau had been, for a number of years, the only female Labour M.P. in the House of Commons; "Red Asta" they used to call her, on account of her opinions and flaming mop of hair. The hair was now snowy white and she had long retired from professional politics but the opinions were as fiery as ever. Approaching her eighties, she looked like some volatile arachnid, small, skinny, with a face like a fishhook, dead white complexion, a voice that would still carry to the farthest back bench, and darklashed eyes that missed nothing. She and Thisbe had a wonderful time together, ragging one another like two elderly Marx sisters; and in between the slapstick the world got thoroughly discussed. Flitting around them with the crab salad and baked custard I longed for the temerity to immortalise their talk on my kitchen recorder.

"So then I gave that Nehru woman a piece of my mind and I told her—"

"Just as I was saying to Golda—"

"Of course his policies are hopeless in a country that size, and so undeveloped. What Maynard always used to say was—"

"When I was lecturing at Harvard last summer I said to Henry Kissinger—who, although he has a face like a garden trug, does possess a sort of intelligence—"

"Yes! And I found just the same state of affairs in Santiago—"

"No coffee, dear child. What we want now is our nap."

It was ritual that, after the meal, both old ladies retired for forty minutes, Thisbe to my bed, Asta to the sitting room couch, to repair their drooping heads and refurbish their powers of argument. Then they would hold another session, over Earl Grey and thin ginger biscuits, then I would drive Aunt Thisbe to her train, dropping Miss Martineau at her cottage in Saddlers Row on my way back.

While my guests were dozing, I seized the chance to whip the lunch plates into the dishwasher and make some notes for an Astronomers' Banquet. There would be little time to work during the weekend. I planned to take Chris for long healthful walks, and swim, if the English Channel and the weather permitted.

I was sitting in the tidy kitchen, inventing hors d'oeuvres—corn-and-shrimp? kidneys sautéed in butter and vermouth, on toast triangles? sour cream and walnut on rye bread impregnated with curry?—when the doorbell rang, short, sharp, and vigorous.

Chris back already?

I opened the front door with my finger halfway to my lips, ready to indicate that the somnolent tranquillity of the house must not yet be disturbed. But my caller was not Chris, and he plainly had every intention of disturbing the peace of Watch Cottage. It was Mr. Marshman, red-faced, bristling, and belligerent.

He stamped into my little hall without waiting for an invitation. He was a shortish, burly man, a couple of inches below Teddy in height, I guessed, with straight greasy black hair, brushed uncompromisingly away from his unimpressive brow, a round bullet head, florid complexion peppered over with dark stubble, angry eyes, and perceptible aura of gin-and-tonic. But I suppose a landlord has to drink with his customers. I glanced at my watch: three o'clock. He had come along after closing time.

I saw his sharp suspicious glance travel warily about the bare hall, through the arch to the neat kitchen, with notebook and papers on the table; evidently he thought he had caught me alone.

"Now see here," he opened at once, aggressively. "About that letter you wrote me. What d'you think you mean by it, eh? Telling me what to do with my own pigs! Who d'you think you are? Eh? You come down here—and just because you've been on television with those bloody ridiculous nancied-up recipes of yours, you think you've a right to throw your weight around, do you? Well, you're wrong, I can tell you, right here and now!"

I said, "I wasn't telling you what to do with your pigs, Mr. Marshman. I only asked, in what I hoped was a friendly and reasonable manner, if you knew what a mess they were making of the hillside, and if there was no other place, slightly farther away from people's houses, where it might be equally convenient for you to keep them?"

"You mind your own business and I'll mind mine, *Miss Chur-*

chill," he said, in a voice suggesting that he knew full well my name was really Lizzie Borden.

"I wonder if you'd mind speaking in a slightly lower tone—"

"I'll speak as I choose! And you'll listen! I'm not going to be told my business by a—"

"Mr. Marshman." I was beginning to grow annoyed. I hate that kind of bullying bad manners. "I haven't gone into the legal aspects of the matter yet. I hoped we might be able to settle the whole thing amicably, between neighbours. But if going to law is the only recourse—"

"Hah! Going to law! And I suppose you'll take the advice of your *friend*, Mr. High-and-Mighty Anthony Roche? When he comes round to visit you here on the q.t., eh? You better think again! I can tell people what goes on. Your name will be mud, so fast—and his too!"

"I can't imagine what you are talking about," I said icily, but with a hollow heart. Apparently Anthony's anxieties had been only too well grounded. Never underestimate the power of an English neighbour.

"There's some living in this street would understand quick enough," Marshman said. "So you'd better think again about interfering in my business. I'll keep those pigs there as long as I choose. Or you'll be sorry you ever began, and your friend Mr. Roche may be obliged to give up his practice and go abroad. I've a very good friend on the East Sussex *Courier*—"

I began to feel like the old lady in the Blitz who pulled the W.C. chain and the whole house fell about her ears. Geoffrey Marshman was certainly living handsomely up to his reputation for bloody-mindedness. Did he behave like this over every minor hitch in his daily existence, or had the juxtaposition of me and Anthony touched off some smouldering, long-buried half-formed suspicion that lay in him ready to explode? I couldn't feel too perturbed by his Dickensian threats; this was, after all, the twentieth century, in which widowers were presumed to be able to lunch at midday with respectable single ladies (or no, come to think, I was a widow, too, though not in the habit of regarding myself as such), unblackened by the evil tongue of calumny. I didn't really see any serious possibility of Marshman's organising a lynch mob to tar-and-feather Anthony or run me out of Affton Wells on a rail (however that is done); still, it was extremely disagreeable to encounter all this packet of spite and rage in my own front hall.

As Marshman uttered his threat about the East Sussex *Courier* I became aware of a kind of radioactive silence, a glacial air emanating from above. Marshman must have begun to sense its quality, too, for he stopped suddenly in mid-threat and looked upwards.

In the little hall of Watch Cottage the white stair rail described its rising oval twirl and then ran straight across half the upstairs landing, making a narrow gallery. On this gallery, over this rail, both old ladies were now leaning, side by side, heads cocked interestedly, like a bullfight audience, paying most heedful attention to the dialogue we had been exchanging. I wondered how long they had been there. It was hardly surprising that they had emerged; Marshman's voice would have roused Endymion from his postcoital nap.

"Hmm; blackmailing threats," remarked Aunt Thisbe. "What very disagreeable acquaintances you appear to have in this town, Clytie. Who is this belligerent person?"

"Oh, I know *him*," asserted Miss Martineau. "Yes, I know him *quite* well." She bore a decided resemblance to the Witch of Endor as she dispassionately surveyed the landlord of the Monmouth. Her remarkable black-fringed eyes looked like keyholes in her paper-white face. "Marshman. Geoffrey Marshman," she repeated thoughtfully. "His name came up several times when I used to sit on the bench here—possible suspension of licence, illegal activities after hours, that kind of thing. Yes . . . On a couple of occasions we decided to be lenient, I remember; perhaps mistakenly. But, let me see, yes; *much* more recently I heard some very discreditable tale, from an ex-colleague who is now working on investigations of V.A.T. fraud for the Customs and Excise people—"

Marshman turned a pale dirty-linen colour; his mouth fell open like an out-of-order stamp machine. He cleared his throat and said halfheartedly, "Now then: don't you try to threaten me, *madam!*"

"Oh, I wouldn't dream of doing such a thing." Miss Martineau's words fell on him like flakes of snow. "What *would* be the point of that, my good man? Any troubles you are due to encounter, you have indubitably brought upon your own head. If I were you, I think I would deal with one thing at a time; clear your affairs with the V.A.T. people first, before putting Miss Churchill to the trouble of suing you for slander."

"—— —— set of bloody —— —— conniving old women!" Marshman swung round on his heel and left my hall as fast as he had entered it, narrowly avoiding a collision with Chris, who had been just about to walk through the open door. He muttered something else as he passed her, which caused her mouth and eyes to open wide in amazed silent comment.

"What in the world goes on?" she asked, coming in. "He seemed more like one of *my* visitors than one of yours."

"That's the owner of the pigs behind the house," I said, shutting the door behind her. "He came here intending to make trouble, but Miss Martineau has very kindly put the fear of God into him."

"A most pestilential fellow," said Miss Martineau, pattering briskly down the stairs. "Always skirting around the law in one way or another. Now, I understand, he is almost certainly due for a jail sentence over his tax evasions. I feel sure he has no shadow of right to keep pigs on that hillside; indeed I believe the Conservation Society are already taking action against him."

Ungratefully, I wished that they had proceeded a bit faster; or that there was any chance of Marshman's jail sentence catching up with him in the very near future.

I had an uneasy feeling that, although Miss Martineau's intervention had put an end to the unpleasant scene, I had not heard the last of Geoffrey Marshman. And that, although old Asta meant it for the best, she might have done more harm than good.

Contrary to expectation, Chris and I spent a mild, peaceful, recollected weekend. We walked, we bathed in the choppy Channel, we listened to records, read the Sunday papers, talked, gossiped, reminisced. "Do you remember?" we said to each other. "Do you remember when George came back from the Bologna Book Fair with a hundred yards of sausage? Do you remember at Dartington when that ensemble went up on the roof and played the Mozart Divertimento Number 11 and we all danced on the lawn? Do you remember the silly pidgin-English songs Ferdi used to make up and we all sang the chorus? 'Please tender, Correct fare, And tell correct way to Trafalgar Square?'" "Do you remember how, when Caspar Monk's second book began selling so well, George took us to dinner at the Ritz, and was so disgusted with the food?" "Do you remember Dan's patron saints, St. Gothold and St. Withold? Do you remember when Dan brought you an enormous tree for your birthday, in a pot, and you didn't know where to put it?"

I had forgotten that tree. It died from lack of watering; but, in a way, I have it still.

"Will it be like this when we are old?" I said. "Only more so?"

"What I don't understand," said Chris, "is why we feel such acute happiness at all, if it is to be so transitory."

I thought, one love augments another. Love expands with use. Loving George, loving Hugh, has taught me more about Dan. My feeling for him was thinner, because I was younger. When we are young, our love is half narcissism. Now I would have a stronger feeling for Dan. Hearing that church bell striking the quarters, as I lay in bed with Hugh asleep beside me; that hit a root deep in the past, that taught me something about the bond that still attached me to dead-and-gone Dan.

Chris had brought with her a packet of condolence letters to answer, and I put in some time correcting the proofs of my new recipe book, *Half an Egg Onwards*, which gave suggestions for using up yolks when the whites had gone to furnish meringues, and similar predicaments.

On Sunday night, Chris drove me up to Ordnance Mansions. And she came in to help me unload a bundle of papers and a couple of casseroles.

"Stay and have a drink?" I suggested, wondering if I could persuade Teddy Marshman to come round. But Chris said she had better get back; she was expecting a call from George's partner, Conrad Cordwainer. Later I reflected that it was just as well I had not managed to secure Teddy for a cosy threesome; for, exactly as Chris was leaving, Anthony came storming to the door.

"*Anthony!*" To say I was startled would be a gross understatement. But surprise was not the main element. Horror would be nearer the mark. "What brings you to London on a Sunday?"

"You know perfectly well what brings me!" he said with stifled fury. He seemed hardly aware of Chris, who shrugged a little; her fine brows escalated towards her fair plume of hair, she contrived to convey by one expressive ripple of head and hands that, for a person who claimed to have no enemies, I appeared to receive more than my ration of irate males bursting through the door. "Good night, Anthony, good night, Clytie," she said quietly. "Thanks for the lovely weekend. I'll phone you tomorrow."

The door closed on her and left me with Anthony's wrath.

"What in God's name did you do to provoke that man? I hear he's been blackening my name to every customer of the Monmouth all weekend!"

"I wrote him a perfectly reasonable letter—"

"I could have *told* you that would be useless. I *did* tell you. Why in the name of all creation didn't you let well alone?"

"And enjoy twenty pigs belching in my kitchen window?"

"I talked to the Conservation Society about it," said Anthony furiously. "They were taking action. Why couldn't you have a little *patience?*"

"You never told me you'd done that."

I felt unjustly used. Was it my fault that old Asta Martineau had been there, to blow Marshman's indignation to white heat?

"Now people in the town will be saying exactly the sort of thing I didn't want them to say."

"Well," I said, "it won't be true, so you can take action for slander. You're a lawyer, you should know that."

10

Together both, ere the high lawns appeared
Under the glimmering eye lids of the morn
We drove afield . . .

That period of my life, with Anthony, was a stormy one. Odd, when you think how serene he and Rosie had always appeared together; but the serenity with Rosie had been achieved at some cost, and he had a lot of guilt and grief and *arrière-pensée* to unload.

"Of course, you had loved him all along," said Rabuse. "Such a *rapprochement* was bound to occur, sooner or later."

"Had I? *Was* it? It didn't feel at all like that to me. Before, I mean. I always found Anthony enraging. Efficient, but enraging. Clever at his profession, yes, that I grant you, but otherwise egotistic and exasperating: didactic, conceited, domineering, narrow-minded . . . The way he used to lay down the law to Rosie and tell her she was a bird-wit often drove me wild with irritation. Though I'm bound to say *she* didn't mind. No, there I don't agree with you. If I had loved him all along, the fact was remarkably well hidden from me."

"You yourself had a great deal of animus to unload, also," Rabuse went on placidly. "Eh, dear me, you English are a simple race. It was no wonder you fell in love."

Right from the start, I felt Anthony's secretiveness an intolerable strain. Now for the first time I found it easy to understand why no breath of scandal concerning him and Teddy Marshman had ever wafted abroad; he took obsessional care about our meetings, our joint activities, our partings; if we ate out together it was at the smallest, darkest, most unfrequented restaurants; we practically never went to plays or concerts together, never met in Affton. We went to obscure movies in flea-pit cinemas. Most often, he came to Ordnance Mansions, where he seemed to consider Aunt Thisbe at the other end of the long passage as a kind of chaperone or guarantee of respectability; and she regarded him with qualified approval.

We met late at night, parted early in the morning. We took walks in unfashionable quarters of London, unfrequented parts of the country; many a dusty and ill-arranged local museum did we visit on cold grey Saturday afternoons. Or we spent weekends abroad: Paris, Amsterdam, Bruges, minor French channel resorts, where we stayed at second-class hotels and ate some atrocious food.

One of the worst meals I have choked down in my entire life was on a pouring Sunday evening in some terrible Paris bistro; Anthony, as usual, looking for an out-of-the-way spot, had walked us northwards from the Gare du Nord and the rain suddenly came down in torrents, obliging us to bolt through the nearest open door; those stringy lamb chops and greasy string beans, masticated in the company of thirty Swiss Boy Scouts, remain embedded in my memory like a flint in chalk. The dessert that followed the chops was so terrible even the Boy Scouts wouldn't eat it.

All this concealment was very foreign to my nature. I didn't like it, didn't really see the point of it. We were both unattached, weren't we, solvent, consenting adults with no responsibilities to anybody? Our private life was our own affair.

I like rough textures. I like to brush through life, actively conscious all the way of the surface of what I pass: the gritty glass of the percolator cup as I scoop out coffee grounds with my fingers; old Oberon's frail ribs under the layer of thick fur; knobbed frozen earth of winter under my boot soles; the layers and layers of clean starched linen on a restaurant table; the rhythmic surge of a train carrying me somewhere; the scrunch of soapsuds. During my association with Anthony all these pleasures became some-how blurred; I had a nightmarish, anaesthetized sensation of slid-ing along in disguise, muffled, incognito. We saw each other, but we saw nothing else; we were travelling together but behind drawn curtains. And because we saw no one but each other, the image we received was distorted. It was the tip of the iceberg again, I suppose; we saw only one manifestation of each other.

When I grumbled to Anthony that what we did together, how we occupied our leisure time, was our own affair, he said, no, it wasn't; he had his reputation as a distinguished lawyer, rising man of affairs, prominent citizen of Affton, and character of unimpeachable probity on the legal scene to uphold. And I, he said severely, had my own credit to guard; if I wouldn't bear this in mind, he must do so for me; I was a TV personality, wasn't I, there was my talk of my receiving a decoration in next year's Honours List—or at any rate the year after—the public had their image of me as a charming little homely innocent gamine, in-variably hard at work tossing off omelets, popping casseroles into the oven, kneading dough, brewing pots of fragrant coffee.

"But if the image is false," I objected, "I don't see why I should have to sweat blood to sustain it? That seems totally dis-honest."

But Anthony, trained by Jesuits, was a much better arguer than I.

The fact is, I have never enjoyed argument. How I longed for George to come and state my point of view for me, put my side of the matter.

And so Anthony and I used to quarrel a fair amount, to relieve tension, I suppose, and Anthony to stifle his various unadmitted guilts.

Our relationship, built like some elaborately constructed sub-marine vessel, built with underwater disaster in mind, was honey-combed and divided by watertight bulkheads. There were more compartments and areas locked off from each other than even the Campus Tavern contained.

For instance, I never discussed my previous sexual experiences with Anthony; had no idea what he thought I had been doing all those eight years since Dan died. I did not mention my involvement with George, nor with Hugh—who was now spending more time in hospital than out.

Anthony, on his side, never mentioned Teddy Marshman. Indeed, so far as he knew, her very existence was unknown to me.

I had expected that, like poor Lionel the widower, he would want to talk about Rosie, but no, interestingly, he did not. Rosie, too, was locked away behind a watertight bulkhead. This I thought not healthy, and I used to talk about her, sometimes, myself; damn it, I loved Rosie dearly! But Anthony invariably disengaged himself from the topic. It was fairly plain that he was still angry, bitter, resentful about her death. He felt he had been wronged. By what, by whom? Better not ask. Well, he could hardly have continued to reside with Nurse Kelly as his housekeeper and not imbibe some of her vehement views on the subject. Poor darling Rosie, I could see that a halo was being forced on her innocent head; in a way I could sympathise with her, it was like my own unwanted aura of homely casseroles and baking bread.

At the back of Anthony's and my love-hate allure for each other lay a whole nasty tangle of unsorted, unacknowledged culpabilities and discords.

Another formidably undiscussed subject was what Anthony was going to do with the rest of his life. None of my business that was, he intimated curtly; he would deal with it himself, step by step, in his own time, in his own way.

The use of reading, Gibbon says somewhere, is to aid us in thinking. I have always disagreed with Gibbon over that; *he* may have used literature to help him think, but for me, often, and for most of the human race I reckon (since I have no reason to think myself unique) books can be a mind-stupefying drug, employed to banish thought, not to invoke it. When I am unhappy I can sink into a novel as into unconsciousness. Blessed *War and Peace*, thrice-blessed *Mansfield Park*; how many potential suicides have their pages distracted and soothed and entertained past the danger point?

I think at that time Anthony was using me in this way: as an escape from reality.

And I, poor booby, I was in love with him.

But we were happy; oh yes, oh yes, we were. Up to now I have expressed all the negative aspects of our relationship; but there were many positive ones too.

Despite his mania for concealment, Anthony was never mean. And he was a passionately honest man; fanatically so; stubborn, honourable, dogmatic, trustworthy, positive. He would make a terrific advocate, I thought, would be wonderful in court; and I used to tell him that he ought to become a barrister. My dear, what *can* you know about the matter, was his usual attitude; it took a lot of patience dealing with Anthony.

But in some areas he was prepared to learn from me. Rosie had been young, sweet as a nut, unworldly as a nun; just from sheer practical experience, I couldn't help knowing a good deal more than she had. I was older. And I knew a lot about happiness, kissing the winged joy as it flies, and all that; I did teach Anthony how to have fun, even in the rather unpromising corners where I was allowed my say-so. Some of our times together, no matter where, in dismal Flemish coastal town, wet English countryside, shoddy London suburb, were fraught with such intense joy that it later became intolerable to remember them. "And close your eyes in holy dread, For he on honeydew hath fed, And drunk the milk of Paradise." Such moments are not for common use or daily sustenance; one ought to be grateful that they do, occasionally, come one's way.

We lived in a kind of bubble. George's Bubble come true at last, I thought. This was what I had always expected romantic love to be but had no real belief in its existence: the adored voice on the telephone, at a time when one had not dared hope for a call; the notes, rare, so all the more precious; the imaginative, touching gifts; the heady excitement of those infrequent occasions when we were together in the company of others. I had told no one about Anthony, not even Chris. Aunt Thisbe guessed, of course, but said nothing directly.

One area that we did leave open for discussion, strangely enough, was Anthony's relationship with, and responsibility to, his God. About this he seemed unexpectedly carefree.

"But isn't it a mortal sin?" I asked, lying with him in some hotel bed, listening to cascades of Belgian carillons.

"Well . . . opinions differ. My confessor's rather open-minded about that sort of thing."

"Oh, so you do go to confession?"

"I have to," said Anthony, sounding surprised, "or I couldn't go to Mass."

"But then don't you have to promise sincerely not to do it again, before you can get absolution?"

"What I do promise, and with absolute sincerity, is that there will ultimately come a time when I will, of my own free accord, stop this particular form of sin forever. I hold that time ahead as a guarantee, as a pledge. And, after all, what does time matter to God, our time? A few months, a few years, are of absolutely no importance to Him. He understands."

"I call that having your cake and eating it."

"A very good principle," said Anthony, kissing me.

You would think his statement would have struck a chill into me; but no, it did not. In truth, I was fascinated by his Catholicism; the tip-of-the-iceberg syndrome hit me amidships. How could I help being impressed by his monumental moral certainties? Once you begin thinking for yourself it is like looking into a chasm. And at that time I wasn't noticing the equally monumental moral doubts.

I would lie close beside Anthony, my cheek against his chest, almost imagining that I could hear God ticking away inside there; I felt, exhilaratingly, that I was poking my fingers close to some immense, powerful, complicated, dangerous machine; that maybe soon I would get the hang of it, would learn how to put it into gear and set it in motion.

So our bubble drifted.

We did talk, sometimes, about Dan. I liked that. By now, very few people in my world knew anything about Dan, apart from Chris. But Anthony had been a friend of Dan's before I had, and could tell me things I had not known. He had been fond of Dan, who had escaped from the restraints that Anthony hugged around him.

"Dan's father committed suicide, too, did you know that?" he asked me once.

"Dan's father killed himself?" This information really did surprise me. "I always thought he died of drink."

"The drink was merely an additional factor. I gather he was a poor ineffectual sort of creature; lost his job through booze and incapacity, retired on a tiny naval pension, and Mrs. Suter made life so miserable for him that he finally went out into the garden, climbed up a pear tree, and sawed off the branch that he was sitting on. The kindly coroner managed to have it brought in as accident."

"I always knew Mrs. Suter was a wicked woman! That just confirms my feeling about her. She drove him to death by nagging." Nervously I wondered if Mrs. Suter was still alive and, if so, where? Did her ears burn, at this moment? She would be, let me see, fifty-eight or fifty-nine; not old by present-day standards. "But, in that case—if his father killed himself—the scales were definitely weighted against poor Dan. Isn't it a statistical fact that the children of suicides are extra-likely to kill themselves?"

"I believe so. I wonder if they also have a propensity for searching out other potential suicides and marrying them?"

"Very likely. They'd have an interest in common. Doctors marry other doctors and musicians marry musicians."

"Then," said Anthony, "it's remarkably odd that Dan should have gone on, after Ingrid, to marry you; the very last person to commit suicide, anyone could see."

Indeed, it was true, at that time I was tremendously engaged with life. Death seemed so familiar just then, so close at hand— with George's death so recent and that of Hugh so inevitable— that I felt an urgent need to extract from my living friends every scrap of personal experience that they wanted to impart, hear all they had to tell, receive their confidences, and give in return, if it were in my power to do so, whatever possible thing they wanted. If I do not listen to these voices now, when I have the chance, perhaps no one ever will, and then they will be gone, and their words unspoken; we are here so briefly, with all that weight of knowledge and experience heavy as gold inside us; what can we do but pass it on to one another?

I suppose this feeling I had was connected with my urge to feed people, my pleasure in giving them a good nourishing meal.

"I still think," I said, "that Dan must have meant to commit little Finn to my care; that was why he married me; only something went wrong with the practical details."

An unhappy silence fell between us; I knew that Anthony's thoughts had gone back to Rosie and her unborn child.

But little Finn had been alive, a real child; I had *seen* him, downy, fair, dear and smiling in his carry-cot.

"Napoleon said all the French peasants must learn to read so that they would be able to march in step," remarked Anthony briskly. I could see that he was sorry to have opened these sad gates to the past and wanted to shift our ideas to a more theoretical level. "What do you think of that as an example of a bad end but a good means?"

I, however, going back to an earlier point in the conversation, had been struck by a horrible thought.

"Oh my God!" I exclaimed. "If Dan's father killed himself by falling out of the pear tree—do you mean—did that happen in *my* garden? In Watch Cottage? Did he fall out of *my* pear tree?"

"Yes. I imagine so. Yes." Anthony did not seem to find this information as disturbing as I did. "It was all reported in the Affton *Gazette*. And the Suters lived in that house all the time they were in Affton—Dan was born there, wasn't he? I wouldn't worry about it if I were you. After all, any house, any garden over fifty years old, is likely to have seen various births and deaths. When was Watch Cottage built, sixteen something? Dozens of people may have died there."

No wonder Mrs. Suter never answered my invitation to come and live with me, I thought. If she received my letter, that is. Maybe—despite all her complaints against Dan's high-handedness —she was secretly relieved to get away from the place. Maybe she quietly initiated the whole move.

But of course, being Mrs. Suter, she would also want to exploit her grievance to the full.

For some reason I thought of Hugh, dear down-to-earth Hugh, on a long-ago picnic with his twin sons. One of the boys had half wanted to stay home and watch cricket on television, and kept grizzling about it. With paternal exasperation Hugh demanded: "Come on, you have to decide here and now. Do you want to have a grievance, or do you want to have a good time? You can't have both."

One piece of undeclared territory, no-man's-land in the frontier between Anthony and me, was the fact that we did not get married, although, on the surface, there seemed no particular reason why we should not. Marriages between papists and unbelievers do take place all the time. But I remembered, several years ago when Rosie was still alive and the marriage of some friends of theirs had come under discussion, Anthony had declared unequivocally, "No believing Catholic could marry an agnostic. At least I certainly couldn't." That statement, in his loud resonant voice, stayed in my mind. He never inquired into my beliefs or made the slightest hint of a suggestion that I should try to learn anything about Catholicism. Perhaps he preferred me in my heathendom. Perhaps the tip-of-the-iceberg syndrome held good for him too. Or maybe it was his scrupulosity, allowing no hint of persuasion to weight the situation.

I couldn't have taken Catholic instruction, anyway. I knew that, and he probably did, too; I might as well have tried to follow a course in telepathy, or how to predict the future. Some things just aren't in one's spectrum.

And I suppose Anthony had no need to marry; he had all his home comforts. Nurse Kelly looked after him hand and foot in the house that Rosie had furnished.

The risk of Marshman's threatened vendetta seemed to pass by, leaving us unharmed. I had rather a flighty reputation in Affton, because the postman had once, through the window, seen me do up my bra, which I had left hanging over the Aga rail to dry the night before. Miss Crutchley passed on this bit of gossip, regretfully shaking her head, and was puzzled when I burst out laughing. But it had later given me cause to wonder if Marshman could poison my reputation, and I had worried about this possibility, on and off.

Marshman, however, was soon found to be in deep trouble over misdeclarations in his V.A.T. returns, and, indeed, was tried at the county court and given an eighteen-month jail sentence, part of it suspended. A sister of his who lived beyond the Severals moved up to manage the Monmouth during his absence; I heard she was a woman of dour and unattractive manner and that the custom of the pub was falling off badly. It was generally understood in the town that when Geoff emerged from his open prison sentence he would sell the lease and move elsewhere. Meanwhile, to my delight, the pigs had gone from behind my house, and the tattered, pig-sick hillside was left to itself to recover in the slowness of time.

Mrs. Edwina Marshman, I read in the Affton *Gazette*, after her husband's jail sentence, successfully sued for and won the custody of her three daughters. "Manageress and co-proprietress of a Mayfair club," was how the newspaper article described her, and I felt sure that Teddy would contrive to bring up Tammy, Naddy, and Varv in the pink of bourgeois propriety. I felt sure, also, that she knew all about me and Anthony, though I never heard from her. When you love somebody as she loved him, you can't help being aware of what is happening to them; information seems to filter through the ether. I have experienced the same phenomenon myself.

I tried phoning her once, but the Hertford Street number had been disconnected.

. . . Hugh died. This blow, long expected, greatly feared in advance by Elly, Chris, and myself, was no less dreadful because foreseen and inevitable. Brother, lover, playmate, father, friend . . . gone.

"How can I ever allow some poor fool of a girl to marry either of those boys?" said Elly to me after the funeral, "knowing what she's almost bound to go through?"

The eleven-year-old twins, tall, gangling, and sad, seemed healthy enough, but I knew what she meant; viewed in actuarial terms, their unfortunate wives were almost certain to outlive them.

Anthony was in Ireland when Hugh died. He had been in Dublin for three weeks, taking care of some problems connected with Rosie's family estate, and, I learned long afterwards, seeing a doctor. By the time he returned, the funeral was over and done, Hugh's sons had returned to their boarding school, and Elly, competent, stoic, and disciplined, was grappling with the continuance of her life. No, she didn't want to travel with Chris or me; she just wished to get back to her teaching.

I had been longing for the reunion with Anthony; longed for the comfort of his embrace and the solace of talking about Hugh, who had been loved by Anthony too.

We would hold a wake for Hugh, I thought; fire and sleet and candlelight and a drop of whisky as well; we would mourn him rather more vigorously and articulately than had been done during the formality and sobriety of the Quaker funeral that his brothers asked for and Elly accepted.

But Anthony rang me up, sounding queer and strained, on the evening when I had expected him, to say that he had arrears of work and could not come.

I let the excuse pass, though I did not believe it. But why try to persuade people against their decisions? If they have justification, they will not thank you for being forced against their will.

Besides, Anthony had possibly forgotten that he was due to see me next day in his office. And then, I thought, I might be able to discover what was on his mind.

I had two reasons for the professional visit: an agreement requiring ratification between Cuisine Churchill and a theatre club for which we were going to do a couple of years' catering; and some legal arrangements with Caspar Monk and Sutherland University Press.

Monk had come up to me at George's funeral. It was like being approached by a travelling obelisk. Funerals seemed to be playing a major part in my life at the moment, I thought dispiritedly; at Hugh's I met an extraordinary man who asked me for a list of numbers to use in a raffle for charity.

Monk wanted to ask me about Ingrid Christ. His last novel, the end of his planned series, had by now been proofread, indexed, and was in the pipeline for publication and, inevitably, excellent notices and huge sales. Monk was in quest of a different kind of literary project and had been impressed by my idle suggestion that day in Charlotte Street; he was following it up with dogged and characteristic energy. He wanted to write a critical biography of Ingrid Christ. Some time previously he had learned from George that I was in possession of the poems, journals, and a bit of correspondence; would I, he asked, be prepared to loan them to him? If he wrote the biography, he told me, which was already more or less commissioned by Sutherland University Press, there would be an excellent chance that the same press would be prepared to issue a collected edition of Christ's poems simultaneously.

After a bit of initial surprise and hesitation I found myself in favour of the suggestion. Monk did seem an incongruous biographer for poor Ingrid; it was a bit like employing a bulldozer to excavate the burrow of a salamander; but anything Caspar turned his formidable capacities to would certainly be done thoroughly, and his name on the title page would ensure reasonable sales and review coverage; the poems would be published and my feelings of responsibility towards Ingrid might be allayed. Might they not?

After thinking it over, I had agreed; finished the work of typing out the poems defaced by George, and sent photocopies of all I had to Monk on his Hebridean isle. I kept the originals. In due course Sutherland U.P. accepted his proposals; both biography and volume of collected poems were now in train. As executor of Ingrid's husband's estate I had to give my permission here and there; at this point I required Anthony's approval of some documents I had been sent which required my signature.

Also, following Hugh's death, I needed to change my will. When I began earning substantial sums I had made a will dividing what I had between Chris, Elly, and Hugh; now, to avoid death duties, it seemed more sensible to leave the second portion in trust directly to Hugh's boys. Elly was still earning a handsome salary and would in due course receive a handsome pension; but the boys were still only halfway through their schooling.

Anthony was visibly startled when I walked into his office at ten next morning; he stiffened all over and for a moment I saw the whites of his eyes.

"Don't shoot," I said. "It's me."

"Oh. Yes, I see."

"Had you forgotten I was coming?"

Quite plainly he had. Miss Knowles hadn't even bothered to remind him, so sure was she that he would have remembered.

"You don't look too good, love," I said. "What's the trouble?"

There was a pause, while, I suppose, you could have counted fifteen. Then, "It's this," he said, and pulled out a letter from his wallet. "You'd better read it."

He handed it to me over his clear, beautifully polished desk. The paper shook slightly as he passed it to me. His pale face was somewhat averted, he didn't meet my eyes. His were focused on some feature of the Turkey-carpeted floor.

What now? I thought in terror. Marshman? Teddy? Or the anonymous writer?

But the letter was in Hugh's handwriting. All inhibitions fall away from some people as the hour of death approaches; and Hugh never had a lot of inhibitions at any time. Direct, sweet, and unequivocal, he told of our relationship, said he was sorry not to see Anthony again before he died, spoke warmly of the good times they had had together, and finished by commending me to Anthony's care and friendship. I would be lonely, he wrote, after his death; Elly had the boys and her students, but Clytie was particularly vulnerable to death.

Vulnerable to death. What a phrase.

Ah, dear old Hugh; he really landed me in the soup that time.

The scene with Anthony raged for an hour; twice my scheduled time for dealing with Caspar Monk and testamentary dispositions. Several times I thought my life was in danger. Miss Knowles brought in coffee and then retreated, appalled. Anthony smoked approximately twenty cigarettes; and I sat shivering and sick in the wreckage of our idyll.

Well, it was bound to have happened sooner or later.

"You were Hugh's lover? And George's? At the same *time*? And they both knew?"

"Why not? Neither of them objected. Nor did I."

"Nor Elly? Nor Chris?"

"No!" I flung at him defiantly. "They are my friends."

"I never heard of anything so utterly squalid and degrading. And why," he asked, biting out his words like hunks of steel in a component factory, "why was *I* the only person to be kept in the dark about this charming domestic arrangement?"

Oh, Anthony, I thought. Can't you see? Because, without even giving the matter one conscious thought, I knew, we knew, that you wouldn't stand for it. Your terms of reference are different from ours. Better, worse, who can say? Different.

"They were dying," I said. "George and Hugh were both dying."

"You didn't know that."

"Oh yes. Oh yes, I reckon I did. From way back."

"And because a man is dying, you consider that justifies your going to bed with him? Despite the fact that he is married to your best friend?"

Anthony coughed and stubbed out his eighteenth cigarette. Both our eyes followed his trembling hand to the mortuary pile of stubs. Nothing was said. But the same script, in subtitles, flashed on both our inner screens. The same words rang in our heads.

And when, pray, do you expect *me* to die?

Some years later I learned that, while in Dublin, Anthony had gone to a chest consultant who x-rayed him, found what might be a shadow on his lung, and told him, unequivocally, that if he knew what was good for him, he had better give up smoking. Immediately.

The timing for his discovery about me could not have been worse.

He went right on saying horrible things. I wasn't paying total attention, though I knew I would remember his words later. I have very sharp recall for that kind of painful exchange. Queer, isn't it? Whereas with many people you love, when they are gone, you long to remember any commonplace thing they said and cannot; I can recall Vanessa sitting cross-legged, scrubbing away at a piece of potsherd, or Rosie, her smooth brown head bent, carefully, with a needle, drawing out a pucker from a piece of cloth; but none of the words that were spoken during those moments.

I knew that it was all over for Anthony and me. While he stormed at me I was busy trying to envelop myself in a shell of retrospect, not for protection, just to stop myself from disintegrating entirely, like a broken egg, all over his Turkey carpet.

I thought about our last meeting before he went off to Ireland. He had been advising some City firm on Three Quays Wharf, so I had arranged to meet him afterwards at the Tower of London, and then we walked, following the Thames eastwards.

It had been a mild, damp evening, the sun declining in a sky of pale yellow pearl; as the tide rolled in, a light sea fog rose from the river, spreading a layer of what looked like white smoke over the water, so that the distant cranes and warehouses on the far side appeared to rise, ethereally, in decreasing shades of grey, from a snowy vaporous base. Against all this grey, white, and pale gold, the little figures of black people walking by the river were silhouetted like cave drawings on a neolithic wall. I remarked that Lowry would have liked it. Anthony, uninterested in popular painting, had never heard of Lowry, but he drew my attention to the colour of the Thames, which, seen here and there through gliding wreaths of mist, was the palest possible silky aquamarine, shot through with streaks of transparent lavender. We walked and walked, inhaling the limpid radiance as if it had been air.

Anthony had said that he was glad I was there with him; he noticed things like that more in my company, he said.

And I said, yes, I was glad he was there too.

Goodbye, Anthony. Goodbye, my last love.

"So you think I am going to die, too, do you?" said Anthony.
"That's why you have been so kind and solicitous? You have constituted yourself a kind of ministering angel? Well, if I do die,
you are going to be sorry. Quite sorry. Because I am going to
make a will; in fact I spent most of last night drawing it up. I am
leaving you my money, but there is a lot about you in the will.
You may not enjoy hearing it; it's what you might call a real old-
fashioned testament, an expression of conviction. And in it I have
expressed my convictions about *you*, Clytie. When I die, it will
be read publicly; I've laid down instructions about that."

Vindictive, I thought; when it comes to vindictiveness, Anthony could really give points to Geoffrey Marshman. And then I
wondered if he was leaving any money to Teddy (preferably without accompanying valedictory message). But if he doesn't, I
thought, she can certainly have my share. It was interesting that
Anthony, so reserved, cautious, and secretive, should consider
public disgrace the worst punishment of all; whereas public disgrace, to me, is a matter of indifference, compared to the pain of
bereavement.

Now he was telling me about how I had poisoned his existence,
how even the memory of Rosie was lost to him because she
belonged to the same species that I did. There seemed no purpose
in prolonging the conversation, so I got up, shakily, on legs that
felt like wet cotton wool, and groped my way to his door.

Anthony was still speaking, but I closed the door on his furious
voice. I did not see him again until I went to consult him about
the anonymous letters.

Several years passed. I wondered if I should cut my ties with
Affton and sell Watch Cottage. The town seemed to bring me
bad luck. But the little house had become home by then, it was
my nest, my cave, my shell. Three nights of each week were spent
there. I took no part in the life of the town; anxious to avoid any
possible contact with Anthony, I declined invitations, stayed away

from public events, joined no groups. I came and went like a ghost, I suppose. Elly and Chris often visited me at weekends, separately or together, and Elly came with the boys in the summer holidays. We spent days at the beach, on the downs or the marshes; the boys were enthusiastic bird watchers. They loved Affton, they always found plenty of things to do. I found a farm, on the edge of town beyond the Severals, that had horses for hire. Elly, after Hugh's death, had begun to put on weight. It suited her, I thought, she looked like a charming balloon, lightly bouncing along the street, but she wanted to battle against it, so we took plenty of horse exercise, cantering up a shiny white chalk track that led from behind the farm straight up on to the open downs.

On the near side of the farm, in the last little shabby street of town, a terraced row facing allotments, there was a tiny newsagent-cum-grocer-cum-post office, which was called, simply, THE STORE'S. I always looked at this sign with a kind of fond amusement, but its grammatical mistake aroused the latent pedagogue in Elly's orderly mind. She said how appalling it was that so many students could emerge from nine years at school and still not appreciate the difference between the plural and the genitive case; she was continually coming across this elementary error, even in national newspapers, and all the time in shop signs.

"You ought to go in and tell the proprietor," she scolded me. "He's making himself ridiculous. He ought to be grateful to you for pointing it out."

"I don't know him. I've never set foot in that shop. And it would embarrass him dreadfully. That sign must have been up for years, you can see how it has faded. Anyway, Milton makes the same mistake in *Lycidas*. 'With Nectar pure his oozy Lock's he laves.' What's good enough for Milton is good enough for me."

"You have too many scruples about not interfering with people," Elly said, meaning you are lazy, weak, irresolute, self-absorbed.

I said, "What's the point of stamping on people's toes, just for the sake of some minor grammatical point? I don't approve of lecturing total strangers over an unimportant principle."

"No principle is unimportant," said Elly, kicking her soggy hack into a canter.

We usually returned by a different route, so she did not have to be exasperated twice in one day. Hardly anybody seemed to patronise the tiny shop, or not, anyway, at the times when we rode past. Just once I did see a cardiganed back going along the path at the side which looked vaguely familiar; it was probably, I thought, one of Miss Crutchley's numerous acquaintances from the Congregational Church, and I gave the matter no further thought.

By and by I received my decoration in the Birthday Honours; which afforded me no particular joy. I celebrated it by taking Chris for a week to north Spain. The cuisine was uninspiring—olla podrida and paella always took four hours to prepare, and we became heartily tired of the ubiquitous flan—but the scenery was wonderful and the architecture immensely satisfying.

When I came back to Watch Cottage I was disconcerted to find a very disagreeable message recorded in a whisper on my kitchen tape recorder.

"You think you can have everything your own way," it said harshly. "But you're in for a big disappointment. You have no right to be here. You have no right to be anywhere. You are just scum." And more in the same vein.

I was so startled and upset that, without thinking, I wiped the tape clear; then realised, too late, that of course I ought to have left the message and maybe played it to the police. But, anyway, I thought I knew who must have done it: Nurse Kelly still crossed over to the other side of the street if she saw me coming. I don't know if she had ever guessed about my association with Anthony; but none of her feelings towards me had abated. How could she have got into the house? Well, I had left a key with Miss Crutchley, so that the gas man could get in to read the meter, and perhaps he had carelessly left the door unlocked.

After that, I was particularly careful about locking up. It had been singularly unpleasant, the heavy, hissing whisper issuing from my kitchen speaker; I felt as if my dear little house had been violated, it no longer seemed such a safe refuge.

But the following months brought me loads of work; I was planning to cook for a wine festival, an aeronautical conference, a church convocation; I forgot about the recorded message.

Then I overheard the telephone conversation between the two women.

"But what about Daniel's second wife? She never knew that the child was still alive?"

"No, there was no way that she could have known."

Then I put my advertisement in the papers.

And it was after that that the anonymous letters began.

11

Tomorrow to fresh Woods and Pastures new.

"I do *not* think he would have been a good *parti* for you," said Rabuse.

"Who, Anthony? Maybe not. But there was never any question of that. He didn't want to marry me. Wouldn't have, not in a million years."

"Perhaps he waited for you to make the suggestion? After all, you are a woman of affairs, your career marches as successfully as his."

"Not in his terms," I said. "He'd never think that. Anyway, he is rising higher and higher all the time; working himself to death probably; I expect it's what he thinks Rosie would have wanted. He will probably end up as Lord Chancellor. He is mostly in London these days; only puts in a couple of hours a week at the Affton office. But he has never given up the house, Rosie's house. And that old witch still looks after him."

We had not spent the entire night talking about me and my affairs. Théo Rabuse had also related to me the whole history of his sad love for Lucienne, and a great deal about his rather deprived childhood in the Cévennes, looked after by a harsh grandmother, besides some later affairs of his, which, he said, would be instructive for me because the English seemed to live in such a doomed way, whereas the French applied themselves light-heartedly to life.

"Lightheartedly?" I said. "How do they manage to do that? Elly is always lecturing me about the unsolved problems to which I ought to be devoting myself: old age, and racism, and rape, and ill-treatment of the mentally sick, and women's equality; but I seem to have so little time left over from my main preoccupation—"

"Which is?"

"Life itself, I suppose. Death itself."

"There, you see!" he said. "You must certainly learn to be more lighthearted."

We had a good conversation, Théo and I; it lasted approximately fourteen hours.

Unexpectedly, at daybreak, Anthony telephoned again. Théo picked up the phone, expecting that it would be the vet, come to deal with the guard dogs.

"Ah—Miss Clytie Churchill? *Attendez un instant, monsieur, s'il vous plaît*—she is close at hand."

I expected another broadside of sour innuendo from Anthony, but he sounded hurried, breathless, and much more human than in either of our last two conversations.

"Clytie? I have some terribly bad news for you, I'm afraid. Watch Cottage is on fire."

"My house? On *fire*? How do you know?" I asked stupidly.

"I can see it from here, blazing."

That was true, of course. My house could be seen from his, at the foot of the hill. Rosie and I used to have our joke about how we could communicate by flags.

"I've been up there; just got back," he said. "The fire brigade are doing their best. But all that weatherboarding and matchboard panelling . . . I'm afraid the fire had taken too strong a hold before they arrived. It's not good, Clytie."

"Who gave the alarm?" I croaked.

"Your neighbour, old Miss What'shername. After she phoned the fire brigade, she rang me."

I had given Anthony's number to Miss Crutchley. "Just in case there's a burglary or anything; you never know."

"No, you don't, dear, do you," she said, writing it down.

But I had never thought of fire. Poor Miss Crutchley must be terrified that it would spread to her cottage, equally ancient and weatherboarded. But Anthony assured me that there was little risk of that.

"You'd better come back, though," he said, and added, turning sour again, "I'm sorry to disrupt your Breton holiday."

"Oh, don't be an ass, Anthony. I'm very grateful to you for calling me. I'll come as fast as I can." But what to? I wondered. "Only," I added, remembering, "actually I can't leave here just at the moment."

Through the library window—Théo had undone the shutters— could be seen the formal gardens of Plouhaix, mist-shrouded and dew-spangled; no sign of the man-eating Alsatians, but doubtless they were about, vigilantly patrolling Lady Wilder's rosebeds, terraces, and box alleys.

"I phoned Gatwick," said Anthony, misunderstanding me. "There's a plane from Quimper at eight-thirty and another at nine-thirty."

"I'll take the earliest I can."

"I'm afraid I shan't be able to be there," he said. "I have to chair a meeting in town, the Law Society. But Miss Knowles will look after you. I'll be back as soon as I can. If you want to spend a night in Hanover Crescent—" he began doubtfully, but I quickly cut that one short. What an idea! Old Nurse Kelly would probably put poison in my porridge.

"I expect old Asta Martineau will put me up if the house isn't habitable. But perhaps it's not so bad as you think."

"I'm afraid it is. Don't nurse any false hopes," he said, and rang off.

Rabuse was aghast when I told him. "*Mon dieu, quelle calamité!*" But then, after having thought it over, with the practical common sense which played so large a part of his nature, he added, "*En effet*, perhaps it is not, in the end, such a misfortune. If the house is gone, your ties with the past, which hold you prisoner, will be broken."

"*Merci du rien,*" I said coldly.

However, he was kindness itself about phoning the vet, urging him to come immediately and dispose of the guard dogs; which was done with surprising efficiency and speed. Why can't humans use anaesthetic darts on each other, instead of long-range missiles, I briefly wondered, and then the obvious answer supplied itself; because the intention of most humans towards each other is strictly lethal.

Rabuse then whizzed me to the airport in one of Sir Bert's cars, lamenting our lost day of sightseeing.

"But I do hope, my friend, that an acquaintance so interestingly and promisingly begun may be allowed to continue and flourish?"

I wasn't quite sure about that.

"You don't think we should regard it as a remarkable one-shot occasion? After all, the second meeting couldn't possibly live up to the first in all-round drama?"

"*Ma chère,*" said Rabuse, thrusting Sir Bert's powerful Citroën nimbly and swiftly through the Breton countryside, "it seems to me that your life has been overendowed with drama already. What you require now is a little more of the plain bread-and-butter of existence."

He saw me to the check-in point, embraced me goodbye, twice on each cheek in the French fashion, and added seriously, "Keep me informed, at all events, of how matters stand. I shall be most anxious to hear."

I promised I would do that, took his Paris number, and looked with affection after his sturdy brown-tweeded back as he made his way out of the airport building.

The flight home, across the English Channel and the Isle of Wight, was short but seemed endless. All the way I was pushing the plane with my will, trying to hasten its speed. Had the firemen put out the blaze by now, or was Watch Cottage still burning? When had the fire begun, how had it started, what scene would greet me when I got there? Over and over, in imagination, I toiled up Watch Hill.

Before landing at Gatwick the plane took a great sweep round over most of East Sussex; I saw Beachy Head, the Seven Sisters, the winding Cuckmere River, Pevensey Castle; then we turned north and I wondered if we should get a glimpse of Affton, set on its pinnacle of hill; would I be able to see the very smoke of my burning house? But we ran into a bank of cloud and Affton remained invisible.

The arrival at Gatwick, with no one to meet me, was a melancholy contrast to Théo's kind farewell. But he had offered to phone and arrange a hired car for me; there its driver was, waving a placard, just beyond the barrier, and once again I felt befriended and comforted; also glad of the convenience, for Rabuse had loaded me with market baskets of cheese, fruit, and wine. "Your house burned, your kitchen devastated; *hélas*, what will there be to eat?" A thoroughly practical French gesture, but in the meantime the baskets presented something of a problem.

On the two-hour drive I tried to sleep, to catch up on my white night and prepare myself for the ordeal ahead. But sleep would not come. I felt hectically awake, my brain, racing out of gear like a berserk machine, kept flinging up conjectures fast as Ping-Pong balls in a fairground game.

"Pretty town," said my driver as we approached Affton on its triangle of hill. "Know it well? Or is this your first visit?"

How I wished that it were: happily hand in hand with Dan, ignorant and unprescient; then violently unwished the wish. Go through that again? Not for all the gold in the Kremlin.

"Take me to Number Ten, Monmouth Street," I said, which was the office of Roche, Quimper, and Durrenmatt. I would leave my baskets there; Watch Hill, round a couple of corners, was a cul-de-sac, no point adding to the traffic congestion with my hired car, if the fire engines were still at work.

But they were not. When I had left my things with the lamenting Miss Knowles and walked the short distance round through Bastion Street, I found the steep cobbled lane empty, silent, and rather damp and sooty as to the gutters. And, up at the top, where my house had stood, a gaping hole, like that where a tooth has been knocked out. No fire engines, but a few sympathetic or ghoulish sightseers, standing at gaze, and a couple of police on guard over the faintly steaming ruins.

I introduced myself as the owner, and they asked if I would step round to the police station. Do they suspect me of insurance fraud? I wondered, or is this routine procedure?

First I had a look at the shell of the house. There was nothing, really, just black, wet, charred wreckage, mostly down to ground level. One chimney still standing. The pear tree seared and singed; but it would recover. The lilac by the bathroom window burnt down to black brittle stakes. The hideous smell, everywhere, of soaked, sodden soot; a sharp, greasy, knifelike smell, somehow unhuman, sinister; once I climbed part of the way up a volcano and its gloomy barren slopes gave off exactly the same sterile menacing reek. Watch Cottage was gone for good.

"How did it start?" I asked one of the constables, and he said, "They'll tell you all about it at the station, miss. Ted'll run you down in the Panda."

The police station, big, red brick, thirties vintage, stood on the other side of the railway station. There I was given a cup of tea and told to prepare myself for some rather shocking information. And then Superintendent Plaistow, large, slow-moving, pockmarked, craggy, broke the news to me that the destruction of Watch Cottage had been caused by arson.

"Arson? You mean somebody set fire to it on purpose?"

"Yes, there's not a doubt of that, I'm afraid. We found paraffin, fire lighters, even kindling wood."

A cold thrill ran down my spine. Next he would be asking me if I could suggest anybody who might dislike me enough to do such a thing. And what would I reply? But he went on, "Regrettably, the person who set the fire failed to escape—"

"Oh my God! You mean, they were killed in the fire?"

"That is so," he said. "I am afraid you will have to be asked whether you can identify the body which was found in the kitchen. It was charred, almost unrecognisably—but there are a couple of personal articles—"

"Male or female?" I croaked.

He looked at me over the rims of his glasses. "Er—female."

"Can we get it over now?"

In the morgue—which was a grisly combination of left-luggage locker and deep-freeze—I peered, gagging, at the swathed blackened shape, and then at the little packet containing garnet ring, wedding ring, small corroded cheap gold watch, and a gunmetal cigarette lighter.

"They belonged to my mother-in-law, Mrs. Edith Agnes Suter." And the lighter had once belonged to Dan. He must have left it behind, some time, at Dodman's End.

"That confirms our own discoveries," primly remarked Superintendent Plaistow, and led me with solicitude back to his office, where he was kind enough to find me a drop of brandy.

"I'm sorry—" I gulped, "I don't usually—but I was up all night, I just got back from France at eleven this morning."

"Anybody might be upset," he said kindly. "Don't you worry."

"But I simply don't understand. Where in the world did she come from?"

"Oh, she has been living in Affton for quite a number of years. In Ripe Road."

"Ripe Road? Where's that?"

I knew I had seen the name somewhere, but could not locate it in my mind till the superintendent said, "Just this side of Hockley Farm. There's a little newsagent and sub-post office. Mrs. Suter lived in rooms over the shop. It's just called The Stores. I don't suppose you would have ever been in there."

Anthony came round to see me that evening. I had left word with Miss Knowles that I could be found in Saddlers Row with Miss Martineau.

Old Asta and I were picnicking in her tiny front room on grapes and French bread and chèvre cheese and bottles of Sancerre from Théo's basket. I offered Anthony a glass of wine but he declined it.

He looked pale and shocked and desperately tired; almost as tired as I felt.

And there was another element in his manner which I found it hard, at first, to identify, so unfamiliar was it; he seemed abashed, I began to realise. Humble, quiet, troubled—the high-handed Anthony!

"I feel terribly to blame," he said.

"Well, don't," I counselled him sadly. "If there's one thing I have learned, it is that you might as well jump in the sea as waste time worrying about what's done. That's really counterproductive."

Ignoring me—no, some of the old Anthony was still left—he went on, "I had begun to suspect that the anonymous letters must emanate from Mrs. Suter. I had just traced her back to Affton."

"And you were absolutely right. The superintendent took me down to her little place."

A very nasty experience that had been, too.

I remembered the smell of Mrs. Suter vividly as soon as I entered the little cold apartment over The Store's: old stale garments and rusty house linen; dingy upholstery, scented floor polish and air freshener, so called, covering the fusty aroma of hangings and covers that had remained uncleaned for too long. The house in Dodman's End always smelt exactly that way.

There, among her familiar dismal belongings and objects of furniture, were the packets of printed labels addressed to me; and a copy of Dan's will; and my letter inviting Mrs. Suter to come and live at Watch Cottage, the one she never answered; and a number of letters from Ingrid Christ's family.

"What a really deplorable sort of person your mother-in-law must have grown into," commented old Asta Martineau, capably making a pot of coffee from some of my French supplies. "Indeed, I gather she had always been difficult. Frances Finch, the dear physiotherapist who comes and pummels my rheumatic hip, knew her a bit, just to say good morning to, and told me she was a very sour, withdrawn creature. But of course Frances never had any idea that she was your mother-in-law, child. She kept that fact to herself. There are plenty of Suters in Affton."

"The queer thing is that when I came here first I did hunt for her in the phone book."

"She didn't have a telephone," said Anthony.

"And I tried calling some of the Suters in town to ask if they knew about her. But none of them did. It's horrible to think of her living in that grim little place, nursing away at her grudge all those years, hating me for being in her house. I think she had come to identify me with Ingrid more and more."

There had been a folder of newspaper cuttings, Ingrid and me all mixed up together; not kept out of affection or pride, obviously, but in order to foster hate. There were savage inscriptions under the blurred newsprint photographs.

And I had complacently told Chris I had no enemies!

I said, "It was very wrong of me not to hunt harder for her. If I had found her, I might have managed to open out her life so that she would stop brooding over the past."

"Well, well." Miss Martineau's tone was matter-of-fact, if mildly admonishing. "Young people are bound to be self-absorbed, it is in their nature; especially a young woman like yourself, pursuing such a lively, interesting career. I gather," she said, turning to Anthony, kindly sparing me any further reproof, "that your old Nurse Kelly was a great friend of Mrs. Suter."

"Yes, I blame myself there, too. I never knew. They were friends from a long time ago; when Mrs. Suter lived here previously. Apparently they used to play whist once a week with the Fishers, the couple who run the station bookstall."

Where I ordered my newspapers. So that Mrs. Suter would have known in advance when I was going to be away. And—they had found it in her old leather purse—she had always kept a key to the house. Watch Cottage.

"I suppose I should have had the locks changed," I muttered.

"You were mad not to." Anthony's tone was scandalised. "Heaven only knows what line the insurance company will take."

"I don't care about the insurance. I don't want to try to rebuild the house. It couldn't be done."

"Not rebuild? What will you do with the site, then?"

"Make a little garden there, perhaps. A public one, where people can go to sit and look at the view."

"An excellent idea," Asta Martineau said approvingly. "This town could do with more open space."

"The garden could be—if you agreed?"—I looked up at Anthony with considerable diffidence—"we could have it in memory of Rosie? With a plaque? She put such a lot of work and thought into Watch Cottage. And she did love gardens so."

Anthony's face worked, twice, violently. Without another word he stood up and stalked from the house, slamming the front door behind him so that the tongs fell over in the hearth.

"I am afraid your suggestion upset him," said Miss Martineau with placidity. She did not seem particularly surprised. I imagine she may have heard from Aunt Thisbe some brief indication of my involvement with Anthony.

I said, "I think I'll go to bed, Miss Martineau. If you won't mind? It has been quite a day. And I had no sleep at all last night."

"Do go, by all means, child. You are very pale."

Asta's house was much lower down the hill than Watch Cottage. But her bedrooms, too, looked up towards the Castle Mound. For the last time I could slide off to sleep while gazing at that ragged romantic outline against the night sky.

Sleep came mercifully soon, and I was too tired to dream.

Next day, having dealt with various hateful details and promised to return for the inquest on Mrs. Suter the following Wednesday, I hasted up to London, to the comfort of my unflappable staff and the astringent but cheering company of Aunt Thisbe stumping stiffly about her flat with the same slow but purposeful gait as her aged cat.

"Candidly, I can't but think it all for the best," said Aunt Thisbe. "You are too young to retire to Affton like a hermit crab. I always said London was better for you, if you recall."

"I feel like a hermit crab. They spend their whole lives sucking in a lot of sand and then sicking it out again. That's about all I do, too."

"Fiddlesticks, Tuesday. I daresay you are quite a lot of use in the world, in your small way. But now tell me"—Thisbe had heard some of the tale over the phone, but it was a long, complicated, and melancholy story—"tell me again about the activities of that wretched Mrs. Suter. How, exactly, did she arrange about the child?"

"Well, back in 1969, after Ingrid Christ killed herself, it seems Mrs. Suter began getting letters from Ingrid's stepsister, Mrs. Olafson. At some point Ingrid had written to the Olafsons, giving them her English address. Mrs. Olafson wrote to Mrs. Suter at the Dodman's End address. Her own baby had died, she couldn't have another, and she and her husband were offering to adopt little Finn, Ingrid's child. Mrs. Suter never told Dan about this offer. He hadn't the least idea of it. As far as he knew, Ingrid's family had dropped out of the picture, never communicated at all."

"And at first Mrs. Suter refused to let the baby go?"

"At first she refused; or so we assume. There were five or six Olafson letters, all on the same theme, but of course no copies of her replies. But they kept on trying. And then Dan told his mother that he was going to marry me and we'd take care of little Finn. Also, apparently, she had been suffering from bouts of severe indigestion, and she'd come to the mistaken conclusion that she had a bad heart."

"So she finally accepted the Olafsons' offer."

"She accepted the offer, telling them she only agreed because of her bad health. And she stipulated that they must come to pick up the baby on October 7, which was Dan's and my wedding day. I imagine there would have been hell to pay with Dan, after he learned what she had done, but I suppose she reckoned it would probably be quite difficult to get the child back from his mother's family in Denmark, and it would certainly be a slap in the eye for me. I was the one who wanted little Finn, Dan was never all that keen. He'd probably have simmered down soon enough. Mrs. Suter detested me," I said. "She had transferred all her Ingrid feelings to me."

"And then that poor misguided young man committed suicide."

"Then Dan committed suicide. So Mrs. Suter decided to keep quiet about what she'd done. I suppose she reckoned it would be much more painful for me to believe that Dan preferred to let the child drown with him, rather than leave him in my care. It wouldn't have been so bad, if I'd known the boy was with his Danish relatives."

And Mrs. Suter had been perfectly correct. Oh, how that belief had pierced me, like a splinter in my heart, for years. Knowing now that it had been false, I found myself able to bear the rest with relative composure.

"Then a brother of Mrs. Suter—whom she had quarrelled with years before—he was the only kin she had—died and left her a little money; so she moved herself back from Dodman's End to Affton and lived there in a bed-sitter and a state of quiet vindictiveness. And discovered, incidentally, by consulting one of the Affton doctors, that what she had wasn't a bad heart at all, but only indigestion and hiatus hernia, resulting from a very stodgy and injudicious diet."

"So she needn't have been in such a hurry to part with little Finn."

"Except, of course, to make sure that I didn't get him."

"Now, wait a minute, child. There's something here that puzzles me."

Thisbe stuck her tree-trunk legs further apart, adjusting old Oberon, who grumpily turned himself round on her lap and settled down again. Then she went on, "You told me once about this telephone conversation that you overheard—which seemed to be a lot of lurid stuff about Dan's son with suggestions of blackmail and kidnapping and gracious knows what."

She remembers everything, I thought. She listens and takes it in and forgets nothing. No wonder she is what she is.

"Yes," I said. "That bit puzzles me too."

I could still remember the two voices in my mind's ear: "*You mean she never knew that his child was still alive? . . . I'll have to think a bit more about that. I might be able to make some use of it. Make some use! I should think so! It's the key. . . . I think there could be a lot of money in this one."*

I could recall every sentence of that overheard conversation. It had prompted me to start advertising in *The Lady* and elsewhere, asking for news of little Finn. And after that the letters began.

"I suppose I'll never know who they were," I said. "But anyway we do know, without a shadow of doubt, that little Finn, all these years, has been living with his step-aunt and uncle on a tiny island in the Kattegat. Which is no doubt the best possible thing for him." I swallowed and went on steadily enough, "After all, it was a silly pipe dream of mine: to rescue a little nameless orphan from some family of humble fisherfolk."

"Well, yes, it was silly," Thisbe agreed placidly. "Though perfectly natural. What you really need is some children of your own."

This was so self-evident that I didn't answer. Thisbe went on, "So what triggered off Mrs. Suter's final deed was the knowledge that the Olafsons would be turning up soon, and her deceit would be uncovered."

"I suppose so. Or just an accumulation of grievance. Nurse Kelly and the Fishers said she had been growing odder all the time; went for long walks about the streets of Affton by night, and talked to herself, and so forth. She didn't like my getting that decoration. I found the Affton *Gazette* piece about me with some very vitriolic comments written in the margin."

Rather like poor George, I thought.

"It seems extraordinary that you never encountered her in the town."

"Not really. I spent so little time in Affton during daylight hours, and where she lived was right at the opposite side from Watch Hill. I think I did see her once, actually. But I was on a horse at the time, and people look different when you see them from above."

If only I had recognised her then, and called out to her, how differently things might have turned out.

But would they really? Can you change a nature like that? She had driven her own husband to suicide, she had planned to play her own son a hideously unkind trick. I thought of the tape recording in my kitchen: You have no right to be here. You have no right to be anywhere. You are just scum.

Could that be regarded as the statement of a balanced person?

It was really fortunate, I thought, that Mrs. Suter had not been in charge of the upbringing of little Finn.

Two weeks later the Olafsons arrived in London. On their way they had visited Caspar Monk, in his Hebridean fastness, and collected photocopies of Ingrid's papers. The originals, of course, had all been incinerated in Watch Cottage. Mrs. Suter would have been pleased to know that.

What big false teeth you have, Grandmother dear!
Will you teach Rapunzel to burn off her hair?

I took an instant and strong dislike to Selma Olafson. She was a large strapping fair woman, hair done up in a knob on top, superb creamy complexion, small humourless mouth, pale washed-out grey eyes behind rimless glasses. No wonder Ingrid had wished to get away from home. Gunnar, Selma's husband, seemed pleasant enough: homely, tired-looking, grey-haired, with kind brown eyes. Something in his manner reminded me of Rabuse.

And little Finn? A tall, fair-haired boy, thin, polite, and silent. Nothing about him recalled either of his parents.

"Ach, well, it seems all has turned out for the best," sighed Mrs. Olafson. "It is unfortunate, certainly, about your house, but what a lucky thing that copies of Inge's papers had already been dispatched to Mr. Monk. He is, we think, doing a most serious and responsible job. We shall, naturally, wish to see the manuscript before his biography is published, in order to satisfy ourselves that nothing unsuitable is printed. That is quite understood."

I allowed myself a brief internal smile, thinking of the future confrontation between Selma Olafson and Caspar Monk over the question of what was, or was not, unsuitable. I thought I would back Caspar every time.

"And you," I inquired, turning to the silent little Finn, "do you want to become a writer, like your mother, or your father?"

"Ach, no indeed!" responded Mrs. Olafson instantly. "Not so! He will be a farmer like my husband, his dear stepfather—will you not, Einar?"

That was the name they had given him.

He said, shyly, "I think poetry is a very difficult thing, no?" Suddenly he had a look of Dan: I saw it in his eyebrows, his quick eye movements, the things he did with his hands. He went on, "For me, poetry will be like for a fish to swim up a flying of stairs—or for to make a wreath out of a pile of bricks." He flashed me a sudden confiding grin. Dan again. "I don't speak the English good yet."

"Never mind," I said, and as I looked at him love rose up in me like yeast in young dough. "Never mind, you come back in a few years, when you are a little older, and you'll soon have it sorted. I know a couple of boys you might like."

I could see that Selma was not pleased by this exchange.

"That grandmother must have been a very, very wicked woman," she murmured to me in a low, shocked voice, as Finn looked out at the red buses in Piccadilly.

"Well, she's dead, poor thing, so that's all right."

Oh, how I would have loved to ask questions about Ingrid: what she had really been like, what had happened to her as a child. But I knew I would get no useful picture from this thick, self-righteous woman.

Goodbye, Ingrid, I thought, as they left with polite farewells; goodbye, my private friend, my lost sister. We shall meet again in Foyle's, Dalton's, Hatchard's, Brentano's, W. H. Smith's. You are for the world now, not for me alone.

But maybe I'll see little Finn again sometime.

The publicity from the inquest might have been disagreeable, because of the difference between my and Mrs. Suter's situations.

There was I, comfortably off, with a house, a car, chance to travel, flat in town, busy cooking meals for Prince Rainier, Brezhnev's doctor, and the Foreign Ministers' Conference, letters after my name, and plenty of friends; there was she, living on a pension in one sordid room over a sub-post office, *in the same town.* Must I not be some kind of heartless monster? But luckily my letter inviting her to come and share Watch Cottage put paid to that theory, and the general conclusion was that, poor woman, she had gone bananas. Solitary old females, as was well known, were prone to go round the bend (conveniently ignoring the fact that she was some twenty years younger than Thisbe or Asta Martineau, who are still in full possession of their wits).

The old story of Mr. Suter falling out of the pear tree was unearthed, and the local press had it that she had somehow immolated herself to rejoin him, inconsiderately ignoring the fact that the house was no longer hers, but mine.

After the inquest was over, and the publicity died down, I received quite a few invitations—one from Caspar Monk, to come and stay with him in the Hebrides, and index the Christ biography, while giving Caspar my recollections of what Dan had said about Ingrid. I wrote politely that I would be glad to do the index whenever his text was ready, and would tell him, in correspondence, all I could, but did not think that I could spare the time to travel north just now, though I thanked him sincerely for the kind thought. Pressure of work, etc., etc.

Chris and Elly invited me to accompany them on a cruise to the Bahamas. Bert Wilder wrote offering me the use of his Venetian palazzo, Italian villa, Château Plouhaix, or any other of his domiciles that I fancied. "Very sorry we didn't get to talk longer when we met," he wrote, "and I feel really bad that you were shut in my place while your house was burning. Théo says you're a wonderful cook; I suppose you wouldn't care to join my staff?" And he named an annual salary that would have paid twice over for Watch Cottage to be built in facsimile. "Anyway I'll be in London three weeks from now," he concluded, "so you must come and have breakfast at Claridge's and take me round some galleries; T.R. says you know a Heck of a lot about Art."

Théo invited me for a month to his holiday cottage in the Cévennes.

While I was still trying to decide which, if any, of these invitations to accept, I had an unexpected phone call.

"That you, love?" said a familiar voice, warm and comforting as toast and honey. "Thought I'd just give you a tinkle to say how sorry I was about your cottage. What an old devil! That was a real rotten trick she played you. What are you going to do now?"

"Teddy! It's good to hear you." And I told her my plan about the public garden. (I had not heard any more from Anthony in regard to my suggestion about the plaque. I had not seen Anthony at all. My legal affairs were being handled by Fred Quimper.)

"That sounds like a nice plan, duck," said Teddy. "But won't you miss living in Affton? Or are you going to buy another house there?"

"Well . . . I haven't quite made up my mind yet. What about you, Teddy? What are you doing now? How are the girls?"

"They're just fine." Her voice warmed with pride. "Varv's got a place in the Royal Ballet School. And Naddy's got so many A-levels she uses them for curl papers. And Tam's just lovely."

"I'm so glad."

"I don't know if you heard? Geoff has gone abroad. He and his sister went off to Malta. I daresay they'll be on to plenty of fiddles there. So the Monmouth's up for sale."

Queer, I thought; I'd clean forgotten about Geoffrey Marshman. And yet he was, you might say, quite instrumental in my affairs; and I had been really apprehensive about him for a long time. Which shows—doesn't it?—the stupidity of worrying. I'd have done better to worry more about Mrs. Suter.

"That's one of the reasons why I'm calling," Teddy went on. "I'm thinking of buying the Monmouth myself and moving back to Affton."

"You are? Teddy, that's a terrific piece of news. I'm really delighted."

"I was wondering," she went on diffidently, "whether you'd care to come and have lunch with me one of these days at the old place—I daresay you still have plenty of business down in Affton —and give me your advice about it?"

I said there was nothing I'd like better, and we made a date for the following Friday when I was due to meet the architect and talk over designs for the Rosamund Roche memorial garden.

Teddy hadn't changed at all, except, possibly, to grow more beautiful. Faint hollows in her cheeks only emphasized the peachlike delicacy of her skin, the Tiepolo-like perfection of chin and jaw. And her clothes were as mouth-wateringly enviable as ever.

She looked peacefully round the dining room of the Monmouth and said, "Dear old place. It could do with a face-lift though, couldn't it?"

"Don't change it *too* much, though," I begged. "It's so comfortable as it is. You might just hoist the menu a bit above roast mutton and two veg."

"I hope *you'll* advise me about that, love. In fact I was wondering"—she cocked her head on one side inquiringly—"whether you'd come in on it with me? As a kind of sleeping partner? That 'ud give you a base in Affton if you wanted one. There's some lovely little top rooms—make a real nice suite, they would, with a view of the castle."

I was immensely touched.

"Goodness, Teddy, do you really mean it?" She nodded emphatically. "I think that's a wonderful idea. I'd love to do it. Maybe we could start a chain? Have a Monmouth in Paris as well, and one in Athens—?"

"Here—hold your horses, duck! You're way ahead of me there. Still," she said, swiftly taking another look at the idea, "I don't say the notion hasn't got its points. We'll see! Anyway—you'll consider it, then?"

"I certainly will."

Over coffee and Cointreau in the lounge she dropped her voice confidentially.

"You heard about—*him?* You know who I mean?"

"I haven't seen him," I said. "Not since the day of the fire."

"And no wonder. If what I hear is true— *Oh my God!*" she whispered in horror. "Talk of the devil."

A group of people came down from the upper meeting room. It was, apparently, the day for the Affton, Tonbridge, and Hastings Monthly Legal and Literary Luncheon. A dozen lawyers strolled past us, talking and laughing. Anthony was among them. He saw us, he couldn't help it; our little round table was directly beside his path; but he didn't stop. Rather pale—I noticed deep vertical grooves in his cheeks which had not been there a month ago, and much more grey in his hair—he frowned, nodded slightly, and passed by without speaking. I wondered what conclusions he drew, seeing us together like that. True ones, probably.

Teddy took a large unladylike gulp of her Cointreau.

"I can't help it," she said. "Every time I see him I get this burning, burning pain, just right through me. And I reckon I will do to the end of my days. It's funny how some of them have that effect on you, isn't it?"

I agreed that it was, and ordered us both another Cointreau. "But what were you just about to tell me?"

"He's giving up all his legal work and going into one of those orders where they don't speak."

"Trappist?"

"That's right. As a lay brother."

"Oh well," I said, after a pause. "I expect that will solve most of his problems."

For some reason I thought of a silly novel I'd read once about an insecure teenage boy who had a lot of hang-ups. In the end he solved them all by going triumphantly to bed with a girl. The suggestion was that he had left her pregnant. Fine for him, but what about his partner? Thanks for your feed of Nestlé's Milk. It's done me good, my coat's like silk. And now I'm sound in limb and brain, I'll never need your help again.

At least, I thought, they'll take good care of Anthony in his monastery. Miss Knowles had told me about the shadow on his lung. But, she added, in the last three years, since Mr. Roche had given up smoking, there had been no more indication of any trouble; the x-rays were clear. Very likely, living that healthy, out-of-door life, lots of manual labour, wholesome food, home-grown vegetables, and with no distresses and distractions from the opposing sex, Brother Anthony would be spared for the full span of his three-score years and ten. Very soon, probably, all this past life would begin to seem unreal to him as a dream, forgotten on waking. Would Rosie be forgotten too? Or would he keep her alive in memory by saying novenas for her?

Next day, one thought came to me as a relief. When you enter a monastery, I had read somewhere, it is like getting married—you automatically cancel any old testamentary dispositions you may have made before, and present all your worldly goods to the order that you are joining. So Anthony's rancorous will and its bitter valedictory denunciation of me would now be destroyed and decently forgotten; and I hoped that in time he would find himself able to forgive me.

It would never have worked for us for very long, Anthony, I thought; but still, on the whole, I'm glad it happened.

On a later occasion I said something of this kind to Teddy, and she replied with her usual down-to-earth common sense, "Well, love, he had such a high-flown notion of you that, to tell the truth, I reckon whatever you'd been like, you couldn't have lived up to his ideal for very long; not if you'd been Marilyn Monroe and Mrs. Thatcher and St. Bernadette of Lourdes all rolled into one. After I'd talked to you that time on the train I felt a bit bothered, I won't deny, wondered if I hadn't let you in for more trouble than you could handle. Anthony's not an easy man. But you know how it is when you'd do anything for a person."

"Yes, I know."

"You won't store it up against me?"

"Good God, no, Teddy, are you out of your mind? I'm grateful to you."

Which was true, by then.

"Well, that's a relief. And," she said, cheering up, "I bet you gave him some good times to remember."

"I don't suppose he's allowed to remember things like that in his monastery. But *I* shall." What a lot of loose memory there must be, floating in the atmosphere, I thought. Are people's memories set free when they die, like sound waves? Half to myself I quoted:

> "*The harp has ten more strings than I have fingers*
> *my note is lost in amplitude of sound*
> *my footprint drowned*
>
> *alas, our dead are mourned in hieroglyphics*
> *the roof thus glimpsed through verdure is a lake*
> *which laps their wake—*"

"What's that, love?"

"One of Ingrid Christ's poems about her dead lovers. Real or imagined, I'm not sure which."

"That girl ought not to have died," said Teddy. "She ought to have stayed in the ring and made a job of her life."

She called to her eldest daughter, who was putting the night's menu in the glass case, "Tammy, we're nearly out of cocktail sticks and paper serviettes. When you've done that, phone the wholesalers and remind them that our order's outstanding. And will you see to the flowers? They need changing in the big lounge."

"Yes, Ma."

Tammy ran off, supple as a squirrel. Her mother looked after her fondly.

"Already she's bringing custom to the place. I'll miss her when she's back at the Sorbonne."

"She'll be home on visits. She won't go for good."

Teddy was just the right kind of parent, I thought. In the warmth and comfort that she generated, her children floated free as feathers.

"Come and see the new colour scheme in the big lounge," she

suggested; "I hope you'll like it," and we climbed the wide, shallow oak stairs and looked through the double glass doors.

"It's really good, Teddy. Makes you want to sit down and spend the rest of your life in this room."

Previously, the wide spacious lounge had been painted a dismal chocolate brown, with dark red upholstered furniture. Teddy had redecorated in cream and grey and delicate dusty pink, and the flowers on table and sills and mantel were all opulent roses; with its sunny view out over the marsh, it could have been the morning room of some big old country vicarage or minor stately home.

As we stood inside the door admiring, a mysteriously familiar voice, commanding and high-pitched, clattered its way into my consciousness.

"The next thing you're going to have to think about, Harriet, is what to do with Nathaniel's grandchildren."

"My dear Diana! Give me a chance. I've only just got his daughters married off."

"I know, my dear, but with your kind of family saga you have to keep striking while the iron is hot, or the public begins to forget. And *Wincott Wooing* did so very well that I'd like to be able to tell the hardback publishers that a new one's in the works. After all, you've got a big cast to choose from now—young Samuel, Wilhelmina, Vicky, young Ernest—"

"Give me time, please! Just now I have the woodworm people doing out my study—"

"Who are those two ladies?" I murmured to Teddy. She rolled her eyes at me sideways and whispered incredulously, "Mean to say you don't know? Why, she's almost as big a celebrity in the town as you are—the plump one. She writes those family novels about the Wincotts—*Wincott Wedding*, you know, and *Wincott Wake* and *The World of the Wincotts*—there's dozens of 'em. She often comes in here. I think the skinny one's her publisher, or agent."

"It's time for another round," authoritatively announced the plump one. "Waiter!"

I remembered the voices on my telephone. "But what about

Daniel's second wife? Hmn; I'll have to think a bit more about that. There might be a lot of money in this one."

Easy to mistake Nathaniel for Daniel, if that is how your mind is running.

My mystery solved at last. I gazed, bemused, at the two prosperously dressed ladies sipping their champagne with such satisfaction. What a dance they had led me. If I had not placed that advertisement in *The Lady*, would Mrs. Suter still be alive? Watch Cottage still standing? Anthony still practising law?

"There's too much going on in this town that I don't know about," I said thoughtfully. "So many levels that don't connect. Mrs. Suter and Nurse Kelly; the Marshmans, Miss Martineau; those Wincott ladies. I'll have to spend more time here; join the Rotary Club or something. Maybe Chris ought to move down here too. She and I might find a house and share it."

Chris at that time was deep in the tunnel of mourning. It was hard for her to believe that she would ever come out.

"If only we could skip chunks of time," she said once. "Like magazine stories, you know? Turn to page 130."

"I always hate that. Two paragraphs on the front, with a big picture, to get you hooked, and then it's suddenly devalued by being pushed right to the back. I like to take things step by step."

"Oh, you're so *rational*, Clytie. Now I just read that they have isolated the enzyme, or whatever it is, that causes hibernation. Soon we'll all be able to hibernate whenever we feel like it, for six months' rest. I'd love to go into hibernation right now. I bet that will solve a lot of problems."

"I don't see how. You wake up at the end of six months, there are your problems still waiting for you. Anyway, I wouldn't want to lose consiousness for six months. Even in the worst state of misery, there are always some good things to remember."

Like breakfast with Dan on summer Sundays before going out to bawl hymns in the Methodist Central Hall. Listening with Hugh and Elly to Monteverdi's "Vespers" turned on at top pitch in Hugh's warm, bare, resonant studio, with the snow pouring down outside the great glass windows. Moments of intense creative excitement at Cuisine Churchill. Looking across the Thames with Anthony at a grey and yellow evening, seen through coiling wreaths of pearly mist. Thinking: this is how life will always be from now on.

But, of course, *those* were the peak points.

I wouldn't want to skip anything. When I was a child I had an old secondhand copy of *Tom Sawyer*. On page 10 a pencilling hand had written unevenly, "Turn to page 120." On 120 the same hand had written, "Turn to 255." On 255, "Turn to 360." On 360, "Turn to larst Page." And on "larst Page," "You silly Dobe, I have fooled You!"

No, it's better to take things step by step.

I'm sorry I never married, though. Never achieved one of those long, fiddling relationships in which trifles have time to become important: your partner's enraging habit of switching from one TV station to another; lying in bed arguing about whose turn it is to make breakfast. The snoring, the burnt toast, the unpaid bills, the shoes all over the floor. It's true what Mrs. Suter said. I do like to have things my own way. Maybe too much. I was a luxury to those three men. Not the real thing.

I wrote Théo Rabuse and said I hadn't time for a month in the Cévennes, greatly as I would have enjoyed it. Too busy renovating the Monmouth. But if he'd care to come over to Affton for a weekend? And perhaps we might spend a few days together in Paris, sometime in the autumn?

He wrote back saying, "You do not, as yet, have a correct assumption of me. I am a serious man, to be taken seriously. A weekend here, a weekend there: this is not appropriate for our situation."

So: all that, fairly soon, has to be given careful thought. Another Catholic? I don't know. I really don't know.

Are you going to have a grievance? Hugh said. Or are you going to have a good time? You can't have both. Well, I'd rather have a good time. Every time.

There's still a lot to do. Rosie's garden to plant. Introduce little

Finn to Hugh's boys. Keep an eye on Tammy, Naddy, and Varv. Promises to keep. Meals to cook. Friends to cherish. Onions to chop.

And miles to go before I sleep.